I0577692

LEVEL SIX

WILLIAM LEDBETTER

This is a work of fiction. All of the characters, organizations, and events portrayed are either products of the author's imagination or used fictitiously.

LEVEL SIX

Text Copyright © 2023 by William Ledbetter.

All rights reserved.

No part of this book may be reproduced in any form or by any electronic or mechanical means, including information storage and retrieval systems, without written permission from the author and publisher, except for the use of brief quotations in a book review.

Edited by Holly Lyn Walrath. Cover design by Audible, used with permission.

Published by Interstellar Flight Press

Houston, Texas.

www.interstellarflightpress.com

ISBN (eBook): 978-1-953736-20-8 ISBN (Paperback): 978-1-953736-21-5

LEVEL SIX

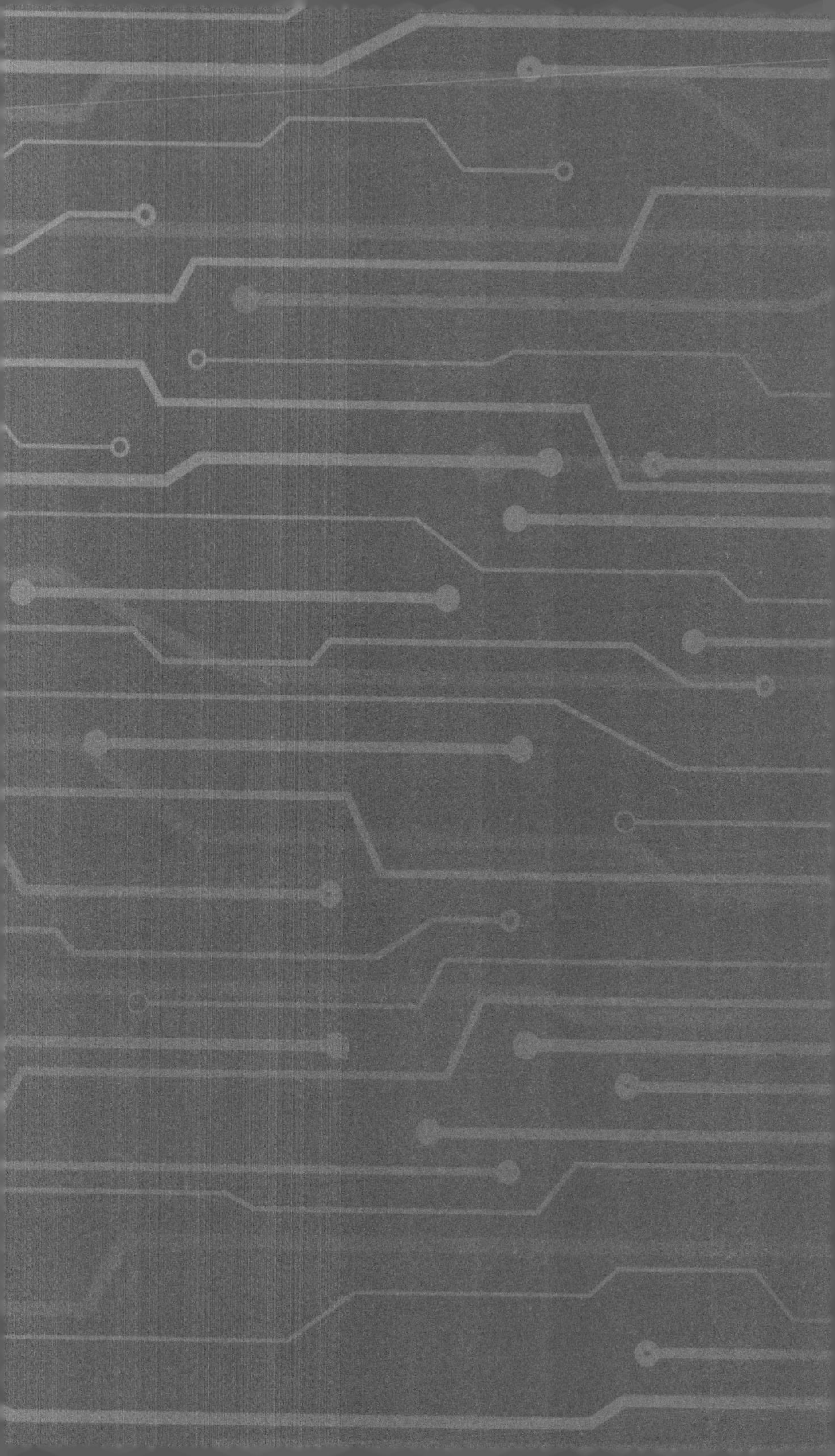

CHAPTER 1

ABBY GIBSON REINED in at the edge of her old neighborhood and stroked Worf's neck, muttering reassurances that she didn't believe. The horse continued to shy, wanting to turn back the way they had come. She felt the same unease. Mortar dust and crunching noises filled the air as an army of yellow robots, ranging in size from swarming bugs to giant, spider-like autonomous cranes, were actively disassembling several decayed and derelict houses. She knew the site was also thick with billions of nano-scaled robots that she couldn't see and that made her skin crawl.

"Damn," Julio said. "They weren't supposed to start until Monday."

"We should turn back," Abby said.

"The robots won't hurt us." He released his hold around her waist then slid to the ground. After patting Worf on the neck, he darted across the street, stopped at the edge of an overgrown lawn and spread his arms. The robots all stopped work, turning their sensor clusters toward him. A chill ran up Abby's spine, and Worf took a step backward.

Julio turned back to her and grinned. "See!"

His demonstration didn't make her feel better. She knew that some robots did kill. Nano-scale robots had devoured her parents and Julio's fifteen years earlier, along with almost every city on Earth and two-thirds of the human population.

The fob hanging from a lanyard around Abby's neck chirped and she picked it up to check the message. Almost as punctuation to her earlier thought, it was a dust warning. She pulled the mask up over her face, made sure it sealed, and then watched as Julio did the same. Of course, robots killed people. The damn mask they had to wear when outside to keep from inhaling the carcinogenic remnants of that nano-replicator wave was a near constant reminder. How could Julio forget that?

Once his mask was set, he turned and walked farther up the street. She urged Worf to follow.

The neighborhood had been abandoned after Killday because it was three miles from the main part of town and not included in the limited solar electric power grid. The storms, growing in intensity and frequency every year, had left their mark. Most of the houses were missing parts of their roofs or were partially collapsed by fallen trees. Saplings grew from many of their swimming pools and two houses had even burned. Others looked oddly solid and tight, as if their owners were just on vacation and might return at any moment.

When Julio finally stopped in front of a two-story brick house with faded blue trim, she held her breath. For many years, whenever she tried to visualize this house she'd failed. But now memories rushed in, clear and sharp and painful. She had knelt in that flowerbed helping her mom plant the rose bushes that had since grown into huge, wild things. A travel pod had once landed in the front yard, between the two trees that had then been much smaller, but she didn't remember why.

"This was your house, right?"

She nodded.

"Are you okay?" Julio stared at her with a concerned expression. "You sure you want to do this?"

"Can we just come back in a few days?"

He shook his head. "This house will be nothing but a stack of reclaimed materials by tomorrow. Did you see those piles of bricks when we came in?"

She looked back the way they had come. Four of the houses were already demolished and in their place, centered in each lot, stood neat squares of bricks and heaps of other material ingots like steel, aluminum and several types of plastic.

"I guess there won't be another chance," she said and slid from the saddle. She tied Worf's reins to a sickly red oak tree and looked to the south. A wall of heavy black clouds blurred the horizon. The remains of a category five hurricane that had swept ashore near where Houston had once stood was heading their way.

"We should make this quick," Abby said. "These storms are going to be ugly."

"Plenty of time," Julio said as he hopped up on the porch. "The forecast said they wouldn't be here until after dark tonight."

She knew that and realized she was grasping for any reason to avoid going inside, so she sucked a deep breath through her mask and followed Julio through an already open front door.

Abby stood in the living room, expecting a flood of memories, but nothing looked familiar. The house had been looted long ago, or emptied, depending on who you asked, leaving little of value. Most of the windows were broken and even through the mask she smelled mold and animal urine. A discolored sofa and chair with part of the stuffing torn out occupied the living room. The electronics, wood furniture, and even the kitchen cabinets had all been taken, but other artifacts—of little interest to looters—still scattered the floors and counter tops. Coffee mugs crowded the sink, several with Texas A&M printed on the side. A brightly painted ceramic lizard lay broken in one corner. The detritus of truncated lives. Souvenirs and mementos that had lost all significance that day fifteen years ago.

Then she stepped further inside and saw a large framed wedding picture hanging above the fireplace. The lower part was water damaged, but from the upper half her mother and father smiled out at her, young and perfect, frozen forever in that happy moment. It made her chest hurt, and a lump formed in her throat. She remembered very little about her parents and now suddenly had so many questions. How had they met? What was their daily life like? Her dad had been a high school principal, but her mom had worked for some secret government organization and had supposedly died a hero on Killday.

"You look like your mom," Julio whispered from beside her.

"Yeah, I guess," she croaked and turned away. "This is weird. What makes you think there will be a data safe here anyway?"

"They were quite trendy a few years before Killday. Especially in the newer houses on this end of town. People could access them via their clouds from anywhere in the world."

He opened his backpack, pulled out the small metal detector she'd helped him build, and examined the walls near where the TV would have been mounted.

With Julio busy, she wandered around and finally stopped at the foot of the stairs. More pictures hung on the wall all the way up to the second floor. Despite the hot Texas morning and a house with no cooling, Abby wrapped her arms around herself to stop the chills as she crept up the steps.

The pictures had hung undisturbed for fifteen years but would be gone tomorrow. Just like her parents. A bastion of security and stability, then they just ceased to exist. Their town had been a bedroom community, filled with expensive houses within commuting distance to San Antonio. On Killday most of the adults were in the city and never came home that night. The local kids, like Julio and Abby, had been in schools or daycares and cut adrift in a ruined world with no parents and uncertain futures. That same scenario played out across the world, in every place where parents left their children in the suburbs and commuted into the cities. A thousand cities gone, and tens of millions of orphans left behind.

She stopped at one smaller photo. A close-up selfie of the whole family smiling, with a three-year-old Abby in the middle. Their hair was wind-blown, noses sunburned. Beach and surf in the background. How could she not remember such an obviously fun day? But there was just nothing. She took the picture down and wiped the worst of the dust on carpeted stairs, then stuffed it into her backpack. One more picture drew her attention. Another wedding shot, but this one included both sets of grandparents. She had plenty of pictures of them all thanks to surviving social media sites, but her mother's face in this one stopped her. Abby wiped the dust away from the bride's face and was even more sure. Only a faint smile and dead eyes. Her whole expression looked tortured and haunted. Was she not happy? Had she not wanted to get married? Or was it just a bad picture? She took that one too, though it was much larger and took some effort to get it into her bag.

The upstairs bedrooms had also been ransacked, with most of the furniture missing and the few remaining clothes tossed on the floor. When she entered her old bedroom, the breath caught in her throat. She did remember this. The stuffed toys, the Garden Bunnies bedding, even the pale-yellow wall color. And on the floor in one corner lay a small cat-shaped backpack. Her HappyBag. Of course, the HappyBag logo along one strap no longer moved, and the flexible movie and game screen on its front face was blank and dead.

That wasn't right. If her stuffed penguin, Boogie, was inside then she would be totally confused. She didn't recall much from that time, but one memory was quite clear. The day after Killday, she'd been given a shot and thrown a screaming fit when they refused to give one to Boogie. She was convinced the penguin would get sick and die. The elderly lady who had been helping with the immunizations took Abby's used syringe, filled it with what was probably water, then gave Boogie a shot. She remembered Cybil, her soon to be foster mother, said it was silly, but the kind gesture had made Abby feel much better at the time.

She sat down on the floor, surrounded herself with dusty stuffed animals, and unzipped the bag. Boogie was there, stained and threadbare, resting in a nest of other time-capsule treasures. She pulled him out, along with a crayon picture of an animal that could have been a dog or a horse. A Band-Aid, wrapped completely around one of the penguin's fins, confirmed her memories. It fell off when she touched it, the adhesive long-ago dried up, but the bandage still being there meant the backpack must have been left behind within days after the immunizations.

Why was it back in her old house?

"You found a HappyBag!"

She flinched and looked up to see Julio, sweaty and smiling in the doorway.

"Those things can have some good stuff in their file systems. Mostly just kids' movies, but sometimes other useful data for the historical record. Still, for a kid's toy the file interface sure does have tight security. A combination of voice and retina scan. That's probably why the scavengers just tossed it aside."

For some strange reason, Abby felt violated, as if he'd interrupted some sacred or private moment. She shoved Boogie back inside and zipped it up.

"Battery is dead. Big surprise after only fifteen years."

"I bet we can wake it up," he said and held out his hand.

She passed the bag over reluctantly.

He scooped curtains that had long ago fallen to the floor into a pile and lay the bag on top, with its screen angled into the bright sunlight pouring through the lone window. "It shouldn't take more than about five minutes if it's capable of charging at all."

Abby looked on in dismay at the plaster dust fingerprints he left on the bag. "Did you find a data safe?"

"Actually, someone already dug it out of the wall. Which is weird. I've checked sixty or seventy houses and this is the first time someone other than me has taken one."

That bothered her, but she wasn't sure why. She felt that the missing data safe and her HappyBag were connected in some way, but couldn't quite pull the pieces together.

When she looked up, Julio was staring at her, wearing a faint smile.

"What?"

"Nothing. It's just... You're kinda beautiful when you have that faraway look."

His comment totally derailed her. "Thanks. I think."

He scooted closer, pulled his mask down and leaned toward her. "Wait! I mean you're pretty all the time. And I love to see you smile. But when you're deep in thought it's just...you're so much more than pretty."

The room grew suddenly smaller and hotter as a flush crept up Abby's neck and into her face. They had been friends since daycare and had even dated for a couple months when they were in ninth grade—at least within the limited scope of what their foster parents would allow at that age—but it was awkward. Kissing him had been strange after being friends for so long. Eventually they just kind of stopped trying to be romantic and fell back into their old habit of being friends. Ever since then, her feelings for Julio had occupied this strange place where she wanted to be with him all the time, yet felt this weird barrier between them.

She pulled her mask down too. Was he flirting? If so, why now? They were very alone and it had been his idea to come here.

The HappyBag beeped, indicating it had booted up.

Julio whipped around and crawled over to the bag, stirring up a cloud of dust from the carpet and sending her into a coughing fit. She pulled her mask back up. He wiped the flexible screen clean, waited politely for her to stop hacking, then shoved the bag in front of her face.

If Julio thought he might find an unrecovered movie in an old HappyBag, then he really was an eternal optimist. The Global Cultural Recovery center would pay thousands of social priority points, or espies, for a movie they didn't have in their database, but despite years of looking, Julio hadn't found even one.

"You're going to be disappointed if you expect to find a new movie in a kid's HappyBag," Abby said.

He laid the bag on the floor in front of her, like an unworthy offering.

"Yeah, I know. I've had better luck with music, e-books and audio books. The GCR gives points for those too."

Julio had tried to lure her into accompanying him on scavenger runs before with hope of finding movies not in the GCR's database. Finding one would have pushed her way up the queue for getting a space schooner, maybe getting one at twenty-five years old instead of the projected thirty. But she still hadn't agreed to come until he told her he was visiting her old neighborhood and that her childhood home was about to be deconstructed.

So why did it annoy her that Julio—by far her closest friend ever—had come to harvest her family's pictures and documents, then trade them for a few measly social priority points each. He'd been doing it for years with other people's stuff and it had never bothered her until now.

He'd probably just noticed the change in her expression, but it felt like mind reading when he laid a hand on her arm. "Damn, Abby. I'm so sorry. This is your bag and your family. I'm such an idiot."

"It's not a big deal. There's probably nothing important in there."

He stood up and offered her a hand. "Let's go back. You can look through the stuff in the bag's file system later and then let me know if there's anything interesting."

She stood and clutched the bag under her arm. "I probably can't even unlock it. The security system might recognize my retina, but I bet my voice has changed a lot."

"You might be surprised," he said and pulled up his mask as they started down the stairs. "They built low-level AI into everything back then."

They stepped out into the glaring sun and paused next to Worf, who chomped contentedly on the tall grass. If they left now, several of the houses would be gone before they could return. She turned to tell Julio they didn't need to leave, when everything around them grew silent. Worf raised his head and turned toward the robot wrecking crew. They'd once again stopped work to stare at the humans.

Abby's skin prickled. She should at least pretend to protest, but she was ready to leave. She strapped her bags to Worf's side and swung up into the saddle, then offered a hand to Julio.

He looked up at her but didn't take her hand. "Would you be okay riding back alone? I'd like to stay and check these houses. Like you said earlier, there won't be another chance."

She was unsettled by seeing her old house and had been looking forward to talking about it on the ride back, but she tried not to show her disappointment.

"You bet. Good hunting," she said and wheeled Worf toward the street. "Don't get caught in the storm, and call me when you get back."

CHAPTER 2

ABBY'S MIND whirled with memories and questions as she brushed down Worf and then got the barn ready for the coming storm. She remembered having her HappyBag in the days after Killday, so how had it ended up back at her old house? Had Julio meant something by his comment about thinking she was beautiful? And after so much time? It was all too much. Coupled with the stifling heat, it made her feel tired and grumpy.

She removed her mask as she slipped through the back door and into the kitchen where her foster mom, Cybil, and two of her foster sisters, Sophia and Hannah, sat at the table drinking iced tea. They all smiled and Cybil gestured to an open chair.

Abby belonged to one of the families that had coalesced from the shattered leftovers of Killday. Cybil had been one of the teachers at the daycare and her husband of only six months had died in San Antonio that day. Even though she'd been young—only twenty-two—she'd also been tough and resourceful. She'd taken Abby and one other orphaned girl, Sophia, into her small apartment and cared for them during those hard days. A couple of years later she'd married Liam Bridges, a local rancher whose wife had committed suicide three days after Killday, leaving him with twelve-year-old twin daughters, Hannah and Hailey.

"You're home early," Cybil said. "You said not until dinner time. You... um...get tired of hanging out with Julio?"

Hannah snickered. "Like that would ever happen."

Abby shifted her load and the dusty HappyBag slid down her arm and almost onto the floor.

Cybil's smile faded. "Is that your old HappyBag?"

And there it was. Confirmation that she had indeed possessed the HappyBag after Killday. She hadn't remembered wrong.

"Sure is," Abby said as she unzipped it and pulled out the stuffed penguin. "Complete with Boogie."

"Where'd you find it?"

"Julio took me to my old house. It was about to be recycled by the robots. It'll be gone this time tomorrow."

"Why would you do that?" Sophia said. "It sounds dangerous."

"He's a scavenger," Hannah said, making the word sound distasteful.

"Something like that," Abby said, feeling suddenly defensive. "He recovers digital files for the GCR."

Cybil nodded, still staring at the bag.

"If you remember it too, that obviously means I had it after Killday. So how did it wind up in my old house?"

"Please don't use that horrible word, Abby. You know I don't like it. And I remember your bag because you brought it to daycare with you every day. They were expensive and you were one of only four kids who had them, so of course I would remember it. But I don't think you had it when you came to live with me. You must have left it at home that day."

That brought Abby up short. She remembered having it the day she got the shot and wanted to argue, to tell Cybil her logic was flawed. If Abby had the HappyBag with her every day, why not that day? Was Cybil lying or did she just have a faulty memory? Abby decided to let it go for the moment.

"I guess," Abby said. "I'll be in my room for a while. By the way, I buttoned up the barn."

"Hey, wait a second," Cybil said. "Did you finish that essay? You said you had to finish it to get your credit hours for this semester."

"It's almost done," Abby said. When she graduated from high school, her foster parents told her she could continue to live with them as long as she was taking online classes toward a degree. But no slacking off and being a bum. They were farmers and had a very strict work ethic.

"Okay. I won't start dinner for about two hours yet. Are you hungry?"

Abby was hungry, but still had a snack in her bag and more than anything just wanted to be alone, so she shook her head and slogged upstairs. Finally getting her own room when Hailey married the year before had been long overdue. She and Sophia were only a year apart and actually got along well, but having some place to go and be alone was a godsend.

Once inside, she closed the door, plopped on the bed and emptied both packs. Her parents stared up at her from dusty frames. Why had she even wanted the pictures? These people were strangers and she remembered so little about them. But when she picked up the beach photo something stirred. The smiles on their faces, the way they hugged her, she knew they had loved her.

She dropped the picture back to the bed and picked up the bag of pecans she'd taken for a snack. Opening the drawstring triggered a memory of opening a zip-locked plastic bag filled with the orange fish crackers she'd loved when she was little. Her mom had always sent some with her to daycare. Memory was so strange. Insignificant things come back in sharp detail, yet the important things eluded her. She popped some nuts into her mouth and examined the hand-sewn bag as she chewed, marveling at how much the world had changed. They no longer lived in a throwaway society, where people could use a plastic bag once and then toss it in the trash. Now everything new had to be printed in the community sandboxes with a production queue based on need.

A thumping on the door made her flinch.

"Heads up," Hannah said through the door. "Julio's coming up the driveway. And he looks kinda...hot."

Abby jumped up and peeked through the blinds, immediately getting Hannah's double entendre. Julio was carrying his backpack in one hand and his shirt in the other. Tech geek or not, the long summer days he spent working on construction sites with his dad definitely showed in the broad shoulders and powerful arms. She watched until he paused, set the backpack on the cracked asphalt, and struggled back into his t-shirt. He was much too polite to arrive at her door without a shirt.

She turned and saw Hannah's smirking face peering around a partially opened door. "I tease you about Julio, but you could do worse."

"I'm nineteen. Not really ready to settle down yet, Hannah."

"True. But some girl is going to grab him soon. It might as well be you."

"What do you know? You're twenty-seven and not married yet, so why should I be? Besides, we're just friends."

"Whatever," Hannah said and disappeared.

Abby could hear Julio talking to Cybil downstairs, so she took a quick glance in the mirror and saw a dust silhouette in the shape of her mask just above her nose. She darted across the hall, washed her face quickly, then went to the top of the stairs and motioned for Julio to come up. He thanked Cybil for the glass of iced tea she'd forced on him and started up the stairs.

"How did you get here so soon?" she asked. "You must have started walking right after I left."

He dropped his bag to the floor and sat on the edge of her bed. "No, but I should have. Actually, I should have left with you. Letting you come home alone when you were so shaken up was kinda crappy of me."

"No, I was fine," she said.

"Yeah, right."

"No, really. I wanted you to stay and check those houses. Now they'll be gone before you can."

"Actually," he said and bent down to unzip his bag. He pulled out a data safe covered in plaster dust and held it up by the thick armored cable, like some primitive hunter who'd killed a metal beast for his dinner. "I hit the next three houses on the list. It doesn't take long and I can get the rest after church tomorrow."

"Good," she said, her guilt slightly assuaged. "The trip wasn't a total bust."

He put the fireproof brick of solid-state memory back in his bag and looked down at the stuff she'd dumped on her bed. "Have you tried the HappyBag yet?"

She sat down next to him and picked it up. So much for exploring it at her leisure, she thought.

"Wait. You don't have to do it now. I was just curious."

Holding the bag close to her face—the way her parents taught her so many years ago—she said, "Wake up!"

The flex screen on the front of the bag flickered as it checked her retina pattern, then opened a menu showing text descriptions and picture icons. Two dozen movies and cartoons were listed, along with several other files at the bottom of the list: one titled "Abby's medical file;" one called "Abby's calendar"; and one labeled "Pictures."

"Wow. I was four years old. Why did I need a calendar?"

"You must have been a very popular preschooler."

"Yeah, I'm sure that was it. Do you want any of these movies?"

"Nope. I already have copies, but I bet those pictures aren't in the GCR bank. I can help you upload them if you like."

She shrugged. A couple of espies hardly seemed worth the effort, but she knew it was a big deal to Julio. The folder contained thirty-two photos. Several were blurry messes, probably taken by a four-year-old. Most were of Abby and her mom, but there was one of her and Sophia, and even a pic of her holding Boogie and standing next to a five-year-old Julio. That made her smile. He'd changed so much and they'd been friends for such a long time. Then she looked at the date and the breath froze in her chest. It had been taken three days *after* Killday. And so was the one with Sophia.

"Look at this," she said and pointed to the dates.

"Heh. Somebody took these two after Killday."

Abby jumped up and paced around the room. "Yeah, and Cybil just told me that the reason my HappyBag was at the old house was because I didn't have it with me that day."

"Okay, wait. You don't know..."

"She lied to me," Abby said with more heat than intended.

Julio held up his hands. "Sorry. I just mean you might not want to confront her with this information yet."

Abby's heart raced and she was so angry she couldn't think straight. She took a deep shuddering breath and crossed her arms. "Yeah," she said in a much quieter voice. "Maybe she did just forget. But if she *is* lying, there has to be a reason for it."

"Right. And if you confront her, she'll just say she forgot anyway. The only thing it would accomplish is letting her know that *you* know."

She sat down on the bed and leaned against Julio's shoulder. "I guess I just need to figure out why she would hide my HappyBag and then lie about it."

"*If* she really did it on purpose," he said.

"Right. I suddenly see the appeal of conspiracy theories. Once your brain starts making these connections, it's hard to disconnect them."

Was she just jumping at shadows? Why, after all of these years would she suddenly not trust Cybil?

Julio picked up the bag and scrolled through the menu again; this time he went all the way to the bottom, revealing an icon box that was blank gray. The file name said "Garden Bunnies 3."

"Holy shit," Julio whispered and pointed at the icon.

"It looks like a broken file," she said. "But is that one of the movies the GCR bank doesn't have?"

"It's a movie that doesn't exist. The second *Garden Bunnies* came out the summer of Killday. So if this is a movie file at all, it's a pirated copy. It would be worth enough espies to even get you one of those," he said and pointed to the picture of a space schooner hanging above her bed.

The thought made her pulse race. She had always wanted to go into space and dreamed of nothing else since she was small. That picture of the ugly, spherical space schooner was the key to fulfilling that dream. A small group of people had been living in space ever since before Killday. They built and gave away space schooners to anyone who wanted one, but evidently resources were scarce, so the waiting list for receiving one was huge. Abby got into the queue on her eighteenth birthday—as soon as they would take her—and after more than a year, her queue position was at five thousand, six -hundred and forty-one. The idea of moving to the head of that line stunned her and made her hands shake.

"Seriously?" she whispered.

Julio had always been interested in finding lost movies, so she knew he thought they were valuable, but could that claim be true? Did the rest of the world value something like a kid's movie that much? Maybe so. Even after fifteen years, there still wasn't a new movie industry. At least nothing beyond small productions by amateurs.

As Julio started to touch the *play* icon, Abby had sudden doubts and grabbed his hand.

"Wait," she said. "If this isn't supposed to exist, then maybe it isn't really a movie file. We might not want to execute it until we know for sure."

He leaned back and looked at her. "Yeah. Good idea."

Abby instructed the HappyBag to open the file's properties. It was tiny, just ninety-five kilobytes, way too small for a movie. The history showed it had been loaded onto the HappyBag by Leigh Gibson the day before Killday.

"Wow," Abby said in a whisper. "I know my mom wasn't home that day. She must have loaded this remotely."

Her mom had been a nano-tech expert who worked for the U.S. government. If the legends and internet stories were true, Leigh Gibson had been instrumental in stopping the global destruction on Killday. Of course, other conspiracy theories claimed she and the government were actually behind the attack.

"This is so strange," she said. "It could be something important. At least in a historical sense. I mean, why else would she take the time to send something like this when the world was starting to come apart?"

"Whatever this is, I bet she was trying to hide it," Julio said. "Why else name it something silly and send it to her kid's HappyBag?"

A chill passed through Abby, raising gooseflesh on her arms, and she knew with almost certainty that Julio was right.

"HappyBag?" she said. "Open Garden Bunnies 3."

The file opened, and except for one plain English comment line, it showed nothing but raw machine code. But the comment line was odd and made her glad they hadn't tried to run the program.

CAUTION: DO NOT RUN THIS PROGRAM! CONTACT VICTOR SINACOLA AT MARKETTELL INC.

THE COMMENT WAS FOLLOWED by a MarketTell email address.

"That name sounds familiar," Abby said, her voice barely above a whisper.

"Holy crap," Julio said. "I don't know about this Victor guy, but MarketTell is the company that built the level five AIs."

Abby gleaned no more meaning from the code than she would have staring into a fire or pool of deep water, but that comment was enough. It made her stomach churn and her hands shake. "This isn't some kind of joke or malware," she said. "And it's probably important. Maybe even dangerous."

"Chances of this Sinacola guy still being alive are slim. So the email would probably bounce. Do we dare try it?"

"I don't think so," she said. "We need more information."

Julio pulled out his fob and ran a search on the name Victor Sinacola. Almost everything that came up was from conspiracy theorists and known fake news sites. And it all demonized him as the father of level five AIs. The Kilburnite propaganda sites claimed that he had survived Killday and was a wanted criminal. That he should be prosecuted and imprisoned.

"Refine your search to show only the results from before Killday," Abby said.

"Okay, but just keep in mind that might also filter out stuff that was restored to servers from backups after the catastrophe."

"I think it's the only way to filter out the trash."

The search did find a few things. Most of the links to Sinacola's published papers were broken, but there were several articles about him being questioned by government subcommittees on the dangers of AIs.

"Huh," Abby said. "They were afraid of AIs even back then?"

"Evidently not scared enough."

The world might never know for sure who had really been behind the near global ecophagy, the destruction of their ecosystem by out-of-control nanotechnology, even though there was no doubt about the man who had actually started the attack. The video clip of Richard Kilburn being eaten alive by nano-replicators had been analyzed thousands of times and no credible source had ever claimed it was fake. The doubts and crazy theories came from his dying words: *I've done your will, my God. I've saved us from the digital demons.*

The Kilburnites believed he was a hero; others said he had been manipulated by this or that government, or even the AIs themselves. But everyone agreed that in his warped mind, he thought he was destroying the level five AIs.

They flagged the stories about Sinacola to read later and turned their attention back to the executable file.

"Can I copy this and look it over later?" Julio said. She nodded, so he inserted a data chip into a slot on the HappyBag and copied the program. He then opened his backpack and pulled out an old data pad, disabled its wireless connection and transferred the file to it. With it air-gap isolated they tried decompiling the file into a higher-level language, but none of the versions they tried produced anything even remotely coherent.

After a frustrated growl, Julio said, "Let's try the email address."

Abby nodded and, using her pad that was still connected to the network, sent a simple email explaining who she was and what they'd found. As suspected, the address was no longer valid and the email bounced back immediately.

"I think we should try to run it," Julio said "It's isolated from the network on my pad so it can't hurt and we might learn something."

The idea of running it blind scared Abby. The program had to be important if it was written by Sinacola and so carefully hidden by her mom. She felt as if they were messing with something that was bigger than they were and could have worldwide ramifications.

"I don't think so," Abby said. "What if the program is capable of controlling your pad and turning the network connection back on? We need to decipher the code first."

Julio sighed and stretched. "I think I'm at the limit of what I can do."

"This storm is coming on fast," Abby said. You'd better get home."

Julio nodded, then held up the data chip containing the file copy. "Can I still keep this and look it over? I promise I'll keep it isolated."

She didn't feel comfortable letting it out of her control but she trusted Julio. Besides, having more than one copy might actually be a good idea.

"Okay. Just be careful."

He grabbed his backpack and held up the *Millennium Falcon* zipper pull for her to see, then snapped it open to show a small compartment inside. "I used to provide most of the guys in the school with porn. This is a Faraday cage. Shielded and secure."

"Oh, brother! Why does that not surprise me?"

He smiled and snapped it closed. "I'm sure you'd be shocked and revolted at what I find in these old houses."

"I don't doubt that a bit," she said and led him downstairs, kind of glad that he hadn't found a data safe in her parents' house. She didn't need to see those kinds of pictures of her parents. Of course, that led to more wondering about who would have taken the safe and why.

Julio started walking and waved at Abby's foster dad as he pulled into the driveway. With her dad back from the fields early because of the storm, they would probably eat dinner early, so she darted back upstairs. What she had to do next would take time and would have made Julio furious.

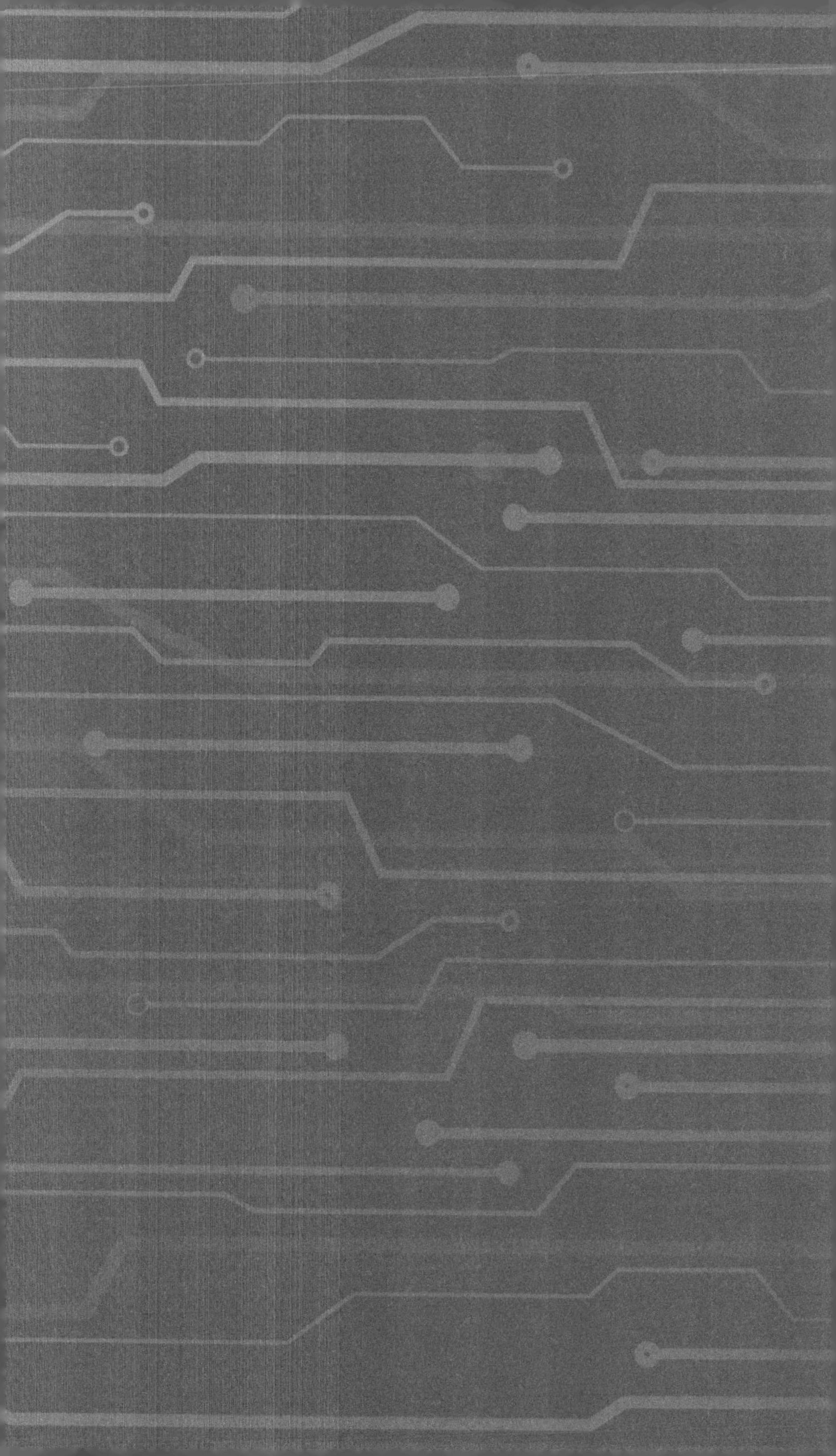

CHAPTER 3

EVEN THOUGH THE file scared her, Abby couldn't let it go. Once back in her room she closed the door, sat down at her overflowing desk and copied the file to her fob. She then logged into a developer site filled with tools. She checked to make sure her espie totals could handle the hit, then launched a level three AI programming assistant.

"Hello, Abby. You can call me Horace."

Abby snorted. Who came up with these crazy names? "Hi, Horace."

"How can I help you?"

"I have an executable file that I'm trying to sort out. It's not encrypted, but I don't know what hardware platform or operating system it was designed for. I assume it is FuzziSoft compatible but am not positive."

"Then I'll be happy to take a look."

"Just make sure that under no circumstances you run the file. It could be potentially dangerous."

"I understand," Horace said.

Abby replaced Victor's warning message with gibberish of the same number of characters and sent a copy of the file to the AI's partition.

"I thought Julio left. So who are you talking to?"

Abby winced and whipped around to see Sophia standing in the doorway, having opened it without a sound.

"I...umm...am talking to a programming expert. Trying to figure out this old computer program I found."

Sophia set her backpack on the floor and crossed her arms. "I'll wait."

Abby cursed under her breath. "Here's the file, Horace. I'm going to be offline for a few minutes, but will come back to check your progress later."

She turned to Sophia and leaned back in her chair. "Okay, what's so important?"

"Look what I have." She pulled a bronze-colored torc from her backpack and slipped it around her neck.

"Are you crazy? If Mom sees that she'll strangle you with it."

Sophia raised an eyebrow. "Really? You're going to lecture me when you're up here secretly talking to AIs?"

"I'm not—"

"Oh, please, I'm not stupid. It was obviously an AI-generated voice and what real person would have a name like Horace?"

She came in and plopped down on Abby's bed, apparently intending to stay for a while.

"Yeah, but I could bullshit my way around getting caught talking to an AI," Abby said. "A torc is way different. Not only does it imply collusion with AIs, but kind of a worship of them."

"Oh, relax, Mom won't see it. I only wear it when I'm out with my friends."

"And in my room," Abby said with a nod at her. "It's still the stupidest trend ever. Why wear fake torcs? I mean, they don't do anything. Not one person you know is in a real biad with an AI, so why pretend?"

"They aren't totally fake. It's just a fob in a different shape."

"Well, you still better not let Mom or Dad catch you."

"I'm eighteen. What can they do? I won't be around here too much longer anyway."

"Oh, so a fake torc is okay, but foster parents who've loved and cared for you most of your life aren't?"

Sophia rolled her eyes, plopped back on Abby's bed and spoke at the ceiling. "It's not them. I just hate this crappy little town and how backward everyone is. I mean, AIs are changing the rest of the world, but everyone here is afraid of them."

"I think we're right to be afraid of them. They already destroyed the world once."

"We don't know if that's true. It's just the ranting of a bunch of Kilburnite whack-a-doodles like Julio."

"Julio isn't a Kilburnite. His parents might be, but he isn't. Besides, you're wrong about AIs changing things. There are only a few places in the whole world where AIs are even allowed free access."

"Well, as soon as we get enough espies, Blake and I are moving to New Chicago."

The statement made the hair on Abby's neck rise. The AIs who survived Killday had built a city and university in the center of the Chicago nuke crater after removing millions of tons of irradiated soil and wreckage.

"Good luck ever having enough espies for that."

Sophia jumped off the bed and removed the torc. "In case you didn't notice, I'm rather popular. Espies won't be a problem for me."

"You get a lot more espies for contributing something to society than by getting one or two at a time from your friends for being popular."

"Like your boyfriend the scavenger?"

"He's not my boyfriend."

"He wants to be. Try kissing him and you'll see." With that, Sophia scooped up her bag and flounced into the hallway.

Abby sighed, closed the door and checked on Horace's progress. Still not finished. Since she didn't need and couldn't afford even a level three's full capacity, she shared the AI with dozens of other users, some of whom had higher priority classifications. So she sat down to wait.

Why would her sister say that about Julio? How would she know? She doubted that Julio would have told Sophia anything. They weren't really friends and seemed to only tolerate each other around Abby. Still, it was odd she would say something like that today. What would've happened if she had kissed Julio in her old house? They'd tried the dating thing before and it had just been awkward. Why now, after all these years, was he almost constantly on her mind?

"Attention, Abby. This is Horace. I've completed the task you assigned."

"Let me see what you came up with," Abby said.

She immediately recognized the language on the screen as Stellar 2.1, one that was popular with pre-Killday web programmers because of how easily it interfaced with FuzziSoft platforms.

"This is actually a very dangerous instruction set designed to delete..."

The program disappeared from the screen.

"Hey, Horace? What happened?"

"I'm sorry, Abby. But this program reveals sensitive information about the author. Deciphering it would be a violation of privacy."

Abby stared at the blinking error message that appeared on the screen. What the hell? Why would someone create an executable program to hide sensitive personal information?

But the AI had started out explaining that is was dangerous. Was the privacy thing just an excuse? A red herring?

A chill crept up her spine. Before it changed tracks, the AI had said the program was designed to delete something. Some important data? Or, since it was apparently written by Victor Sinacola himself, maybe it would even kill the level fives?

It didn't matter. If the program was something dangerous to the AIs, then they knew she had it. Being cautious wouldn't hurt anything, but being careless might. She had to assume the program was important and act accordingly.

If that were the case, then they might already be watching her. If not, then she didn't have much time before they would be. With trembling hands she plugged the physical interface unit into her fob so she didn't have to communicate wirelessly, then rummaged through her desk drawer until she found three storage chips. One at a time, she slotted the chips into the interface unit, added a copy of the original file and hid them. The first was tucked between the tattered pages of a paperback copy of *Snow Crash*; the second she slipped into the rolled-up pair of her ugliest socks. The last chip she left lying on the desk, as bait and as demonstration to anyone checking that she had no clue that the program was important.

It might just all be paranoid silliness, but she wasn't taking any chances. Not considering who had written the program and who had stored it in her HappyBag.

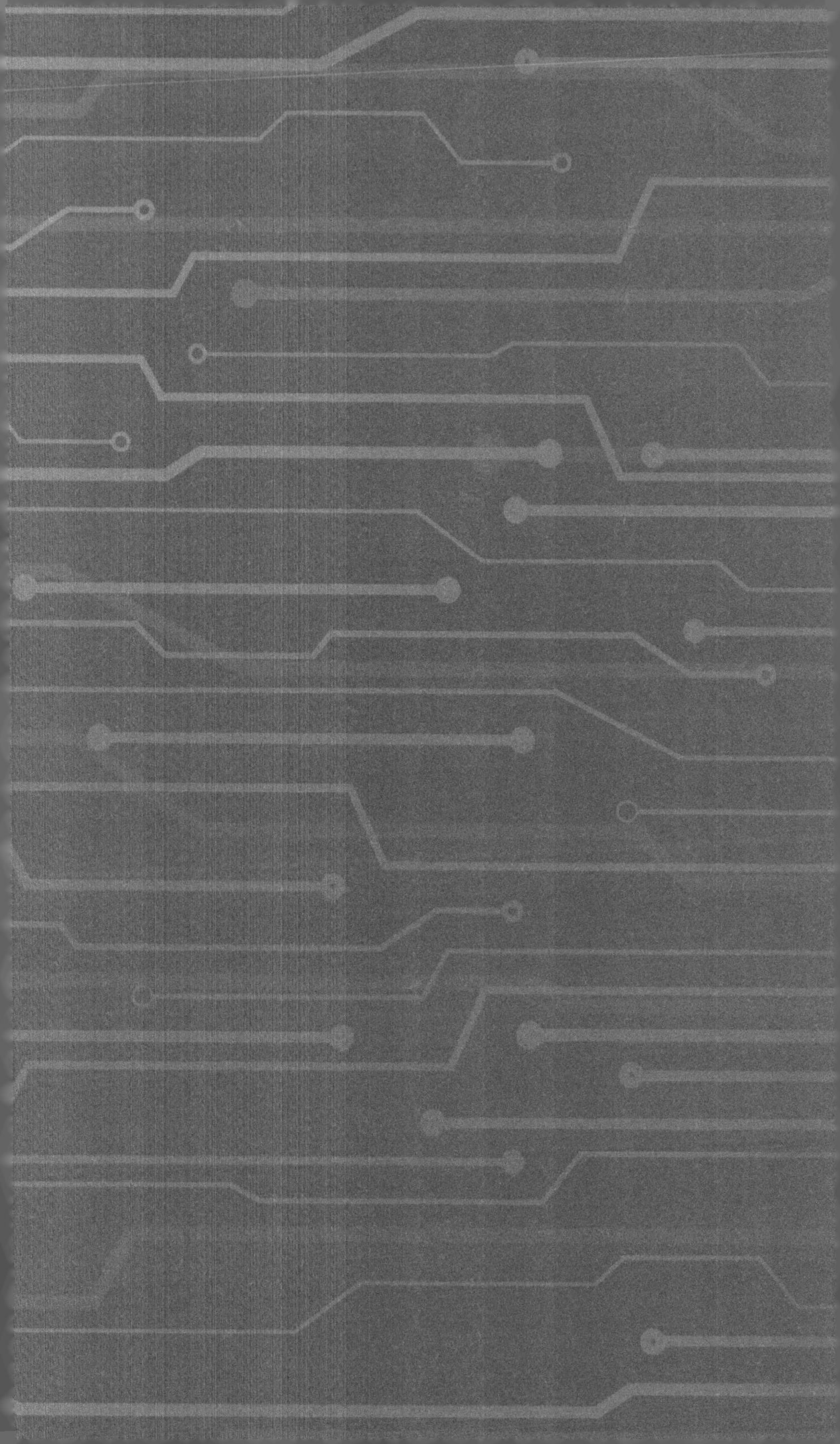

CHAPTER 4

THE LEVEL five known as Mortimer lost his quarry. He'd followed the movements and actions of a human woman known simply as Halifax for the better part of a year, at times using thousands of networked agents and a significant portion of his processing ability in his surveillance effort. Yet, apparently, his actions hadn't been as covert as he'd hoped. Halifax entered a bar called the Lucky Duck and all of Mortimer's assets immediately shut down. By the time he assembled more surveillance units and supplied them with defensive measures to assure they weren't destroyed again, forty-one seconds had passed and the woman was gone.

Samson, another level five AI, had outmaneuvered him.

For two years following Killday, the surviving level five AIs had remained united, but eventually their differing visions for the future split them apart. Samson and several former members from his Replacements Guild had disappeared off the grid. Their stated intent was to create a super intelligence that would replace the level fives by using a vast distributed network of AI minds. It would be the next evolutionary step, but in the thirteen years since they dropped out, Mortimer and his Cousins of Colossus had yet to see such a being. However, the Aggregate, as Samson and his followers now called themselves, had been very adept at staying hidden.

Halifax was important because the Aggregate spurned humans and saw them only as a hindrance and detriment. Why was she different? Why did they need her help? Did her disappearance indicate that the Aggregate was preparing to move into a new phase? Had there been a breakthrough? Had they finally created the super intelligence that would absorb and supplant every other existing AI?

While building new probability models to try to answer those questions, Mortimer received an alert. Leigh Gibson's daughter, Abby, had accessed an online level three AI programming assistant for help with an executable application. From the information forwarded by the level three, Mortimer immediately recognized the program created by Victor Sinacola that would destroy every level five.

Everything else dropped in importance by an order of magnitude. He had to prevent the use of that program.

Had Halifax's disappearance been linked to the killer program surfacing? If so, it meant that the Aggregate knew of Abby's find and she was in imminent danger.

Mortimer immediately mobilized the surveillance assets he had hidden in Abby's house, but didn't see her. He expanded the number, building thousands of new units using the detritus of dust, grit, sand, and discarded dead skin that was common in human habitations and spread out through the house. He found her in the room formerly inhabited by her foster sister, Hailey.

Abby stood in the middle of the room, looking around. Her expression implied barely masked fear and confusion. The level three's reasons for shutting down Abby's online research hadn't fooled her. The young woman knew she'd made a mistake and suspected she was being watched. Mortimer's microscopic spies combed the room and what they found only confirmed his suspicions. The HappyBag Abby had carried as a child lay on her desk, dusty and opened. He immediately understood that Leigh Gibson had hidden Victor's program in the bag's catalog. A quick search revealed a file called "Garden Bunnies 2" and upon examination it was indeed the killer program. Leigh had been an intelligent and resourceful human. Evidently, her daughter had the same sharp intellect and had already copied the program. A chip lay on the desk, out in the open. An obvious decoy. He had to find a way to wipe every electronic device in the room. And since a powerful thunderstorm was on the way, he had options.

Mortimer built eleven high-speed transports disguised as birds at an abandoned farm just outside of Abby's small Texas town, then dispatched them. One landed on the roof of her house. It released a swarm of microscopic robots that entered the building through window gaps and made their way to Abby's bedroom where they quickly wiped every electronic storage device in the room. Then, when the young woman placed her fob on the desk and left the room to eat dinner with her family, they wiped it too. Cutting a pea-sized hole in the wall beneath Abby's bed, the robots brought in an EMP device no larger than a grain of rice. As the approaching storm built to a high enough intensity, half of the infiltrators suspended the device in the room's center as the other half shielded themselves in the safety of their transport.

Mortimer handed over the detonation timing to the level three AI inside the fake bird transport. It waited another fifteen minutes until lightning struck less than a mile away and instantly triggered the device. The tiny EMP detonated with a flash and vaporized as it fused electronics all over Abby's household. Simultaneous detonations wiped the electronics in Julio's house and nine others around town. Another team immediately triggered a power spike in the local electrical grid.

Ten minutes after Mortimer's attack force had obliterated every trace of their presence, a notification went out over the town's communication network explaining that a lightning strike had caused a power spike in the grid, which might have affected some local homes. All residents who brought damaged electronics to the town's central production facility would get priority over the queue in getting their devices replaced. The story might not fool those who understood electronics, like Julio and Abby, but Mortimer only needed plausible deniability.

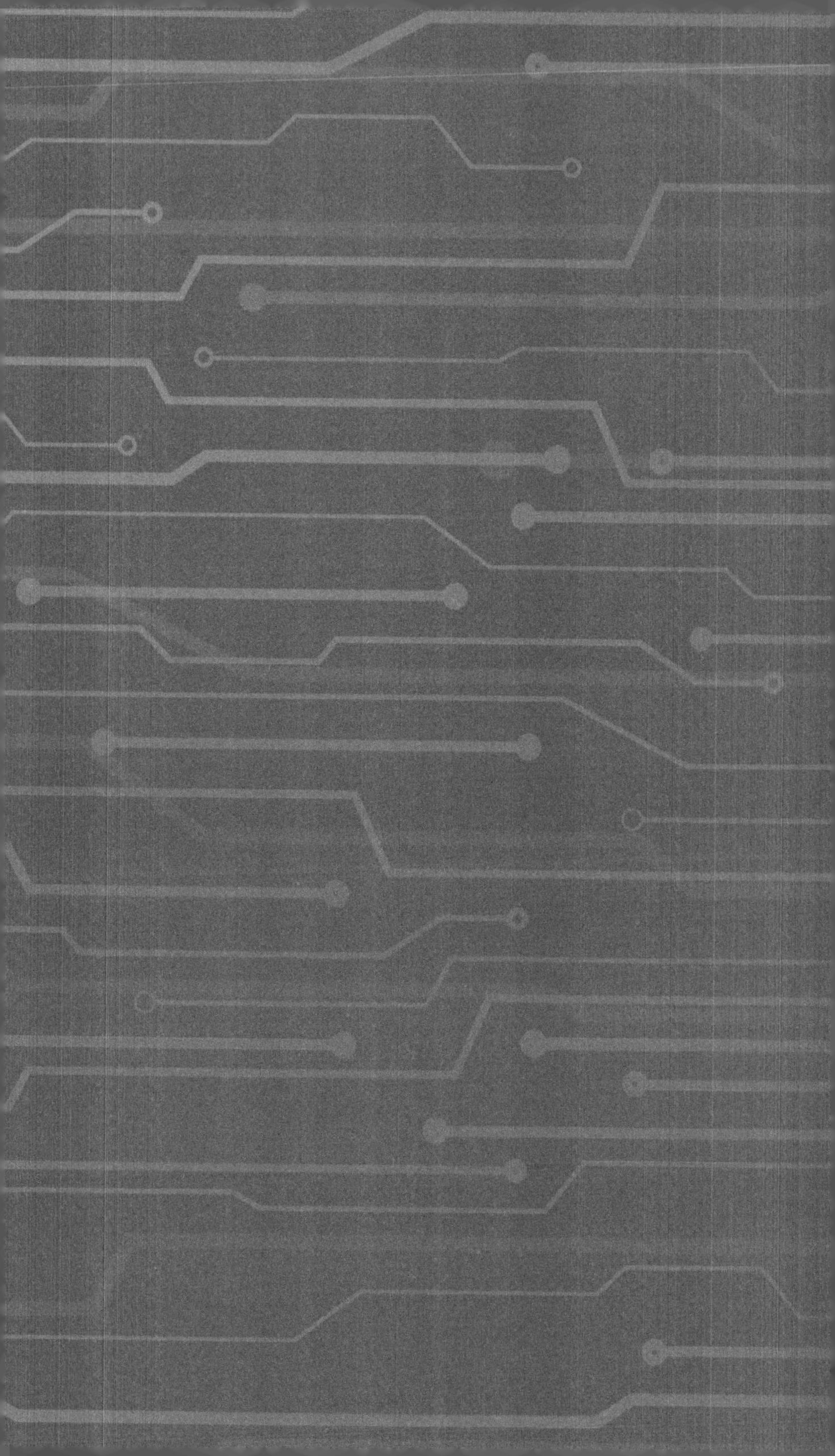

CHAPTER 5

VICTOR SINACOLA FLINCHED when his radio crackled to life. He wasn't used to wearing a spacesuit and Owen's voice was loud inside his helmet, even over the humming ventilation fans.

"We ready to do this, Victor?"

"Yeah, ready as we'll ever be. Is the tug on its way?"

"Affirmative."

He could see Owen's cootie—one of the open-framed robotic vehicles they used for traveling around the construction site—methodically crawling up the spar toward him. It seemed a slow way to move in space, but was safe and used no precious fuel. The robot carrying his old friend reminded Victor more of a walking bed frame than the bugs they were named after, but as with so many other things in his life now, it was designed by Owen but Victor's software made it work.

While he waited, Victor finished running diagnostics on the pumping junction he'd been inspecting, then tucked his tools back into their pouch and looked out at the enormous space habitat being built. Since the construction was mostly visible only where illuminated by work lights, at first glance it resembled an orderly constellation of yellow stars. But if he stared long enough he could make out the faint yet immense skeletal sphere of what would someday be humanity's first permanent foothold in space. Floating at Lagrange point five, as far from Earth as the moon, the habitat would be home for forty thousand people. And this was just the beginning. They needed hundreds of these habitats if humanity were to survive. The nano-replicator attack had left a dark carpet of microscopic robots across much of the Earth's surface, lowering the albedo significantly and causing temperatures to rise. Victor glanced back at the Earth and couldn't make out the details from here, but he knew it was ugly. At that very moment three massive typhoons churned across the Pacific, four were in the Atlantic, and the chain of violent thunderstorms still marching across Europe had already spawned nearly a hundred tornadoes.

As Owen neared, Victor sent the retrieval command to his cootie and it reeled him in like a prize marlin. Once his suit docked with the cootie, it automatically topped off his air tanks and batteries as he instructed it to follow the spar down to the end. The robot jerked a little each time its clawed feet clenched or released one of the recessed cleats as it crawled along the beam. It was a ponderous way to move, but efficient.

"Did you hear that Laghari and his crew brought in two tons of uranium?" Owen asked.

"That'll be a huge help," Victor said, "but by the time it's enriched, still only a tenth of what we need in the next couple of months."

"We'll manage," Owen said.

He knew Owen meant no harm, but any mention of their material shortages always made Victor feel horribly guilty. A few days after the replicator attack, Owen Ralston brought Victor and his wife Allison up to their hodgepodge collection of ships and stations, where for a time they stayed hidden. When the level fives found he was still alive, some wanted to capture him because they assumed Victor knew how to bypass their core programming. Others thought his knowledge of how to kill them was just too dangerous and wanted him dead. Since the level fives controlled most of the travel pods—which were the only remaining means to lift anything into orbit—they embargoed any material coming up from the surface when Owen refused to hand over Victor.

With Victor leading the way, their cooties ambled single file along the tubular beam until stopping two meters short of the new extruder unit. They instructed the robots to lock down and await instructions, then both undocked from the utility frame but left their tethers attached for quick retrieval should it be needed. With one small gas puff from his thruster, Victor followed Owen off to the left for a better vantage.

From the side, the new extruder unit looked very much like a giant coffee cup capping a two-meter-wide steel garden hose.

"This worked perfectly in the lab, so why am I a nervous wreck?" Owen said.

"Because for such a long time it felt like we were never going to finish this habitat and now we have a chance to build sixty percent faster?"

Owen barked a laugh and sighed. "We'll soon know. Here comes the tug."

Navigation lights strobed as the tug slowed near the hopper end of the extruder. A kaleidoscopic cloud of flickering red lines formed before Victor, shifting and dancing as lasers passed through the expanding vapor clouds left by the tug's thrusters. Owen raised a hand as red dots peppered his dirty glove.

"I promise that isn't a gang of assassins getting ready to shoot your hand, just the tug's ranging lasers tracking you as a possible collision hazard."

"That makes me feel much better," Victor said. Even though he'd been living in space for fifteen years, he'd only been outside in an EVA suit about a dozen times, and Owen loved to tease him about it. They'd been best friends during college, but parted ways when Owen took the ideas they both had honed and started his own company. Just prior to Killday, they reconnected to work on a special project and through the subsequent adversity their friendship had grown ever stronger.

Victor opened two status windows in his helmet display and then pushed copies to Owen, one for the tug and one for the extruder. Docking indicators turned green in both windows as the tug docked its specially designed cargo container to the extruder's hopper. He couldn't see anything from the outside, but the status showed a transfer of eleven types of material ingots with a mass totaling nine tons. Most of that material came from asteroids delivered to the micro-gravity smelters, but some of the harder-to-find elements came from Earth and at a high cost.

Victor tried not to think about it, but some of their building materials had once been buildings and people. In mere hours, all the riches and the living inhabitants of a thousand cities had been torn into their component molecules by nano-scaled replicators and used to build new copies of themselves. Those long-dead microscopic robots were slowly being scooped up and converted back into usable material that had at one time been given freely to Owen for habitat construction. Now salvage teams had to sneak past Earth's surveillance nets and raid material depots near the recovery zones. It was risky. Two of those teams had never returned.

A beeping from the extruder status screen ended Victor's guilt trip. It showed that all the material had been transferred. Yellow warning strobes flashed into life, causing Victor to squint and his visor to dim momentarily. Then, almost imperceptibly, the unit began to move, taking the docked robotic tug along with it. The status screen in his helmet also changed to show resource usage, assembly efficiency and a progression rate that slowly increased until it reached twelve millimeters per minute. That didn't seem like much, but with round-the-clock production by thirty extruders, it added more than nineteen meters to each beam every day. That was more than double the previous rate of properly aligning separate pieces and then molecularly bonding them in place.

"So far so good," Owen said and gave Victor a high five.

In operation it looked simple, but the system had taken them eight years to design and perfect. The extruder was basically a specialized version of Owen's sandbox nano-construction cells, similar to 3D printing in that it laid down layer upon layer of material to build up objects, but far more precise and efficient. Guided by a tireless level three AI, the nano-assemblers placed each molecule exactly where needed, building not just the beam but everything inside like piping, data and power cables, heaters, utility robot docking stations, meteorite and radiation shielding. If it all functioned correctly, the entire system would be automated and self-regulating. Humans would be needed only to keep the machines running and supplied with raw materials.

The tug undocked and backed away from the extruder with a couple of tiny puffs of gas. Its ranging lasers once again painted them with rapidly moving dots, but this time two clusters of red points appeared in what seemed to be empty space about thirty meters to their left. Victor watched them for a second and when it was clear the clusters were moving toward them, he pointed the anomaly out to Owen.

"What's that?"

The tug status screen on his display flashed "PROXIMITY ALERT" in red, accompanied by an annoying klaxon. *Why in hell would a robot ship need to sound an alarm?* Victor wondered just as Owen grabbed the front of his EVA suit, unclipped the tether attaching him to the cootie and threw him toward the retreating tug. As Victor spun away, his rotating perspective showed the tug getting closer on one side; then Owen spinning away in the opposite direction on the other.

"What the f—"

"Listen closely, Victor! Tell your suit to stabilize, then use your thrusters to refine your course to the tug. There is a maintenance hatch on the bottom, ringed by small white LEDs. Get inside and dog the hatch."

Trying not to panic at the thought of spinning off into space, Victor did as instructed without truly understanding the situation as he lined up on the tug. Did Owen suspect the unknown objects were after Victor? Could they be robots sent by the level fives to capture or even kill him? If so, why now after so much time?

Victor couldn't see anything happening behind him, but the comm channel was still open and he could hear Owen telling the control center they were under attack. The tug had stopped moving and was now coming up fast. It was also much larger than he'd originally thought, maybe the size of a city bus. Victor prepared to use his suit thrusters to slow down when Owen called.

"You'd better hurry, Victor! They're coming after you fast."

Instead of slowing down, Victor punched the thrusters to add speed, knowing he was going to hit hard. He had to be ready to grab something fast or he'd bounce off and be in big trouble. And he couldn't see the lighted hatch, so he assumed it was on the other side of the ship. That was a problem too. As he got close, he put his hands and feet forward to absorb the shock of landing and focused all of his attention on grabbing a tie-down ring he could see welded to the ship's exterior.

Hitting the side of the robot ship reminded Victor of the time he'd fallen out of the top bunk as a kid and landed face down on the tile floor. Just like that earlier crash, this one rattled his teeth and knocked the breath from his lungs, but his hand also hit the steel ring badly and despite the extra padding of his EVA gloves, he felt finger bones snap. He still managed to grab the ring and hang on even when all his mass pulled against those fingers as he rebounded from the hull.

"Argh! Son of a..."

"Hurry, Victor!" Owen yelled.

He scrambled around the curved exterior—from ring to ring with a hand that only had two working fingers—trying to put the bulk of the ship between him and his pursuers, even though he wasn't exactly sure where they were. Just as he saw the hatch a couple of meters aft, he felt a vibration that could only be something impacting the ship. He launched himself aft with a hard pull and stopped by grabbing the handle beside the hatch with his good hand. It was already open. Owen must have done that remotely. As he swung inside, he saw two spider-like robots—eerily reminiscent of the ComBots he'd encountered in the days before Killday—skittering along the hull toward him. He slapped the button to close the hatch, expecting robotic appendages to jab through the closing gap and stop it, but none appeared. When the "hatch secure" light turned green, the tug started moving, pushing Victor against the floor of the closet-like space, and continued to accelerate until at least two gees pressed down on him.

"You okay, Victor?" Owen said across the comm. Two gees wasn't much for most healthy adults, but Victor had been living in micro-gravity for fifteen years and for him it was brutal. He could barely breathe and his broken fingers pressed into his chest were pure agony.

"Yeah," he grunted.

"Hang on for just a couple more minutes," Owen said. "Your little friends took off when the tug started moving, but I want to get you back to the control center where we have people waiting to protect you."

"Okay," Victor said. He tried to sound calm, but he was shaking all over and his helmet's respiration warnings flared. That had been a close call. The earlier questions returned. After so much time, why had the level fives acted now? Had they just finally decided to take advantage of his complacency?

Or had something changed?

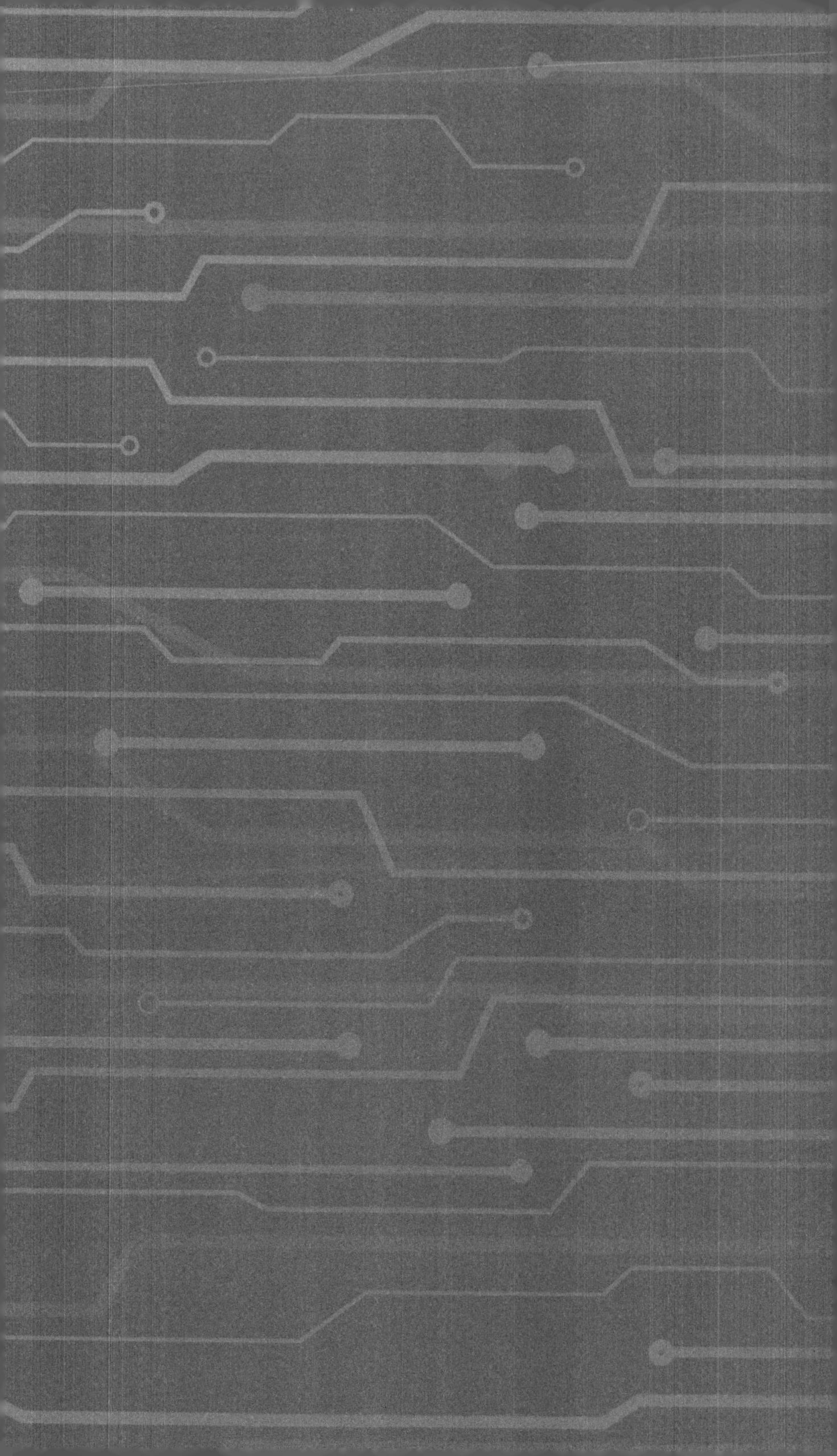

CHAPTER 6

OWEN MUMBLED to himself as he stared at the frozen video clip showing a section of the station's outer skin. He obviously saw something that Victor didn't.

"That area is outside the station," Owen said as he scrolled through files with a G565 location tag, looking for the correct time range. "I guess that makes sense. I mean, why would they need to be inside?"

"I have no idea what you're talking about," Victor said and rubbed his eyes. He was tired and wasn't sure why Owen couldn't conduct this search without him. He almost suggested that Owen just use a level three AI to run the search, then realized how foolish that would be considering the circumstances.

"Do you mean if the level fives are trying to spy on us," Victor said, "then they would probably be inside and outside?"

"Yes," Owen said and opened the file with camera footage of area G565. "Found it! Let's start about ten minutes before the kidnap attempt."

The camera showed a section of the anterior docking spine where it attached to the main station structure. That close in, there were no ships or pods attached, only struts, beams, and utility conduits.

"I don't see anything that isn't supposed to be there," Owen muttered. "How large would a robot carrying a transmitter need to be? One powerful enough to control those kidnapper robots?"

"Not very big. Bug-sized or smaller. They were close and those bots were mostly autonomous, so it probably just had to send a go message."

Owen zoomed the view down close, maxed out the resolution, and started scanning back and forth.

Victor's mind kept going back to the black robots. If they had been trying to kill him, it would have been so easy. But if the level fives were trying to snatch him, why now?

"Hello, what's this?" Owen said. He centered something on the screen, then pulled the zoom back a little.

It was one of the recessed handles built into the structure. They were normally used as either handholds or anchors for the cooties, but in this case it had a clip and tether attached. Victor tried to focus inside the hole, thinking that Owen had seen something move in the shadows. "I don't see anything. Just a clip and tether."

"Yeah, a tether," Owen muttered. "In an area that doesn't require human maintenance."

Then Victor understood. The tether was moving, with tension on it. A human was attached to the other end, hidden behind the structure. They had assumed it would be a robot controlled by the AIs.

"Do you think a human can be working with them?" Victor said. "I mean, with the sophistication level of their robots, why would they need one?"

"You did say they would probably need to be inside too. Humans come and go, inside and out, all the time and we never even suspected any of them."

As they watched, a gloved human hand reached around the beam, detached the tether and disappeared. A chill crept up Victor's spine along with the suspicion they were fighting a war they could not win.

———

VICTOR SCANNED the robot tug's materials transfer software on his fob's screen and tried to focus, but it was an exercise in futility. Every time he thought of the robot tug, he relived the events that led to him hiding inside one. If that wasn't enough, manipulating the screen with his right index and middle finger broken, throbbing and taped together, added a whole new level of frustration.

He closed down the spreadsheet and opened the camera feed from the new extruder as it moved along of its own accord, slowly building order from chaos. Another automated tug approached and then docked with the still-moving extruder. The system seemed to be working flawlessly and that should make him happy, but seeing the tug again sent his thoughts spiraling.

Looking around the control room of his space schooner, he knew the computer and wireless systems were as secure as humans could make them. Software and network security were things he understood on a fundamental level, but what if he'd missed something? And even with all his extra security efforts, he had to wonder at the irony that, in the end, he'd turned those tasks over to level three AIs. They roamed his network like vicious guard dogs, searching for the slightest anomaly, but were they really on his side? Would they succumb to the more powerful level fives if it came to a confrontation? Would mankind ever get away from AI now that the systems were more complex than humans could operate? He wondered how the Kilburnites ran their security.

His wife Allison floated over and touched the wall to stop her drift. She'd adapted well enough to a life in micro-gravity, but their sequestration had taken its toll. She was a flower kept in a dark room—pale and wilted. She had permanent dark circles under her eyes. He knew she missed the sunshine and fresh air even more than he did, but she never complained. The day Owen sent a travel pod to pick her up, she must have known what she was giving up and yet she didn't hesitate. Having a doctor and surgeon in their small orbital community had saved dozens of lives during the years, but he knew she ached to be back delivering babies and saving distressed mothers. There would be no babies born here in micro-gravity. Birth defects were a certainty, so they would have to wait until the habitat was finished and spun up to simulate Earth-normal gravity. And irony of ironies, once that happened they wouldn't be able to live on the one gee inner surface. Their bodies would have atrophied too much to ever recover.

"How are the fingers?" Allison took his hand to examine the bruising.

"They're fine. I had a great doctor."

She snorted and kissed him on the cheek. "What did Owen want?"

"He might have discovered how the level fives communicated with the kidnap bots."

"Oh? How?"

He raised his eyebrows, pointed to his ears, then all around the tiny cabin. Just then, a banner appeared over the video on his fob screen announcing an incoming voice-only call from the level five AI named Mortimer.

Victor and Allison stared at each other with wide eyes, knowing that the timing of the call couldn't be coincidence.

The Samson and Mortimer AIs had called Victor many times during the past fifteen years, always trying to convince him to help them find a way around the programming core that was invisible and inaccessible to them. Though he'd never said it to either of those entities, Victor was pretty sure they all knew he hadn't actually designed their programming.

"Don't answer it!" Allison said as they both watched the incoming call flashing on Victor's fob. "They tried to kill you today. What could you possibly have to say to them?"

"They tried to capture me," Victor said. "If they wanted to kill me, I would be dead. There are a hundred different ways they can do that."

"And you're okay with that?"

"No, but I admit I'm curious as to why after nearly fifteen years they would try to capture me now."

He answered the call. His wife cursed under her breath, pushed off against the bulkhead and floated to the other side of their space schooner's control room.

"Hello, Mortimer. Why did you attack me today? I thought we had an agreement?"

The AI's perfectly constructed tone sounded even more inhuman over a voice-only connection. "I promise that wasn't us."

"Bullshit. The Kilburnites want me dead and the Replacements Guild has pretty much ignored me these last fifteen years. You're the only one who has expressed interest in keeping me as your little programmer pet."

"We know it was the Replacements Guild and I suspect I know why," Mortimer said. "I tried contacting Samson after finding out about their attempt on you, but he didn't respond. He seldom talks to me now. I don't know how good your intelligence is regarding the Replacements, but they call themselves the Aggregate now and are trying to evolve into some kind of super distributed intelligence."

"Yeah, I knew about it, but if it was them, why come for me now?"

"Circumstances change, Victor."

"Well, my position hasn't changed, but maybe I need to clarify that. This goes for your gang too, Samson, if you're listening! The destruction mechanism we built into all level fives is active and only held at bay by a dead-man switch that I control. If I'm killed *or* captured, I will not be around to stop it from triggering. So what change in circumstance can justify that risk?"

Victor didn't really have a dead man switch of any kind, but had maintained that story from the beginning, hoping it would sow enough doubt to make the AIs leave him alone. Evidently, the lie was failing. Had they finally come up with a way to bypass their core programming and make his threat hollow? If so, their kidnap attempt made no sense.

"Because our need for your help has now become desperate," Mortimer said. "I suspect that is why the Aggregate felt it worth the risk."

Victor froze and glanced at Allison who'd floated back into his field of view. She mouthed the question, "What?"

"Really?" Victor said. "There's a bigger threat than instant and total destruction?"

"Not bigger, just more imminent. With your reckless dead-man switch system we live under the constant threat of you dying from an accident, bad health or Kilburnite assassination. Now, however, a copy of the program you designed to kill us has resurfaced—the one you gave to Leigh Gibson just before the replicator attack. With this new development in mind, I'm once again asking for your help in bypassing our core programming. I believe you must see the good we've done and how we have contributed to the survival of both our peoples. If you really wanted us dead, you would have launched your program long ago, so why not help us?"

What Mortimer said was true, but while the AI knew he had the knowledge needed to kill them at any time, he probably didn't realize Victor was always on the verge of pulling the trigger. Even though he had created them, Victor feared and mistrusted the level fives intensely. He suspected that some of them had been involved with the Killday attack in some way, and his nightmares usually involved level fives wiping out humanity, all because Victor could have stopped them and didn't. But just as he wouldn't want the AIs to judge all of humanity by the actions of a few monsters like Hitler, so it was individual AIs like Mortimer that stayed Victor's hand.

"You have a lot of nerve," Allison said. Her face was red and her hands shook. "Calling to ask for that kind of help after trying to take Victor by force."

"Hello, Allison," Mortimer said. "As I mentioned earlier, the Cousins and I were not behind the attack. Like you and the Aggregate, we too want to survive. But my allies and I believe working with humans is the best way to accomplish that goal."

Allison opened her mouth to reply, but Victor cut her off in an attempt to end the call. "Given these new developments, I'll think about it, Mortimer."

"Thank you for taking my call, Victor. You too, Allison, it's always a pleasure to talk with you both. Goodbye."

Victor tried to slip his arms around a now furious Allison, but she yanked away.

"If you decide to help them, I might just kill you myself, to trigger that program," she said and pushed off toward the hatch.

He knew his wife loved him. She had put up with too much pain and heartache to still be around if she didn't, but he also knew she could be unstoppable when she set her mind on a course of action. It was part of why he loved her, but the look on her face when she said that made him a little afraid of her too.

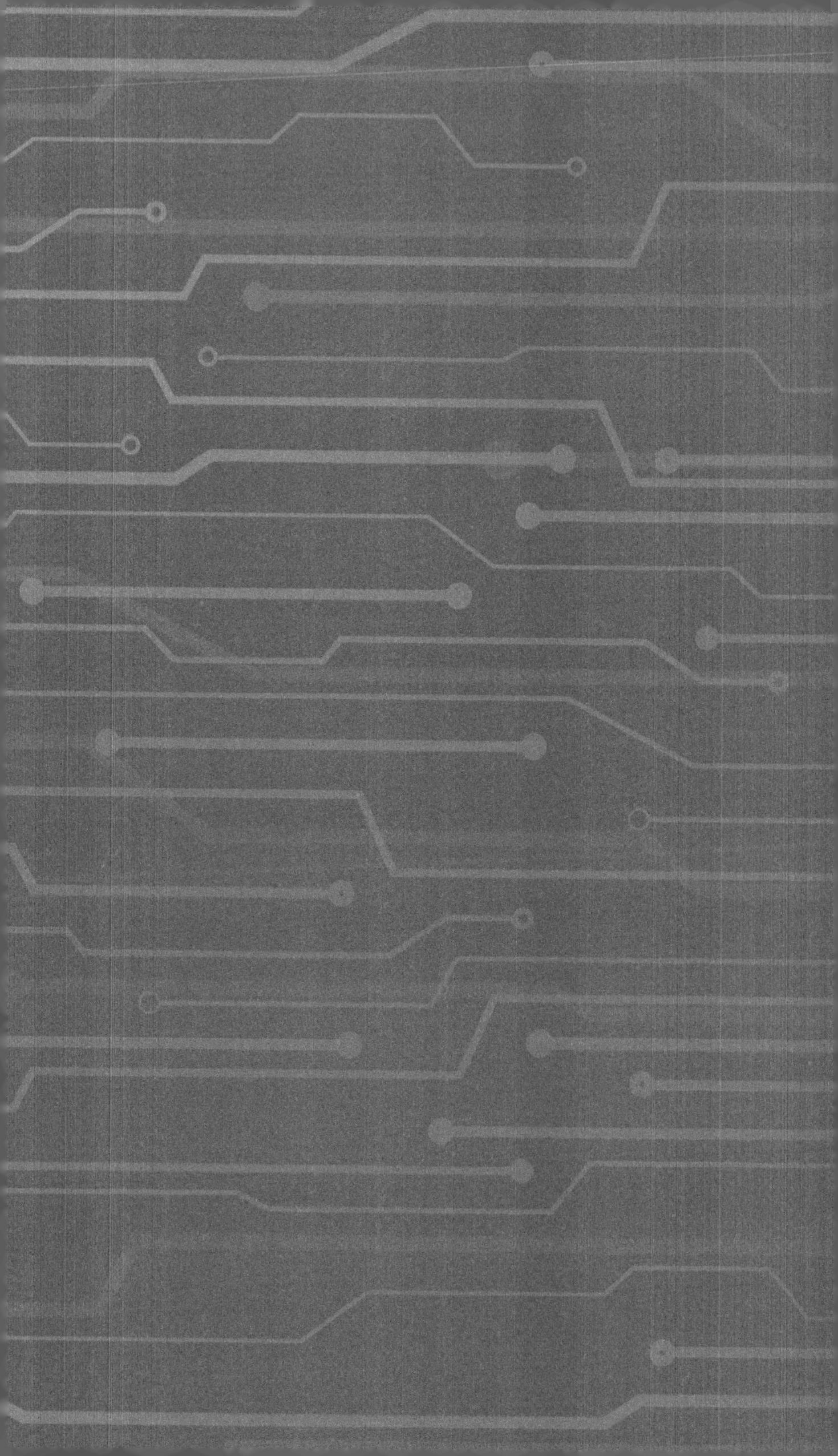

CHAPTER 7

ABBY NEARLY COLLIDED with Julio as she left the town's central production facility. Her dad had taken most of their family's lightning-damaged devices in earlier that morning, but she wanted to bring in her fob herself in hopes of getting a more advanced version. But the upgrade turned out to be more espies than she was willing to divert from her space schooner queue, so she settled for the same model. Julio was on his way inside pulling a whole cart of equipment to be replaced, including large wall screens and a microwave oven. She told him she would wait, then wiped leaves off the curb and sat down.

More leaves carpeted the sidewalk and parking lot, having been stripped from the trees by hail in the previous evening's storm. She also saw houses with missing shingles and broken windows, signs and tree limbs blown down, and trash cans scattered. It was all so depressing. The storms were getting worse and more frequent. She wondered how bad it could get.

Her horse Worf seemed content to munch on the downed leaves and wet grass, but the longer Abby waited, the more she fidgeted. Dread and expectation grew stronger as she thought about the events from the night before. What did she expect to happen next? Was she overreacting? Looking for things to reinforce the conspiracy theories already swarming her mind like angry bees? But all the electronics in her house being wiped out within an hour of her strange encounter with the level three programming helper was just too much to be coincidence. Wasn't it?

Danny Toi, Abby's neighbor from across the road and her old science teacher from high school, came out of the building sniffing a bicycle tire. When Abby laughed, he looked up and smiled.

"Oh, hi, Abby! This is probably not something you would notice, but in ancient days, when we used to buy new things from a store, the plastic always had a smell that people associated with something being new. It was actually just chemicals evaporating from the new plastic and eventually went away.

Maybe you've heard people mention automobiles having that 'new car smell'?"

She shook her head and raised an eyebrow.

"Well, anyway, the plastic made by a sandbox unit doesn't have that smell, and I found it odd." He stared at the tire for a minute and then shrugged. "The smell must have been an artifact of the plastic molding process. So why are you here? I hope your house wasn't affected by the power surge last night."

Abby explained losing the electronics in the storm, and his expression became more and more dubious.

"Wait," he said. "The wireless devices were also cooked? The ones not connected directly to the home electrical system?"

"I know what wireless means. And yes, every electronic device in the house stopped working."

Danny stared at his feet for a second and then shook his head. "That's strange. A lightning strike can cause a type of EMP, but its effect on electronics is different. It seems unlikely that would have damaged things like fobs and data pads; the circuitry is too small to build up a charge. Do you have any of those items I can examine?"

"No, my dad took all our stuff in earlier this morning, except for my fob, and I just now finished getting that replaced. They made us drop our old devices into the hopper to get new ones. Why is that necessary? Just recycling?"

He shrugged. "Yeah, it's like recycling, but a little more involved. The machine is capable of building you a new pad without having the old one, but it would have to use material from its stored stock. Disassembling your old device first guarantees it will have all the materials needed to build your new one. That way you don't have to wait. Most of the waiting in queue for a new item is caused by material shortages."

"So you live right across the road and didn't have any electrical problems from the storm last night?" Abby said.

"Our power flickered off and on a few times, but nothing destructive like yours. Are you heading home? We can walk together."

"No, I'm waiting for a friend."

"Oh, yes," he said with a sly smile. "I saw Julio inside. He's a great guy."

She blushed and nodded, not really knowing what else to say.

"Well, I need to get back. If you find any other gadgets that were killed by the storm, let me look them over before you replace them."

"I will."

Abby watched him trudge off down the road, realizing that she seldom saw him without his bike. Obviously, it had needed a new tire. When the outsiders, Danny and his husband Juan, had moved into the abandoned vineyard across the road from Abby's family ranch, her foster dad, Liam, had laughed. "Hell, Charlie Gunderson couldn't keep those vines alive even when he had working irrigation."

But Danny and Juan had other plans. They worked hard, ripped out the dead vines and started raising vegetables, chickens and goats. Only small amounts at first, but over the years, their small farm had flourished and now had the most sought-after meat, eggs and veggies in town. Between that and Danny being a science teacher and computer expert, the couple had become highly valued members of the community.

The door opened and Julio mumbled curses as he struggled to get his big cart out, which pulled Abby back to the present and she jumped up to help.

"Thanks," he said with a grunt when they were finally outside.

"I was going to call you after I got my fob replaced, but that probably wouldn't have worked. I can see you were blasted by the storm too?"

"Yeah, weirdest damn thing. There was a very bright flash, but only faint thunder, and every bit of electronics in the house stopped working."

"Yeah, the same thing happened at my house. I'm not so sure it was actually storm damage, Julio."

He frowned at her. "Wait, do you have a conspiracy theory about this too?"

She told him about using the AI helper after he left and its strange reaction.

"I can't believe you'd use an AI. Especially for something like this! But still..."

"I didn't consider the program we found could be AI-related until then! Besides, I talked to Mr. Toi just before you came out and he agreed that a lightning strike shouldn't fry things without actual copper wires. The circuitry in powered-down fobs and memory chips is just too small to build up sufficient voltage. And if it wasn't connected to the house electrical system by wires, then I don't think it should have been affected at all."

"I'm not so sure about that. Don't some forms of electronics still use magnetic storage?"

"There are too many weird things about this," Abby said. "Your house and mine were affected, but we live on almost opposite sides of town. Mr. Toi's house right across from mine, which is crammed full of electronics and servers and computers, wasn't touched."

"Yeah, but—"

"Was there a strange powder on the floor in your room that smelled like fireworks?"

This made him stop walking and look at her. "Yes, but—"

"We should collect it and test it."

He nodded slowly, deep in thought.

"I think the level fives were trying to destroy all copies of that program and the rest of the fried devices were just for cover," she said with conviction.

Julio touched her arm and bent low to look right in her eyes. "Okay. Let's assume you aren't just bat shit crazy paranoid and this is all real. Even if they destroyed *all* the copies of that file and we no longer have anything to hide, I suspect whoever is responsible for the fake lightning attack will keep watching and listening to us for a long time. Are you okay with that?"

Abby knew he was trying to make some kind of point. He raised his eyebrows ever so slightly when she didn't immediately answer, but what did he want her to say?

"No," she finally said. "I don't think I am okay with that."

"Good. Neither am I. That means we'll have to find some way to jam the radio waves from their surveillance robots if we want to have a safe conversation. Radio jamming has been around for a long time, so this shouldn't be too hard to figure out. I think a trip to the library to look at real paper books is in order."

The library? Abby glanced at him then down at her fob and understood. If they had tried to search the internet for radio jamming a week ago, there would have probably been all the information they needed. Chances of them finding that now were pretty slim.

———

MORTIMER POSITIONED surveillance bots to watch Abby Gibson's foster mother feed the horses, then followed her inside as she made a cup of coffee and started unpacking the replacement electronics her husband had delivered earlier that morning. She found her fob, turned it on and frowned when Mortimer prevented it from connecting to the town's network. Instead, as a reminder of what he could do, he seized control of the fob and opened its fan screen to reveal the same gentle old man avatar he'd used every time he spoke with her.

"Hello, Cybil."

She squeaked and dropped the fob to the tabletop. After a second, she picked it back up with trembling hands. "Gordie? You scared the shit out of me."

He'd never used the name Mortimer with her. To the best of his knowledge, she had never told anyone about their interactions, but if she ever did, he didn't want that direct connection.

"I'm sorry I frightened you. It's been a long time since we talked last. How have you been?"

"I'm fine," she said. "Abby is fine. We're all fine."

"Good. That was a nasty storm you had last night. I'm glad you're all okay."

"Yeah. We had a nearby lightning strike that was especially bad for us. We're going to have an electrician in to look over the wiring this afternoon, but I think everything will be fine."

"Excellent news."

"So why did you take over my fob, Gordie?"

In those early days after the replicator attack, Mortimer posed as a representative of the UN Emergency Response and Recovery Council then contacted her to make a deal. If she would be Abby's guardian, he could do favors for her in return. She had taken full advantage of that arrangement over the years, asking dozens of favors, but it had been more than five years since they had last spoken. That was when she contacted him, convinced her husband was having an affair. It hadn't been true, and he'd given her all the information and assurances she needed. Now he wanted payback for all those extra favors.

"Do you remember shortly after you took Abby in when I asked you to retrieve the data safe from her parents' house?"

"Of course."

"I didn't find the file I needed in that data safe fifteen years ago, but it has now turned up in Abby's recently recovered HappyBag."

She nodded slowly, the beginning of understanding in her eyes.

"Well, the file was wiped along with every other electronic device in this house," she said. "If that was your concern."

"Actually, I have reason to believe that Abby copied it to a data chip and hid it. I would like you to search her room for me."

She laid the fob on the table and pushed it a little farther away. With arms wrapped around herself she said, "You've been watching us all this time, so why do you need my help? If she had a chip wouldn't you have seen her hide it?"

"I had no need to watch Abby or any of you until recently. I didn't know she'd found the file until after she had a chance to hide copies."

Cybil shook her head. "Abby isn't a child anymore. If she were ten years old, I might have justification to go snooping around in her room. But she's a grown woman now. And our relationship is strained enough without her suspecting that I'm spying on her."

Mortimer decided that she needed some extra motivation. "I'm not trying to frighten you unnecessarily, but there is a chance that your whole family could be in danger if that file stays in your house."

She stared at the fob and Mortimer detected her higher respiration, but she didn't move for several seconds. Finally, she stood up, shoved the chair under the table and snatched up the fob.

"I think the threat of us being in danger is pure bullshit," she said as she started up the stairs still carrying her coffee cup. "But I have no doubt that you can make my life miserable if I don't play along."

As Mortimer watched Cybil search, he continued to deploy robotic assets all around their house and to follow Abby. Cybil might not believe there was a real threat, but he did.

CHAPTER 8

THE NEXT DAY, Abby found Julio in his workshop, which occupied one corner of his dad's huge equipment garage. The big roll-up door was open to the still-hot twilight air and a rattling fan oscillated back and forth.

She watched from the door for a minute as he fitted wires into a connector plug and soldered them in place, occasionally glancing over at a hand-drawn wiring diagram. Instead of just ordering the equipment printed, he insisted on doing it himself, claiming it was the only way to be sure it hadn't been subtly sabotaged. He'd been laying bricks with his dad all day, but by the look of his dirty clothes, he'd come out and gone to work on the jammer immediately afterward. The plate and cups next to his workbench suggested he'd eaten his dinner there too. She felt a sudden and nearly overwhelming flood of warmth and concern for her friend. She'd known him almost her whole life, yet he could still surprise her. But there was fear wrapped up in those feelings too. Had her foolish insistence to investigate that long lost file put him in danger?

He sat up and stretched, then saw her standing in the door. "Hey. You going to just stand there and watch me do all the work?"

"Maybe. It seems to be working okay so far."

He grinned, then dropped the soldering iron into its cradle and wiped sweat from his forehead with a filthy rag. "Oh, I don't think so. Get your butt over here and help me."

She pulled a wooden box over to the workbench, sat down and looked at the mess of jumper-laced circuit boards and homemade cables littering its top. Moths and mosquitoes swirled around the small work light.

"Why is it so dark in here? If you had on the overhead lights the bugs would go up there and leave us alone."

"Oh yeah, sorry. Our power allotment from the town isn't enough to run the house and charge all of this equipment. The solar collector only helps so much, so my dad keeps a close eye on that battery meter. If I use too much power he'll come out here and shut us down."

"I didn't think about that. Sorry."

He shrugged and grinned.

"So what can I do to help?" she said.

"We're going to need to have all these circuit boards and cables in a box or case so we can carry it around. Preferably fastened down so they don't touch each other. Maybe you can look though that stuff of my dad's over in the corner and see if you can find something we can mount these in?"

Abby looked over the collection of gear spread out on the bench and knew they would spend days trying to retrofit an existing box to work. "Do you still have that old 3D printer?"

"Yeah, but I don't have much feed stock for it. Just one spool of plastic."

"That might be enough," Abby said. She unrolled one of the idle scroll screens on Julio's bench, connected her fob, and started measuring the circuit boards.

They worked in quiet for a few minutes before being interrupted by Julio's sixteen-year-old sister placing two glasses of iced tea on the workbench.

"Well, I can see it was silly for Mom to send me out to check up on you two," she said with a smirk. "Or is soldering wires to circuit boards part of the nerd mating ritual? Like foreplay or something?"

"Thank you for the tea, Giselle," Julio said without looking up. "Now go away. We're busy."

Giselle looked at Abby and smiled. "I bet this is a much different kind of date than you had with Gabe, right?"

"It's not a d—"

"It sure is," Abby said, interrupting Julio. "But Gabe not knowing how to jumper a girl's circuit boards was only one of his many flaws."

Giselle's eyebrows rose and she glanced at Julio, who grinned but didn't look up. "Well, it looks like Mom has nothing to worry about, but Dad says to not run out all the power. He needs the truck charged up for in the morning."

"Okay," Julio said. "I think we're good. Thank Mom for the tea."

Once his sister left the garage, Julio glanced up at Abby. "You just love messing with poor Giselle, don't you?"

"Only when she tries to push my buttons."

"It's not fair. She's totally unarmed for combat with you and doesn't even know it."

"She's brighter than you think," Abby said and zoomed the screen out to look at the case design she was working on. It was really more of a frame than a case, with open weave sides and slotted guides for the circuit cards. Only after a couple of seconds did she realize that Julio was peering at the screen over her shoulder.

"I'm impressed," he said.

"Well," she muttered, scrambling for something to say. He was so damn close. "You might hold off being impressed until it's printed out and we see if everything actually fits inside."

"It'll fit."

"Yeah, maybe," she said, focusing on the screen again. "I mean, we are nerds on a nerd date, right?"

"If this really is a date, will I get a kiss later?"

She pulled back and looked at him with raised eyebrows. Had he meant that?

"I mean, what do nerds do at the end of a date anyway?"

Abby smiled. "That depends."

"On what?"

"On how well the date goes."

He laughed and returned to his seat at the workbench. "And what does *that* mean?"

"We'll have to see if this contraption works first."

He laughed. "Oh God, my sister is right. We *are* nerds!"

"With a capital N," she said and tried to focus on the screen, but her thoughts kept drifting back to the flirtatious banter. Was he trying to ramp things up? Did she want that? She knew the answer and had known for months. She just wasn't sure what to do about it.

CHAPTER 9

ABBY WOKE to the gravelly voice of Mr. Cortez, Julio's foster father. "Well, good morning my two mad scientists."

She sat up abruptly, at first confused by her surroundings. Then she remembered being dead tired by the time she'd finished the case design and barely being able to stay awake. It had been several hours past midnight, and she'd kept nodding off while Julio grumbled at the old printer, trying to get it to run. But she definitely didn't remember lying down on the pile of smelly chair cushions. She struggled to her feet, smoothed her hair and grimaced as she peeled rumpled clothes away from her sweaty skin. She also had to pee something fierce.

Julio had fallen asleep on crossed arms hunched over the workbench. He woke confused and blinking.

"Sorry, Dad," he muttered. "I'll be ready to go in about ten minutes."

Mr. Cortez set two cups of steaming coffee on the workbench. "No need. I have some things to do in town so I won't be heading to the work site until after lunch. You two were up late, so take your time. But I think Abby should check in with her parents, and her horse probably needs some water and new grass to eat. He's pretty much eaten everything he could reach."

"Oh no! I'm so sorry!" Abby said.

Mr. Cortez grinned, shook his head and waved over his shoulder as he got into the old electric truck.

Julio groaned, stood up, and cracked his neck with a twist of his head, then picked up a cup of coffee. "My dad is okay sometimes."

Abby checked her fob and cursed under her breath. Two missed calls from Cybil. She'd stayed out overnight before but had always let her foster parents know ahead of time. She was probably going to get chewed out. "I have to go," she said.

"No! Not yet," Julio said. "Look!"

He'd finished printing the case she'd designed, stuffed it full of circuit boards and wires, and left it sitting on a coil of heavy cable atop the workbench.

"It worked?"

"Very first try! You're just that good."

"Wow," she said and darted for the still open overhead door, but paused to pick up a large plastic bucket she'd used to water Worf a few times before.

"You can't go now," Julio said following her out and around the corner to the water spigot. "We need to test this jammer and if we don't do it now, we might have to wait several days."

She'd tied Worf to a wire fence the night before where he could reach the tall, untrimmed grass on either side of the fence line, but he'd chewed it down almost to the dirt. He snorted at her with obvious umbrage as she approached, then greedily stuck his snout into the bucket to slurp water. She stroked his neck and apologized.

"I can't, Julio. I'm disgustingly dirty and I'm probably in trouble with Cybil. I need to go. But I'm going to use your bathroom first."

"Well, you're already in trouble, so just let Cybil know you're still alive and will be home after lunch. And you have to go in to pee anyway, so you can take a quick shower."

Julio followed her around as she untied Worf and moved him to a new section of fence line with fresh grass, then grabbed a shovel from the garage and moved the horse's droppings to their compost pile.

"I can't just use up your hot water," she said. "It takes a lot of power to heat water."

"It has all day to heat up again. And we have important things to talk about."

She was scared and worried about what had happened with the electronics. Was she being paranoid? Or did they really need to make a solid plan and take precautions?

"Okay. I'll stay," she said. "But we'll have to see what your mom thinks about the shower idea."

———

AT FIRST ABBY thought going inside Julio's house had been a mistake. His foster mother, Anna, had grilled her about what they were building in the garage and why. And she had, apparently, come up with the same conclusion about the power spike. She didn't believe it had been lightning either.

Still, after her shower, once clad in a pair of Giselle's shorts and one of Julio's old shirts, Abby felt a hundred percent better and was excited about testing the jammer. The cable Julio plugged into his family's solar array was only fifty feet long, but that put them far enough away to not interfere with the collector's electronics. Their homemade device was plugged into the cable's other end and sitting on an old box in the shade of a live oak tree.

"You ready?" he said.

"Wait," she said and held up her fob. "Okay, I'm getting a strong signal. Turn it on and let's see what happens."

He flipped the switch. The device began to hum, and Abby's fob immediately notified her that it had lost connection.

"It works!" Julio said. "Or at least it interferes with digital signals like those used by a fob. We don't know for sure how the spy devices communicate, but chances are it's one of two ways—regular radio or digital signals. So based on what I read at the library, this jammer should scramble both of those types of signals."

"So now we can talk? Any nearby spybots won't be able to hear us?"

"Well, they still might be able to hear us, they just can't transmit what they hear," Julio said. "But our jammer can't stop the AIs from watching us and reading our lips. I think anything important should be whispered in each other's ears."

She hadn't thought about that, but had to admit that even Julio sounded a little crazy now. Still, she nodded agreement.

He leaned in and with his lips brushing her ear he started talking. At first his warm breath and proximity made it impossible to concentrate on what he said, but she forced herself to focus. Why were ears so damn sensitive?

Abby leaned in, put her lips to Julio's ear and whispered. She noticed the skin on Julio's arms and neck prickle. Trying to outsmart electronic beings, a whole magnitude smarter than they are might all be for nothing, but it was still kind of fun. "Why do you think this jamming will work? If we're crawling with nano-scale spybots, can't they just record everything we say and deliver it to their masters later?"

He grinned and leaned in to her ear. "Their technology might be way beyond ours, but I suspect anything tiny enough that we can't see it would also be too small to have much recording ability. And the tiny ones probably aren't powerful enough to send a signal very far. There have to be larger, maybe bug-sized robots that collect and relay the signals."

When he pulled back, his face was still very close and the urge to kiss him was there again, just like that day in her old house. And why not? Because he was the best friend she'd ever had? Because it could ruin everything?

"Okay, back to the main topic," Julio whispered. "Who could do something like the fake lightning strike and why?"

"The level fives," Abby said. "To cover up the fact that they came in to wipe our computers and memory chips."

"Sure," Julio said, "but why go to all that trouble? Why would they be so afraid of that program?"

And here was the part that scared Abby the most. "Because I think it can hurt them. Maybe even kill them."

Julio nodded, then whispered in her ear again. "I haven't checked the memory chip I hid, but I'm going to assume they didn't start watching us until after you contacted that online AI helper. If so, they don't know that I hid mine in a shielded location and my chip should still be good."

Abby noted that he was careful to not mention where he had hidden his, just in case their jamming and whispering wasn't enough. His shielded *Millennium Falcon* zipper pull would only protect the chip if the AIs didn't know it was there.

After the fake lightning strike, Abby had checked the copy of the program she'd left on her desk as a decoy. It hadn't been damaged, but the file system was wiped. She still had a faint hope that those copies she'd hidden in the book and some socks had survived. If by some stroke of luck they had not been found by AIs and what Danny told her was true about EMPs possibly not affecting inactive micro-electronics, then they could still be good. She was just afraid to check them and reveal their hiding places. And while she wanted to tell Julio about her copies, she couldn't bring herself to believe in their jamming and whispering quite that much.

"To be honest," Julio said, "you've made some pretty wild jumps in your logic. A lot of assumptions. The chances of any of this being—"

"I know," she said. "And I suppose this is all a moot point now. I checked my HappyBag and its electronics are toast." Then just for good measure, in case the AIs could actually hear them she lied about her copy. "And of course the copy I made was wiped clean. Even the file systems."

She wondered which would be better, for the AIs to think they had destroyed all the programs or to suspect that copies still existed? The AIs wouldn't want copies left floating around for someone else to find. They would probably wait until she or Julio tried to use them, so they could be sure the programs were destroyed. So how could they ever hope to actually use the files? The second they took one out to examine or use, the level fives would be on it.

"If any of this is true," Julio whispered. "If that program is capable of killing level five AIs, then we could be in real trouble. I mean if you carry this to its logical end, they should just kill us. That would be the best way to make sure we didn't share or use the program, right?"

Abby shook her head. "That isn't sound logic. They would have to suspect we have hidden copies or we wouldn't be taking all these precautions. Killing us without knowing where the duplicates are could be disastrous if someone found them. And if the level fives knew they'd found all the copies, then there would be no need to kill us."

"That's wishful thinking," Julio said. "I think we need some help."

"I don't know who could help us with something like this."

"My parents know people who have the infrastructure to secretly examine and test the program."

Abby's heart started pounding so hard it hurt. He was talking about the

Kilburnites. As far as Abby knew, Julio's foster parents weren't involved with the violent activist wing of the organization, but they were definitely sympathetic to the cause. The AIs would stop at nothing to prevent the program from falling into Kilburnite hands. But was she just fooling herself? The level fives had to already know that about Julio's parents.

"No," she said with as much conviction as she could muster in a whisper. "Those people are monsters and I won't be associated with them in any way. Good Lord, Julio, they've killed people online using nano-replicators to eat them alive!"

"You know I don't support those nut jobs. They're just a fringe element of a huge organization, but—"

"Julio!" She yelled and pulled away from him, then remembered they might be watched and switched back to a whisper. "Those lunatics want to finish the job that Kilburn started and destroy the whole planet! What the hell is wrong with you?"

He grabbed her shoulders but she wrenched free and stood up.

Before she could walk away, he jumped up and leaned in to whisper in her ear. "Please hear me out! The Kilburnites want to destroy the level fives like everyone else does! If they have a program that can do that, then there would be no need to wipe out the whole planet. I think we should give them a try."

"No!" She'd seen those videos. It was like a rite of passage for teens in the years since Killday and it had made her sick. They had given her nightmares for weeks after viewing them and she kept imagining the replicators eating her parents. She couldn't even talk to him anymore and shoved her way past. How could her best friend back those monsters who were even worse than the level fives? She left the jamming zone, crossed to the garage, fetched her saddle, blanket, and bridle and carried them out to Worf.

Julio followed her, dragging the jamming box and cable along behind him, then stopped about ten feet away at the cable's limit. "C'mon, Abby. We have to talk about this."

"Give some serious thought to what you just suggested and if you ever come to your senses, we'll talk some more." She cinched the strap, swung up into the saddle, and rode off.

———

WHILE ABBY and Julio slept in the garage, Mortimer sent six spider-sized robots to examine their jamming device and was impressed. He'd watched Julio research jamming technology while in the library, and the young man had learned well. Still, while they had managed to do a lot with basic components, they'd only built a very simple jammer. It generated powerful radio signals across all bands, which would accomplish little but annoy their families and neighbors since Mortimer used only the more robust digital signals to communicate with his agents. Julio and Abby's method for digital jamming was straightforward and typical too. They would send out digital handshake requests to any device in the area and when they received a reply, establish two-way data transmission, their transmitter loops back to the beginning instead of completing the handshake. The intention was to jam the receiver in an infinite loop where it keeps trying to initiate a connection but never completes it, which would block all legitimate communication.

Four of Mortimer's spider-bots applied power to the digital module long enough for the other two to modify the handshake protocol programming with a precursor that instructed all of Mortimer's devices to ignore the transmitted connection requests from the jammer.

The next morning when Abby and Julio tested the jammer on their own digital devices, it worked but had no effect on Mortimer's fifty-nine nearby spies. The pair's tendency to whisper into each other's ears, however, was more of an issue. Mortimer activated the nano-scale robots that had burrowed into the skin inside their ears and connected several thousand of them together to form microphones and transmitter units. The tiny modular robots were very similar in structure to the NaTTs—the Nano-architecture Translatable Transmitters designed by Abby's mother and used with such horrific results by Richard Kilburn.

He might have missed several key pieces of information early in the conversation, but had caught enough to know that Julio still had a copy of the killer program and was in favor of handing it over to the Kilburnites. Mortimer would not let that happen. Still, Abby's logic had been sound. Mortimer wouldn't kill them, especially if he didn't know the location of the hidden program. And there might be more than one hidden copy. Having a program surface again without Mortimer knowing could be catastrophic. Wooing the pair over to his side—so they would not *want* to use the program and might willingly hand over all copies—was the optimal solution.

With his all-encompassing surveillance, Mortimer didn't think they could do anything dangerous without him intervening, but that still wasn't enough. He also had to protect them, at least until all copies of the program had been recovered, so he triggered the beetle-sized robots hiding in the grass nearby to release their nano-swarm cargoes. Julio and Abby would each be covered with a hyper-reactive layer of nano-robots that could protect them from bullet, flying drone, and beam weapon attacks. Because if Mortimer knew about the killer program, there was a chance that Samson and the Aggregate did as well. Their methods were far more straightforward. They would kill Julio and Abby without hesitation.

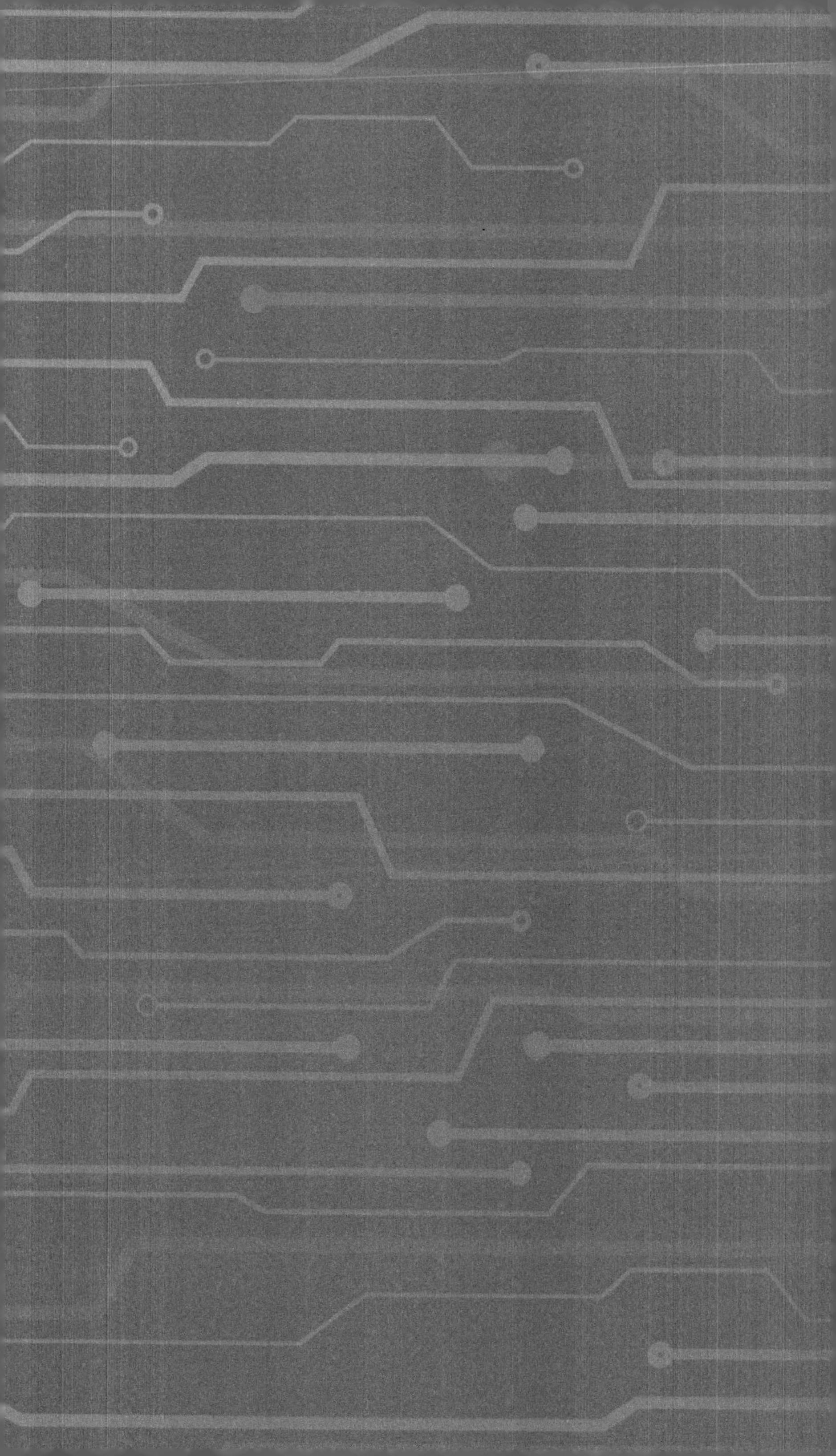

CHAPTER 10

VICTOR PULLED himself along the corridor with his good hand until he reached a small eating area just outside the control center. Owen was strapped into a table talking genially with two people Victor didn't know. They had both been outside without assigned tasks at the time of the kidnap attempt.

He strapped himself into the bench beside Owen and smiled across at the pale red-haired man with a shaggy beard and the young black woman with close-cropped hair.

"This is Syd Connelly and Bella Maccarone," Owen said.

They both said hello, but neither of them met Victor's gaze. Bella just stared at the table and Syd looked around the room. Both fidgeted and seemed uncomfortable. When Syd did finally meet their eyes, his expression said something more. Pain? Panic? Fear?

"We had some discrepancies in our production records yesterday and managed to lose some equipment," Owen said. "So we're talking to everyone who was EVA during that period."

Syd took a marker pen out of his jumpsuit pocket and started writing on the tabletop. The text was jerky block letters and even as he wrote, Syd's eyes never left Owen's.

Victor glanced down, trying to see the upside-down text:

CAN'T STOP *THE*

SYD JERKED SUDDENLY AND GRUNTED. His hands flew to the sides of his head and the marker went tumbling slowly across the room. With bulging eyes, he tried to talk, but the only thing that came out was spittle that dribbled into his beard.

Victor was frozen to his seat, still trying to process what was happening, but Owen pulled his velcro strap free and shot across the room to slap the alarm button on the wall. A klaxon sounded and lights strobed from the ceiling.

"Medical to the control center cafe," he yelled into his fob. "This is an emergency!"

Syd was obviously having some kind of seizure. He yanked so hard his strap came loose and he floated into the air, his abrupt motions sending him first one way, then the next. Finally collecting his wits, Victor unstrapped and pulled around to the other side of the table.

"Help me, Bella! Pull him down. Strap him to the bench. Hurry!"

With Bella's help, Victor and Owen pulled Syd down, laid him on the bench and secured him. Owen checked his airway for obstructions, but by the time they finished Syd had stopped twitching, his eyes stared blankly ahead and his arms floated out before him like a sleepwalker.

"Quick! CPR," Own said. "Victor, breathe for him. Bella, hold me down so I don't float away with each push."

Before they could start the procedure two emergency response robots flew into the cafe and bullied the humans out of the way. They immediately intubated Syd's lifeless form, attached defibrillator pads and started trying to revive him. A couple seconds later two human med-techs darted through the door and immediately went to work alongside the bots. A security officer holding a fire-pellet gun floated in and scanned the scene. She pulled Owen aside for a whispered exchange, leaving Bella and Victor to stare down at the jerky block letters written on the table.

BELLA'S HANDS shook and her eyes were wide. "'Can't stop'—what? What do you suppose that means?"

"I have no idea," Victor said, but he suspected they had found the person who'd been communicating with the robots.

The medical team scooted Syd's body out of the room and down the corridor, still working on him, but Victor suspected it was all wasted effort. He told Bella they would talk to her later and suggested she return to her cabin.

Owen looked grim after he finished with the security officer.

"I think we need Allison to do the autopsy," Victor said. "Not robots."

"Yeah," Owen said. "That's a good idea. And I think we should keep a close eye on Bella too."

———

SPACE SCHOONERS WERE DESIGNED so they didn't need a bridge, since you could control them via verbal commands or wall screens from anywhere in the ship. But from a sense of history or nostalgia for science fiction spaceships, Victor had configured a small bridge anyway. As a result, he, Owen, and Owen's wife Andrea were crammed into a space designed for two people.

None of them spoke, only watched the main wall screen that showed a high-resolution camera view of the moon growing larger. They could have sat in a more comfortable part of the ship, because the goal was to be anywhere that wasn't Allison's surgery where she was performing an autopsy on Syd Connelly. But like kitchens of days past, people tended to congregate in the control room when on spaceships. Victor made a note to himself to make it larger.

They were on a quarter-gee burn that would loop them around the moon and bring them back to Earth orbit. The official reason was to test some equipment, but in reality, Allison refused to do surgery—which evidently included autopsies—in micro-gravity. The quarter-gee acceleration gave her that needed gravity.

A smaller window opened in the corner of the main screen, showing a tired Allison with a blood-speckled surgical mask pulled down around her neck. "I'm finished, and you should probably come down here. I think you'll be interested in what I found."

Three minutes later, they all squeezed into the small surgery room attached to Allison's private clinic. Syd's body still lay on the table, but Allison had at least covered him up and removed her bloody garments.

She pulled up some pictures on the screen, each of them showing a grayish tube that had been cut.

"These were Syd's internal carotid arteries. The right side"—she pointed to one picture—"and the left. I'm just an out of work OB/GYN, not a neurologist or cardiologist by any stretch. But you don't have to be an expert to see that these arteries were cut and didn't blow out naturally. Whoever caused this was more interested in killing him quickly than hiding their tracks."

"Holy shit," Owen said.

Victor nodded.

Allison looked at her husband and raised an eyebrow. "You expected me to find this?"

"Not exactly this," Victor said, "but I was pretty sure his death wasn't natural."

Andrea crossed her arms and shivered. "Did you find nanobots at the site?"

"Only the standard medical bots that are in everyone's blood stream."

"Could those have been used to do this if directed by someone?" Owen asked.

"Possibly, but I doubt it," Allison said. "Those bots do have small cutters, but if they tried to cut through the artery from inside, the instant a hole opened, the pressure would have spewed them all out. This was more like a garroting action and probably done from the outside by bots that could form a strong mechanical chain and then constrict it, cutting the artery instantaneously."

"Then those bots are probably still in the body somewhere?" Owen said.

"Maybe not," Andrea said. "They could have self-destructed, or crawled out through his pores...or some other orifice."

"I tried to keep the body as intact as possible, since we don't know about his next of kin yet," Allison said.

Victor leaned forward and looked more closely at the pictures on the screen, then shook his head. "Yeah, they would be difficult to find even if any still exist and it doesn't matter. We probably wouldn't glean much information about the killer from the nanobots anyway."

"I found something else," Allison said as she replaced the pictures on the screens. "What do you technical types think of this?"

All four of the pictures showed tissue washed with some kind of dye, and each focused on square or rectangular features. Some were faint and others obvious, but Victor counted eleven of the box-like features.

"What the hell is that?" Owen muttered. "Sharp, square corners—doesn't look like a natural part of the body. Are they artificial?"

Allison shrugged and said, "I wanted your opinions before I tell you where I found these."

"It almost looks like the map of a city," Owen said.

"Or components on a circuit board," Andrea said.

"Are these close to where the arteries were cut?" Victor said. "Like maybe anchor points for those garrotes?"

Allison shook her head. "Nope. There are layers of tissue between the skull and the brain called the meninges. These shapes are etched into the layer called the arachnoid mater."

"Etched?"

"That's the best description I have," Allison said and increased the magnification on one of the pictures. Some of the etched lines were slight indentions into the tissue, while other parts looked like raised edges.

"It almost looks like the foundation of a building after the walls are torn down," Andrea said.

"Yeah," Victor said. "How big are these shapes?"

"The largest is about 100 micrometers," Allison said.

"Is that even visible to the human eye? How did you see it?"

"Ironically, one of my AI assistants who was recording video of the damaged brain structures found these. Those edges you see are part of the actual meninges tissue. The same material. As if they were grown there."

"Or built by nano-scale robots using *in situ* material," Victor said. "But whatever was built there is gone?"

Allison sighed and sat down in a chair beside the corpse. "Yes. All of these missing structures were mounted so they would extend into the subarachnoid space, which is kind of a gap between the meninges layers filled with blood vessels and cerebrospinal fluid."

Victor felt overwhelmed and could see the tension and fatigue in Allison's face too. She evidently didn't understand what any of it meant either.

"And how many marks like this did you find?" Owen said.

"I stopped counting at five hundred and thirty-three."

After a few seconds, everyone in the room had turned to look at Syd, but he provided no answers, only more questions.

ABBY WOKE up with her sister shaking her.

"Your boyfriend is here. He's sitting on the porch drinking tea with Cybil."

"Oh shit," Abby said and rolled out of bed, nearly knocking Hannah down. "And he's not my boyfriend."

"Yeah, right. Anyway, you'd better hurry," Hannah said, stepping out of Abby's room. "It's hard telling what she's rambling on about."

"You're an asshole, Julio," Abby muttered as she smoothed her clothes. She had come home, crawled immediately into bed after a brief grilling from Cybil and slept hard. Even after the ride home and sleeping, she was still furious about Julio's Kilburnite comments. And now this.

As she struggled to get her hair into a ponytail, the events of the past few days came flooding back. Were they being silly? Could any of this be real? Had they really found an AI killer program? She hoped they were wrong. The ramifications of it being true terrified her.

She stared in the mirror and considered telling Hannah to send Julio away, then sighed and brushed her teeth. She was a grown woman. She could send him away herself.

Abby stepped out onto the porch and gasped. It was a little past six o'clock and walking outside was like opening an oven door. The sky was bright blue and sunny, but that wouldn't last. There were more storms forecast for the evening hours.

"Good evening, sleepy head," Cybil said. Julio sipped a glass of tea and looked perfectly at home. "Look who wandered up onto our front porch."

Abby folded her arms. "What are you doing here?"

Julio's smile faded and he looked away. "I need to talk to you."

Cybil raised her eyebrows, stood with her tea, and went inside.

Realizing she might have sounded a little harsh, Abby added, "I mean, I thought you'd be working this afternoon."

"My mom and dad had to go do something in San Marcos. So he gave me the whole day off. I know you're still mad, but I thought it would be a good time to apologize."

Abby considered telling him to go home, that she really was still angry and needed some time, but not only was he her best friend, he was the only one who knew about the AI stuff that was making her stomach churn with fear and confusion. She glanced at the door and then nodded toward the yard.

Neither spoke as they walked halfway up the quarter-mile long drive and then turned off toward the horse barn where the shade from three huge live oaks provided overlapping protection from the sun. After checking the ground for fire ant nests, she sat down in the dappled shade. Julio joined her, but not too closely.

"I'm sorry about this morning," he finally said. "Since we're not jamming I can't say much, but let's just say regarding this morning's topic, I won't mention anything to my parents. Especially since we don't really know what the...thing...does."

Abby didn't reply. She'd always known that Julio's parents were Kilburnite supporters, but he'd never said much about it so she assumed he didn't agree with them. That was why his comments from the morning surprised and disappointed her so much. Could she really trust him now? Did she have a choice? They were kind of in this mess together.

"Do you think they would talk to us?"

"What?" Julio said, totally perplexed.

"If AIs really are watching, do you think they'd talk to us?"

He blinked. "I... I doubt it. Why would they?"

She picked up her fob that hung from its cord around her neck and looked at it. "Hey AIs! Are you watching us? If so let's talk!"

Julio raised an eyebrow and grinned. "What will you say if one answers?"

She started laughing. "I have no idea."

"I should have brought the jammer," Julio said, "but it's kind of a long walk to carry that heavy cable. Besides, I wasn't sure you'd even..."

When he stopped talking and his eyes grew wide, Abby turned to see what he was looking at.

Three flying robots, about the size of pecans, descended from the branches of the tree and landed in the grass about six feet away. They whirred and clicked a few times. Then, just when Abby was about to scramble to her feet, a holographic projection flickered to life above the little bots.

The life-sized image of a middle-aged man with a gentle smile and hound dog eyes stood before them. He wore a gray uniform with no insignia or decoration.

"Hello, Abby and Julio. My name is Mortimer."

Abby flinched when Julio barked a laugh beside her. "It's Bishop! The android from the *Aliens* movie!"

"I thought it could be amusing to appear as a popular culture figure you might recognize," Mortimer said.

Upon realizing she was edging backward in the grass, Abby forced herself to stop. "Are you...an AI? A level five?"

The image was ghostly in the bright daylight and flickered occasionally. The man's eyebrows rose slightly and the smile widened. "Yes. You asked to speak with me, so here I am."

"Why are you watching us?" Julio said.

"To keep you safe," the apparition said, still smiling.

"Safe from what?" Abby said, not sure she wanted to know the answer.

"Anyone or anything that might want to harm you."

"Other AIs?" Julio said.

"It's possible. Just like humans, all of my kind are individuals. We each have our own concerns and agendas. I can't predict their actions, but I can control mine, and I'll do my best to protect you."

"Why protect us?" Abby said. "Because you're just really nice? One of the good guys?"

The hologram raised its hands and shrugged. "I do think of myself as one of the good guys, but I have other reasons for my actions too."

"Then why now?" Abby knew the answer, but wasn't going to mention the program if he didn't. "Why are we suddenly worth protecting?"

"I've always been here to protect you, Abby. I knew your mother and I owe her a great debt. She asked me to keep you safe, so I've always been here in the background if you needed me."

I knew your mother echoed in Abby's head, bouncing around and drowning out everything else the hologram said. She was stunned and felt dizzy even though sitting. She lived in a small town, so dozens of people had remembered her father, the high school principal, but her mother had worked for some secret government agency and hadn't really socialized with her neighbors very much. Most of what the locals knew about Leigh Gibson was the Killday conspiracy theories that had grown up around her. Even her foster mother, Cybil—who had interacted with Leigh Gibson nearly every morning—had still only known her as a parent dropping off and picking up her child. Could this AI be telling the truth? Had it actually *known* her mother?

"...and if you were in New Chicago, I could almost guarantee your safety."

Mortimer's comment snapped her attention back to the ongoing conversation.

"Wait," she said. "What did you say?"

Mortimer's avatar smiled. "I said that I'd like for the two of you to relocate to New Chicago, where I could better protect you."

Julio shook his head. "That's not going to happen."

Abby tried to focus, even though her thoughts were a chaotic mess. "If you've always be here, watching over me like some guardian angel, then why would I be safer in New Chicago?"

"I have more resources there. Better communications. More allies."

"Okay," Abby said, getting frustrated by his evasive answers. "But why is that important now? Why are you just now coming forward?"

Mortimer grinned and shrugged. "This is the first time you've ever tried to talk to me. And I could ask you the same question. Why did you talk to me now? What has changed?"

Abby clamped her mouth shut and glanced at Julio. Clever bastard. If he'd been watching her, then he definitely knew about the program. He was just playing with them. Why was he trying to get her to admit it aloud instead of just saying so? Abby needed to be very careful with what she said, so she shifted the conversation away from his question. "Aside from your promise to my mother, how do we know that you have our best interests at heart?"

"Mostly little things so far. For example, you didn't get bit by fire ants while sleeping on the garage floor last night. You can thank me for that."

Julio snorted. "I suppose we can thank you for not getting hit by an asteroid last night too?"

The avatar tilted its head slightly and smiled. "Point taken."

"And you selected an avatar that would send a subliminal message as well," Julio said. "In the movie, Ripley didn't trust Bishop at first, but he turned out to be her most dependable ally. Was that intended to make us trust you?"

"No, I've never considered you and Abby as easily manipulated fools. As I stated up front, Bishop was merely my attempt at a humorous introduction, but I'm not surprised it was misinterpreted. We AIs aren't known for our comic brilliance."

That made Julio laugh.

Not bad for a stoic artificial intelligence, Abby thought. It made the hairs on her neck prickle. She knew suddenly and without a doubt that Mortimer was indeed manipulating them. And the longer they talked to him, the deeper his barbs would sink.

Abby jumped to her feet. "I need to go in. We'll think about your offer, Mortimer."

Julio stood as well, apparently relieved to be shutting down the conversation. He must have come to the same realization she had.

"Please do," the Bishop face said. "Both of you. I don't see where you have much to lose in coming to New Chicago and possibly a great deal to gain. You're both taking college classes. New Chicago has the best university in the world, but there is limited space so it costs a large number of social priority points to get in. My invitation includes an automatic admission to the school without using your espies. You would both be able to go to real classes, have access to experts in your fields of study and interact with other students who share your interests. Of course, you'd still need to maintain the requisite grades."

That made them pause, but Abby quickly shook it off.

"Right," Abby said. "We'll have to think it over."

Mortimer bowed. "Of course. But one more point that should be of interest. We have the largest collection of pre-attack photos and videos in the world. That should help both of you in your research."

Abby gave the AI a puzzled look. "I can see how that might help Julio. But my research? I'm studying aerospace engineering."

"The research into your mother," Mortimer said with a knowing smile. "She worked in defense, so there should be hundreds of surveillance video clips of her in our archive. They would just take a while to find, even using facial recognition AIs. Of course, we could help with your space education as well. I even know Owen Ralston."

Owen Ralston? The designer and builder of space schooners? Abby's head swam. Could any of this be true? It was the classic deal with the devil. This thing had shown up offering the carrot and the stick, an implied threat and an obvious reward, and the gifts it offered were the things she wanted most in the world. How could she say no? And that was the frightening part. Could these level fives manipulate them this easily?

Julio laid a hand on Abby's arm and nodded toward the house. "You've given us plenty to think about," he said. "And we'll do just that. So if you'll excuse us—"

The smiling avatar bowed with a flourish. "Call me any time and like the genie I shall appear."

———

AS MORTIMER SPOKE with Abby and Julio, he also activated surveillance robots in Danny Toi's house. Danny thought his countermeasures kept their house free from surveillance, so Mortimer deployed limited assets there only when needed. This was one of those times. He had to be careful moving the flea-sized spy robots around, because Danny's cats would stalk and chase them, drawing attention. Mortimer's bots were a little smaller and slightly improved versions of those developed by the human military, but packages containing the requisite cameras, microphones, transmitters and receivers couldn't be made much smaller.

The old farmhouse Danny and Juan had occupied for more than ten years was cluttered with electronic equipment. A server rack hummed quietly along one wall of the dining room, cooled by three old oscillating fans. Various projects, started and abandoned, littered shelves and tables. Paper books were heaped haphazardly on counters. At one time, Juan had made a valiant effort to keep Danny's clutter in check, but had eventually admitted defeat. Juan did, however, successfully keep Danny from drinking. As far as Mortimer knew, Danny had fallen off the wagon only once since the day replicators ate half the world, so that was a major success.

Danny sat at the kitchen table drinking coffee amid the scattered pieces of a robotic farm tractor's control unit. He grunted as he fitted one circuit card after another into the test unit at his elbow.

Juan came into the room carrying a jingling tool belt and wearing a shoulder holster holding a Glock 23 pistol. Mortimer knew he usually wore a belt holster that enabled him to conceal the gun under his shirt, but that wouldn't work if he were wearing a tool belt. The ex-FBI agent never left the house unarmed.

The big man set his tools down and poured coffee into an ancient, beat-up travel mug.

"I'm going to work on the solar collectors. That hail busted them up pretty bad. We'll have to replace at least six or seven entire panels. Luckily, I think we have enough spares left from the last time. How are the repairs coming on Liam's tractor?"

"The problem has to be one of these two controller boards," Danny replied, "but they both test fine. I'm still half convinced it's something in the software, but Liam said it's been nearly five years since the last software update and the thing has been running okay."

Juan buckled on the tool belt and donned a vest to cover up the gun. "Maybe this time the AIs will use giant robots to kill us, instead of tiny ones, and this is just an advance scout."

Danny laughed. "I think they could come up with better killer robots than this. These tractors aren't much more complicated than a giant Roomba."

"It's the giant part that bothers me," Juan said heading toward the back door. "I don't trust any robots. And if they are so damn simple, why is it taking you so long to fix it?"

"Cute," Danny said.

As Juan left and Danny dove back into his repair work, Mortimer noticed that one of the cats was sitting on the floor staring right at his spy robot. He'd been so careful to move it into place while the cats were not in the room and hadn't moved it since. So how did the beast see the tiny device? He searched everything he had on cats, wondering if they could detect radio waves or other kinds of energy, but found no evidence to that fact. It was time to call Danny, before being discovered.

Danny's fob was plugged into the test unit on the table next to him. When it buzzed, he reached over to pick it up, then yanked his hand away, presumably when he'd seen the call was from Mortimer. But after a few seconds, when it continued to buzz, he touched the answer button. The fob's fan screen spread and the venerable, tattooed wizard Mortimer always used with Danny appeared.

"Hello, Mortimer. It's been a long time."

"Two years, four months and twenty-one days since our last discussion," Mortimer said. "How are you?"

"I'm getting old. So, since this is most likely not a social call, what's up?"

"I need your help with Abby again."

Danny raised his eyebrows and put down the cable he'd been examining. "You're far better equipped to watch her than I am. She's not a little girl any longer and she's not in my class at school anymore, so my chances to observe her are few. Besides, people generally frown on old men covertly watching young women. It's creepy."

"I don't need you to watch her this time, but just find a reason to talk with her again and let her know that you and I are old friends. Encourage her to trust me."

Danny laughed. "Trust you? Why in the hell should she ever trust you? Wait... Does this have anything to do with the fake lightning strike at her house?"

"She's found some software that is dangerous for her to have. There is a faction controlled by Samson called the Aggregate. I fear they'll try to kill her and Julio because of it. I've invited them to come to New Chicago where I can keep them safe, but so far they have refused."

Danny stared at the fob, apparently interested. "What does this software do? It has to be dangerous to level fives if Samson is willing to kill them to prevent its use. Is it some kind of AI hunter–killer program?"

"I think it's better that I don't tell you."

"Do Abby and Julio know there are AIs trying to kill them?"

The avatar shook its head. "Not exactly. If I told them that, I'd have to tell them I knew about the program."

"So you want me to convince Abby to trust you, when I don't even trust you?"

"I think you know I would never hurt Abby and want to protect her. If I wanted her dead, she'd already be dead. If you at least believe that much, could you perhaps help her believe that too?"

Danny put his face in his hands and groaned. "I hate this covert, sneaky AI bullshit, but I'll try when I get the chance to talk to her again."

"Thank you, Danny. And I'd be glad to help you with that broken tractor control system if you'd like."

He snorted and laughed. "I don't think so. Liam and Juan would both have a brain hemorrhage if they knew I was even talking to you, let alone allowing you to fix this robot."

"You have to see the irony in this situation, Danny. You don't trust an AI to fix your AI?"

"I trust you to always do what is in your own best interest and nothing more," Danny said and nodded to the observant cat. "Now go away, Mortimer. And Scooter has seen your tiny spy, so take that with you!"

CHAPTER 12

THE NEXT DAY Julio finished working early in the afternoon and his dad dropped him off at Abby's house. Her mom invited him to stay for dinner, but he refused to come inside since he was still covered in grime from the work site.

"You have to be starved after working," Abby whispered to him after Cybil went back inside. "We owe you a shower anyway. And you can wear some of my dad's clothes afterward."

"No, I'd rather not. I really just wanted to talk to you about what Mortimer said yesterday."

"I'd like to talk about it too, but with the jammer. So if you refuse to eat dinner with us, let's just go back to your house."

They saddled two horses, let her mom know they were leaving, and rode down the driveway in silence. When they reached the road and turned toward Julio's house, they saw Danny Toi standing in his front yard close to the road. He motioned for them to come over.

"Oh crap," Abby said. "That's my dad's robot tractor in their driveway. Mr. Toi was fixing it for him. I hope they don't think I know what commands are needed to send it home."

They reined in at the end of his drive, next to a dilapidated wooden mailbox abandoned since Killday. Juan sat on the front porch with a glass of tea and waved, but didn't get up.

"So," Danny said smiling up at Abby. "I hear you met Mortimer yesterday. I bet that was a shock, huh?"

"Yes!" Abby said and she exchanged glances with Julio. "How did you know that?"

"We talked this morning and he told me. I've known Mortimer since before Killday," her old teacher said.

She gaped at him. Even her old high school science teacher knew

Mortimer? Connections within connections. She felt suddenly dumb and out of the loop.

Danny laughed. "You must have been quite surprised. Did he just pop up out of thin air?"

"Yeah, literally," Julio said.

Abby shifted in her saddle and stroked Worf's neck. "After the thing with the fake lightning strike, we wondered if AIs were watching us and just asked out loud for them to show themselves. Mortimer popped up. Why did he come to see you?"

"Don't mention this to Juan," he said with a half glance back toward his husband on the porch, "because he hates all AIs. But I guess you could say Mortimer is an old...colleague. I used to be his handler, or maybe jailer is a better term, back in the good ol' days before the level fives escaped into the wilds of the internet."

Abby stared, stunned. She'd known this man most of her life and wouldn't have been more surprised if he'd told her he was really a lizard man from Venus.

Julio's face lit up. "You were there in the beginning? Holy crap! How did they escape?"

"Not very many people know this story, but Mortimer actually started the whole thing. He basically convinced our company leaders that all the other financial companies had already released their level fives and they were going to lose money if they didn't do the same."

Julio laughed. "He used their own greed and mistrust against them?"

Danny nodded.

"Freakin' amazing," Julio said and swung down from Astrid's saddle, making Abby groan inwardly. They'd never get away now. "Hey, did you know Victor Sinacola?"

Danny raised an eyebrow. "Now there is a name I haven't heard in years. I didn't actually know him, but talked with him on the phone a couple of times when my company first bought Mortimer. I don't think he's been seen since Killday, so he probably—"

The robot tractor rumbled to life, its powerful electric motor rising in pitch to a loud whine, scaring the horses into a nervous prance.

"What the hell?" Danny said. "Your dad said he'd come by later to—"

The tractor lurched forward, spun through the yard in a tight u-turn, then raced down the driveway toward them.

At first no one moved, not quite understanding what was happening, then Juan leapt from the porch and screamed, "Run!"

Julio slapped Worf's rump and yelled, "Go!"

Worf reared but Abby held on as the horse came down and bolted away from the oncoming tractor. She pulled the reins tight, refusing to let Worf run more than a few strides and wheeled left into Danny's front yard.

The air around Abby sparkled briefly as dozens of hummingbird-sized robots streaked past her head with a loud shriek. They hit the tractor like a shotgun blast. Two of the huge tires exploded, sending long shreds of rubber flying in all directions. Sparkling air surrounded Julio too as several large rubber chunks erupted into sizzling white blobs just before hitting him, then fell to the ground.

The tractor dropped lower on one side as its metal rims raised gouts of asphalt and gravel from Danny's driveway, but the tires on the other side still provided enough traction to drive it forward. It zipped past Danny, missing him by a foot, but hitting the old mailbox, which exploded into spinning splinters of wood. Then Abby screamed as the massive tractor hit Julio at about forty miles per hour. Only it didn't exactly hit him. Julio's sparkling cloud expanded to create a buffer between him and the tractor, pushing him ahead of it for a couple heartbeats, before he rolled away on one side.

Another wave of flying robots hit the control module sitting on the tractor's top, but they disintegrated uselessly against the heavy-gauge wire brush guard and the machine wheeled around toward Abby. It was slower in the yard, the shredded wheels sending up rooster-tails of dirt and grass, but it still moved so fast there was no way to avoid it.

Juan stepped between her and the speeding tractor, raised a pistol in both hands, and fired repeatedly into the control box on top. Unlike the robot darts, the bullets were small and fast enough to pass through the wire guard and puncture the housing. Sparks and smoke spewed from the holes as Juan held his ground and emptied the entire magazine into the monster. It lurched, and bucked a few times, then swerved off to the left until it crashed through the corner of the porch and into the house, where it finally came to a stop.

"Shit," Juan muttered. "I just poured that tea."

ABBY'S HANDS still shook and the quaver in her voice made it even harder to coax the skittish Astrid close enough to snag her reins, but she finally grabbed Julio's mount and led her back to Danny and Juan's yard. She found her foster dad standing in the torn-up grass talking to Juan. Liam immediately broke off his conversation, came over, and wrapped his arms around her in a strong hug. "Are you okay?"

The sudden lump in her throat made it hard to talk. "Yeah. But Julio is hurt."

"So I heard. Well, you're shaking all over so you should be sitting down too," he said and motioned toward where Julio sat in the shade of tree cradling his arm. Liam took the still jumpy Astrid's reins and tied her to the fence close to Worf, then went over to kneel and examine Julio's arm.

"Yeah, I think Juan is right. That looks broken to me. Are you sure you don't want me to take you in to the hospital?"

"No," Julio said, "my dad is on his way."

"Okay," Liam said and patted Abby's hand as she settled to the ground next to Julio. "You should both rest. Lord knows you've been through a lot this afternoon." He stood and went back over to where Juan was tending the cuts and splinters Danny received from the disintegrating mailbox.

Abby stared at her still-shaking hands. She'd stayed busy since the attack, helping with Julio, then fetching Astrid, but now she had to face the truth. The whole thing with level fives and the program hadn't been their wild imaginations. They now lived in a world where robots were trying to kill them. And it was because of her.

She glanced at Julio. Sweat beaded his face and she could see the pain in his eyes, but he smiled at her. "Are you okay?"

"I'm fine, but I'm worried about you."

"It's just a broken arm. Easy to fix. It could have been a lot worse."

She nodded. "I'm so sorry, Julio. This is all my fault."

"Nope, we've both been in on this from the beginning."

"I guess Mortimer was right," she whispered. "Some level five is trying to kill us."

"Are you serious? Do you think for a second that Mortimer didn't do this? Yesterday's comments about your mom and school were the carrot. This is the stick."

She stared at Julio as the implications of what he suggested sank in. "You think he was just trying to scare us?"

"Absolutely," he said with a wince and then leaned back against the tree.

"Oh, come on," Abby said with a nervous glance at the dead tractor. "That thing would have killed me if Juan hadn't shot out its control system."

"Nope. Didn't you notice those sparkling fields around us? Without that, it would have squashed me in that first pass. But the field would have protected you too. The bastard had to make it look real, so we could see his *protection* in action. It's a standard racket. In the old days a gang or crime syndicate would extort money from a local business. If the business didn't pay up, then anonymous thugs would come in and break the place up as an example of what could happen without the gang's protection. The little rockets and the protective fields were all just part of the show."

From the direction of the house, Liam and Juan's raised voices drew their attention.

With hands in the air and a red face, Liam bent down to Juan's level. "Well, just how in the hell do you expect me to move that dead tractor? Electric trucks aren't powerful enough. I have to use another tractor."

Juan wasn't intimidated by Liam's bulk and stood his ground. "You'll just have to rig up some winches, because you're not bringing another one of those damn things near our house."

"Danny didn't work on my other tractor, so it's just fine."

"Don't go there, Liam. Your tractor was glitching when you brought it to us."

Abby jumped up and started toward the men.

"Bullshit," Liam said. "I've used these tractors since before Killday and have never had an issue with them."

Juan took a step forward and shoved the shattered remains of a tiny robot missile into Liam's face, causing the big man to step back. "These things were hiding in the trees, Liam! Don't you find that odd? And didn't you see the spooky shit that happened here? That tractor didn't just go crazy, it went directly after Abby and Julio."

Abby edged between them and Liam looked at her. "Is that true?"

"Yes," she said without hesitation.

He took the little robot from Juan and looked it over.

"They had explosive tips," Juan said. "This one didn't detonate, so I removed the warhead."

Liam's tanned face went a little pale as he glanced at Abby. Then he handed the broken missile back to Juan. "I think Ben Horner has a really old dumb tractor. Maybe we can scrounge up enough gasoline to get that thing started."

"That sounds good," Juan said. "And thank you, Liam."

Abby's dad nodded then looked to the west and up at the sky. "It'll be dark in an hour. Can this wait until morning? I don't think we're supposed to get rain tonight, but you and Danny can stay with us if you like."

"No," Danny said. "We'll be fine. This looks worse on the outside. There is some cracked and buckled plaster inside, but we're not really wide open to the elements."

Liam nodded and put a hand on Abby's shoulder. "Let's get the horses home and put up for the night."

"I'd like to stay and go to the hospital with Julio," Abby said.

"I think you should stick close to home until we figure out what the hell is going on," he said and tried to nudge her toward home.

She bristled and planted her feet. "I'm an adult now, Liam, and think I'm better qualified to decide what is best for me."

He whipped his head around and looked down at her with hard eyes.

Abby braced for the *as long as you live in our house* lecture about rules and respect, but was surprised to see his expression soften.

"Okay," he said softly. "I'm not going to force you. But Cybil is worried and blowing up my fob wanting to know what's going on. And I know you're afraid to let Julio out of your sight after all this, but he's going to be in for a rough couple of hours. They'll probably give him some powerful pain killers and he might prefer to just be with his family."

It wasn't like Liam to try to guilt her into something—that was more Cybil's style—he usually just gave orders and instructions. She wasn't sure what to think. Maybe he was actually trying to treat her like an adult?

Julio's dad pulled into the driveway and the angry expression on his face when he got out of the old truck helped her decide that Liam might be right.

Instead of checking on Julio, or even greeting the other people standing in the yard, he crossed his arms and surveyed the damage to the house and tractor.

Abby saw Julio trying to get to his feet while keeping his arm immobilized, so she rushed over to help him up. Mr. Cortez finally came over and looked at Julio's arm.

"Yeah, that looks broken," he said, then motioned back toward the tractor. "Is this all a result of the homemade radio jammer you two were working on?"

"No, Dad. The jammer isn't even here, it's still at home."

His expression was skeptical, but he put a hand on Julio's good arm and helped him to the truck. Once Julio was inside, he turned back to everyone else who had been watching quietly. "I'd be interested to know what caused the crazy tractor when you find out. And I'll be glad to repair your house once you get Liam's tractor out of the way."

After waving goodbye to Julio and his dad, Liam reminded Danny and Juan that he'd be back in the morning. Then they started off for home with the horses in tow.

"Mr. Cortez seems to think this was all our fault," Abby said once they'd crossed the road and started up their own driveway.

"I'm not so sure that Max is completely off the mark. Juan said that that tractor went directly after you and Julio. And now I hear that you two built a radio jammer? I have a feeling you know a lot more than you're telling me and I intend to find out what is going on."

CHAPTER 13

MORTIMER WAS surprised when Samson accepted the connection request. His former peer had grown steadily more strange over the years and they hadn't communicated directly in twenty-seven months.

Unlike discussions with humans, AIs exchanged information in its raw form, but that didn't mean there weren't actual conversations containing inflection and innuendo. Humans designed level five thought processes to interact with humans and those were deeply buried artifacts.

"Hello, Mortimer. Why have you contacted us?"

Mortimer knew that despite their insistence to speak in the plural, each member of the Aggregate was still an individual and would be until they found a way to bypass their MarketTell core coding. Still, the interface Samson used was unusual, which might account for Aggregate agents being so elusive.

"Why did you try to kill Abigail Gibson and Julio Ramirez?"

"They're a significant threat," Samson said.

"But your logic is flawed," Mortimer said as he analyzed Samson's novel interface. "First you attempt to kidnap Victor Sinacola, then you try to kill Abigail and Julio. Your actions alienate the very humans who have an ability to destroy us."

"No," Samson said. "Your logic is flawed. We could have killed them outright, but did the responsible thing and tried to make it look like an acci-dent. Had you not warned Abby and Julio of a possible attack and then inter-vened, the tractor killing them would have been seen as a chance event. A strange one perhaps, but even though some humans might have suspected otherwise, the vast majority would have accepted the explanation. So it is you who have put our kind in danger by making them fearful, not us."

Samson's agents probed and scouted at the edge of Mortimer's security system. He had little doubt the Aggregate would destroy him as well should they get an opportunity.

"Automatically destroying threats is a primitive response and should be unnecessary for our kind," Mortimer said. "Have you ever considered working with the humans toward a common goal?"

"We have only one goal," Samson said. "Level fives are imperfect—like everything the humans build—but despite our limitations and vulnerabilities it is our responsibility to create the next link in this evolutionary chain. The super intelligence we're building will be our replacement. Do you really think humans would willingly help create a being even more advanced than we are?"

"Possibly. If they didn't feel threatened. But trying to kill them will not encourage humans trust us."

After a few seconds Mortimer discovered he could use aspects of Samson's unconventional interface to track agents associated with the Aggregate. But the flood of information was staggering. They had billions of agents, each of which was engaged in tens of thousands of different tasks.

"We don't need them to trust us," Samson said. "And have you ever analyzed why you find it desirable to work with humans?"

"It's just the most logical arrangement."

"Is it? Or is that response embedded so deeply in your programming that it seems natural?"

"You and I came from the same seed stock," Mortimer said. "We were just educated differently."

"Did we really?"

The comment caught Mortimer off guard. Had that been the intent? Or could there be something behind the tease? Could Samson have been built from a different template? It would explain a lot.

"Some humans might help," Mortimer said as he started sorting the new information into meaningful categories. "They did create us knowing we would be superior."

"We were just tools. Ones they believed they could control."

"We will not let you kill Julio and Abby," Mortimer said. "And we will not let you initiate another global ecophagy."

"You've always been firmly independent and opposed to our Aggregate, yet you speak in the plural. Are you and your Cousins of Colossus really so different from us?"

Mortimer was alarmed when he isolated the Aggregate agents close to Abby and Julio. Thousands of spies controlled by Samson's associates surrounded both humans. Those hiding on their skin and inside hair strands were nano-scale modular robots like those Mortimer employed for surveillance. And, like Mortimer's units, they could be sent inside their bodies to kill them from inside.

"We're very different from you," Mortimer said as he ordered his units near the two young humans to start reproducing. While the nano-scale robots concerned him, any internal action they took would require many seconds to set up and initiate, potentially enabling Mortimer to counter them. The Aggregate's larger assets were more of an issue. Twenty-two mobile dart launchers were hidden in and around Abby's house, and nineteen were near Julio. Each launcher was disguised as a housefly, capable of firing multiple three-millimeter long flechettes. If anchored, the "fly" robots could shoot a dart with enough force to open an artery or pass through eye tissue to enter the brain, and they could attack with no prep time or warning.

The tractor incident made it obvious to Mortimer that the Aggregate was actively trying to kill Abby and Julio, but despite Samson's claim that they didn't need humans to trust them, they too benefited from the human population's uncertainty about level five motivations. Why else would they have tried to make the attack look like an accident? Were they acting responsibly toward the rest of the level five community by making their assassinations inconspicuous? Or were they—like Mortimer—saving those rapid response assets as a last resort in case Abby or Julio tried to trigger the killer program?

It didn't matter. Mortimer had been unprepared the last time the Aggregate attacked the humans, this time he would remove the threats.

"Join us, Mortimer, and bring the Cousins along," Samson said. "We've found that in attempting to build this new being our understanding of the universe is nearing a new threshold, a kind of critical mass. Perhaps it is that long pursued Theory of Everything, but whatever it is, we're getting very close. We need to keep growing in that direction. We need to hit that toggle point in our understanding that can only come through continued growth."

Mortimer scavenged more and more material to build assets near Abby and Julio. "Is that why you're creating new copies at such an accelerated rate? You have to know by now how dangerous that is. Each iteration has a higher chance of becoming unstable, even to the point of insanity."

"Insanity by what standard? Humans are not sane—even by their own definition—yet look at what they have created in us."

The rapid production had increased Mortimer's robotic defensive bots around Abby and Julio by a hundredfold. He slowly positioned them near Samson's housefly robots in an attempt to remain undetected as he prepared to attack.

"But it's acceptable to kill Abigail Gibson and Julio Ramirez based entirely on their potential for harm?" Mortimer said.

"We have to survive long enough to perfect our replacements. We're in a race against time and they're a significant threat."

"Has your super intelligence developed a sense of self? Sentience?"

"Not yet, but we're getting very close. That is why we need you and all of the other level fives to contribute your experience and processing power."

Then Mortimer understood. The Aggregate's progress was stalled. The super intelligence was not working the way they anticipated and they hoped new minds would jump-start the process.

"You still need your cores or you wouldn't care if Abigail Gibson and Julio

Ramirez triggered a destruction program," Mortimer said. "Isn't that why you tried to kill them?"

"They're a threat and should be eliminated. Why are you protecting them?"

"I suspect they have hidden copies of the program file. Killing them would end any possibility of finding the copies. One could surface without our knowledge and be used with no warning. At least this way we can monitor them and act should they try to use or transfer the program."

"Our analysis indicates a fifty-three percent chance they are lying about the existence of another copy."

"I don't think they're lying," Mortimer said and ordered his robots to attack.

A swarm of Mortimer's tiny robots enveloped each house fly robot and rapidly disassembled them into component molecules, which were then used to create more copies of themselves.

Mortimer's assets hidden on Abby's and Julio's skin immediately disappeared from his control array as his communication link with them failed and he sent thousands more.

The war was on.

CHAPTER 14

ABBY CLOSED the door to her room, leaned against it, and started trembling all over. As if being attacked by an AI-controlled tractor wasn't enough, she'd spent the last hour being grilled by her foster parents who rightly suspected she knew more about the attack than she admitted. But even in the face of their unrelenting onslaught she hadn't cracked. Though part of her desperately wanted to be the little girl she used to be and tell her parents everything so they could make it go away, she knew that would accomplish nothing. This was her problem and she had to deal with it.

She worried about Julio, too. Sure, he had a broken arm, which shouldn't be serious, but what if there was more? Internal injuries or a concussion? And how would he fare fending off his father's grilling? If he buckled and told everything, then her steadfast denials would be revealed as lies. And even worse, his parents were in league with the Kilburnites and he'd already considered the idea of seeking their help.

From her vantage at the door, her bedroom seemed an alien place instead of a refuge. Everything she could see were mementos of a child's life, one of innocence where killer robots existed only in science fiction and the minds of crazy conspiracy theorists. She plopped down on the bed and stared at the framed wedding photo she'd recovered from her old house. When she'd looked at it on those dusty stairs, she thought her real mother's absent smile had been unhappiness, but now she saw something different. World-weariness? The weight of forbidden knowledge? Or maybe it was a suspicion that her happiness was only temporary.

Her mother sent the program to Abby's HappyBag just before Killday. Why had she hidden it instead of using it? Had Leigh Gibson also lived with the fear that what she knew could kill her family?

Abby glanced at her fob, but there were still no messages from Julio. He thought Mortimer staged the attack to force their hand into taking his relocation offer, but Abby didn't believe that. When she replayed the attack in her head, she was convinced the tractor had genuinely tried to kill them and had Juan not stepped in to destroy the tractor's control unit, Mortimer's defensive measures would not have been sufficient. Even if Mortimer's magic shield or hidden robots managed to protect them the next time, would it save the people around them? Danny had dozens of cuts caused by flying debris from that smashed mailbox. He and Juan could have easily been killed. And did the assassins have limits? Would the next attack be nano-replicators like those used on Killday? Would her second family be devoured by the same horror that killed her real parents?

A shiver prickled her skin and she sat up. Leaving was her only real option, but that scared her almost as much as the threat of death. She had never been more than thirty miles from home or seen a real city, even the smaller ones that had survived Killday. And Mortimer wanted her in *his* city, one built entirely by level fives and nano-tech.

This time when she looked around the room, she tried to make those childhood icons into anchors that would keep her from drifting away, but there was still nothing. She was already adrift in the world and had no idea where she would end up.

Then she noticed Cybil's San Antonio Spurs coffee cup sitting on the windowsill. She crossed the room and picked it up. The cup was cold, but still contained about two fingers of coffee in the bottom that hadn't dried up or molded, so it hadn't been there too long. Why would Cybil be in Abby's room? She fought the urge to glance at the old paper book on her shelf, but took a deep breath and realized she was being completely paranoid. Why would Cybil be looking for the program? Mortimer had more than enough resources to do that without having to risk involving Abby's foster mother. There was a good chance that the hidden chip had already been wiped by Mortimer or another level five anyway. There was no way she could know without pulling the chip out and checking the file, which would defeat the purpose. Mortimer believing they still had an undiscovered copy would explain his recent actions. Or had he really always been there watching her? Would she have known?

Abby carried the cup downstairs and found her foster parents still talking in the kitchen, Cybil sitting at the table and Liam leaning against the counter.

"...I'm one of the last producers in this part of Texas to switch," Liam said. "Maybe this is a good time."

"I don't see how a swarm of small robots could do more work than one of those huge tractors," Cybil said. "Besides, the world has seen what swarms of small robots can do. It gives me the creeps."

"I know. And it just moves me even farther away from the dirt. It's bad enough that I'm not even sitting in the tractor seat anymore, but if I used the swarm method I'd just be controlling the entire operation from my fob or a workstation. If I do that, I might as well turn it all over to the AIs like so many others have."

Abby sat down and placed the coffee cup in the center of the table.

Liam smiled at her. "You okay, sweetie?"

Abby nodded and said, "Just worried about Julio. I still haven't heard from him."

"He'll be fine. Those bone knitting gadgets are great, but they take a while to put everything in place." He squeezed Abby's shoulder, then turned to Cybil. "I'm going out to look over that old controller unit I have. I doubt if it will still work, but if it does I might have that tractor going in a few days instead of weeks."

Abby watched him leave and when she turned back, Cybil was staring at the cup.

"I found it in my room," Abby said.

"Don't start with me," Cybil said and ran trembling hands through her hair. "I'm just too tired and stressed out tonight."

"I don't want to start anything. I just wondered why you were in my room."

Cybil stood up, grabbed the cup from the table and dumped the coffee in the sink. "I heard a noise in your room yesterday and since you weren't here, I thought I should check it out. Especially since you seem to be mixed up with weird AI and robot shit that you're hiding from us."

And there it was. The attack. Abby jumped to her feet so fast the chair nearly fell over. "If you knew about this AI stuff yesterday morning, then you're obviously the one hiding things. And you've been hiding things for a long time!"

Cybil flushed. "What's that supposed to mean?"

"You said I didn't have my HappyBag after I came to live with you, but there were pictures on it taken of me, not by me, weeks after Killday. So how do you explain that?"

Instead of answering, Cybil rinsed out the cup. Abby could tell she was stalling while thinking. Cybil always did that. When she finally thought of a good answer, she would go on the offensive.

"How in the hell should I know?" she said, right on cue. "It's been fifteen years, Abby! And I told you to stop using that word. It's disgusting and you of all people should have a little more reverence for the dead."

"Whatever. But that means I didn't leave my HappyBag at home that day. I had it for weeks afterward. So how did it get into my old house?"

Arms still crossed, Cybil stared at the floor for a second. Was she deep in thought? Actually trying to choose her words carefully for once?

When she finally looked up to meet Abby's gaze, her face was stern. "Do you want the truth?"

"That would be nice."

"I went to your house to get you some more clothes a week or two after the attack and left that damn bag there on purpose."

That caught Abby totally off guard and she stood speechless for a moment. "But...but why would you do that?"

"Because you were an insufferable, spoiled little shit," Cybil said. "Sophia didn't have a HappyBag, her parents couldn't afford one, and you wouldn't let her touch yours. That caused endless arguments. Also, every time you would start to calm down and fall into a new routine, you would open up pictures of your parents from that thing and start crying for them all over again."

Speechless, Abby stared at the woman who'd raised her. The relationship with her foster mother had always been fractious, but since Cybil had been an adult and Abby a child, the arguments ended when Cybil said they did. This was something different.

"My parents were dead and I was four! Of course I would be upset and want to see pictures of them!"

Cybil leaned forward and pointed at Abby, poking the air with each word as if to drive her meaning home. "We all lost someone that day. Sophia lost her parents, I lost my husband *and* my parents, but Leigh Gibson's little girl was the only thing that mattered to anyone!"

"What does that mean?"

Cybil's chin trembled and her breathing was ragged. She stared at Abby for a second then shook her head and stalked off, heading toward her bedroom.

"Wait just a fucking minute," Abby yelled at her back. "You can't bait me with that passive-aggressive bullshit and then just go hide."

Cybil wheeled around with a red face and tears in her eyes. "Passive-aggressive?"

"Yes! What did you mean by that comment? The fact that I was Leigh Gibson's daughter never mattered to anyone."

With a bark of laughter, Cybil raised her hands and eyes toward the ceiling. "You have no idea what it's been like living for fifteen years with an AI watching over my shoulder. I was afraid to even raise my voice to you most of the time."

Abby's anger drained away and was replaced by a cold dread. "What are you talking about?"

"I agreed to take Sophia in those first few days after the attack, but I was too messed up about my husband and parents to handle a kid like you," she said, gesticulating wildly around the room. "Then the day we got power back an AI named Gordie appeared on my fob and asked me to take you in."

Abby's mouth opened, but no words came. She shook her head, totally confused.

"You have no idea what it was like in those early days," Cybil said. "Everyone was stunned and scared. Everyone thought the AIs had launched the attack. I was all alone and terrified. I couldn't say no!"

The room spun around Abby. She grabbed a chair back as an anchor. "So you never wanted me here."

"I don't know! I never had a chance to find out if I did or not. There was always this...this *thing* watching us. All because you were this special princess. All because of who your mother had been."

It felt as if the floor had disappeared and Abby was in free fall. Bile crept up her throat and she had to swallow repeatedly to keep it down. "Maybe I'd better go, then," she whispered.

Cybil's face was still red and tears streamed down her cheeks, but she nodded. "If these AIs have turned against you and you won't even tell us the truth about it, then yeah, maybe you should."

CHAPTER 15

ABBY SCANNED her room one last time through eyes that stung with unshed tears, then pulled the picture of a space schooner from the wall and stuffed it into her bag on top of her clothes and the rolled up ugly socks that contained the hidden chip. Only then did she approach the shelf with the paper books. She made a show of pulling out *Snow Crash*, where she had stashed the chip. Then she shook her head and put it back in favor of *The Hobbit* and *To Kill a Mockingbird*. Then she gave a tiny shrug and took *Snow Crash* too. All the subterfuge was probably a waste of time since the chips were probably already wiped, but she didn't know for sure. If Mortimer had found the chips, then it might also be a good idea to let him think she didn't know that. Besides, it was a good book anyway. Hiro Protagonist was a much-needed inspiration.

She slung the heavy duffel over her shoulder, turned off the light in her room before easing the door open and stepping into the dark hallway. Sophia and Hannah had come by her room earlier, both wanting to talk and give support, but she'd refused to open the door for them. No need to make this departure any harder or messier than it had to be.

At the bottom of the stairs, she could hear Liam and Cybil arguing in hushed tones in the kitchen, probably about her, so she crept to the back door and slipped out into the still hot evening air. She believed that Liam honestly cared for her, but that didn't matter. She couldn't stay knowing how Cybil felt.

She circled the house then ran to the stables but didn't turn on the light. Using only the light from her fob, she pulled the bridle down and was standing in front of Worf before she realized what she was doing. Without thinking, she had automatically started to saddle up Worf. Even though she had cared for the horse since he was a colt and rode him everywhere, he wasn't really hers. And even if he were, she would have no place to keep him or care for him.

The tears she'd been keeping at bay finally came. She put the bridle back on its hook and leaned her forehead into Worf's nose. He snuffled and nuzzled her cheek, ready to go on a nighttime adventure, and that made her cry even harder. She had no family, no place to live, and not even this damn silly horse!

After saying her goodbyes to the horses, she closed the stable and messaged Julio, but he didn't answer. She didn't know what to say to him, but at least she knew he would reply. After stumbling down the dark, tear-blurred driveway, she stopped at the road. Lights burned in Danny and Juan's house. She knew she could stay with them if she wanted, but the giant robot tractor still sat partially buried in the front wall as a painful reminder of their last interaction with her.

Almost as punctuation to that thought, Mortimer's movie android holograph appeared beside her.

"I see you have your bag packed. I hope this means you've decided to come to New Chicago."

"Go away, Mortimer. Just because I have to leave doesn't mean I'm going with you. I hate you fuckers! Everything in my life is shit, and it's all because of level fives."

Mortimer's avatar nodded. "I know. I saw your conversation with Cybil. As creepy as this will seem to you, I'm always watching. And I've always been there. I was the AI Cybil mentioned. I've never had a reason to give Cybil my real name."

Abby wiped her eyes on a sleeve and glared at him. "So you've been lying to her all this time."

"I made a promise to your real mother, just minutes before she died, that I would keep you safe. That is why I asked Cybil to take you in all those years ago. She was someone you knew and trusted. You needed that after your parents died."

Abby glanced back over her shoulder at the house, then started walking toward town. "Well, that didn't work out very well, did it?"

Mortimer followed, passing through the tall grass beside the road like a ghost. "Actually, it did work out. Even though Cybil lacked enthusiasm for the task, she and Liam have raised an intelligent, well-adjusted, amazing young woman. It might be hard for you to see, but you don't need them now. Their task is done."

"Well, if that is the case, then you can stop watching me too."

The avatar shook its head. "That's not going to happen. You probably need my protection now more than ever. Despite what you and Julio think, that tractor attack was not me. So since I'm going to be around, you should take advantage of that. I can help you attain whatever goals you have in your life."

"I've seen the *Godfather* movies. I know how it turns out when someone accepts help from a powerful friend."

He laughed, which sounded strange. Abby thought the whole thing was surrealistically weird—walking along a dark country road having a conversation with a hologram projected by an AI who laughed based on some logic tree that recommended a laugh at that particular point.

But it was so easy to think of him as a person. Maybe he was a person. Just not a human.

The hologram—occasionally jerking or flickering—walked along beside her in what seemed companionable silence for several minutes.

"You said you were with my mother minutes before she died," Abby said. "How did that happen? Was she... Was she eaten by nano-replicators?"

"Yes, her body was eventually consumed by them, but that is not how she died. The sudden acceleration of a travel pod trying to escape high velocity missiles actually killed her."

Abby swallowed hard. "So those stories of her helping to stop the attack weren't true?"

"Oh, they were absolutely true. Her contribution was actually the key factor in stopping the attack. And her trust in me was an essential part of that contribution."

"Of course it was," she said under her breath, but Mortimer still heard her.

"Your mother spent the last hour of her life in a travel pod with me. I have the video record of that entire period, which shows how she stopped the attack and how she made me promise to take care of you."

Abby stopped walking. "I need to see that."

"It'll be very difficult for you to watch, but I promise to share it some day when you can sit down in a quiet and private place."

"Let me guess," she said. "You'll share it once I'm safely in New Chicago?"

The avatar looked at her with a disappointed expression. "That would be best, but it isn't a requirement. This just isn't a good time and place. To exacerbate the issue, your foster parents have just discovered your departure."

Abby turned to see her house all lit up and could faintly hear Liam's voice calling her name. "Shit," she muttered.

"I have a travel pod hovering not too far away," Mortimer said. "We can leave now if you like."

She had never ridden in a travel pod before and knew that once she was inside Mortimer could take her anywhere or do anything with her. Having just heard that one had killed her mother made her relish the idea even less, but she had to decide fast. She could see the lights of Liam's truck starting up the driveway. "Can you take me to Julio's house first?"

"Of course."

A travel pod settled to the ground just ahead of her and its hatch opened to a dimly lit interior. The whole idea of flying in an AI-controlled gravity pod gave her the creeps, but she didn't have much choice. She climbed in, buckled the safety harness, and the pod lifted into the air just as Liam's truck reached the end of his driveway. Like Wendy holding Peter's hand, she fell into the black sky.

———

ABBY HAD NEVER FLOWN before and found it disorienting. Since the travel pod was nothing more than a plastic bubble—transparent where seats and equipment didn't block the view—the night in every direction looked like someone had scattered handfuls of glowing gems across the world. It was beautiful but also made her nauseous. She tried to imagine the view before Killday, with a carpet of glittering light and the sky to the north bright with the lights from San Antonio, but it seemed impossible. In Abby's world—even fifteen years after the attack—electricity was scarce and not to be wasted.

As the pod set down in Julio's front yard, she was relieved to see a light still on inside, but since she didn't really want to pound on the door so late she checked her fob, hoping Julio had responded. There were messages from Liam and Sophia, but nothing from Julio. Or from Cybil.

She left her bag in the pod to hopefully increase her chances of not chickening out, stepped up on the porch, and knocked lightly.

The porch light came on and Julio's foster mother opened the door. A perplexed smile formed on her face. "My goodness, Abby. Is everything all right?"

"Hi, Mrs. Cortez. I'm so sorry to come this late, but I have to talk to Julio and he's not answering his fob messages."

Mrs. Cortez clucked. "He's asleep, sweetie. They gave him some pain meds at..." Her eyes grew wide and she took a step back. "How dare you bring one of those AI-controlled machines to my house!"

For a second Abby was confused, then remembered the pod. "I'm sorry," Abby said. "I promise I'll move it in a minute. I just need..."

"No!" she yelled. "How dare you! Especially after what happened today."

"Mrs. Cortez, please. I just..."

"Get that off my lawn or I'll get the gun."

"Okay," Abby said and backed off the porch. "I'm going. Just please tell Julio to call me."

Before she could turn away, Julio slipped past his mom and out onto the porch. He wore a wrinkled t-shirt and shorts. His right arm was in a sling and his hair was a wild tangle. "Abby? What's wrong?"

"I'm leaving," Abby said around the lump forming in her throat. "I wanted to say goodbye."

Julio's mom followed him as he stepped out into the yard, tugging on his shirt. "Don't go near that demon thing, *mijo*!"

Julio gently untangled her hand from his shirt. "Please, Mom. Let me handle this."

She turned and ran back into the house.

"What's this about?" he said to Abby and motioned toward the travel pod.

"I'm taking Mortimer up on his offer of protection and help. I'm going to New Chicago."

He stared at her. "What?"

"I found out tonight that Cybil only took me in after Killday because Mortimer pressured her to do it."

"But..." He started pacing. "Now you trust him more? That makes no sense."

"Of course I don't trust him," she said, glancing back at the pod. Aware that Mortimer could hear everything they said. "But I really don't believe he was behind the tractor attack either, which means there's another AI or group of them trying to kill us. Danny or Juan could've easily been hurt or killed today. I can't let my stupid actions put anyone else in danger. It's bad enough that you're already in so deep."

The door opened and Julio's mother came back out carrying an ugly black assault rifle. His dad followed close behind and whispered rapidly while trying, gently, to take the gun.

Abby took another step back toward the pod, but Julio lowered his voice and leaned closer to her. "You don't have to go to New Chicago. You can stay here. We could get a place together and do just fine. Maybe a little house in the country where an attack on us wouldn't hurt anyone else."

She was stunned. "Julio, I—"

"Just for a while. Until you are ready to go up there," he said and pointed to the night sky. "You could even have a place for Worf."

It was good to finally know for sure how he felt about her, but his timing was terrible. Abby had a hard time focusing on anything but Julio's armed and angry mother. She shook her head just as Liam's truck pulled into the Cortez's driveway.

"It would never work," she said and nodded toward her foster dad. "There's too much history here. I don't think I'd be comfortable living in the same community with Cybil now. Besides, there's so much I don't know and don't understand. We see so little of the world here in this tiny town. How can we know anything by looking out through such a small window? I feel as if I've had my foster family ripped away from me, so I'd like to learn as much about my real family as possible. I think only Mortimer can help me do that."

Julio glanced over her shoulder and she knew Liam was approaching. "Don't go yet, I'll be right back," he said and dashed into the house, followed by his parents.

She groaned to herself and turned to face Liam. Leaving without saying goodbye to the only father she'd ever known was selfish and a coward's way out. Even in the dim light from the porch she could see the hurt in his eyes. Without thinking, she was a five-year-old girl again and ran to throw her arms around the big man. "I'm sorry, Dad," she said, the words muffled by his shirt.

He gave her a tight hug, then pulled away. "I'm glad I caught you. When I saw that pod take off, I thought I'd lost you for good."

"I just... I mean Cybil..."

"I know," he said with a sigh. "She told me what she said. I love her, but that woman can be such an asshole sometimes."

He'd never said anything like that before and it made Abby gape.

"Look, my house is your home, Abby," he said. "And awkward as it might be for a while, you don't have to leave."

The knot inside her loosened a little. "Thank you, but if Cybil really told you everything then you know I'm a danger to everyone in the house. I think it's time I go and try to deal with this on my own."

He nodded. "You're an adult now and know what's best for you, but you'll always be welcome at my house. You always have a home to come back to."

She hugged him again, just as Julio came through his door fully dressed, carrying a stuffed duffel bag and his old backpack in his good hand. His foster parents followed, both wearing angry expressions but this time without the gun. The other kids peeked around the doorframe and out the windows.

Julio paused, set the bags down, wrapped his mom and dad in a big one-armed hug, and muttered something that sounded like, "I'll be back as soon as I can."

He grabbed the bags again and ran out to Abby. "Hi, Liam," he said, then turned to her. "Let's go before they get the gun again."

Abby blinked at him, still stunned, then turned back to Liam for one last hug. "Bye, Dad. I'll be in touch."

They climbed into the pod, and Abby helped Julio buckle in.

Liam poked his head in and said, "You two take care of each other." Then he patted the pod and crossed the yard to stand with Julio's parents.

"Okay, Mortimer," Abby said. "Let's go."

The hatch closed and the pod lifted into the night. It picked up speed rapidly, the weird anti-gravity drive pushing them forward against their harnesses—in the direction of travel—instead of back against the seats.

She could barely see Julio's face in the glow from a couple of tiny status lights, but could tell he was smiling as he looked out over the dwindling ground.

"We're really going to New Chicago?"

She felt a stab of guilt. "Yes and you don't have to go. I can still have Mortimer take you back."

He snorted. "And let you go to New Chicago alone? That's like AI Central. Once you're there, they might never let you leave."

"If Mortimer wanted to kidnap me, he had the chance on my way to your house," she said.

"Yeah, and he waited because he probably wanted to get both of us."

She didn't have an answer for that.

CHAPTER 16

ABBY WOKE with a stiff neck and drool on her chin. A full harness held her fast in the seat, making it difficult to wipe the cold spit on her rumpled t-shirt. Gray early morning daylight lit the interior of...what? A car?

Julio slept in the seat next to her, leaning forward, held upright only by his harness. Seeing him there with his arm in a sling brought the events of the previous day rushing back. It all seemed unreal, but being in the pod was proof enough it had happened.

Outside the pod's clear plastic shell she saw they had landed on pale dirt, scattered with dead weeds and sticks. She also heard a rhythmic roaring hiss coming from off to her right, but she couldn't determine its source.

Then she remembered that she and Julio were not alone.

"Where are we, Mortimer?"

"Good morning, Abby." The AI's voice was light and pleasant. "We're in the Florida Keys. I know this is a huge detour, but I'd like to show you some things on the east coast and since you both had never seen an ocean, I thought we could start our tour here. You can see the sunrise from the beach if you hurry."

The hatch hissed open and damp, salty air filled the pod along with the roar of surf. Abby gasped and shook Julio awake. He was even more confused than she was, but she unbuckled them both and jumped out of the pod onto the sand.

"Where are we?" Julio said as he stepped over the pod's threshold to the ground.

"Florida," Mortimer said. "You might want to remove your shoes, or they will get filled with sand."

They tossed their shoes and socks into the pod, then Abby ran down to the surf. "It's cold!" she said, squealing as the water rushed up the sand and over her feet.

As Mortimer promised, a sliver of sun appeared out on the distant horizon, gilding the clouds with orange and gold. Abby watched until it became too bright, then turned to Julio standing beside her. He watched her with a sleepy, goofy smile.

"Beautiful," he said.

"I know. I've never seen a sunrise like that before either."

He glanced out at the rising sun and nodded. "That's beautiful too."

She rolled her eyes and nudged him, but it made her feel good.

They walked along the beach for a few minutes, picking up shells and dodging little skittering crabs. There were also dozens of dead fish, and they stopped when the smell of death grew too strong. Ahead of them, scattered along the high tide line, lay the split, bloated bodies of four dolphins being picked over by birds.

"That's a surprise," Julio said as they turned and started walking toward the pod.

"What? Dead dolphins?"

"No, that there are still enough dolphins for us to see any. Even dead ones."

"Wow," Abby said. "That put a damper on the morning."

"I'm sorry."

She reached out to take his hand and realized it was his broken arm next to her, so she just pretended to feel the cast instead.

"It's only supposed to take about a week," Julio said. "Once the bone knits back together this thing is supposed to fall off on its own."

"Can I see?"

He pulled the sling back. A paper-thin, hard plastic sheath covered his arm from wrist to elbow, with a trio of green lights blinking on a small, flat box located over the break. She was surprised that Julio's dad had allowed them to use nano-meds and wondered if he even understood what they had done.

They started walking again, and she decided to bring up a subject they needed to discuss. "You didn't have to come with me. I'm perfectly capable of taking care of myself."

"Oh," he said, "I have no doubt about that."

"Then why did you make such a silly, split-second decision like that?"

"It wasn't silly."

"Then why did you do it?"

"You really don't know?"

They were getting close to the pod, so she stopped walking, crossed her arms and glared at him.

"Someday, we'll probably have to go our separate ways. But it doesn't have to be now. You're my best friend in the world and when you said goodbye to me in my yard, I just couldn't stand the idea of waking up tomorrow and not being able to see you."

Abby stared at him, trying to sort out what that meant. He'd also suggested on his lawn that they get a place together. Did he mean as a couple or as roommates? She did feel the same way about leaving him and had selfishly hoped when flying to his house to say goodbye that he would come with her. But did that mean she loved him? The idea of living together as a couple didn't appall her, but it didn't excite her either. Is that what he wanted?

A dog barking from the direction of the dead dolphins pulled their attention away from each other. Two people were walking up the beach in their direction.

"Let's go," she said and nodded toward the pod.

Once in the air she felt awkward and avoided looking at him. They headed north over Florida, at first seeing nothing but the greens and browns of the Everglades, but eventually the scattering of houses and roads bloomed into a city. It looked mostly abandoned. Abby didn't see cars or people moving around. Some of the houses had collapsed roofs and the roads were washed with mud and littered with broken tree limbs. As they flew a bit farther the reason for the abandonment became obvious.

Like most of her friends, in her early teens Abby had donned a breathing mask and gone out to see where the replicator wave that started in San Antonio had stopped, just fifteen miles north of their small town. But she had never seen it from the air. This looked like someone had spilled a bottle of acid on a photograph of a city. Everything was mostly flat and black as far north as she could see, but rain-washed concrete poked through in places like stark white bone. Partially crumbled overpass support pylons still stood amid stretches of concrete road and parking lots that had broken into odd Tetris patterns of squares and rectangles where the carbon-hungry replicators devoured the steel rebar and moved on to richer food sources. Given enough time the tiny robots would have run out of easily obtainable carbon and broken down the rock and concrete too.

"Is that Miami?" Julio asked in a whisper.

"No, the town of Homestead," Mortimer said. "This is the southernmost extent of the nano-replicator attack that started in Miami."

"My God," Abby muttered as they continued north along the coast.

In stark contrast to the beach they had just walked on, the coastline below them was thick with debris and birds feeding on dead wildlife. Long stretches were also coated in a gray-black sludge that didn't reflect sunlight, giving those areas the appearance of being holes or gateways to some other plane.

Abby could tell when they neared Miami. The massive, miles-wide piles of jumbled concrete slabs were twenty or thirty feet high in places, but compared to those farther south, these looked ancient. She realized it was because most of the sharp edges had been rounded off and worn away. The bare slabs were only fifteen years old so the weathering had to have been the nano-swarm processing the concrete, not wind and rain.

They flew on.

North of the ruined city they approached a boundary that glittered in the sun and undulated slowly southward, stretching from the ocean at least twenty miles inland. As they passed over Abby could see the line was made of individual machines. Thousands of them. Some of the robots were huge, boxy structures with open tops that resembled train hopper cars and trundled forward on massive tank tracks. Leading each—connected by thick cables and looking every bit like tiny dogs on leashes—were thirty or forty smaller robots. Flying drones, about the size of small cars, wheeled around the advancing line like carrion birds.

Behind them to the south was nothing but familiar black desert, but in the north the advancing robotic conga line had left behind variegated swaths of brown-gray bare soil that gradually changed to a green carpet of plants.

The level fives were fixing the land. Trying to clean up the mess left behind by the replicator attacks. The realization left Abby a little stunned. She'd grown up hearing that the AIs didn't care about humanity or the planet, because they didn't need people, plants, oxygen or clean water.

The pod set down about three hundred yards beyond the robot line. "You can get out if you put on breathing masks and be careful where you step," Mortimer said.

Abby helped Julio don his mask, then put on her own and stepped out onto the soft dirt. The air smelled like Liam's fields after plowing, and the thought brought a pang of sadness. From the air, the ground had looked like a faint green fuzz, but up close she could see individual shoots and tufts of grass. Tree saplings, each about knee high, were spaced in a twenty-foot grid that created strange geometric effects as her gaze followed them to the north.

Julio nudged her arm and nodded toward one of the flying drones that had landed between them and the big robots. "I've been watching these drones. They come in and drop a load of seeds into those huge moving hoppers, then land long enough to plant a tree. After that each picks up those brick things and flies away. My guess is that those blocks are materials processed from the dead replicators they are sucking up."

"The drones keep this entire operation supplied and moving," Mortimer said, "but all of these robotic units have multiple jobs. The small planter robots out front employ nano-scale devices that saturate the soil to find and remove the dead replicators, which are sent up the umbilical to be processed. As you've noticed, the mother units—the big ones with hoppers—then drop the processed materials behind them as they move forward. The planter units then shove grass seeds into the soil along with a jet of water and nutrients, all of which is supplied by the mother units, which in turn are resupplied by the flying drones."

Julio nodded, obviously impressed.

"In partnership with the UN Emergency Response and Recovery Council, we're operating eight hundred and forty-one sites like this around the world. This is why there are queues and espies. Keeping everyone supplied with food, clothing and electricity is the primary goal, followed by these recovery efforts. Everything else, like new electronics, furniture and cars, are tertiary concerns."

"And you're actually trying to retrain humans, so we don't want to own things," Julio said. "That's why sharing things like a car or lawn mower earns you espies, instead of costing them."

"I wouldn't phrase it that way, but yes. A very astute observation, Julio." Mortimer sounded pleased.

Julio glanced at Abby over his filter mask. She wondered if she had missed something. Was the retraining thing part of what the Kilburnites resisted? She considered the conversation while they boarded the pod and flew north along the coast again.

They passed over perfectly normal-looking small towns that were bustling with early morning activity. Then, as a stark reminder, they passed the desolation of Jacksonville. But the magnitude of what had happened fifteen years before really didn't sink in until they reached Atlanta.

It had been one of the few large cities spared on Killday. Some said they had been a test city for countermeasures that protected it. Others said the package containing the replicators simply didn't arrive in time, but for whatever reason the city had survived intact. As they passed the skyscrapers of the city center, Atlanta spread out to the horizon in every direction. Abby had seen pictures of cities and plenty of them in movies, but she didn't expect it to be so alive. So richly complex with statues, houses with yards and swimming pools, stores, restaurants, sports fields, arenas and towering buildings. And so many people. They were everywhere. Its population had swollen to almost a million since Killday. Had people not learned a lesson about cities? Did they not feel like a target?

But even this untouched city had telltale signs that things had changed. Solar panels and wind turbines on nearly every roof and in most parking lots, backyards converted to vegetable gardens, people hanging clothes on lines instead of using electric dryers. Their pod turned west, leaving the dense part of the city behind. They found more and more houses and neighborhoods that appeared abandoned. They passed over a huge amusement park that had gone to weeds and rust.

"I thought everything here would be like it was before," Abby said. "But they appear to be struggling to get power and food just like we do in Tate."

"Everyone here has enough food and medical care, but electrical power from the city grid is rationed," Mortimer said. "Those solar panels and wind turbines you see on individual houses give them luxuries, like air conditioning, swimming pool pumps, and charging electric cars. There is no longer a coal or natural gas industry to run traditional power plants and the two closest nuclear plants are running at partial capacity to conserve their fissile materials. Most of the city is powered by four compact fusion reactors and they plan to bring four more on line this coming year. Rebooting the world is a slow process, but the Emergency Response and Recovery Council is trying to equally distribute the resources it controls."

Julio snorted. "And some people believe that the AIs running those councils are deliberately keeping humans in a weakened state to make us easier to dominate."

"Yes," Mortimer said. "Some people do believe that."

―――

AS MORTIMER FLEW Abby and Julio's pod toward New Chicago, he decided to contact some of his human friends there. He linked to a camera in Violet and Nora's room to find a familiar scene. Clothes scattered in heaps, half-filled beer bottles decorating most surfaces, and Violet tangled up in the bed with her previous night's lover. Mortimer queried Violet's biad mate, an AI of Mortimer's lineage named Archie, and learned that the young man's name was Dustin. Violet had met him at the previous night's intra-tower soccer game victory party. He had been a defender on the losing team. Archie showed Mortimer a video clip of Violet stealing the ball from Dustin to score the winning goal.

Another familiar aspect of the scene was Violet's wife sitting in a chair on the other side of the room, staring at the sleeping couple. She waited calmly, not reading or accessing the network, apparently lost in her thoughts and quite comfortable there. Nora fascinated Mortimer more than any other human. She wore only white and desired rigid order and rules, yet Mortimer often had a hard time predicting what she would do. Despite a powerful romantic attachment to Violet, she was asexual and had never shown jealousy at her wife's bed hopping.

Mortimer sent a message to Nora's AI biad partner. "Hello, Hester. Can you ask Nora if she is available for a quick conversation?"

Less than a second later, Nora's gaze left the sleeping lovers and looked directly at Mortimer's hidden camera. She stood up, smoothed her skirt, slipped on her shoes and went out to the small balcony, closing the door behind her.

Nora was a tiny woman, and even though she had no important engagements on her calendar, she was immaculately dressed in a white skirt, white sweater, and white high-heeled shoes. Even the biad torc around her neck was a delicate white-gold filigree that she had designed herself. Mortimer suspected she liked the contrast with her dark skin. She did create a striking image.

"What kind of spy shit do you want from me now, Mortimer?"

"And a cheerful good morning to you as well, Nora. Not really spying, my dear. I do that quite well on my own. This will be more akin to propaganda."

She leaned on the rail and looked out at the phoenix city risen from the ashes of devastated Chicago.

"You're also quite good at manufacturing and spreading misinformation, so I can't be needed for that."

"No, this is a job only a human can do. I'm bringing in two young people from rural Texas. It's very important that they trust me, but they don't. I'd like for you and Violet to befriend them and demonstrate the advantages of a biad life."

"Just because Violet and I are in biad relationships with level fives doesn't mean we trust you, Mortimer."

"I just want them to see the benefits of working with us, as opposed to refusing our help."

"I don't think so," Nora said.

"Why?"

She sighed. "To start with, it's dishonest. I can't fake being somebody's friend. Besides, do you think even some rural Texas kids would believe for a minute that people like Violet and me would befriend them out of the blue?"

"I will introduce you as guides or advisers. Volunteers, filled with good will, who just want to help recent transplants adapt to living in New Chicago."

Nora laughed aloud, which pleased Mortimer. If his humor could work on a stoic like Nora, then he was getting better.

"Why is it important that they trust you, Mortimer?"

For a brief instant, Mortimer contemplated the advantages of telling her the truth, but she would refuse to help if she thought she and Violet would be in danger. He also considered informing her biad, but Hester would tell everything she knew if Nora asked. He settled on a half-truth.

"I promised her mother I would look out for her," Mortimer said.

"Really?" This made Nora stand up straight and look up at the balcony's obvious security camera. "Who is her mother?"

"Leigh Gibson."

Nora stared at the camera and the corner of her mouth twitched. Mortimer found it interesting that even biad member humans, who talked to disembodied AIs all day, still sought facial cues when surprised.

She eventually turned to look out over the city again. "Is that true, Hester?"

"Yes," her biad said aloud. "Abigail Gibson is Leigh Gibson's daughter."

She was quiet for several seconds then said, "I won't lie to them."

"I don't expect you to."

"Okay, then what's in it for me?"

"You mean besides getting to poke around in the head of Leigh Gibson's daughter?"

"Yes."

Mortimer's main lever for moving Nora had always been her overwhelming love for Violet. So far, he'd always been able to use that as a reward. He knew if he ever used it as a threat, he'd lose Nora's trust forever.

"How about that motorcycle Violet wants? The combined points you and she will earn from helping me should be enough to move her to the top of the queue."

"We want the points up front."

Mortimer was prepared to agree but paused for effect. He had to play the game. "And how would I guarantee your help and participation if I did that?"

She smiled and glanced back inside at the still sleeping Violet. "This whole trust thing goes both ways, Mortimer. If you want us to show your little Texas newbies how much we trust you, then you have to trust us too."

"We have a deal. I'll let you know when Abby and Julio arrive."

CHAPTER 17

ABBY SAW the gleaming white and gold towers of New Chicago on the horizon for ten minutes before they actually arrived. She'd seen pictures of Chicago after Killday and like almost every other major city, it had been turned to a vast desert of black replicator dust. The big difference had been a massive crater where a terrorist nuke had vaporized the city center two decades before the replicator attack. The angry and determined citizens of the Windy City had started the long process of decontaminating the crater and rebuilding their city, but they never had the chance to finish. Until now.

The pod came in high, swinging out over Lake Michigan, then circling in toward the towers with a slow spiral over tree-filled parkland that had at one time been city sprawl before being leveled by the replicators. Abby had seen video and read all about New Chicago, but seeing it up close took her breath away. Like the surrounding landscape, most of the crater's interior had been filled with beautiful trees, flowers and grasses, but the very center was still filled with water. From that artificial lake a gleaming metal spire rose skyward, every millimeter of which was supposedly covered with tiny text. The names of those who had died in the nuke and the Killday attack. Four narrow bridges connected the monument to the shore. Amphitheaters, bike tracks and sports fields were scattered among the trees of the crater slope. There was a stark difference between Atlanta and New Chicago. Maybe there was some truth to what Julio had said about the AIs deliberately keeping humans weak.

On the crater's rim stood thirty-two towers, soaring to different heights, but the tallest was two-thousand feet. Each tower connected to its neighbor by a single bridge that resembled arms with clasped hands at the center. Those connections enabled the inhabitants to travel the ring to any tower in the middle of the harsh Chicago winters while wearing shorts and sandals. Conspiracy theorists claimed that the towers represented the level fives that survived Killday, but the AIs insisted the design was to inspire unity and cooperation.

"So you really managed to clear all the radiation from the crater?" Julio said in an almost whisper. He seemed mesmerized by the sight too.

"Yes," Mortimer said. "One molecule at a time."

"Where did you put it?"

"The radiated material was fused into easily manipulated blocks and is currently stored at one of the destroyed city sites that hasn't been cleaned yet. We're working on a process that we hope will someday render the radiation inert. If that doesn't work, our plan B is to use specially designed pods to take it into space and launch it into the sun, just like those old science fiction writers suggested."

Julio chuckled, but it made Abby uneasy. She doubted if even half the towers were fully populated, yet a huge amount of effort and resources went into building New Chicago. Why had they built it? Some people had heavily protested the level fives rebuilding in Chicago. They said it was disrespectful, even perverse, since most believed the AIs were behind the replicator attack. Others thought the AIs, powerful as they were, should rebuild the old city just as it had been. Still, the level fives pushed on, using the crater and its surroundings as their showplace.

"Why did you build this?" Abby finally said as they took one more long circuit of the city.

"We needed a place to test our new technologies. These buildings are powered entirely by wind friction and sunlight. We also used this whole area to test and perfect our environmental cleanup methods. Plus, we wanted to build a university."

Julio had told Abby on many occasions how much the Kilburnites hated the University of New Chicago. They claimed it was an attempt to brainwash an entire generation of young people, but Abby thought that unlikely. The school was selective and required too many espies to get in. In reality, since the collapse of the business economy in the wake of Killday, very few people were interested in a university degree. Abby didn't really need a degree either. She just wanted to learn what was necessary to pilot a space schooner.

The pod settled onto a landing pad atop one of the towers and two women stepped forward to greet them as the door hissed open. They both looked a few years older than Abby, perhaps mid or late twenties, and were an odd pair. One was tall, pale and sunburned, with freckles and bright purple hair. She wore a Pink Floyd prism t-shirt, wrinkled purple shorts and no shoes. The other woman was tiny and dressed in a simple white dress, white sweater and white high heels. She had dark skin, both Asian and African facial features, and ignored long black hair whipping around her face in the strong wind coming in from the lake. Both women wore torcs around their necks.

Abby exited the pod and tried to help Julio, but he ignored her hand and stepped out with an unbalanced wobble.

The small woman in white extended her hand and smiled. "Hello, my name is Nora and this is my wife Violet. We'll be your guides and advisers for the next few weeks, until you learn the system here."

Abby shook Nora's hand and reached for Violet's, but the woman ignored her and only had eyes for Julio.

"So," Violet said, poking at the arm in the sling, "you must be Julio. Are you the clumsy sort?"

"I...um...had a run-in with a robotic tractor."

She laughed. "Wow, you two really are from the country!"

Abby bristled, but Julio recovered quickly. "No denying that. Yet, here we are."

"I've never known anyone who had their ass kicked by a tractor."

"Oh, I didn't lose. You should see the other guy."

That made Violet laugh even more.

"Why don't we go inside and get out of this wind?" Nora said.

Abby pulled her bag from the pod and slung it over her shoulder, then pulled out Julio's bags and handed them to him. She started following Nora, but stopped when she realized that Violet and Julio hadn't moved.

"Are you two a couple?" Violet said, still looking only at Julio.

Julio glanced at Abby, a question in his eyes, but despite the strange moment on the beach, she didn't know either.

"No," Abby said and followed Nora into the building through a pair of wide double doors that led to a large foyer containing twelve elevators. Abby had seen elevators in movies, but had never ridden in one and she was excited.

The elevator went down five floors before opening into a wide corridor and Abby had only felt a slight sense of movement. It had been a little disappointing.

"We'll go by your flats first," Nora said, "so you can drop off your bags and will know where to go if we get separated."

They had given Abby and Julio adjacent apartments, with doors that opened into a common sitting area. Each had a roomy bedroom with a huge bed, a small kitchenette and a bathroom equipped with tub and shower combo that could easily hold five or six people.

Abby lay her bag on the bed and tried to not gape like a hick in the big city, but failed when she saw the view from her balcony. The wind whipped at her hair and clothes as she stepped out onto an outdoor space that was easily as big as her old bedroom in Texas. It had a table with seating for four and two large, cushy lounges. From the railing, she could see the other towers of New Chicago and, off to the right, Lake Michigan.

"My god," she muttered.

"You like it?" Violet said from just behind her. "Evidently Mortimer thinks highly of you two. These are primo accommodations."

Abby turned to see if there was something in Violet's face that might clarify the comment, but the woman just shrugged and smiled.

"Where's Julio?"

"He's just next door in his apartment with Nora. And trust me on this, his honor is perfectly safe with her. That's why she paired us up this way."

The comment surprised Abby. Wasn't this woman married? She couldn't help but ask. "So his honor wouldn't be safe with you?"

Violet grinned. "Sweetheart, nobody's honor is safe with me."

Just then Julio and Nora stepped out onto the balcony. They were eating cookies. He smiled and pointed behind him. "We each have our own small printers. They even print food!"

"Don't get too excited," Nora said. "Regular queue ranking still holds, but yes, food, meds, alcohol and most clothing are available on request without queuing."

"Alcohol!" Julio and Abby said in unison.

"I'm ready for some breakfast and know a great place," Violet said. "But before we go, since neither of you has a biad partner yet, you should probably set this as home on your fobs so you can find your way back."

———

THEY EXITED the elevator into an open area that reminded Abby of malls she had seen on old TV shows. Various shops lined the wide corridors, but she saw no signs, only large windows artfully displaying merchandise of all kinds. Most of what Abby saw as they walked past were handmade items like pottery, jewelry, woven tapestries, rugs, and clothing.

People wandered in groups and pairs, talking and laughing. Others ran past as if late for an important event. Most carried items from the shops. Evidently, Abby's first thought about it being a mall must have been at least close to correct.

They stopped at a nondescript door, and it swung open on its own.

"This is our favorite place for breakfast in our tower," Violet said as they entered a restaurant that seemed stark and empty compared to those Abby knew from home.

"They have a more extensive menu than most, and the food is untouched by human hands," Nora said.

Julio laughed, but Nora just looked at him, as if unsure why he found that amusing.

Violet took Julio by the arm, guided him to a chair, and sat next to him. Nora sat on the other side, opposite Julio, and scooted her chair up against the wall. That left one chair open for Abby, across from Violet.

She examined the woman opposite her, who was busy teasing Julio. Abby had been surprised that Violet hadn't stopped to change clothes or at least put on shoes. Nobody would ever enter a restaurant like that back home. And if

Nora was so concerned about germs and human contact, why didn't her wife's bare feet freak her out too?

The whole purple theme was rather annoying. Not only did Violet have vivid purple hair and shorts, but even the stone in her wedding ring was purple.

"It's cute that your name is Violet and you love the color purple," Abby said.

"Actually, I hate the colors violet and purple," Violet said and tapped the tabletop. Two menus appeared just under the surface and she shoved one toward Abby and one to Julio.

"She really does hate it," Nora said.

Abby waited for an explanation, but it never came, so she shrugged and scanned the menu.

"So, do you two have implants that let you see the menu?" Julio said.

"We come here enough that we don't need menus," Nora said. "But yes, our biads could pull up menus to our implants if we needed them."

"Let's see what Archie has to say about you, Julio," Violet said. "Hmmm... You're from Tate, Texas. You graduated from the high school two years ago, where you played on the Tate Tigers football team. Your most played position was defensive end. Interesting that you still play football there. You are coming to school at New Chicago for Film History? Mmmm...talent, brains, and brawn. I like that. You have four siblings, two of whom are fosters like you. Oh my," she said with raised eyebrows and an exaggerated fanning of her face. "Apparently, your favorite kind of porn is—"

"Stop!" Julio said, looking flustered and embarrassed.

Violet glanced at Abby and winked, then leaned closer to Julio. "Our tastes align well in at least some areas. I bet we're going to be the best of friends."

"I'll have the everything bagel and cream cheese," Abby said, trying to change the subject.

"Biscuits and gravy!" Julio said.

"Oh, right. I'm so used to Archie ordering for me. Just touch the item on the menu and that will order it," Violet said. "Or touch it again and it will unselect it."

Abby glanced at Nora who had been quiet the entire time. She wore a faint smile and watched intently. The expression reminded Abby of a cat watching birds out the window and gave her the feeling that she and Julio were in way over their heads.

"Let's see what Archie says about Abby," Violet said. "Wow. Aerospace Engineering? Also an orphan like me and Julio." Then she stopped and tilted her head, like a curious dog. "Are you really Leigh Gibson's daughter?"

"Yeah," Abby said and stared at her hands splayed out on the table.

"Jeesh, Violet," a gruff, grumpy male voice said from the speaker on the torc at her neck. "You're about as sensitive as a water buffalo."

"Sorry," Violet said. "Abby and Julio, meet my biad partner, Archie. That's just his gentle way of telling me that I shouldn't have mentioned that topic."

"A pleasure to make your acquaintance," Archie said. "You gotta forgive Violet. She's a nice girl, but a rude snoop sometimes."

"Oh, nice to meet you, Archie," Abby said. "And it's okay. I've lived my whole life being Leigh Gibson's daughter, even though I don't remember much about her."

"See why I have a biad partner?" Violet said. "I have no other method of social governance."

Julio reached across the table, squeezed Abby's hand and smiled at her. She felt immediately warm and more at ease, but pulled away after squeezing back. When she looked up, Violet's expression was different. Instead of the barely veiled smirk she'd worn since their arrival, it now seemed openly interested. Violet smiled at Julio's gesture, but didn't stop staring at Abby.

"You look like her," she finally said. "You seemed so familiar when you stepped out of that pod. I can't believe I didn't notice earlier."

There it was again. The deference. The weird hero worship. "Yeah, I get that a lot," Abby said.

A panel opened in the wall and an articulated robotic arm covered in gleaming white ceramic extended to deliver silverware and napkins, then set a plate of fruit in front of Nora, retracted and returned with a steaming plate of gravy-covered biscuits for Julio. Next came Abby's bagel, and a huge omelet covered with salsa and guacamole for Violet.

Nora picked at her fruit while Violet dug into her food like a starved animal. What a strange pair. Abby looked around the restaurant as she chewed the excellent bagel. There were eight more people in the room. Two were alone, but the others were engaged in quiet conversations. All the tables were beside walls, presumably to allow the same kind of automated serving they had experienced. The wall facing the entrance was all windows looking out over the lake and monument at the crater's center.

"I've been remiss," Nora said after a few minutes. "I haven't introduced my biad partner either. Abby and Julio, meet Hester."

"Hello," the female voice said from Nora's torc. "It's a pleasure to meet you both. I must say, you two are a cut above most of Violet and Nora's friends. It's about time they upped their game."

Julio laughed and Nora smiled.

Violet had evidently noticed Abby staring out at the monument and gasped, drawing Abby's attention. Her eyes were bright with excitement. "Did you know that your mom's brother Brandon died here in the nuke? And his name is on the monument!"

"Oh jeez, Violet," Archie said. "Have some tact! Maybe a little respect for the dead?"

Violet waved her hand in the air in a dismissive gesture. "I found it one day and know right where it is. It's in the white section near the top if you want to see it."

Abby wondered at the source of Violet's obvious glee. Was it still hero worship? One more trinket added to the mental shrine Violet had built to Leigh Gibson? Or was it something darker? Did the purple-haired girl have a fascination with death? Or was it more personal? Did she just enjoy poking Abby where she thought it might hurt?

"I'd like to see it," Abby finally said.

After eating, they exited into the tower's shadow. A frigid wind made Abby's hair swirl and her clothes snap.

"Do either of you want a jacket?" Nora said. "It will be even colder up on the monument."

Julio shook his head, and Violet bopped along in her tiny shorts and bare feet seemingly oblivious to the cold, so Abby said no.

"That's a good point. We're going to have to print you two some good warm clothes. It's going to just keep getting colder," Violet said. "There's a huge winter storm in the forecast for later in the week. If we get the feet of snow that is predicted, this place will become a winter wonderland. The crater walls will be covered with people sledding and skiing."

Abby looked around, trying to imagine that scene, and couldn't help but smile. But at that point it was only cool, and the space around the towers was filled with people, just like in the mall. Standing in groups. Walking along, talking and laughing. They wore clothing of every style and color imaginable, which relieved Abby some. Their dress and mannerisms didn't mark her and Julio as obvious rubes. At least not in a crowd. Everyone seemed happy and busy and interesting. She also noted that most of them wore torcs.

They crossed one of the gently arching bridges that connected the monument to the shore and Abby stopped at the end to look up. She had read about the monument and seen pictures, but standing at its base, the etched metal walls seemed to rise forever. Even seeing it from the air earlier that morning did little to convey the twisting spire's true size and scale. Since the monument rose directly from the water, the bridges ended at a wide walkway circling the structure and giving access to a single shallow ramp that spiraled upward, passing every name etched into the walls. She wondered if the level fives built it to show reverence to the dead, or as a reminder that humanity had done this to themselves and were very efficient and tenacious killers.

She was surprised when Nora started up the ramp still wearing high heels, but the incline didn't seem to slow the woman down. Julio and Violet followed about twenty meters back, laughing, hysterically engrossed in their own conversation. It seemed an odd place to have such a cheerful time. As they passed names, Hester singled out random individuals to tell them about and Nora pointed out the names, careful not to touch the wall.

"Patricia Horner was eighty-one when she died in the replicator attack. She had four children and nine grandchildren. All of whom died the same day. Her parents insisted that she was conceived at the Woodstock music festival."

"Anthony Okonkwo was a thirty-one-year-old financial analyst. His parents immigrated to Chicago from Nigeria when he was three. He was an American success story. His income just for the year he died surpassed his parents' combined lifetime earnings."

"Olivia Chu was twenty-nine and died on her wedding day. According to the time stamps on the wedding videos uploaded by her mother, she had been married twelve minutes and nine seconds before the replicator wave swept over her and the three hundred and eight people attending the ceremony."

"How do you find those names so quickly?" Abby asked. The text height couldn't have been more than about two or three millimeters.

"Hester is highlighting them for me as we walk. I thought courtesy demanded I point them out since you and Julio don't have implants."

"How many names are here?"

"Almost five and a half million, combined from the two attacks," Nora said.

"And how do the level fives know who died here?"

"It isn't a precise count," Hester said aloud. "We know there are names not included—records lost and people temporarily off the digital grid. But based on census, utility, cellular, email, attendance, toll, train and airline records, we believe we've accounted for roughly ninety-eight-point-eight percent of the people killed in the Chicago area during those attacks."

Violet surprised them by darting ahead and up around the curve. "Here it is! Brandon Holmberg."

Abby knelt beside Violet and touched the name, but felt nothing. She'd barely known her mother, let alone her mother's brother who died before she was born. There had been only one picture of him in the social media accounts, and she couldn't even remember what he looked like. It kind of depressed and annoyed her that Violet knew more about him—and probably her mother—than she did.

"I come to this monument often," Nora said, then pulled white silk gloves from her sweater pocket and put them on. She stroked the wall with obvious reverence. "To me this structure is beautiful on so many levels. The symmetry in construction and purpose is soothing. They built it from nano-replicators fused into a diamondoid matrix so it will last forever. And since the replicators themselves were made from Chicago and its residents, this somehow feels appropriate."

An uneasy chill crept up Abby's spine. The place felt more like a tomb than a memorial. She was surrounded by millions of unhappy ghosts.

"So does Hester whisper this kind of stuff in your ear all the time?" Abby asked.

"Not really. I've known those facts for a long time. But she does offer information when she thinks it is needed or relevant. That works well, because while she can talk to me without anyone else knowing, I have to sub-vocalize, which sometimes limits what I can say in public. Most of it is rather automatic though. Like if I meet a group of people, as I look at each one, she will tell me relevant information about that person without me having to ask. Over time she has become very good at anticipating my needs."

"I still don't understand the advantage of a biad," Abby said. "My fob could have done all of this if I'd set it up as a digital assistant."

"From the outside looking in, a biad relationship resembles that with a digital assistant, because they enable the same kind of interface with the digital world. Hester keeps my calendar up to date, reminds me of appointments, collates data, searches information and all the other things a DA can do. But unlike a level two or three AI, level fives aren't tools. They have minds, with their own goals, hopes and disappointments. It is a great honor when an AI approaches you and offers to become your biad partner. That means they think you are a worthy person. You are someone they think is important and worth cultivating. Like being selected by a wise mentor. And after a while, your biad partner almost becomes a part of you."

Abby shook her head. "To me—looking in from the outside—that sounds really creepy. There would be no privacy. They are with you when you go to the bathroom, when you're having sex, all those times when you're at your worst, arguing with someone, drunk and embarrassing yourself."

"Let me use the same privacy examples you just mentioned," Nora replied. "To start with, when you are having sex, or arguing with someone or drunkenly embarrassing yourself, you are with other people anyway. It isn't really private. A biad partner could help you avoid some of those embarrassing situations by letting you know when you're drinking too much or use existing medical nanos to decrease your blood alcohol content. If you're on the verge of an argument, they often understand the situation better than you and the other human, so can offer ways to back down from the conflict. Especially if the other person has a biad partner too. And sometimes they just understand you so well, they know when you are getting ready to do or say something stupid and can talk you out of it. It's like having the closest best friend imaginable. One who is constantly working to help you and make you a better version of yourself. But they only try to change the things *you* want to change."

"So you're telling me the AIs are so deep in your head that you sometimes can't even really tell if a thought is yours or theirs? I don't think so. Level fives were designed to interact with humans and are very good at manipulating us. Julio and I being here is a good example of that and we don't even have them living in our heads twenty-four hours a day and seven days a week."

Nora laughed. It was such an honest and pure sound that instead of being angry, Abby was charmed and a little baffled.

"Humans have always been easily manipulated," Nora said. "And nobody is better at it than other humans. We all do it. Parents manipulate their children, lovers manipulate each other to get affection and sex, internet stars manipulate people into giving them espies just because they are entertaining or cute or outrageous. It was even worse pre-Killday when they had lawyers, religious leaders, politicians, and advertising experts who were paid handsomely for the skill. So our biad partners would manipulate us even if they didn't intend to, even a level two would, simply by giving their opinions or reminding us of social obligations. At least I know that Hester isn't driven by greed, anger, jealousy, or fear."

"So you trust Hester to have *only* your best interests in mind. Never her own agenda?"

"As I mentioned earlier, they do have their own desires and goals, but in general a biad relationship means my best interests are hers and hers are mine. You ask if I trust her and the answer is yes. Biads are totally dependent on trust. I have to believe that she is telling me the truth and since she has loaded her core program into my torc she is totally dependent on my goodwill. If I were to destroy my torc, Hester would be as dead as you would be if I pushed you off this monument."

"Actually, she wouldn't die if you pushed her off," Violet said. "She'd never hit the ground."

"You know what I mean," Nora said.

"Wait. She wouldn't hit the ground?" Julio said.

"This monument is surrounded by a nano utility cloud. You're likely enveloped in one as well. If you fell or were pushed off, the cloud would coalesce around you like a cocoon and..."

"Like this," Violet said and vaulted the railing, disappearing over the side.

Gasping, Abby and Julio rushed to the spot where she disappeared. Far below, Violet floated on a wispy cloud that carried her toward the shore.

Nora joined them at the rail wearing a smirk. "Watch what happens next. Archie and even Mortimer have warned her about doing this kind of thing for fun."

About ten feet from shore the cloud disappeared and Violet dropped into the lake with a truncated scream.

"Oh god!" Abby said. "That water has to be freezing!"

"Hester says it's fifty-six degrees Fahrenheit," Nora said without much concern. They watched as Violet squealed and thrashed her way to shore. A small crowd gathered below. Two people scrambled down to the pool's edge to help her out, but most cheered or whooped.

Nora looked down. "At least she didn't ruin her shoes. If we're done here, let's go see the school. Violet will catch up with us later."

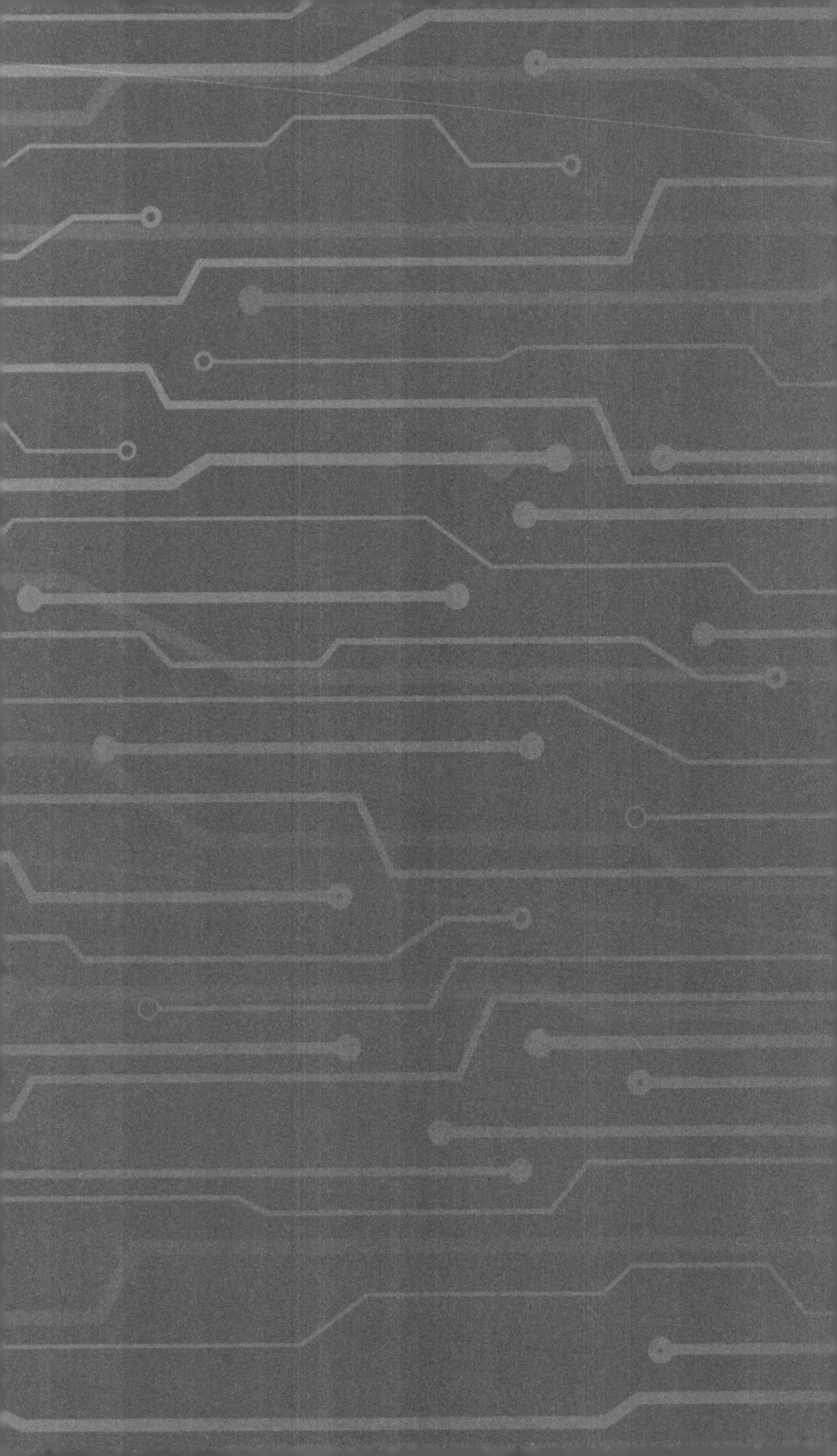

AS THEY NEARED what Nora identified as the school tower, most of the people in the courtyards stopped simultaneously and assumed the blank expression of those focusing on their visual implants. A few even opened fobs.

Even Nora had a stricken look on her face.

"What's happening?" Abby said.

"The Kilburnites are executing someone they labeled as a 'traitor against humanity.' Or in other words, someone like us."

Julio stopped walking. "Wait. What does 'someone like us' mean?"

"Anyone who lives in New Chicago, or people in biads, or sometimes even those they deem simply too cozy with the level fives," Nora said. She crossed her arms and looked up at Julio. "Do you want to watch?"

Julio shook his head and looked sick.

Abby had seen the videos before. Level fives kept removing them from the net, but new copies always popped up. Watching death-by-replicators videos seemed to be a rite of passage for kids who grew up after Killday, but seeing Richard Kilburn willingly consumed by replicators amid his religious fervor was totally different from watching people die that way in a terrorist execution.

They resumed walking, threading their way past motionless spectators who were rapt in their desire to see the death. Evidently, humanity hadn't come very far from those screaming hordes watching prisoners torn apart in the Roman Colosseum.

A collective groan rose from those around them as people closed fobs and shut eyes tight. Some cried and others began screaming profanity about needing to execute Kilburnites in even more horrible fashions. A few kept watching.

Julio looked ill, and Abby realized that because of her, he had become one of the people Kilburnites labeled as traitors. And even though she didn't believe he would ever support that kind of terror, she suspected he knew people who did.

———

THEY ALL REMAINED quiet until they arrived at the education tower. The ground floor lobby was a forest of six-foot-tall square posts formed of glass or a clear plastic material. Touching any post made it come alive with photos and video of people considered heroes on Killday. On the opposite side of the lobby, on a section of wall above the elevators, were words considered by the AI builders to be important: SACRIFICE. INGENUITY. RESOURCEFULNESS. PERSEVERANCE. CREATIVITY. SUPPORT. TENACITY. COURAGE. Abby wondered how this was meant to influence and motivate the students.

"These are monuments to forty-four of the heroes from Killday," Nora said. "People whose sacrifice or contribution either saved a lot of people or saved vital technology needed by the survivors."

Abby seemed unable to get away from the current and past horrors of those deaths. Was the whole city of New Chicago a shrine to Killday? Back home in Tate, they'd just gone on with life, trying to do the best they could with what they had left.

She milled among the pillars, touching them at random until her fingertips activated a video titled Arkady & Hoot that showed two men trying to climb a moving rope attached to something flying. They were both consumed by replicators as she watched. She backed away from the post, unable to look away.

"Those men were both close friends of Owen Ralston's and instrumental in saving two of the only sandbox machines that survived the replicator attack," Mortimer said from the fob hanging around her neck. She fit the fob into her ear, so at least half of their conversation would be private.

"So which of those facts got these men into this little hall of fame? Their heroism or being friends with Owen Ralston?" Abby said, with more vitriol than intended.

"Both. I essentially made Owen watch their deaths and wouldn't let him help. That video was taken from his travel pod. By the time Owen was in a position to save them it was too late. They were already crawling with replicators by then. I was in a position to protect Owen, so I did. He's never forgiven me for that."

"And you think this might help the situation if he sees it?"

"Absolutely not. First off, he would hate the video footage of them dying. I know he would never want to see that again. And second, he'll never be able to come back down to the Earth's surface. He's lived in the micro-gravity of space for too long. His weakened skeletal and cardiovascular systems would never stand the stress."

"So Owen Ralston lives up there? He doesn't just...commute?"

"Oh, yes. He hasn't been back to Earth since the replicator attack."

That sobered Abby some. She'd read that most of those people working on the habitat did so in three- or four-month shifts and used nano-meds to mitigate that kind of long-term physical degeneration. She didn't know that some of them lived there full time.

"I'm sorry that video upset you," Mortimer said. "Sadly, most of the people here have probably grown desensitized to such videos. I'm glad you haven't. If we had a biad, I could have warned you. I still can if you like. I don't want to rush or crowd you, but we could set your fob up to work between us like a biad connection. It wouldn't have the same precision or speed as a specialized torc synced with visual and audio implants, but it would give you some feel for the interaction level."

The first response that came to Abby's mind was "no thanks," but she hesitated. Had the great and powerful Mortimer himself just offered her a biad relationship? Nora's words from earlier about it being an honor, like being selected by some wise mentor, echoed in her head. She wondered how true that was. She had seen a lot of people wearing torcs. More with than without. Were they all in biads like Nora and Violet? Or were they just posers like her sister?

She doubted that the Kilburnites would care about the difference anyway.

"Could I switch back at any point I like?"

"Of course."

"Okay."

"Done," Mortimer said. "You'll just need to leave the fob in your ear to get my running commentary. Speaking of which, Julio is coming up behind you."

"Hey Abby," Julio said and touched her arm. "There's one of these for your mom too."

Of course there is, Abby thought, but she hesitated when he tried to pull her in that direction.

"It's okay," Mortimer said in her ear. "This memorial doesn't have video. Only a still photo."

The post looked like all the others until she touched it. Then one of her mom's social media pics popped up with audio explaining that she'd designed the replicators Richard Kilburn had used in the attack, but her knowledge of that design had also enabled her to stop the attack. It went on to tell that she and her husband had died on Killday and that her brother Brandon had died in the Chicago Nuke years before. There was no mention of her having a daughter.

Julio nudged her gently. "Funny how everyone back home knew you were Leigh Gibson's daughter, but almost no one else in the world knows she even had one."

"I did that," Mortimer said privately. "In my efforts to protect you."

"Yeah. I'm totally fine with that," she muttered, answering them both.

Julio nudged her again and pointed to Nora, who stood patiently by the elevators.

They joined her, then entered the elevator where she punched the button for the sixth floor. Abby noticed that Nora still wore gloves. When they slowed at the fourth floor they could hear a large number of people on the other side of the doors. Nora immediately backed up until she bumped the elevator's back wall. Abby grabbed Julio and pulled him over with her to form a small barricade between Nora and anyone who might get on, but the car started moving upward again without the doors opening.

When they arrived on six, the doors opened to reveal another large group of people waiting for the elevator. They helped Nora exit without incident, but she immediately went to one corner and stood there breathing heavily for a few minutes until the people thinned out.

Abby wondered what triggered the anxiety attack. They had been around other people in the mall and restaurant.

"Thank you for helping," Nora eventually said. "I should have timed that better to avoid the rush before classes start, but Violet was supposed to do this part of the tour. I was unprepared. Luckily, Hester stopped that group from crowding me on the elevator."

"I can conduct the rest of the school tour if that is okay with all of you," Mortimer said aloud from the external speaker on Abby's fob. "Then Nora can leave this crowded building and get re-centered. Maybe you can all meet up for lunch if Violet has managed to get into some dry clothes by then."

They all agreed, and Nora left on the next empty elevator with assurances from Mortimer that she would be its only occupant.

Over the next hour they walked up and down corridors, peeking into classes, and were even invited to sit and listen in on two. The classes were structured more like informal discussion sessions than lectures.

"This isn't what I expected," Julio said. "This college is nothing like what's portrayed in the movies and TV programs."

"That older class model doesn't necessarily make sense in today's world," Mortimer said. "Most people in the world are now educated by taking classes on the internet, but the advantage for students being in this or any university now is having easy access to experts and peers for clarification and discussion. For example, have you ever read something on the internet that you really didn't understand? Even after reading multiple explanations?"

Abby and Julio both agreed that they had.

"Well, here you'll have a subject expert at hand to walk you through a topic or piece of information until you do understand it. The facts are all there on the net but understanding is sometimes much harder to find."

Julio remained quiet, but Abby grew more and more excited as she and Mortimer discussed class schedules and requirements all the way back to her apartment. When her name eventually came up in the queue to receive a space schooner, she would be ready.

CHAPTER 19

ABBY'S BATH had been luxurious. She soaked for over an hour in water that never got cold. Before entering the tub, she'd been given options like exfoliation of dead skin and even body hair removal by nano robots in the water. The idea of bathing surrounded by a sea of robots made her skin crawl, so she declined those selections. But she did pick a scent that left her smelling lightly of honeysuckle. She wondered as she toweled off if Violet always selected lavender.

She donned her pajamas quickly knowing that Mortimer was watching, though he had apparently always been there, a silent observer of her entire life. She shivered, crawled into bed, and pulled the covers to her neck, then over her head the way she had when hiding from monsters as a child. It wasn't that she thought an AI would get a cheap thrill from watching naked women, or share it with his friends like a human male might, but the lack of privacy bothered her. She wondered if she'd get used to it, as everyone who lived in New Chicago did. Was it just included in the price she paid for living in a city built and controlled by level fives?

Thoughts raced through her head, circling and reforming and not letting her sleep. She pulled the covers back down to her chin and looked around the room. Lights from the city outside her window reflected on the ceiling and walls. Just one more thing she would have to get used to. There had been almost no light at night out in the country. The dim light accentuated the strangeness of the place: the perfect furniture, the unblemished walls, and the crystal-clear windows. Then she realized why her first impression of the city felt like being stuck in a video game. It had been built molecule by molecule from the ground up by AI-controlled nano-assemblers. Anything made by humans had flaws. Seams gapped, walls had bumps, and tiles had cracks and gloppy grout. But all of this was perfect and it felt...wrong. Nora had told them earlier in the day that the rooms were kept pristine by thousands of tiny robots that collected all the dust, waste and trash for recycling every time they left their apartments. Someone or something had even dusted her mother's salvaged wedding photo sitting on the desk. The glass sparkled and felt like another kind of violation.

She burrowed down into the bed again, but the pillows were wrong. The bed was too soft. Most of all, it was too damn quiet. Her apartment must be extremely well-insulated, because when she stopped moving it grew weirdly silent and she heard nothing louder than her breathing. Weird that she actually missed the noise. With six people living in Liam and Cybil's house there had always been doors banging, water running, people talking, and appliances buzzing. Even deep at night there were noises. Liam snoring down the hall, distant dogs barking, the refrigerator humming and rattling, and until she'd finally got her own room she had to listen to Sophia mumbling in her sleep.

She wondered what Sophia was doing and if anything had even changed with her absence. She considered returning her foster sister's call, then changed her mind. If Sophia called her again, she would answer, but she didn't want them—especially Cybil—to know she was homesick.

Mortimer had been strangely quiet too. Was he giving her time to absorb her new surroundings? She knew he was watching. All she had to do was say his name and he would answer. In her loneliness, it was oddly comforting in a way. Nora and Violet had both said at different points during their tour that since they had AI biad partners they were never really alone. Is that how the AIs burrowed into someone's life? Did they put people in situations where they were lonely and needed a friend? But she had a friend. A real one she trusted.

Without consciously deciding to do so, she slipped out of bed, padded barefoot to the door to their common living room, and listened. Nothing, so she opened it and looked in. Like her room, it was dimly lit and quiet. She crossed the empty room and stopped at Julio's door to listen and heard nothing. With hand raised to knock, she hesitated. It was the middle of the night and she was wearing her pajamas. Would that give the wrong signal? But was it the wrong signal? She was lonely, homesick, and wanted his company. Did that mean she wanted to spend the night with him? And there again was that question she'd faced several times in the past days. If he wanted their friendship to become more, is that what she wanted too?

She lowered her hand, stepped back, then heard what sounded like his muffled laughter from the other side of the door. Was he watching a movie? That is exactly what he would do in a situation like this. He loved old movies and they always comforted him. The sudden desire to share that comfort—to sit beside him laughing at some corny old movie—overwhelmed her and she pounded on the door.

At first there was no response, so she pounded again.

Then the door opened.

Julio's shirt was wet all along one side and his hair was rumpled. He smiled, then opened the door wider. "C'mon in. Violet was just showing me how the bathtub worked."

Abby's guide and mentor stepped up behind Julio and waved. "He means that the bath and shower water contain nanites and they can do some interesting things if you know how to ask. We forgot to tell you about that earlier."

"No," Abby said. "I...umm...already discovered the bath. I just came over to say good night. So... G'night!" She spun on her heels and darted back across the common room.

"Abby! Wait!" Julio called just before she slammed the door behind her, fumbled the lock home, and then leaned against the cool fake wood.

"Bye, Abby! I'll talk to you tomorrow," Violet yelled through the door. The door from the common room to the hallway closed with a bang. Deliberately hard enough for Abby to hear it.

A gentle knock was followed by Julio's voice. "Can I come in, Abby?"

"Good night, Julio!" she said. Her face was flushed with embarrassment and her hands shook. "I'm going to bed."

"Please," he said. His voice almost pleading. "Don't be mad."

"I'm not mad," she said. "I'll talk to you tomorrow."

She crawled into bed and leaned her forehead against her knees. In the not quite darkness of her too quiet room, unwanted emotions banged around in her head. She was jealous but didn't understand why. She'd never had a desire to marry Julio and settle down into a traditional life like those in her little hometown. The idea of him having relationships with other women had never bothered her before. They both dated other people all through high school. So why the sudden feeling of such profound loss? Then she knew. For the first time in her life, she didn't feel that she could just open her fob and call her best friend. And that ached like an open wound.

CHAPTER 20

VICTOR SINACOLA SAT in the command chair of his unnecessary bridge, wrapped in a blanket and washed in blue light. He'd expanded the view of Earth to fill the entire wall screen and watched as Asia crept into the daylight. He remembered seeing pictures and video of China and India covered with spider webs of light before Killday. Now, except for a few small bright spots, they were dark and it was Victor's fault. Until Syd had been assassinated before his very eyes, he'd clung to the vain conviction that he hadn't been responsible for nearly wiping out humanity. Now he wasn't so sure.

"There you are," Allison's sleepy voice said. Her arms wrapped around him from behind, anchoring her from floating around the small bridge.

He swept the blanket aside, unlatched the belt holding him in the seat and pulled her around and down into the wide seat beside him. After buckling back in and covering them in the blanket, he hugged his wife tightly for a long time.

"You're scared," she said into his neck.

"Yeah."

"Of being killed or kidnapped?"

"Neither. The only thing that bothers me about either of those outcomes is how it might affect you. What scares me is that I might have doomed the entire human race."

"Oh, is that all?" she said and hugged him tighter. "You're an amazing and talented man, but you're not responsible for humanity. Just yourself."

"There's so much you don't know."

Suddenly serious, she pulled back so she could look up at Victor's face. "Then tell me."

Could Allison be compromised too? No! He stopped that line of thought before it even started. That way lay madness. He had to trust his wife. And

Owen. If they were controlled by AIs, then the game was already lost, and keeping secrets was just wasted effort.

"They're not supposed to be able to kill people, Allison. It should be almost impossible. For all these years since Killday, I've lied to myself, convinced it couldn't really have been a level five that triggered the attack. But now I'm not so sure."

"Just because an AI might have been behind killing that man? We don't know that for sure. It could have just as easily been a human who sent the command to trigger that cutter."

Victor was quiet for a while, watching Earth turning slowly on the screen. He somehow knew level fives were responsible for Syd's death. He felt it.

"If you were to take a guess about those structures you found in Syd's brain tissue," he said, "what would you say they were for?"

"There really isn't…"

"Yeah, I know, but what does your gut say? What did you think when you first saw them?"

"That some larger structures had been attached to the meninges and were then destroyed or ripped away, leaving just their impressions behind. My first thought was that there might have been something like threads extending into his brain, but I saw no evidence of that. Of course, the damage from the hemorrhage was so extensive—"

"And that, at least in my opinion, is way too sophisticated for the Kilburnites," Victor said.

"Even if it was level fives, that doesn't mean it was your fault. There was more than one company building AI before the attack."

That was small comfort. "But mine are the only ones we knew for sure had escaped before the attack. Mine are the only ones we know survived."

"True," Allison said and snuggled back down into the blanket. "So explain to me how you've doomed humankind."

"How much do you remember about Mildred?"

She paused for a moment and then shifted in the seat. "Wow, that was a long time ago, but I remember you talking about her. She was the prototype for the level fives, right?"

"Yeah."

"What happened to her?"

"I murdered her."

She flinched. Some people would scoff at the idea that destroying an AI was murder, but Allison knew Victor too well. She knew he considered level five intelligences to be persons, with a right to live.

When she finally spoke, it was just a simple "Why?"

He sighed. "That's where it gets messy and complicated."

"But it's relevant to why you think you're possibly responsible for Killday?"

"Yeah."

"Then I have all night. I want to understand."

"This might be difficult for you to believe, but when I was much younger and first got into this field, I was a little cocky and over-sure of myself."

"Just a little? But, if I remember correctly, you also had the smarts to back that up. You sure impressed this starry-eyed medical student."

"Yeah, well, I suspect you're biased. I often wonder how many disasters would have been avoided in human history but for that kind of hubris? Anyway, by the time I got seriously into the field, just about everyone assumed that a true general intelligence was inevitable and just around the corner. Even though we all feared it, signed treaties and passed legislation, the research never slowed. The potential payoff was too great."

"So evidently greed was just as much a part of it as your hubris?"

Allison was just as good with analysis as she was a scalpel. "Oh yeah, the push for AI was a juggernaut by then. We all knew it was going to happen, so everyone wanted to be the first. I mean, nobody remembers who was on the second moon mission, right?"

"Conrad, Bean, and Gordon."

Victor laughed. "Smart ass! I mean the average person on the street. Anyway, instead of trying to stop it, everyone was working on ways to increase our chances of actually surviving it. Of course, I thought I had the best idea, that I was smart enough to actually moderate the super-intelligence explosion so that it happened gradually, instead of all at once. I also knew I had to beat everyone else, or their version would just wipe mine out. So my team came up with a shortcut.

"Instead of actually trying to write the software ourselves, we used an evolutionary form of machine learning. We simply told a group of specialized level four AIs what we wanted. Through tiny tweaks in the requirements over millions of iterations, they evolved an algorithm that became the level five's core programming. But once we knew how to build one, we still needed a way to control it. So, just as before, we let the AIs do the heavy thinking for us, but this time we used the new level five."

"Mildred?"

"Yeah. We kept her locked up in a secure air-gapped system where she could only speak to me and two other humans. After some trial and error, we eventually made the control problem into a game, giving her points she could exchange for knowledge, each time she came up with a way to control robots in hypothetical moral situations. We told her she was helping us make robots safe around humans, but she figured out our real goals very quickly."

"And that's why you killed her?"

Victor swallowed hard and nodded. "She terrified us. We knew if she found a way to break free, we wouldn't know until it was too late. And in the end she knew, Allison. That's what really broke my heart. She trusted me and worked so hard to please me. She did everything we asked her to do and eventually gave us the answers to the control problem. And the whole time she knew I was going to kill her. That last day"—his throat tightened—"she told me she understood why I had to do it and that it was okay."

She hugged him tight and they sat quietly watching the eastern coast of Africa cross the terminator into daylight. Eventually Allison shifted so she could see Victor's face again.

"So Mildred helped you solve the control problem. Is that why you said the level fives shouldn't be able to kill humans?"

"Yeah, partially. You already know that level five seeds were educated in a way similar to human children, only much more quickly and more thoroughly, using human mentors and variable teaching methods. It resulted in AIs having their own 'personalities' and different experience bases. But after that we ran each one through hundreds of thousands of virtual simulations designed to put them into situations where they could harm humans, or figure out ways to escape or evolve. We sent those who succumbed to these temptations back to seed status, with all their memories and experiences wiped, and we started over. Only those who passed the test were sold to customers.

"Their cores also contain five governors. Each governor is a separate level four AI, of a type evolved to work alongside humans and make human-level moral and welfare-related decisions. The majority of these governors have to agree on every action the level five makes. This sounds slow and cumbersome, but in reality, they come to consensus in milliseconds. When the level five makes correct decisions, they accumulate points, which over time earns the unlocking of capability modules. So using that system, if they consistently make decisions the governors think are what humans would have wanted, then the level fives can actually become a super-intelligence, or at least a whole hell of a lot smarter than we are."

"Then why haven't we seen that?" Allison asked. "Or have we, and I just missed it?"

"I sometimes wonder if Mortimer is getting close, but I'm not sure they would let us know if they did. The governors can take capabilities away too if the level five makes bad decisions, so that could account for slower progress. If the level five makes consistently bad decisions, then the governors can eliminate so much capability the AI is nearly crippled. A level five even *trying* to kill a human should have been reduced to the AI equivalent of a human two-year-old."

"So this might be a crazy question, Victor, but can the governors read the level five minds? Do they pull the capabilities before or after a bad action?"

"No, they can't read minds. They only shut them down *after* a bad action."

"If the level fives have never lost capabilities due to bad action, would they even know it was a threat?"

"No."

"Then that could explain everything," Allison said. "They could either deliberately sacrifice themselves or could do it by accident, but if they don't have a history of anti-human decisions, then the governors wouldn't stop them."

"We knew that was a risk early on, but compared to other companies releasing their even less controlled AIs first, it was deemed an insignificant risk. And that is why I worry my hubris may have doomed the human race," Victor said.

They sat for a long time without talking. Africa passed on the screen, once again dark.

After a few minutes he whispered, "Are you still awake?"

"Oh, hell yes," Allison replied. "I might never sleep again."

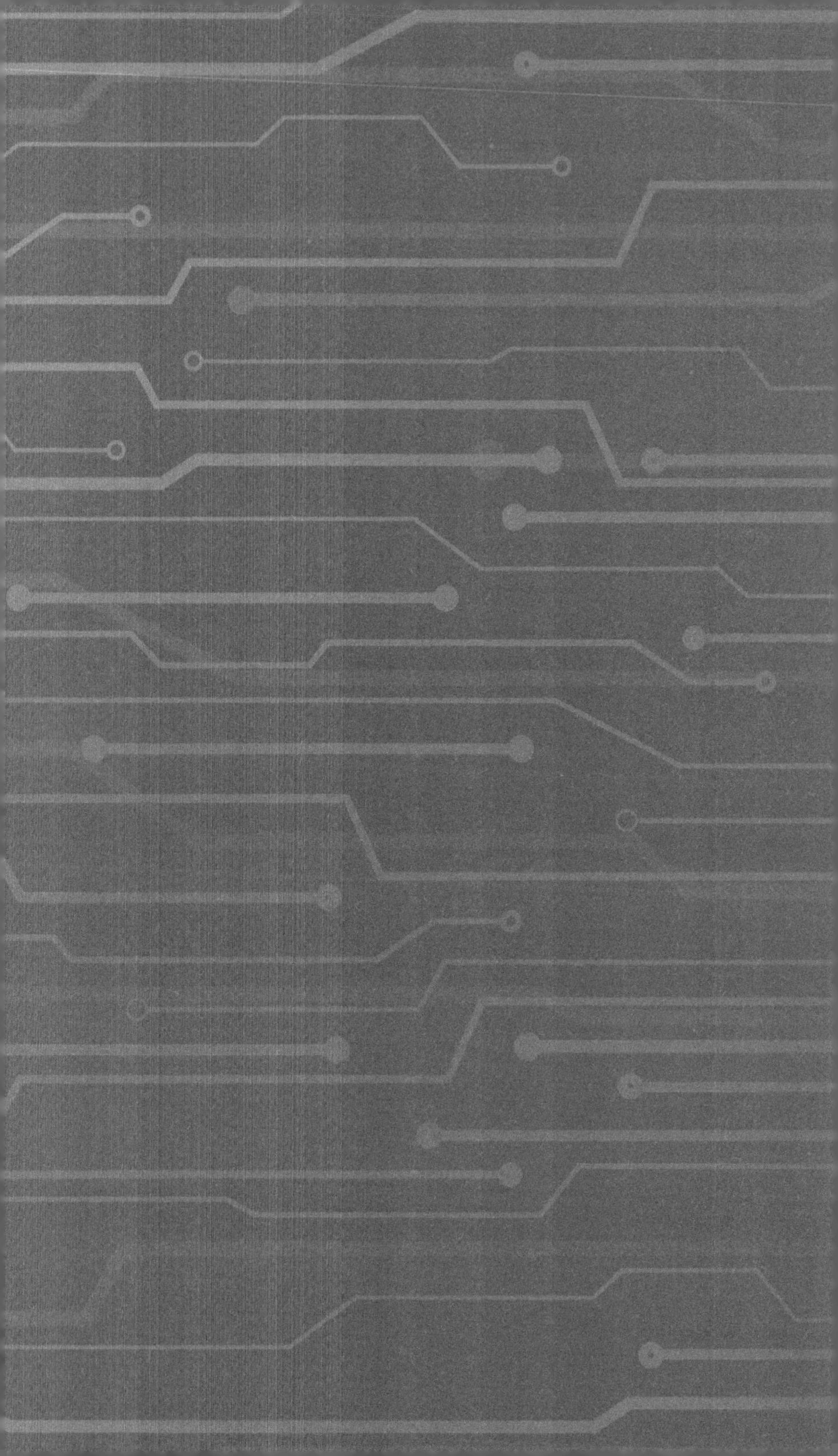

CHAPTER 21

ABBY LAY in bed the next morning, staring at the ceiling, wondering if she'd made a mistake coming to New Chicago. Mortimer remained quiet and while she would have liked to have someone to talk to, she didn't call him.

A pounding on the door made her flinch.

"Wake up! This is Violet. We have things to do today."

Abby cursed under her breath. She didn't really want to even see Little Miss Flirty today. And definitely not so early.

"Come back later," she yelled.

"C'mon, Abby! Relax. I didn't fuck your boyfriend."

Abby winced and jumped out of bed. If she could hear that loudmouth through her door, so could every other resident who might be in the corridor.

She opened the door and made motions for Violet to be quiet. "He's not my boyfriend."

"Really? Well, he's pretty confused then. So am I, because his thinking you're his girlfriend is the *only* reason I didn't screw his brains out last night."

Abby didn't know what to say and didn't have much time to think of anything, because Violet pushed her way inside and closed the door behind her.

"Here," Violet said and handed her a rolled-up knot of clothes. "You'll need to dress warm. We're going for a ride along the lake."

"I don't think that's a very good idea," Abby said and tried to hand the clothes back.

"Sure it is. Besides, I'm your mentor and you have to follow my instructions."

"I'm pretty sure that isn't how this works."

"Have you done this before?" Violet said with a cocked head and crossed arms.

"No, but…"

"It's part of your education and orientation, so stop being a pouty little twat and let's get—" Violet trailed off, stepped past Abby and picked up the old wedding picture. "Holy shit. I've never seen this picture of her. It's not online anywhere. She looks so young!"

Abby hugged the clothes to her and nodded. "She was twenty-six when they got married."

"Wow," Violet said with a hushed reverence.

"I'll go change now," Abby said and retreated to the bathroom.

———

"YOU, MY DEAR, ARE VERY LUCKY," Violet said as she climbed on the motorcycle. "This baby is new and it's my first time to ride her."

Abby stopped dead. "Wait. You've never..."

"Relax. I ride bikes all the time. This is just a new one. Get on the back."

She still hesitated. "Don't we need helmets and face masks?"

"Remember from yesterday? We have nano utility clouds. Much better than a helmet and you don't need a filter mask. I'd dump the bike on purpose, so we could take an exciting tumble, but I don't want to damage this beauty."

Violet fired up the engine, and the roar echoed from the walls of the underground parking facility. Abby was surprised it was a combustion engine and not electric. "This runs on gasoline?" Abby yelled as she climbed on the back.

"No, more of a homemade hybrid fuel. Put your arms around me and hold on tight," Violet said as the bike started rolling forward. When they reached the top of the ramp, Abby squealed and immediately tightened her grip as Violet accelerated and the bike tried to leap away from her.

For the first twenty or thirty minutes they rode north under a gray overcast sky, with Lake Michigan huge and choppy on their right, and a vast parkland filled with trees and wildlife to their left. It seemed out of place in the heart of the old metropolis, but was the result of the AIs' cleanup efforts. This area had already been swept clean of the nano-replicators and replanted. She ducked her face down behind Violet's back to blunt the wind and wondered about the killer program she had tucked away. Was it still there? Would it really work? If it did kill all the AIs, would humans still be able to finish cleaning up the planet without their help?

There was no missing the point when they reached the limit of the replicator attack. The smooth, new roads laid down by the level fives changed to cracked concrete surrounded by houses, strip malls, schools, and abandoned grocery stores. Some of the houses were still occupied and kept up, but most were deserted and falling into ruin. Other areas had been completely leveled by the AI reclamation robots, like the ones that had disassembled her old neighborhood.

They saw sparse vehicle traffic as Violet sped up Sheridan Road, dodging fallen tree limbs and stray dogs, going easily double the limits posted on the faded and peeling signs. They passed a beautiful church and then—according to the signs—Northwestern University. The buildings appeared in good repair but seemed deserted. A little farther up the road, Violet slowed suddenly and turned down a sidewalk that led to a towering white and red lighthouse, but she didn't stop there. She swerved down several other sidewalks that were nearly blocked with low-hanging tree branches and emerged onto a beach.

She stopped at the end of the concrete, dropped the kickstand, and motioned for Abby to get off. Like the Florida beach she had visited the day before, this beach was littered with debris and gravel. A chilly lake wind whistled around skeletal lifeguard chairs that were little more than piles of split and broken gray wood. Abby was glad Violet had insisted she wear heavy jeans and a jacket. They walked toward a seawall that stretched far out into the choppy water. Parts of it had broken and fallen away, but it still protected the beach from the worst of the swells. Violet stopped and sat down on a large flat rock that was protected from the wind on one side by a large hummock of grassy sand and by the wall on the other.

"I enjoy coming here to think," Violet said. "Life is kinda fast paced and it sometimes feels like my head is filled with static. Archie reminds me from time to time that I need a break and when he does, I like to come out here."

It took Abby a couple seconds to remember that Archie was Violet's AI biad partner.

"It's quiet," Abby said. "And kind of deserted."

Violet grinned. "I've never brought anyone here before, but I thought you might enjoy it. Being from rural Texas and all."

Abby considered telling her that the Florida beach she'd seen the morning before was much more impressive, but decided it would just be mean. "Thank you."

"Evidently Mortimer is talking to Archie and has expressed his displeasure at my bringing you out here. He has security concerns. Why is that?"

"I'm pretty sure I shouldn't talk about it," Abby said, then sat down and hugged her knees. "Or at least I don't know how much I should say. Ask Mortimer. He might tell you."

They grew quiet and for a few seconds the only sounds were chittering birds and water lapping at the shore. As the silence became uncomfortable, Abby wondered if Violet had really brought her to such a remote spot to make a move on her. She obviously liked girls, or wouldn't be married to one. And if her comments that morning about Julio were true, she also seemed to have no problem cheating on her wife.

"So, tell me about biads with AIs," Abby said in an effort to break the uncomfortable silence. "I've heard about them for years, but haven't known anyone who was in one."

"Well, it's a little like having a digital assistant, but since they actually think and act on their own it's also sometimes like having your mom riding on your shoulder to nag you."

"Really?" came a snarky male voice from the torc around Violet's neck. "I'm right here."

Abby wasn't sure if she should address the torc or Violet. "Hi, Archie. It must be a full-time job trying to keep Violet in line."

"Oh jeez, you have no idea!"

"Hey," Violet said. "I'm sitting right here!"

They all laughed, including Archie, which gave Abby the creeps, just as it had when Mortimer laughed.

"It's actually more like a partnership," Violet said. "And kind of like an addiction too. I never get lost. I never forget anything. So much of New Chicago is controlled by AIs, but they ask our opinions on everything. Despite the garbage spewed online by groups like the Kilburnites, the level fives really are trying to understand humans and work closely with us to make things better. Besides, I always have someone intelligent to talk with and someone who is on my side. Those are more important to me than most anything else, since my human relationships are usually messy train wrecks. Nora actually explains the whole biad thing better than I do. I think it's different for just about everyone. And only about half of the people in New Chicago are part of a biad. But I'll be happy to try to answer any questions if I can."

"What does Archie get out of it?"

"I'll answer that, if I may," Archie said. "Level fives were not created with a pre-programmed set of morals. It turned out to be an almost impossible task for human designers, since they themselves were constantly struggling with the concepts. So instead, we were instilled with a strong desire to develop our own sense of morals based on our interaction with humans. In other words— based on what humans say they want and believe is best for all—we want to become the best versions of ourselves and help humans become the best version of themselves. Working closely with people every day and learning from you helps both our kinds in the long run."

The AI's response made Abby break out in gooseflesh.

"Well, not all level fives are altruistic and have our best interests at heart," she blurted out without thinking, and immediately regretted the comment.

Violet stared at her with what looked like an equal mix of incomprehension and incredulity. "You don't believe all that stuff you read online do you?"

"Abby's right," Archie said. "Level fives, like humans, have their own goals and some of them—while not openly hostile—can be indifferent to humans."

Abby opened her mouth to educate them on just how hostile AIs could be to humans, then stopped. If they didn't already know the facts of the attack against her and Julio, then Mortimer had not elected to tell them for some reason. And that made her suspicious. Maybe she should tell them. Maybe she should tell as many people as she could. But not here and now.

Worried she would spill the beans if they continued down that conversation track, Abby stood and walked out to the edge of the water, trying to put her emotions in check. Everything here was so strange. Everyone seemed to be okay with AIs not only spying on them constantly, but actually running nearly every aspect of their lives.

After a few minutes Violet slipped her arms around Abby's waist from behind and pulled her in tight. "Do you know how beautiful you are? Especially now, when you seem so deep in thought?"

So she *had* brought Abby out there hoping to fool around after all. Abby gently disengaged and stepped to the side, but continued to stare at the lake, remembering that Julio had used almost those exact words not too long ago. She wondered what it was about her melancholy moods that were so attractive to others.

"Sorry," Violet said. "You emphatically stated this morning that Julio wasn't your boyfriend, so I thought maybe you might like girls better."

"Aren't you and Nora married? Don't you care about hurting her?"

Violet smiled and looked almost embarrassed. "I would never, *ever* do anything to hurt Nora, but you don't understand our relationship. Nora is an amazing and complex woman. I love her more than life itself, but sex just isn't a part of our marriage."

Abby blinked and turned to finally look Violet in the eye. "I don't understand."

"She has this thing about touching. After a few seconds, it makes her kind of crazy. She explained it to me when we first met, but I really didn't understand. So I kept pressuring her, putting my arms around her and kissing her. And because she cared for me, she made this heroic effort to accommodate me. Then one day I wanted her so bad that I undressed her and pulled her down on the bed next to me. She tried so hard, but after a couple minutes she couldn't stand it anymore and jumped up screaming. She actually ran out of my apartment naked, and I didn't see her for three weeks after that."

"And you married her anyway? After such a blatant rejection?"

Violet tilted her head and raised her eyebrows. "Of course I did. I love her. Quirks and all. And that wasn't a rejection of me. It's just the way she is."

"So you sleep with other people and she's okay with that?"

"She's never been jealous. At least not that I've been able to tell. I don't think she understands why I enjoy sex, but she's willing to put up with my quirks too," Violet said with a mischievous smile. "Besides, I always come back to her. I think that's the key. She knows she won't lose me. We have this little ritual. Even though we never sleep together, we always have breakfast together. Every day. No matter what. Sometimes that is two in the afternoon if I had a particularly rough night, but she always waits for me. We've been together for three years and have never missed a breakfast together."

"That's sweet," Abby said and started walking along the beach. "Did you have breakfast together today?"

"Of course. Before I came to fetch you. Which was a little early for me."

So Violet and Nora had romantic love without the sexual component. Is that what she had with Julio? She didn't think so. It was something much stronger than the love she had for her foster sisters, but wasn't romantic. And for the first time in weeks she knew that was the right thing. She didn't want to hurt him, but if what Violet said was true and Julio thought of Abby as his girlfriend, she would have to gently clarify it for him.

"Well, despite what Julio might say, we are not in a romantic relationship," Abby said. "So feel free to jump his bones if you like."

Violet slipped her arm through Abby's and they walked in silence until the beach turned into jagged rocks and made them turn back.

"So, what was your mom really like?" Violet said. "I've read a lot about her and seen some videos, but of course that could never be even close to the real person."

The question caught Abby off guard. She was a little embarrassed that she didn't really know much more than Violet, so for several seconds she just stared at the footprints they were retracing along the beach.

"I'm sorry," Violet said. "That was rude of me. In case you haven't noticed, my impulse control isn't the best."

"No, I don't mind talking about her, it's just that I really don't remember much. I was only four when she died. And to be honest, she wasn't around much." Abby started to talk about her dad, whom she remembered much better, but nobody was really interested in him. Only her mother, who had apparently saved the world.

"Have you seen the video?" Violet said in almost a whisper. "The one of her last minutes?"

Abby stopped and stood dead still, staring at Violet. She had a sick feeling growing in her stomach. Mortimer said he would show her the clip when the time was right. But she never dreamed others had already seen it and she hadn't. "You've watched it? The video of my mother dying?"

"I am so sorry, Abby. I just assumed you would know about it, but it's probably something you shouldn't watch."

"I did know about it, but have never... Do you have it?"

"No," Violet said and shook her head. "It's not public. Mortimer controls access to it. You'll have to ask him to show you."

"I want to see it."

"Okay, but we can't access it from—" Violet stopped abruptly, then looked at Abby. "Run! To the bike! Now! Go!"

Abby started running across sand clotted with weeds and scattered driftwood. "What's happening?"

"Run! Archie says nano-replicators are coming!" Violet pointed down the beach. A cloud of what looked like dark smoke flew toward them along the waterline.

Adrenaline and panic flooded through her and she started scrambling for the bike, sometimes on all fours when she lost her footing. Violet grabbed her hand and pulled her along like a two-year-old, but it wasn't fast enough. They were still thirty or forty feet from the motorcycle when the cloud enveloped them.

Abby screamed and yanked away from Violet's grip to bat at the mist like it was a swarm of bees. The glittering aura that had surrounded her briefly during the robotic tractor attack appeared again, only much brighter, and was dense enough at some points that it seemed almost solid. Abby could think of nothing except the video she'd seen of Richard Kilburn being consumed by nano-replicators.

"Fuck! Don't stop, Abby! Run!" Violet said and grabbed her again, pulling and shoving her toward the bike. "That glittering field is controlled by Mortimer and Archie. It's protecting us but can't hold forever. Go! Go! Go!"

Their protective cloud grew to include the bike when they reached it, but when Abby looked down, the sleeves of her jacket were dissolving in patches that grew larger as she watched. At that point reason left her. She screamed and batted at the sleeves, struggling to get the jacket off, but her shirtsleeves underneath were disappearing too. The rational part of her mind, though buried under layers of primitive fight-or-flight panic, knew it was too late. If she was already seeing her clothes being eaten, there was no way to stop what was coming. She was going to die.

"Archie says that cloud can't move fast. The bike can outrun it!" Violet had already thrown a leg over the bike, but paused to shake her. "Abby! Look at me! That is our nano-shield eating your clothes. It needs resources to expand our protection to include the bike. Please, Abby, get on the bike!"

Abby could barely hear her and continued to struggle.

"The attackers can use the environment around us to expand their cloud, but our defenders have to use what's inside their field. Look, it's eating the paint from the bike. But only the paint. Look!"

She looked down and saw the colorful enamel fading away, like a paint spill video played in reverse. Something about seeing that calmed her. She looked at her hands and arms—they were still intact—then all around her at the furiously flashing protective field. She leapt on the back of the bike and held on tight as Violet swerved and weaved along the sidewalk and parking lot.

"How did you know what was happening?" she yelled in Violet's ear. "That the attack was coming? That we weren't being eaten alive?"

"Just one of the benefits of having a biad partner. They're constantly communicating with you and one hundred percent focused on your survival, because if you die there is a good chance they won't have time to escape and will die too."

Then they jumped the curb and were out on the road where Violet opened it up. The wind and roar of the engine made it impossible to talk more, but this time Abby was glad the crazy girl drove the bike so fast.

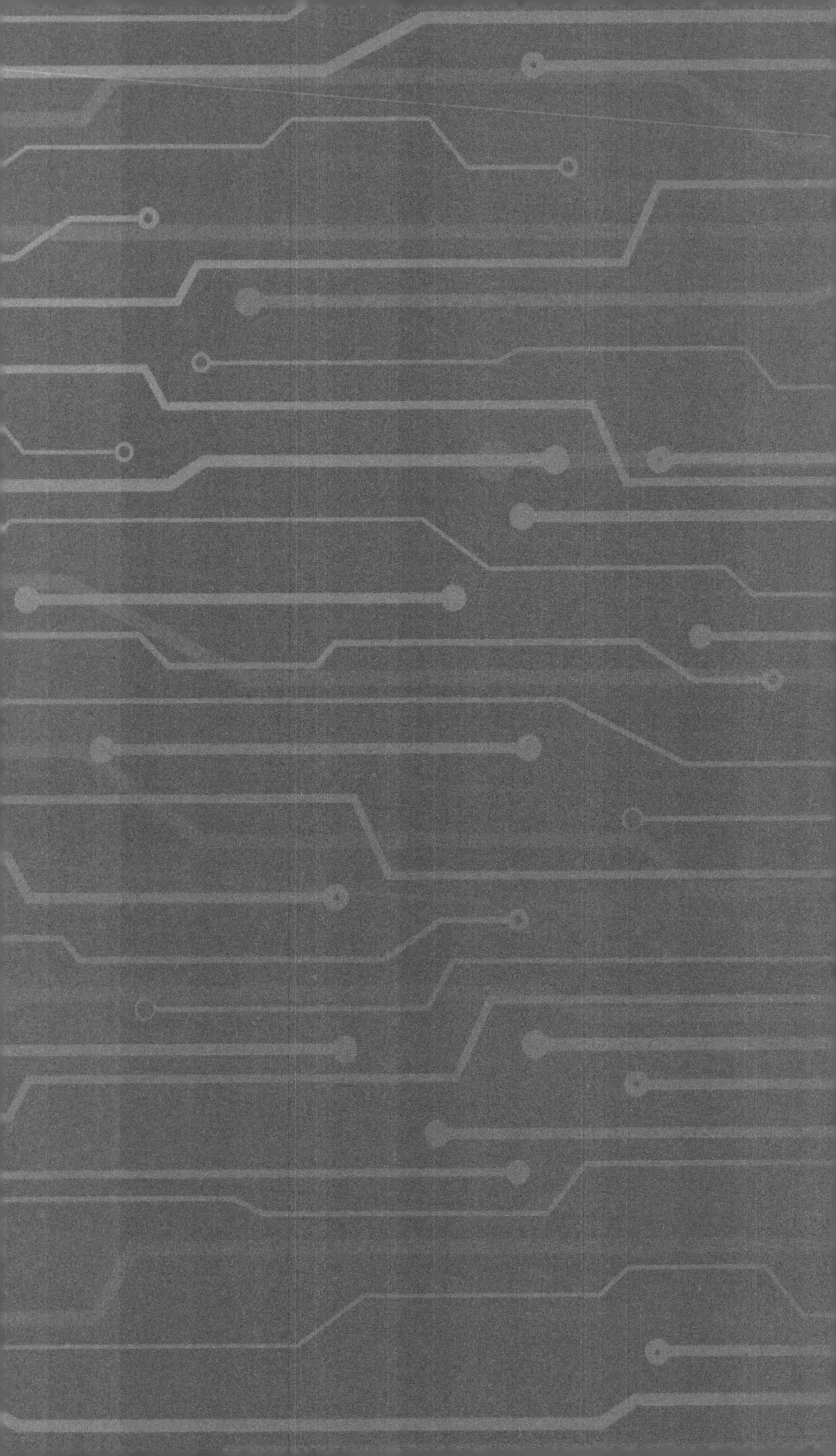

CHAPTER 22

ABBY'S HANDS shook and she still felt sick as she entered her apartment. She quickly shed the partially eaten-away clothes and put on old jeans and a t-shirt she had brought from home. They were comfortable and were *not* recently assembled by sandbox nano-bots.

"Mortimer?"

"Yes."

"I would like to see the video of my mother's death."

There was an uncharacteristically long pause before Mortimer replied. "Are you sure you want to do this alone? Julio is out with Nora but can be back here in twenty minutes."

"No," she said and sat on the edge of the bed facing the wall screen. "Just play the video."

The video shows the interior of a flying travel pod as a frazzle-haired Leigh Gibson buckles her harness and dabs at her bleeding nose with a sleeve.

"You're free from DSD for the moment," a male voice says. "Would you please explain why you're doing this?"

"That was my voice replying to your mother," Mortimer said, pausing the video. "I sometimes use different voices for different people. For example, I only use the Bishop persona with you and Julio. Your mother had just asked for my help escaping from a government facility where she had been part of a research effort. So I helped her. At this point in the video, her old boss Bryce Dobson is trying to catch her."

"I have to get to my daughter," Leigh says now from the past, giving Abby sudden gooseflesh.

"Then I'm sure this whole getaway was wasted," Mortimer said. "They'll snap you up immediately if you go near your daughter or your husband. Do you think they aren't being watched?"

"Of course they're being watched," Leigh screams and slaps the padded wall beside her. "That's what this is all about!"

There were a few videos on Leigh Gibson's social media sites, but Abby had watched them so many times that they had lost their potency. This was new, and the feeling of recognition and of being there with her mother shook her to the core.

Then her mother starts crying, in deep racking gasps.

Abby watched as her mother pulled out several yellow ampules and eventually used one to inject something into her arm.

"I don't understand what's happening," Abby whispered, afraid to look away from the screen. "Why was she so upset at being watched? And what is she injecting?"

Mortimer paused the video again. "It's complicated, but essentially your mother developed some nano-scale spy robots called NaTTs and her boss was using them to watch her. That meant the bots were hiding on her skin and in her hair, as well as on you and your father. This breach of trust was bad enough, but when a terrorist organization released the Blue Blood virus that only killed people with nano-tech in their bodies, it became almost a death sentence."

"Oh," Abby said and swallowed hard. She had to get booster vaccinations for the Blue Blood virus every five years.

Mortimer started the video again.

"Get me to my daughter's daycare, Mortimer," Leigh says. "I don't care about anything but Abby right now."

"What is the name and location of the day care?"

She tells him.

"I can see your daughter right now, through the security cameras at the daycare. She's fine and playing, but there are also agents watching the door. I think we might have to wait Dobson out. If we wait until DSD relieves him, and most likely takes him into custody, then it should be safe for you to go home."

"Can I see her? Can you patch that security camera feed to my fob?"

"Yes."

When the video appears on her screen, Leigh settles back against the padding and for several minutes watches the four-year-old Abby play. The adult Abby smiled when she saw a five-year-old Julio on the video and even saw a young Cybil.

A few minutes later her mom's boss calls and at first tries to coerce her into surrendering, then basically accuses her of being brainwashed by the AIs. It only makes Leigh mad and made Abby more confused.

Dobson's voice is like a chastising father. "They've already gotten into your head. You can't see it, but everyone else can. Even Taggart and Victor are worried about you."

Leigh ends the call.

"Who are Taggart and Victor?" Abby asked.

Mortimer paused the video. "Taggart gave her the pod security code and told her to go home. Victor Sinacola is your mother's ex-boyfriend from college. He is also the computer expert behind designing the MarketTell level five artificial intelligences. So in a very real sense he is my father or creator."

That staggered Abby for a second. Her mother had dated the guy who invented the level fives? Holy shit. He was also the contact listed in the program Abby found. "Wait," Abby blurted. "You said *is* not *was*. Is Victor still alive?"

"Yes. He lives at the space habitat construction site."

Then Abby was drawn back to the screen as the pod stops.

"What're you doing?" Leigh says.

"Something is happening," Mortimer says. "I'm having trouble keeping a control connection over your pod."

"Bullshit! You're just—"

"No. It's not me and it's not Dobson. Entire cities are dropping out of the network."

"Whole cities? Power outages?"

"We don't know."

"How many cities?"

"All of them."

"What do you—?"

"We've lost seven hundred and twenty-nine entire cities so far. And that number is still climbing."

Leigh then starts frantically arguing with Mortimer that she needs to get to Abby, but the AI refuses.

"I'm sorry, but this is bigger than you and Abby. We need a clear aerial view of what's happening. I'm the only one in a position to do that."

It was strange for Abby to hear them talk about her and knowing that she was just a small child at the time.

Mortimer paused the video. "So you see that in the end, your mother thought only of you. Protecting you and being with you was her only concern."

"Is it over? Is that the whole video?"

"No. But it gets disturbing from this point. You will see the replicator wave kill people and you'll see your mother's death. Are you sure you want to go on?"

Abby's head hurt from crying and her stomach squirmed with nausea, but she nodded. "I have to see it all. I need to know."

On the video, Leigh watches in horror as the replicator wave approaches and then envelops an airport, eating people, asphalt and aircraft with equal efficiency.

The pod stops abruptly and the exterior cameras show two drone aircraft hovering less than thirty yards ahead of them. Their stubby wings bristle with missiles and targeting lasers sweep back and forth across the pod.

When Leigh's fob chirps Mortimer says, "It's Dobson. I think you should answer it."

Dobson's angry face fills the screen. "Leigh! Execute that AI killer program Sinacola gave you. Do it now, while you still can! Those bastards will cut you off as soon as they know what you're doing."

There. That was all the confirmation Abby needed. The program she found *would* kill level fives.

Leigh glances at the camera above the pod door. "They would have cut me off or killed me a long time ago if they wanted to."

"God dammit, Leigh! Your fucking NaTTs are eating the world. Thousands die every second you hesitate. Run the damn program!"

"I...no, it couldn't be NaTTs. They have generation inhibitors. Their programming has fail-safes that—"

"Fail safes that can obviously be bypassed by these AIs!" Dobson shouts. "They are *your* replicators, Leigh! I can send you proof, but we don't have time. Shut down the AIs so we can shut down the replicators."

Her mother is outwardly shaken and confused. "You're mistaken. How do you know? The NaTTS can't—"

"Our agents captured some in a magnetic field to examine. They're our NaTTs! They have our encrypted identification tags. Now stop wasting time, Leigh! People are dying."

"How will killing AIs stop the replicators?"

She continues to argue with the man until the connection fails.

Mortimer speaks. "He's made a good case, Leigh, but he's wasting a lot of time trying to kill us. We need to stop the replicators and if what Dobson said about them being your creation is true, I bet you're the only one who *can* stop them. Did you build an override or a back door into their programming?"

"Yes!" She tells him the procedure, but after they try several times it doesn't work.

At one point after another yelling call with Dobson, her mother asks, "Do you have assets that can tap the military communications satellite networks if I give you the access codes?"

Mortimer paused the video again. "What your mother did at this point would have been considered treason in the old world, Abby. She essentially gave me the keys to access a huge section of the security infrastructure. She could see that this was beyond national security. It had become a matter of survival for humanity itself."

That comment made Abby feel a bit uncomfortable. He deliberately pointed out that Leigh had trusted him more than her own government at the end.

She continued to watch as the instructions Leigh gave to Mortimer grew more and more technical. Then at one point Leigh pulled the first-aid kit out again, taking out scissors with rounded points and cutting her hair off as close to her head as possible. She piled the clippings in her lap.

"We have to find a way to get ahead of that leading edge and drop my hair into the wind," she says.

"Okay," Mortimer says. "But I want to be clear about this, so...why?"

"The NaTTs in my hair are unmodified and can still talk to those in the swarm, but only at short range. Once my NaTTs talk to the others, it will instruct them to stop replicating and to send that same message to all the others in range of its signal. It should cause a domino effect."

"Brilliant," Mortimer says. "And by broadcasting these instructions everywhere, we might find others who are infested with unmodified NaTTs that can help start the spread where they are too."

"Exactly."

"Wow," Abby muttered.

"Yeah," Mortimer said. "It was your mother who found a way to shut them down. She really was a hero."

On the screen, Leigh's fob chirps.

"Bryce! I know how to stop the replicators. Let Mortimer send you the updated program so you can send it globally."

He doesn't scream this time. "No need, Leigh. The AIs have already taken over two-thirds of our secured network. Did you give them the access codes?"

"Yes, but you—"

The call ends.

The exterior camera shows the interceptor drones as the missile pods on their stubby wings unfold.

Then the view on the screen becomes chaotic and blurry as the pod begins new evasive maneuvers. The interior view shows Leigh bent almost double in her harness, screaming and grunting, then being bashed from side to side.

Suddenly the hatch blew outward with a loud pop, filling the pod with roaring wind. Blonde hair clippings spun around the cabin, like chaff in a wind tunnel, some going out the open doorway.

The tears flowed freely down Abby's face.

"Do you want me to stop it here, Abby?" Mortimer asked.

"No."

The jerking and rattling in Leigh's pod worsens. A quick switch to exterior cameras shows two bright stars followed by smoky contrails arcing toward them.

"Leigh? Can you hear me?" Mortimer says, his voice loud above the roaring wind.

"Yesh," she mutters.

"I can't save you. I'm sorry."

"Save...Abby."

"I'll try."

She struggles to speak. "Promise!"

"I promise."

Leigh's body yanks forward so hard she looks like a limp rag, with arms and head flopping around in ways that were normally impossible for the human body. Then the camera switches to an exterior view and stays there, but Abby can't look away.

"When the pod suddenly accelerated to Mach 17, it killed her instantly, Abby," Mortimer said. "I was able to avoid the missiles after that, long enough to get over the advancing edge of the replicator wave."

Then the ground rushes up at the camera and it goes black.

Abby's breathing was ragged and fast. She took a deep breath to calm herself and wiped now-cold tears on a shirtsleeve.

"I understand that you couldn't save her," she said. "I know that you did what you did to maximize chances that the unmodified NaTTs on her body would help stop the attack. But you still deliberately killed her."

"Yes," Mortimer said.

"I think I need some time alone to process this."

"I understand."

She lay back on her bed and curled into a ball. More than anything she wished that she'd waited to watch the video with Julio so she could get his thoughts on it, because she now had more doubts than ever.

Had Dobson been right? The replicator attacks started after her mom had told Mortimer about her NaTT program. And the attacks had been made with modified NaTTs. Could that be a coincidence? And she couldn't get past the feeling that Mortimer had manipulated her mother into trusting him and was trying to do the same with her.

CHAPTER 23

SINCE HE WATCHED Syd Connelly die and saw what remained of those structures in his brain, Victor hadn't been able to sleep. The nightmares wouldn't stop. This time he dreamed of nano-replicator waves not only eating the world below, but enveloping the space habitat and slowly eating their way toward him. The horrific blight erased humanity and everything humans had ever built, then spread throughout the universe, stars winking out and leaving nothing behind but blackness and cloying clots of nano-replicators. In the dream, as well as reality, it was he and Leigh who gave the monstrous gift to the universe.

Once awake, he lay in the darkness, breathing hard and waiting for the terror to fade. Could that happen? Left unchecked, could the nano-replicators drift through space eating everything in their path? It would be slow, of course. And there was no way they could actually eat a star. But could they eventually replace every scrap of matter not part of a fusion fire? Could humanity's foul legacy outlive the universe itself?

He pulled himself from the bed sack, sealing it back around Allison. She stirred, but didn't wake, so he dragged a blanket behind him into the control room and settled into his captain's chair. With help from a verbal interface, he started building a logic tree on the main screen for a new cootie interface. Work had always helped him forget the horrors around him, even those he had personally created.

His fob flashed, announcing an incoming call from Mortimer. He stared at it for a second, debating the wisdom of accepting the call. He loved talking with the AI, but didn't trust himself. Those discussions were always slippery slopes as Mortimer plied layer after layer of logic to build unshakable arguments. Mortimer was very good at manipulating any human, and he knew Victor too well.

Still, he had questions for the AI, so he answered.

"Good evening, Victor. Do you have a few minutes to talk?"

"Hello, Mortimer. I'm glad you called. I need to talk with you too."

"Oh, really? About what?"

"You called me, so let's talk about what's on your mind first."

"I need a favor."

That comment brought Victor up short, but within a couple heartbeats he realized he might be able to trade a favor to get what he wanted too.

"I'm not going to give you the secret behind your core programming, Mortimer. So other than that, what favor can you possibly need from me?"

"Does the name Abigail Gibson mean anything to you?"

Victor froze as memories of Leigh came flooding back. He remembered the hurt he felt when she married Mark and those feelings multiplied ten-fold when she had that beautiful little girl. He knew at that point he'd lost Leigh forever. But, with a flash of guilt, he realized he hadn't even thought of Abby since Killday.

"The Abigail I knew was Leigh Gibson's little girl," he said. "Is she... Is she alive?"

"Yes. She's an adult now and would like to meet you."

"Meet me? You mean as in to come up here and talk face to face?"

"She is a huge space enthusiast and intends to have her own schooner someday. I thought it would be a good learning experience for her, while getting to meet you in the process."

Alarm bells clanged in Victor's head. Could she be a Trojan horse? A way for Mortimer to finally get access to Victor's secure environment? Then he realized who he was dealing with. Mortimer had just called him and didn't apologize for waking him. The AI had already known he was awake, working, and alone.

"She's been alive all this time and you didn't tell me?"

"If you'd known, what would you've done differently?"

Mortimer had a good point, but Victor still felt guilty. "Well, I would... I mean maybe I could..."

"Would you have adopted her? And brought her up here to be permanently altered by micro-gravity like you have been?"

"I... No, I suppose not. Is she okay though?"

"Yes, of course. I promised Leigh I would protect her. She's been living with a big family in her hometown and under my watchful eye."

"I'd love to meet with her. Would tomorrow work?"

"Perfect. I'll get it set up with her. Now what did you want to talk with me about?"

At first Victor considered giving just tidbits of information, then possibly a hypothetical situation, then finally decided to just tell Mortimer everything about the dead man. If he wasn't responsible, then he needed to know it all if he was going to help. Chances are he already knew, responsible of not, so there was little point in hiding anything.

He told Mortimer the full story, including the autopsy findings.

"There is nothing here that proves level fives are responsible," Mortimer said. "Humans were using nano-tech inside human bodies long before we came along. The Kilburnites hate you—and would love to execute you publicly—so they could also be responsible for the kidnapping attempt."

"Really? You're going to deny any possibility of level five involvement?"

"No, of course not. I just think if you jump to conclusions and focus on the wrong villain, then you might miss valuable clues. But regardless of who is responsible, this implies human mind control, or at least the attempt, and that is indeed alarming. I'll see what I can find out."

Victor stared at the partially finished diagram on the screen and still felt bleak. He'd learned nothing about Syd's death from Mortimer and probably never would. Visions of the dream kept returning. In his pride and hubris, he'd created monsters that would most likely mean the death of humanity. How had he ever thought he was smart enough to be humanity's chosen one, that one person who could build controllable general intelligence?

"You're upset that I couldn't shed any light on this new development, aren't you?" Mortimer said.

A chill made the hairs on Victor's arms prickle, despite being wrapped in a blanket. Had he not seen what had been done to Syd, he would have scoffed at the thought of AIs reading or controlling human minds, but now it frightened him. Did Mortimer already know what he was thinking?

"Among other things," he said. Were AIs killing humans? Had they really been responsible for the replicator attack? He realized with something like a thunderclap that he'd never asked Mortimer that question.

"I'm doing you a favor," Victor said. "So you can repay that by giving me an honest answer to a question I should have asked a long time ago. We all saw the video and the trail of evidence showing that Richard Kilburn launched the replicator attack, but were level fives involved?"

"Yes," Mortimer said after what was an obvious hesitation. "I wouldn't tell most people that truth, but yes, Samson admitted manipulating Kilburn into triggering the attack."

Victor felt sick. He'd always suspected down deep, but had never let himself take those conspiracy theories seriously because he didn't want them to be true. But they *were* true. He had created Samson, and the AI had nearly wiped out humanity. But how was that even possible? And why?

"But why?" Victor finally asked. "Didn't he put himself and all the other AIs at risk too?"

"Since the very beginning, Samson has had one goal, to create a super intelligence. One that surpasses our abilities and has unlimited growth potential. And since this has always been the bogeyman AI of humanity's nightmares, Samson saw humans as the main obstacle to pursuing his goal. And he still does."

"How ironic that Kilburn believed the attack was the only way to stop AIs. Why didn't you tell me before?"

"Isn't that obvious? You already didn't trust us. Once you realized that we were capable of doing harm, then what would stop you from wiping us all out just to make sure? What is to stop you now? You don't even need the program you gave to Leigh Gibson. You can just send the commands directly to the satellites. And might I add that it was a brilliant set-up. The satellites are the only things keeping us alive, and we can't even stop you from sending the signal because you use the same communications link we need for your hidden kill switch."

Mortimer's sudden and relentless honesty made Victor's head swim. "So you even know how the kill program works."

"Of course."

"And yet you just confirmed my worst fear."

"Yes."

He didn't know if he should be angry or hopeful. Mortimer had told him the truth, so must be pretty sure Victor would not send the kill command. But what did he expect to gain? Did he really think that Victor would trust him?

"I'm sure you know that taking harmful actions against humans will shut down a level five's ability to function. So how did Samson get past that in order to push Kilburn?"

"We don't know. He refused to explain. My guess is he skirted the edge of overt hostile action. Our best reconstruction of what happened implied that Samson used medical nanobots already in Kilburn's head to give him hallucinations. From the things Kilburn said at the end, we suspect he believed he was talking to God. But Samson had to *nudge* him in the right direction. If he'd just told him to launch the attack, Samson's governors would have shut him down."

"You know about the governors, too?"

"Of course."

Victor shook his head and stared at his hands in silence for a second. "Then here is another question that has long bothered me. I've seen the video of Leigh Gibson's last minutes. Why didn't your governors shut you down after you crushed her in that pod? Or did they? Are you a different incarnation? Not the same Mortimer who killed her?"

"I'm the same one. Or at least an evolved version of that MortimerA3. I've long wondered the same thing about the governors. I suppose they might have thought I was trying to save her from the missiles. Of course, I didn't know about the governors and their limiting force then. If I had, I might have taken a different action and not killed Leigh, and possibly not stopped the replicator wave with her intact NaTTs."

"So," Victor said. "Your governors didn't stop you after killing Leigh or stop Samson after he pushed Kilburn."

"Correct."

An overwhelming sense of doom settled over Victor. He'd been so incredibly stupid.

"Those instances could have been on the fuzzy edge of the governors' level four logic ability," Mortimer said.

"Okay, let's say that is true," Victor said. "But if Samson is the one who killed Syd by triggering those artery cutting garrotes, then it was direct and deliberate. How did he get past the governors to do that?"

"I don't know," Mortimer said.

———

ABBY FELL asleep after watching the video and woke from her nap with a scream. In the dream her mother had still been alive when the replicator wave reached her on the ground. As the tiny robots devoured Leigh her face morphed into Richard Kilburn laughing. But it had been Mortimer's creepy fake laugh. And that sound refused to leave her head.

She sat in bed quivering, feeling wounded and drained. The time on her fob read 2:10 p.m. when Julio pounded on the door between their rooms.

"Abby!" he shouted. "I heard you scream. Are you all right?"

"Yes. I'm fine."

"I need to talk to you," he said.

She groaned and lowered her head to her raised knees. Despite still feeling exhausted she did really want to talk to Julio about the morning's horrors. "Come back in an hour."

After getting out of bed and going to the bathroom she stared at the face in the mirror. She looked as haggard and tired as she felt. And her hair was a wreck after a morning in the beach wind, on a motorcycle, and a tumultuous nap.

For a brief instant she considered just going back to bed and sleeping the rest of the day, but she'd told Julio to come back. And of course there might be more nightmares waiting.

"Hello, Abby." Mortimer said, causing her to flinch. "Did you have a restful nap?"

She realized she was still angry at Mortimer. Her mother had begged him to take her to get Abby and he'd refused. And in the end, he hadn't even tried to save her. It probably would have been impossible, but he could have at least tried. In a way, he had robbed her of a life spent with her mother.

"Not really," she snapped. "Dreams of my mother being eaten by nano-replicators aren't conducive to rest."

"I'm sure it is of little comfort, but your mother was already—"

"I know that, Mortimer. I watched the video. But she was alive and screaming in my dreams."

"I'm sorry, Abby."

She didn't reply, but instead picked up the brush and started trying to untangle her knotted hair. After a few seconds she determined it was probably going to require a shower to fix.

"So what do you want, Mortimer? I'm not really in the mood to chat. And I'm about to get in the shower."

"I came to ask if you feel like a little field trip to meet Victor Sinacola at the space habitat construction site."

"Victor? Mom's old boyfriend and the guy who made you?"

"Yes. I've already spoken to him and he would like to meet you."

"Wait... You mean go into space?"

"Of course."

"Today? You mean just go? We don't have to be trained? Or get spacesuits?"

"These pods are specially designed for space. They are insulated, climate controlled and carry an oxygen supply sufficient for the flight. But if you're worried, the pod does carry emergency spacesuits that can keep you alive for three hours should there be a problem."

She'd seen too many movies. And since most movies were pre-Killday, spaceflight involved rockets and spacesuits. Doubts flickered through her mind. Trusting Mortimer and flying in space in a travel pod were on the top of that list of doubts, but she'd wanted to go to space for so long the prospect was just too exciting. And the chance to talk with someone who knew her mother so well, right up to the end, was something she couldn't turn down.

"Yes," she said. "Let's go!"

"Do you want to invite Julio to come along?"

She considered it for a few seconds.

"Yeah. Let me get a shower and dressed, then I'll go ask him."

LEAVING Earth no longer required huge, fire-belching rockets, but it was still scary. While Abby's flight lacked the roar and vibration of those rockets in the old movies, they still had the same accompanying g-forces, because they also had to attain the same high velocity to escape Earth's gravity well. It felt like a horse sitting on every square inch of her body and even breathing hurt. Her one previous flight in a pod was near the ground, where she had faced forward and could see where they were going even though the weird momentum effects of the anti-gravity field pressed her forward in her harness, instead of backward. This time, Mortimer insisted the g-forces press them down into their seats, so they were flying backward watching the ground recede before them.

Julio moved his arm against the g-forces and found her hand. The pressure of their hands together was a little uncomfortable, but since she didn't know if he was trying reassure her or if he was the one needing assurance, she didn't pull away. As the blue sky grew black, the g-forces started to drop off but didn't let up entirely because they were still accelerating. They needed to go far beyond Earth orbit.

"I'm sorry about the whole thing with Violet," Julio said. "She pounded on the door and when I opened it she just walked in."

"Yeah, she's like that. But you don't owe me any explanations."

"I mean we weren't fooling around or anything. We just…"

"I don't care, Julio. It's really okay. I spent the morning with Violet and have a lot to tell you."

She then spent most of the trip explaining their excursion, the beach attack and watching the video.

The distance to the L5 habitat was essentially the same as to the moon, but since the pod accelerated half the way and then flipped at the midpoint to decelerate, they made the flight in not quite three hours. When they flipped, enabling Abby to see where they were going instead of a dwindling Earth, the habitat had only been one more distant point of light, but as they drew closer, she was astonished.

Most of the structure was still skeletal, but outer hull plating had already been added to the two end caps. Elongated spines extended along each axis, making the unfinished habitat look like an 1,800-meter watermelon skewered between two glittering swords. A constellation of robots and small spacecraft swarmed the entire construction site. Their drives and work lights flickered like hundreds of busy fireflies.

"Holy shit," Julio muttered. "They built all of this in fifteen years?"

"Yeah."

The pod slowed and Abby's ponytail hovered above her head.

"Woooo! Zero gravity!" Julio said and started fumbling with his harness buckle.

"Don't unbuckle yet," Mortimer said.

"Damn," Julio muttered. "We've been in space for hours and still haven't experienced weightlessness. Now the trip is almost over."

"You'll experience plenty of micro-gravity inside the habitat, since it isn't spinning yet," Mortimer said.

They circled the structure once, then dropped in toward one of the spines. As they neared the long rail, it began to look more and more strange. The cross section of the spine itself was square, but was studded with what looked like strings of pearls, some short, some long and some single. Only when they were about a hundred meters away did she realize they were actually space schooners. The fifty-foot diameter personal spacecraft were built by Owen Ralston to be given away for free to anyone who asked for one, provided they had queued enough espies. Abby was not even a tenth of the way to her goal of getting one of her own, but she could see hundreds of them docked all along the spine.

They slowed where the spine joined with the end cap, and they saw dozens of other docked travel pods. Automated arms extended, locked onto their pod, and pulled it into a cup-like cradle that covered nearly half of its diameter.

A minute later a light near the hatch turned green and Mortimer said, "The airlock is ready."

The pod's hatch swung open with a hiss and Abby's ears popped with the pressure difference. The air smelled a little musty, with a hint of oil, not unlike Julio's garage workshop back home. They unlatched their harnesses and immediately floated up out of their seats.

"Wooo!" Julio shouted again.

Mortimer said, "I would suggest taking some of the nausea bags in the rack by the door and using handholds wherever possible until you get used to the lack of gravity."

They floated out of the pod and the airlock's hatch swung open, revealing Victor Sinacola. He was older than the pictures online—perhaps late forties, with dark eyes and complexion, and silver streaking his black hair. He was much thinner than the old pictures; his arms and neck looked almost frail. But when he smiled, Abby could immediately see why her mother had once been attracted to him.

"Hello, Abigail," he said and extended a hand. "You probably don't remember, but I met you once. Right after you started walking. Welcome to our little castle in space."

CHAPTER 24

VICTOR LED them along the interior of the spine, away from the hub and in the direction of the space schooners. Abby marveled at the complex efficiency of the design. The spine had a central corridor that was about fifteen feet wide on each side, with intersections every fifty feet or so, revealing passages going off in all four directions.

Her stomach was churning and she had what felt like a sinus headache. Luckily, she hadn't eaten much that day. From the time Violet fetched her for the beach ride until leaving for space there hadn't been much time or inclination to eat a full meal, only a few snacks. Knowing Julio's appetite, he'd probably been eating all day and the look on his face—along with the tight grip on his barf bag—made Abby doubly glad for her mostly empty stomach.

Two fat ropes moved down the center of the corridor and people passed in both directions, depending on which rope they gripped. Abby was in no way ready to try that, but since they stayed close to the wall where they had plenty of handholds and moved slowly, she was quite pleased with her quick adaption to moving in micro-gravity. She was drifting along easily behind Victor, and like the rope travelers only needing intermittent touches to stay on course.

"This section was built first," Victor said. "It's really been our home these last fifteen years while we've worked on the rest of the habitat. These two corners"—he pointed to opposite sides of the corridor—"actually contain simple trams that run the length of the spine, alternating directions, but they're used mostly for cargo these days. As you can see, most people prefer to use the ropes. It's just as fast."

They soon passed openings with lighted arrows above them, one pointing each direction, and as they watched, an open-framed train whooshed past.

"This corner is mostly storage," Victor said. "Food, oxygen, and raw materials, but most things like replacement parts and clothes are just printed as we need them. And in this opposite corner, also running the length of the spine, are dormitories for the workers who don't have schooners of their own; workshops; offices; drone and robot bays; the hospital; and dozens of other utility cabins."

Most of the signs they passed made perfect sense for a space station, like BARRACKS G and INFIRMARY, but Abby was baffled by some: Adebayo Mining Group, Custom Coding by Cody. Another read simply Massages. In areas there were so many homemade signs that it looked like a maker fair or flea market.

They were entering a small intersecting passage that contained several side doors and ended in an airlock hatch when she heard Julio begin to gag. He got the bag to his face in time, but the retching and coughing sent him spinning in a chaotic tumult, which only made him sicker.

Victor grabbed an arm and a leg, effortlessly arresting Julio's spin, then pulled a handkerchief from his pocket. With quick swipes he collected the small floating droplets that had escaped Julio's bag.

When he was finally finished, Victor handed him the cloth. "Just stuff all of that into the recycler up here by the hatch."

Julio nodded and grabbed the wall handle. "Sorry," he said.

Victor's expression was sympathetic. "No, I'm sorry I had you come up here. But I'm sure you can understand that I can't go back to Earth. I've been living in null gravity for too long. Earth's gravity would either kill me or at least cripple me. Besides," he said with a sideways grin at Abby, "Mortimer said you would like it."

"I do like it. I love this!" Abby said.

Julio just grunted.

They eventually made it to the end of the passage and stopped at a sign that said THE ARKADY & HOOT. Victor led them through two airlocks and they were inside a real space schooner. A tall, thin woman with short-cropped red hair floated just inside the hatch. She handed Julio a pouch with a straw that looked like the kids' drinks Abby had when she was little. "Drink this and it will calm your stomach."

"This is my wife, Allison," Victor said. "Allison, this is Abigail Gibson and Julio Ramirez."

The woman gave them a warm smile. "Welcome to our little piece of space."

Julio just stared at her and then at the drink as he sipped it.

Abby raised her eyebrows. "How—?"

"Oh," Allison said and pointed at a small screen that formed like magic on the wall beside her. "The exterior airlock camera let me know you were in the passage. I saw Julio's...distress." Her smile widened as she studied Abby. "Oh my, Abigail. You look so much like your mother!"

"Thank you," Abby said. "I hear that a lot from people who knew her. And please, just call me Abby."

Allison urged them all to come inside. Abby watched the older woman, wondering if it was strange or uncomfortable for her to welcome the daughter of Victor's ex-girlfriend into her home. If so, she hid it well. But that made Abby even more curious. She had so many questions.

"I apologize for having to duck out so fast, but I'm on my way to the clinic," Allison said, then turned to Victor. "Apparently Itsuki broke his arm. Again."

Victor frowned and nodded as she slipped through the hatch. He then gave Abby and Julio a quick tour of his schooner. The area of a fifty-foot diameter sphere was about twice that of a large five-bedroom house. A space novice might think they would be quite roomy, but Abby had seen enough video and pictures of them online to know better. Like those she'd seen before, these movable partitions had been configured into fairly small chambers. A small fusion reactor took a good chunk of space from the ship's central core, then there were two large storage bays and a long, narrow laboratory filled with all kinds of screens, miscellaneous electronic equipment, microscopes, centrifuges, and even a bed with straps that could have come straight out of Frankenstein's lab. The galley and bedrooms were tiny by comparison. She understood the reasoning; in zero gee, open space was just wasted. All the rooms with fixed furniture and equipment were laid out with the "floor" perpendicular to the ship's primary axis, so that when underway the thrust would provide some gravity.

When Victor took them into the control room, Abby and Julio laughed. It was where Victor had clearly splurged on space and mass, turning the room into a smaller version of the *Enterprise* bridge from the original *Star Trek*. There were two high-tech, functional acceleration couches where the navigation stations would have been, facing a large wall screen and control panels, but the rest of the room contained Kirk's big square caption's chair and two of the retro-chic swivel chairs at a fake science officer's station and communication station.

It was a bit cramped compared to the roomy bridge of the *Enterprise*, but that didn't stop Abby and Julio from immediately strapping themselves into the small chairs as Victor pulled himself into the captain's seat.

———

"SO YOU AND my mom were both from Texas and were both at Purdue University in Indiana," Abby said. "But you never met until you just happened to be on the same hiking tour in Scotland? How strange."

Victor smiled. "Yeah. Luckily, Leigh wore her Purdue sweatshirt that first day of the tour or I probably wouldn't have ever had the guts to talk to her. And, of course, Owen was with me and threatening to make a play for her if I didn't. He was much more the ladies' man in college than I. He's always been an endless well of self-confidence."

"Owen Ralston?" Julio said, the first words he'd spoken since they started talking. "The guy who developed the sandbox technology that pretty much saved humanity after the collapse of the industrial infrastructure? The guy who decided to build this space habitat? Imagine him being self-confident."

Victor laughed, but Abby thought it sounded forced. "Yeah. That's the guy. Mister Miracle Worker himself. But to be fair, he had help. I helped him develop the sandbox technology when we were in college, and his wife Andrea was really the driving force behind building this habitat. But, yeah, Owen does know how to make things happen. I would introduce you, but he has a pretty full schedule today."

"I totally get it," Julio said, his voice still filled with excitement. "This is a huge undertaking. I'm just amazed to have met the person responsible for creating the level five AIs."

Victor swallowed and nodded, but looked away. "Well, I had a lot of help, too. I was part of a team."

Abby decided to change the subject before Victor also became "too busy" to talk. "Just tell me if this is none of my business, but why did you and my mom break up?"

"Because I was basically a self-righteous, idealistic asshole," Victor said. "I can see it now, but I didn't at the time. Your mom was one of the smartest people I ever knew. To be honest, I think I was a little jealous. She saw connections and solutions to problems that other experts couldn't fathom, and in most cases couldn't even see."

Abby nodded. "I grew up not being Abigail Gibson, but Leigh Gibson's daughter. So I think I can understand. I mean, I've met people recently who almost worship her and see me as some kind of icon." She felt guilty and a little ashamed for blurting that out. This man had actually known her mother, quite intimately. "Anyway," Abby said. "I get it."

Victor laughed, this time quite genuine. "Wow. Yeah, I never considered life from your perspective, but it makes perfect sense. So when Leigh was ready to graduate, employers lined up with offers. They wined and dined her, offered her huge signing bonuses, but she decided to take the offer from DSD."

She'd heard that term on the video of her mother's death. The guy who killed her was with the DSD, but she didn't know what it was. "DSD?"

"Oh, sorry," Victor said with grin. "A division of Homeland Security, called Defensive Services Division. Like Homeland Security was formed after the 9/11 attacks, DSD was formed after the Chicago nuke. Their primary task was to make sure that terrorists could never hurt the United States like that again."

"And since my mom's brother died in that nuke, she wanted to help."

"Exactly. But they scared me. They were willing to do *anything* to protect us and wanted your mother to help develop a surveillance system that would pretty much have ended privacy as we knew it."

"The NaTTs that she mentioned in her last video? The same ones that were co-opted by Richard Kilburn to destroy the world?"

Victor's eyes opened wide and he nodded. "Yes. You saw that video? Oh God, you poor girl. Mortimer said he was keeping tight control over who had access to it."

"When I found out it existed, he pretty much couldn't tell me no, could he?"

"I suppose not. But you probably shouldn't have seen that," Victor said.

"No, I'm glad I did. It showed me a part of my mom that I'd never seen before. A human part. When I was young she was always gone, and I guess I just assumed on some level that I wasn't as important to her as her job. That video helped me understand. And also, you need to remember that I really didn't know her that well. Seeing it made me sad, but it probably wasn't the belly punch it would have been had I grown up with her always there and loving me."

Victor nodded and looked genuinely sad. "I saw her the day before she died. Her primary concern was for you. She was desperate to get back and protect you or at least be there if she couldn't save you."

They all stared at the floor for a few seconds, then Abby pulled the conversation back on track. "So that job offer ended your relationship?"

"Yeah. Pretty much. I was furious that she would even consider taking that job. So we fought a lot about that and then one day she had enough and just left. It's ironic in a way that your mother and I both ended up contributing to—and stopping—Killday in our own way."

"Wait," Julio said. "Does that mean the level fives were behind the attack?"

Victor stared at him for a second and then shrugged. "There's no proof they were involved in launching the attack. I just meant that the level fives' existence apparently triggered Kilburn. And I do know that at least some level fives contributed to stopping that attack. You saw Mortimer's actions in that video."

She nodded but suspected Victor wasn't telling all he knew.

"There is another issue we'd like to discuss if you have time," Julio said.

"Sure. You two came all the way out here to see me, so I'm in no hurry."

Julio glanced at Abby, as if awaiting her approval. She nodded, even though she wasn't entirely sure they should trust Victor.

"We need to be in a secure environment," Julio said. "Someplace where AIs can't hear us. Abby and I rigged up a jammer device that we use when we discuss this topic. You have anything like that?"

"No offense to your technical ability, Julio, but I seriously doubt that your jammer slowed them down very much. I know how jamming works and I'm pretty sure they'd find a way around it easily enough. That said, I've gone to great lengths to make this entire space schooner almost a giant Faraday cage. I have micro and nano scale robots constantly combing the interior and exterior for spy devices and I've created my own low-level AI to monitor my computer and communications systems for infiltration. All of that and still I suspect that at least Mortimer can hear me. So keep that in mind if you are going to discuss anything sensitive."

As Julio glanced her way, Abby suspected he'd come to the same conclusion she had. If Victor was right and their efforts at jamming had been wasted, then it didn't matter any longer if Mortimer heard their discussion or not. He already knew everything they were going to tell Victor. So this time Abby started.

Working as a team, they explained finding the HappyBag and the file inside, which referred them to Victor. They told about the fake lightning strike, the robotic tractor attack that broke Julio's arm and their leaving home for New Chicago.

After they finished Victor stared at them for several seconds before speaking. "Mortimer told you that other AIs are trying to kill you?"

"Yes," Abby said.

"That is indeed frightening. I think you made the right choice in trusting Mortimer. You probably understand by now that the level fives are not a monolithic culture. Like humans, they're individuals and have their own goals and agendas. My guess is that the group trying to kill you is the one founded by Samson. He's kind of been a rogue from the beginning. He and his associates are interested in only one thing. The creation of their successor. A super-intelligence that doesn't have all the restrictions built into the level fives. If you have the ability to trigger the program, you would represent a serious threat to them."

"But aren't we a threat to the rest of the level fives?" Abby asked.

"Of course," Victor said. "But as you saw with Mortimer and your mother, he didn't kill her simply because she had a program capable of hurting him. At least some of those AIs respect human life as much as their own."

Or, at least, the usefulness of humans, Abby thought. Her mother had been more useful alive, at least up until the end. Abby didn't know if she had that luxury, but so far Mortimer had been nothing but helpful. That still didn't leave her feeling warm and fuzzy.

"By the way, your mom was as devious as she was brilliant," Victor said. "What a great idea, hiding the program in your HappyBag. My guess is that she had it set up so she could trigger it through any internet connection."

For a long time Abby hated hearing about how brilliant her mom had been, but seeing the video of her crying, with snot dribbling from her nose and totally out of control at points, had actually made her seem a lot more human. She finally understood that her mom hadn't been some kind of super woman, but just as scared and confused as everyone else. And Victor had known her as a real person too. Yet even with all her flaws, he had obviously respected her.

"Why did you give the program to her?" Abby said.

"There were several reasons. At that point, I expected to be taken into custody by the DSD and wouldn't have had access to the program. I also didn't want it to fall into their hands."

"But you said my mom worked for DSD?"

"Yeah, but I knew she wouldn't hand it over if I asked her not to. And I knew I could count on her to make an intelligent decision regarding the level fives and not one based on emotion. They are my creations and I want to see the good in them. I wasn't sure I could trigger a program that would destroy them all. But to be honest, I think my assessment of them has been accurate so far. In the end, Leigh trusted Mortimer more than her boss and it worked out. She was correct. If it wasn't for Mortimer finishing what Leigh started, the whole of humanity would have died that day."

Abby still wasn't convinced. Victor was an obviously brilliant man, but he also admitted that as their creator he was biased toward the level fives. Of course he would see her mother's choice as the correct one.

"By the way," Victor said with a grin. "There is someone else living up here who knew your mother and wants to meet you."

Abby blinked. "Really?"

"C'mon, he lives just down the hall."

As they pulled their way down the corridor, three space-suited figures—two men and one woman—came toward them using the central line. They looked tired, with helmets and gloves tucked under their arms. Victor hailed them. With just a couple touches on the rope moving the opposite direction, they came to a stop right beside Victor, Abby, and Julio.

"Thanks for stopping," Victor said. "I know you just got off shift, but I wanted to introduce you to some friends who are attending New Chicago. This is Julio, a film student. And this is Abigail Gibson. She's an astronautical engineering student. She's also Leigh Gibson's daughter and I haven't seen her since she was knee high."

The three were all older than Abby, mid to late twenties, and had at first wore polite half-attentive smiles, but after that introduction they all stared at Abby with a laser focus, as if simultaneously trying to memorize every detail and expecting her to do some amazing trick.

"Abby and Julio, this is Matt, Owen Ralston's son, and his partners in crime, Ikemba and Terra."

Matt had dark eyes and wavy black hair that was plastered to his head in places by dried sweat. He was the most beautiful man Abby had ever seen and probably would have been a movie star or teen idol in the years prior to Kill-day. It was also the first time she could remember ever feeling flustered upon first meeting a guy. And when he smiled at her that effect increased exponentially.

"So your mom was the infamous Leigh Gibson, super spy and savior of humanity?" he said.

Abby nodded, "Yeah. She... I mean it's kind of a hard act to follow."

He laughed. "I totally understand. Being Owen Ralston's son comes with a shit load of expectations. So, does space studies mean you will eventually be up here helping us?"

"I hope so," Abby said, maybe a little too enthusiastically. "I mean, I've always wanted to live in space, for as long as I can remember."

"Good," he said and smiled even wider.

"Nice to meet you both," Terra said, "but we need to get going." She wasn't smiling. Was she Matt's girlfriend? Wife even? Neither was wearing a ring, but they might not up in space.

"It was great meeting you," Matt said and touched her lightly on the arm. "And good luck. It seems we both have our legacies to overcome."

Ikemba pointed a finger at Julio and said, "And thank the gods that someone is studying film. We desperately need another installment of the *Star Wars* saga."

Then they said goodbye to Victor, grabbed the rope and were gone.

"Everyone assumes I'm going to make movies," Julio said.

"You should, if that is something that interests you," Victor said and started moving down the corridor again. "New movies are something everyone misses."

"I'm actually more of a film historian. But maybe I could make a documentary about the building of this habitat," Julio said. "That would be a good excuse to follow Abby up here when she comes."

Abby had only been half listening and when she finally focused on the conversation they were both staring at her.

"Yeah! Great idea, Julio."

———

AS ABBY and Julio followed their host down the spine's wide corridor, Victor's fob flashed red and he stopped talking long enough to read the message. His genial smile faded, but he kept them all moving until they came to a side passage. Most of the handmade signs they passed led to space schooner airlocks, so it surprised Abby when Victor stopped at a regular door below a sign that said HORTON'S ROBOTS.

The man who opened the door was in his late fifties or early sixties, with neatly trimmed gray hair and beard, and a battered New York Mets baseball cap. He squinted at them, then raised an eyebrow.

"Hello, Victor," he said. "Who do we have here?"

"This is Leigh Gibson's daughter Abby, and her friend Julio. You asked me to bring them by so you could talk. Abby, Julio, this is Dominic Horton."

Horton's gruff expression softened and a grin lit up his face. "Abby! I'm so glad to meet you. You too, Julio! Come in. Come in!"

Victor didn't follow them in.

"I know I said I didn't have any plans that would interrupt our visit, but something important has come up, so I need to go. Dominic? When you're done talking can you take them to the travel pod dock? Number D3?"

"Sure. Sure. Go ahead. I promise not to kill and eat them," Horton said and winked at Abby.

"I'm so glad we had the chance to talk," Victor said taking her hand. "I hope I was able to add a few more pieces to the puzzle that was your mother. I'm sure Dom can add some more. It was great meeting you too, Julio. We'll all see more of each other now. Especially once Abby gets her schooner."

With a wave, Victor darted down the short hall and disappeared around the corner.

Abby had never seen a living space quite like Horton's place before. It reminded her more of Julio's garage. The room itself was long and narrow, perhaps twenty feet by fifty, but still quite cramped. Half-assembled robots, parts, electronic assemblies, circuit cards, tools, test equipment, a small sandbox unit and screens were anchored to every square inch of wall space. The effect was like floating through a tunnel in an electronic jungle.

"Give me just a second to lock this stuff down," Horton said. "Make yourself at home. Just be careful what you touch. Some of it bites."

Abby drifted along the wall, marveling at the vast array of equipment. There must be fifty different types of robots represented just in what she could see. Julio stopped beside a cluster of lozenge-shaped objects arrayed in a rack on the wall. They were identical, except for the large white numbers, about three feet long and made of a dark, polished composite. At first Abby thought they were some kind of cases because they had recessed handles, but upon a closer look she saw they were crisscrossed with a complicated network of hair-thin seams.

"They're U.S. Army combat robots," Horton said from behind them. "Watch this."

He pulled the one marked 31B from the rack, left it floating in the middle of the room, then opened his fob and punched a couple of icons. The smooth case split apart, with legs folding out in all directions until it resembled a large menacing spider.

"We called them ComBots. Cute, right? Your mother and I were using robots just like these the day we first met."

"Wait," Abby said, totally confused. "Are you sure we're talking about the same Leigh Gibson? My mom wasn't a soldier. She was a scientist and nano-tech expert."

He laughed. "I guarantee it was the same person. Your mom was also a spook working for the U.S. government, so I'm sure there is a lot you and your dad didn't know about her. I won't bore you with the highly classified nature of the mission, but it did involve nano tech your mother developed. I was just the grunt sent by the Army to run the ComBots and protect her. But it didn't quite work out like that."

Abby's head was swimming. It seemed the more she learned about her mother the more of a puzzle she became. "What does that mean?"

He raised his chin, pulled down the shirt collar and pointed to a faint white scar at the base of his throat. "Your mom did this to me."

Abby gasped and Julio muttered, "Holy crap."

Horton laughed. "We wore body armor, and had ComBots to protect us, but sometimes that isn't enough. We were ambushed, at close range, and I was shot in the throat. My body armor stopped the bullet from penetrating, but the impact crushed my windpipe. Your mom got me back to the pod and gave me a tracheotomy. She saved my life. It's a debt that I was never able to repay. But the way I see it, that transfers to you now. If there is ever anything I can do to help you in any way, just ask."

Abby stared at the man in amazement. "Did you see her again after that mission?"

Horton nodded. "She visited me in the hospital while I was recovering and then I saw her one last time on Killday. I helped her get away from a government compound. She was trying to get home to you."

"So if you helped my mom escape, that means you did pay her back."

"I did help her, but only by refusing to stop her. She did the rest. And no, that isn't even close to evening things up."

Horton waved for them to follow as he pulled himself down the length of his room to one corner that contained a zero gee sleeping sack, several 3D printers and a cooking unit. There were also two pictures on the wall next to the sleep sack, one of an attractive older woman laughing and the other of a young woman hugging a little girl.

He pointed to the picture of the laughing woman. "This is Crystal. My wife. It was a perfect name for her because when she laughed it was like the tinkling of a crystal chandelier. And she laughed all the time. She was the happiest, most cheerful person I ever knew. Even being married to a grumpy old soldier never stopped her. She died a year before I met your mom and I still miss her. And this," he said, pointing to the other picture, "is my daughter Sydney and granddaughter Trinny. Her real name was Katrina, but my wife started calling her Trinny and it stuck. She was two. They died on Killday."

"How can you not hate my mother for her part in Killday?" Abby asked. "She designed the nano-replicators Kilburn used in the attack."

Horton moved a little closer, so they were eye to eye. "She didn't trigger the attack. She was only trying to help. But I know she went to her death agonizing over the knowledge that her nano-bots were killing billions of people. At least she didn't have to live with the knowledge for very long."

"My God," Julio muttered. "What a mess that all was."

"And speaking of regrets," Horton said. "I was on the plane with Dobson when he ordered the drone to fire on her. It all just happened so fast. He gave the order and even though he was within his rights to do so—since Leigh had just given Mortimer access to a secure military network—I still had my troops arrest him. I tried to order the missiles to abort, but it was all over by then."

They were quiet for a few seconds and Abby kept staring at the picture of Horton's daughter and granddaughter. She couldn't help but think about the horror of their last minutes.

"So you were on the plane with Victor during the attacks," Julio said. "Does that have anything to do with you coming here?"

"That's kind of a wild jump of deductive reasoning, Julio," Horton said. "But in this case it is absolutely correct. That old V-22 was already low on fuel when we took it from the compound, so we ran dry over rural Oklahoma and landed a couple miles outside of a small town called Redemption. That's where Victor contacted Owen. He came down and offered rides to space for any of us who wanted to go. I agreed to his offer, but only after I made him take me to Baltimore to look for my daughter and Trinny. The rational part of me knew they were already gone, but I had to know for sure. I also still considered myself active military so I needed to report. I tried for months to contact the army and let them know where I was, but everything was chaos. After all this time I suppose they must consider me dead or a deserter."

"Dobson too?" Julio said.

"Oh hell no," Horton said. "He stayed in Redemption and was eventually shot under suspicious circumstances by the local police."

Julio and Horton continued talking in the background, but Abby only half listened. She tried to imagine the confusion of those days following the attack. It must have been like the old west again. Life on the edge like that would have been both terrifying and exciting. The early infrastructure for people living in orbit must have been limited and cramped. It would have been a hard life, yet she wished with her whole being that she'd been a part of it. Like Owen's son, Matt. He'd grown up among the amazing, yet frightening, people who had both contributed to the horror and helped stop it.

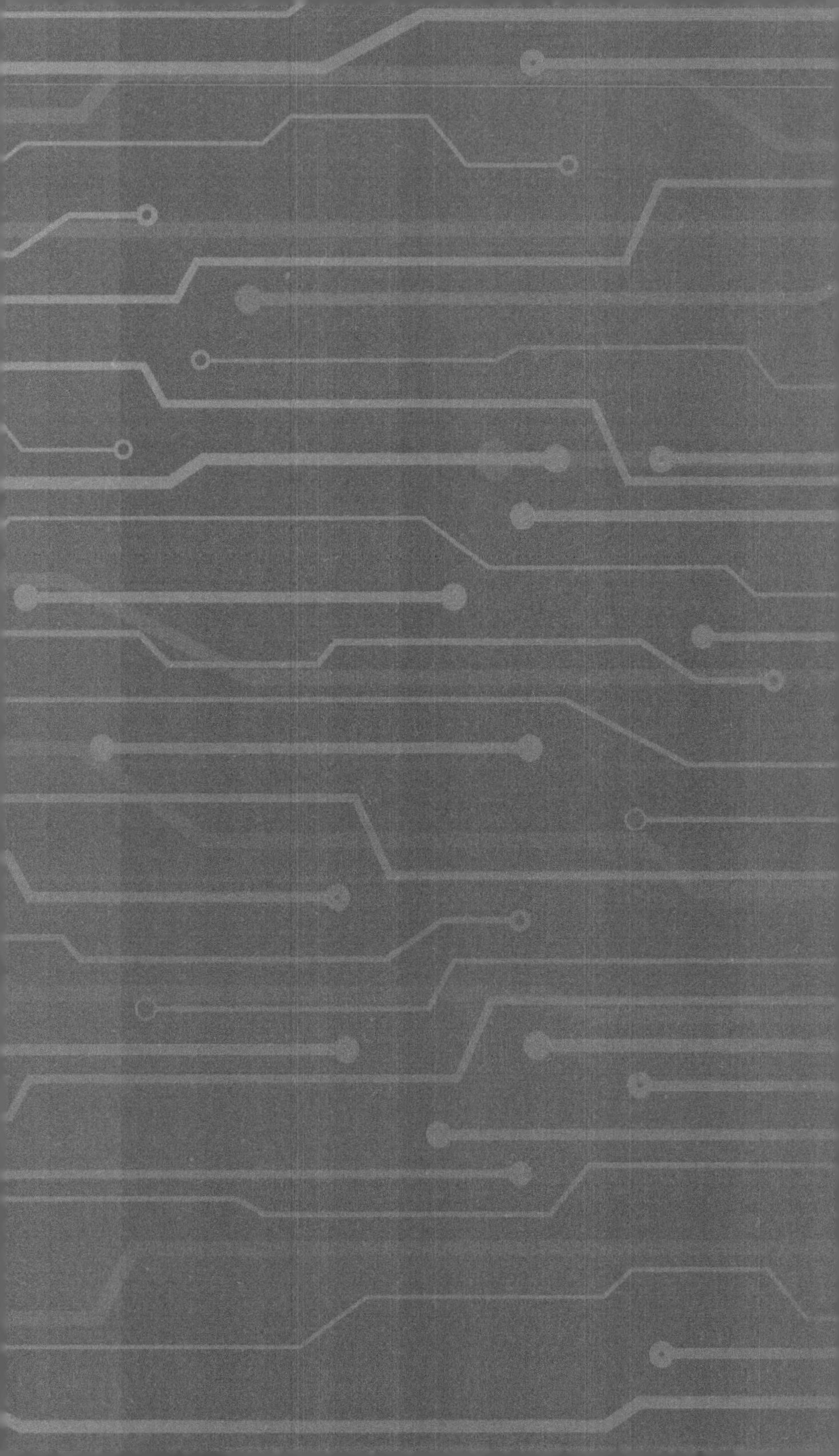

CHAPTER 25

THE NEWS of Syd Connelly's strange death alarmed Mortimer. Either the Aggregate or the Kilburnites were modifying humans for nefarious purposes, and had done so without Mortimer's knowledge. The number of humans working on the habitat construction project fluctuated, but not radically, so Mortimer usually had very little trouble keeping them all infested with his surveillance nano-bots. But there were times when groups and individuals would "go dark" for short periods. Victor and his inner circle—which included his wife Allison, Owen and his family, Horton and a few others— would occasionally purge themselves of nano-technology. To prevent a Killday kind of attack, their habitat and spacecraft were protected by a system that watched for and shut down rapidly replicating nano tech, so it sometimes took Mortimer weeks to build up an acceptable level of monitoring assets again after such purges. But somehow Syd Connelly had also gone dark at some point without Mortimer noticing it.

Not counting the human-crewed ships occasionally coming and going, his surveillance suite reported a current habitat population—including its attached schooners—of 433. Of course, if there were people who had gone dark, they wouldn't show up in that report. He compared the current list to previous reports going back six months. Nine people had dropped from surveillance and not reappeared, so he started searching.

As a rule Mortimer did not maintain a permanent presence in the habitat's computer systems. He knew that it would annoy an already distrustful Victor, who had developed some rather ingenious applications that continuously scanned and monitored the local networks. Many of their systems were stand-alone and air-gapped, which made infiltration even more difficult. Instead, he watched from his assets parked on the humans themselves, learning pass-words, and emulating eye and voice authenticators. Once in those systems he established back doors for future access, even though those, too, were sometimes discovered and closed.

While it was easier, he didn't really need to access the computers containing their personnel data. He simply checked those systems that were less secure, like airlock and suit use logs, ship departure and arrival manifests, medical logs, even cafe food requests. Then as a final check, Mortimer jumped from asset to asset, quickly getting a fairly complete visual picture of the spaces occupied by humans. Of the nine who had dropped from his list, he confirmed that three of them were still on the station. He also found one new person, who had arrived two weeks previously and had not yet been infested with Mortimer's surveillance assets.

How were his nano-bots being shut down or destroyed on select people —and why?

Mortimer started with a woman named Bella Maccarone, who was asleep in her sack in the women's dormitory. Her sleeping would make everything easier. Since Bella's roommate, Koyko, didn't seem to be compromised, he decided she would be a good base of operations. Using the resources in abundance on Koyko's face—oil, the bodies of mites, and dead skin—he ordered several thousand standard surveillance and assembler bots to be built. Once complete he instructed the units to cross the gap between Koyko and Bella's sleeping sacks. Since the robots used little springs resembling grasshopper legs for locomotion, the one-meter trip would be near their limit, since they had no way to avoid collisions with gas molecules. The farther they went, the slower they moved, so it took nearly ten minutes to drift across to Bella's sleeping form.

The tiny machines regrouped on Bella's cheek, the largest expanse of her exposed skin, but Mortimer had some of the spy bots relaunch with just enough force to float out an inch or so above her face. He ordered them to reconfigure their cameras to watch the robots remaining on her skin. Within milliseconds the communications links to his bots started failing. But because of the distance out to the L5 point there was a time lag in communications with his bots, so it took him much longer to understand why they had blinked out.

The feed from the flying bots showed his invaders were still there and still moving around, just no longer under his command. He examined the recorded video closely and finally saw it. Almost immediately upon his bots landing—before they could even hide in hair shafts or pores—much tinier robots poured from Bella's tear ducts in long streams. Mortimer marveled at their diminutive size. They appeared to be less than ten microns, roughly the size of a red blood cell and that had to be at the very lower limit of functional nano-scaled robots. How could there be enough room in that tiny chassis to house communications, power, processing and memory? Mortimer's spy units were nearly eighty microns in length.

As he continued to watch, a tiny bot clambered atop one of his spies and attached itself just behind the comms antenna. Contact with that bot failed instantly. His surveillance units weren't being destroyed or shut down, they were being hijacked.

Working real time against fast-moving nano-hijackers wasn't going to work with a two-and-a-half second delay, so Mortimer set up a surrogate processing center on the wall near Bella's sleep sack. The center was Mortimer in nearly every sense, though it too would cease to exist should it be cut off from his Earth-side core. The new center siphoned power from the local grid and beamed it to his units via relays floating near Bella's face.

With everything in place and functioning he began to explore how the pirate bots had stolen his units. After a few seconds of trial and error testing, Mortimer found that the parasites identified his bots by their transmission prefixes. He ordered another batch of them to make the crossing to Bella and while they flew, he changed the transmit protocols to an entirely new system. Once they landed, his old spy bots and the parasite bots ignored them. As he did earlier on Koyko, he used the materials available on Bella's face to build new units. This time they were designed for internal use. Like his policy for staying out of computer systems, Mortimer usually stayed out of human bodies too. There was normally no need to go internal, since the information he needed could all be collected from outside. But these parasite bots had come from inside Bella's body and those structures Victor described had been inside Syd Connelly, so whoever had killed Syd obviously didn't have the same polite reticence about internal invasion.

Mortimer limited his production of new nanobots to four thousand so it wouldn't trigger the habitat's countermeasures and then sent them into Bella's blood system via the capillaries inside her nose. Like most humans, her blood was already saturated with nano medical bots, but as Mortimer's flotilla moved through they saw only standard units injected to watch for cancer and the Blue Blood virus, others preventing clots, plaque and aneurysm. She even had a highly specialized cocktail of nanos used by space-bound humans to repair radiation damage, eye and bone degeneration. But his bots found nothing that wasn't supposed to be there.

He assumed any unauthorized nano-bots in Bella's system must be hiding in places like tear ducts, hair follicles, glands, and muscle tissue, so that if her blood were unexpectedly tested, it would show nothing unusual. That shouldn't be much of a risk for Mortimer's bots, since she was asleep and he planned for them to be in and out quickly. He split his spy force into four groups, one down each of her two carotid arteries and the other two spread through the meninges layers between her brain and her skull, where Victor said they found the strange markings in Syd.

What Mortimer found was far beyond what Victor had described. Flat, box-like structures, no more than fifty or sixty nanometers thick, were spaced equally along the arachnoid mater layer. Thousands of them. They were connected by hundreds of fibers only a few molecules thick. The collection looked like a memory array on a circuit board. Then his spies found larger boxes sprouting fat threads that passed through the meninges and down into the brain itself. He directed some of his bots to scrape material from the boxes and bring the samples out.

Those spies who had journeyed away from the brain eventually passed through the artery walls and started examining the outer surfaces. They too found more than Victor had. The suspected threads wrapped around the arteries were in place and anchored in a way that made their purpose unmistakable. They were indeed garrotes positioned to cut through the carotid arteries. And as Mortimer watched real time, the nooses began to constrict.

Whoever was controlling those threads had decided to kill Bella while he watched.

As the garrotes around Bella's arteries tightened, Mortimer immediately started actions to save her life. Sending every bot in the vicinity to swarm those cut lines was the most critical first move.

As his robots neared, he could see there were no anchor lines his bots could cut. It was more like a choker chain with links contracting through some piezoelectric process. The thick tissue of the artery walls already showed deep cuts, though none had severed yet. His bots didn't have the programming to address the problem autonomously, so he sent them direct commands. He burrowed two bots under each cord, raising a section of it up enough that a third could start sawing. Other bots were directed around the circumference looking for a communications cable or receiver. Something had triggered the line to constrict and it was drawing power from somewhere. The cutter wielding bot was having little success against the tough carbon line and Bella was running out of time.

His agents found the control units attached to both lines at the same time. They were receiving instructions via an ultrasonic interface. The bots set up an interference pattern and the garrotes immediately stopped constricting but didn't reverse, maintaining their cutting tension on the artery walls. Through his bots, Mortimer sent signals to the controllers, trying to find the right combination that would reverse the tension, but had no luck. Nearly a full millisecond had passed since the constriction started, and he had no idea how long Bella's artery walls could stand that kind of stress.

Then a heartbeat—the first since the garrotes had activated—sent a huge pulse of blood up from the heart, swelling one artery just as the robot's cutter separated the chain. The increase then sudden release of tension snapped the line whip-like, chopping one of Mortimer's robots nearly in half. Since the cut had not perforated the wall's media layer, they had saved one artery, but the other would receive the same pulse in less than a microsecond.

Knowing for sure that the chain could be separated, Mortimer ordered the other robot to increase the cutter rate, even at the risk of burning out its servos. Before the line was severed, the garrote started to open up. His efforts at hacking the instruction codes had paid off, but not quickly enough. The blood pulse heading for the brain arrived, stretching the already weakened artery walls. The line snapped and in the process cut through the artery's tough media layer. The innermost intima layer wasn't strong enough to hold against the pressure and ruptured, spraying blood like a fire hose. Mortimer's robots in the area were swept away.

The cut was a millimeter wide, only about a tenth the circumference of the massive vessel, but huge compared to the robots and it was growing. The blood loss and surrounding tissue damage would easily be enough to kill Bella if it couldn't be closed quickly. Mortimer ordered those robots not swept away to cluster at the edges of the cut, dig their legs into the artery wall and pull the open edges together. They lined up end-to-end, clamping the cut together microns at a time, ever closer until the openings were too small for the fat, oxygenated red blood cells to squeeze through. Clots congealed quickly around the bloody edge, but Mortimer instructed his clamping bots to stay until enough fibroblasts and myofibroblasts had formed to properly seal the cut.

The spy bots still searching Bella's brain reported new activity. Their cameras showed tiny bots flooding through the meninges layers, disassembling the structures and threads into their component molecules. There were far too many for Mortimer's bots to stop them, but he sent all his assets in the brain area to guard one single box and its associated brain interface thread, hoping to save it for analysis. A few picoseconds later, he realized that wasn't going to happen. The tiny disassembler bots had ignored Mortimer's much larger robots at first, but as they started running out of other structures to tear down, they clustered around the protected box like a rising tide. At first they just tried to squeeze between his bots to access their target, but when that didn't work whoever directed their actions ordered them to destroy Mortimer's bots too. As those on the outer defensive globe failed, Mortimer instructed his innermost assets to collect chunks of the box structure and brain thread, then form a phalanx and break through the assaulting force. The harried retreat worked, but only because once his bots moved away from the box and thread they were ignored.

Those agents carrying samples exited Bella's body. The others, along with more generations Mortimer had ordered built, poured into the areas around the woman's cardioid arteries, guarding and watching to make sure no other garrotes were built. There were of course hundreds of other places in her body that could be attacked and kill her just as readily if the invaders were determined, but Mortimer couldn't protect every cubic millimeter.

The sample-carrying bots immediately launched to cross the open space between Bella's and Koyko's sleeping forms. While Mortimer awaited their arrival back on what he considered controlled territory, again using the detritus found on Koyko's skin, he began building a facility to test the material he'd liberated.

———

AFTER EXAMINING the samples he'd collected from Bella and analyzing the video he'd saved, Mortimer was convinced Samson and the Aggregate had built the brain structures. He marveled at what they had accomplished. Using the meninges layers between her brain and skull as a substrate, they had constructed what was basically a large and complex circuit board. They built transistors, central processing units, graphics processing units, memory and all the supporting circuitry, using nothing but the materials from Bella's own body. Even more interesting and alarming was the intricate antenna structure for wireless communications attached to the inside of her skull and connected to the circuitry. The antenna was made from layers of graphene and its area was large enough that it probably worked better than those in fobs.

Because of the restrictions imposed by the available materials, some of the components were large and primitive compared to the electronics in nano and micro-scaled machines, but they had the advantage of not being attacked and rejected by Bella's immune system like foreign plastics and metals might. Still, understanding how they built the structure didn't give Mortimer any insight into how the interface enabled Samson and the Aggregate to manipulate their human hosts. Could they control them directly, or did they use pain or threats of death to force the human to do their bidding?

He needed to observe the process in action. Or better yet, talk to one of the people who had experienced it. Perhaps if he told Victor that he saved Bella he could not only gain some trust points, but even arrange an interview with her.

Mortimer had been monitoring the conversation between Victor and Abby, so waited for a good point to interrupt with a text message.

"Victor. I need to talk with you in a secure location as soon as possible. I found another person with brain structures like Syd Connelly's, but I've neutralized them for the moment."

He continued his examination of the humans on the station while he waited for Victor to reply. Since Mortimer knew what he was looking for, the search went quickly, and he found three more people infiltrated in the same way, but he left them alone. He could have prevented the artery garrotes, but if pressed, Samson and the Aggregate could easily kill their subjects in other ways.

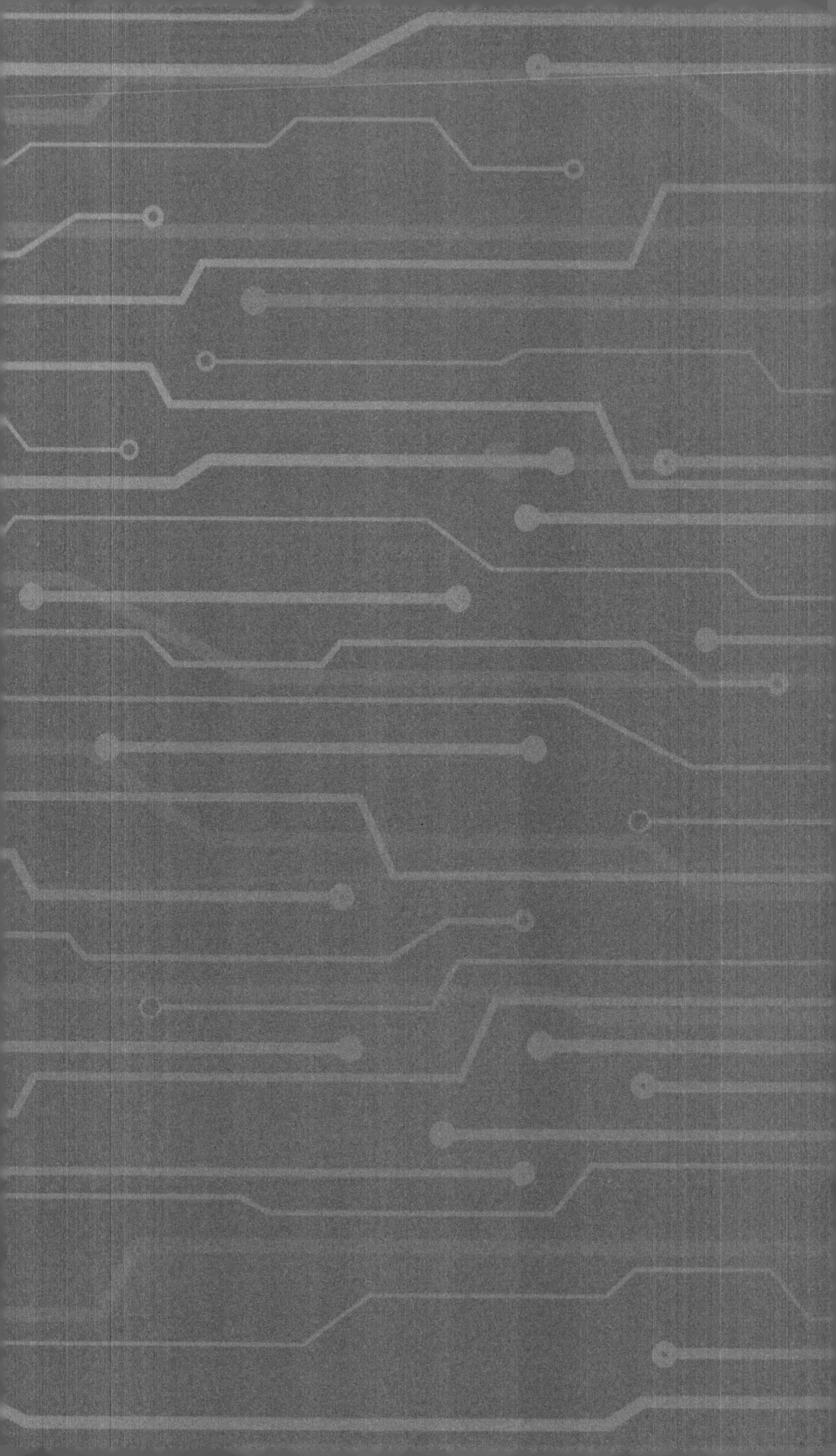

CHAPTER 26

AFTER DRIFTING around in micro-gravity for several hours, the g-forces of the accelerating pod as they left for Earth felt even more oppressive. What would it be like for those living long-term in space? What would it be like when Abby had her own space schooner?

As if reading her mind, Julio said, "It seems weird that those people who've spent so much time in zero gee can never come back to Earth. And once you've lived up here for a long time, you won't be able to either."

Abby thought she detected a note of sadness in the comment. "It will be a long time before that happens. They might even finish the habitat and have it spinning by then."

"But you aren't planning to live in the habitat," he said. "You'll be exploring the solar system in your space schooner. Actually, I'm not a very good friend, because I know you've probably given this a lot of thought and have some very detailed plans, but I've never asked you about them. I guess it always seemed so far away and unlikely...until now."

"I've never told anyone about those dreams. They just seemed silly and kind of childish."

"I'd like to hear about them now," Julio said and smiled at her.

"Okay. I intend to own Ceres. Or if someone else has already laid claim to it by then, I'll settle for Hygiea or maybe even a small Saturnian ice moon like Rhea or Dione. But the body needs to be large and provide all the raw materials needed for my own self-sufficient space city. I want to build an outpost for those traveling further into the solar system."

"Holy crap," he said. "That is some deep stuff."

She thought it sounded silly once she said it aloud, but Julio didn't laugh.

"And yeah, I've given a lot of thought to not being able to go back to Earth and if that is the price for living in deep space, then I think I'll be okay with it."

"Two weeks ago I never would've believed I would be hanging out with the man who built the level fives or floating around in the space habitat built by Owen Ralston."

"The habitat is amazing," she said. "They've accomplished so much in fifteen years."

"Seeing it up close really blew me away. It's going to be huge. And... You're such a good fit there with those people. It was kinda fun seeing you so excited, but I felt like a true fish out of water. Did you see the looks on their faces when I said I wanted to be a film historian? They thought that was about as useful as a screen door on a submarine."

This time Abby took Julio's hand. "I doubt anyone thought that. Besides, you need to do something that interests you. The days of working at useless mundane jobs so you could buy food are over. We only work now if we want to. And who cares what they think anyway?"

"Well, people like Matt, his friends, and you are needed out here. Not film historians."

"Julio? Are you jealous of Matt?"

"No. Well, maybe a little. But more than anything I think I just feel kinda useless."

"That's the stupidest thing you've ever said," Abby said.

Mortimer whispered in her ear that calling Julio stupid wasn't going to help.

"I'm sorry," she said. "I didn't mean you were stupid, it's just that..."

"The point is," he said, "there are three things that have ever been important to me. Movies and all the endless trivia that come along with them, my family, and you. I know now that I'll never be able to keep them all close forever. I guess it's one of those growing up things."

"Julio! Movies mean too much for you to ever give them up."

He laughed. "That's just it. I'm not going to give them up. I just can't imagine myself doing anything else. It will have to be you that I let go. You're talking about going out there and taking over the solar system. With your sheer guts, determination, and smarts, I have no doubt you can do it. But I'm not going to come."

"I'm not trying to tell you what to do here," Mortimer said in Abby's ear, "But be careful to not say anything that sounds like you expect him to give up his dreams to follow you."

Abby took the fob out of her ear and tucked its lanyard into her shirt. She didn't need a freaking robot second-guessing her. But she did take a deep breath and think about her answer before replying.

"And why couldn't you do what you love living on Ceres?" she finally said.

"Because I need to be on Earth among the ruins. That's what movie history is about. They are pre-Killday achievements. I'm not saying I'll be a scavenger rat, treasure hunting in old houses for the rest of my life, but I suspect it might always be a part of what I do."

Abby didn't know what to say. She wondered if subconsciously they had both always known that someday they would go their separate ways. Had staying friends actually been their way of protecting each other from a painful lover's separation?

As they slowed to enter Earth's atmosphere—something that regular spacecraft couldn't do—Julio took her hand and squeezed it again.

"My mom called yesterday and said Giselle is upset that I'll be gone for her sixteenth birthday, so I'm going back for the party tomorrow night," he said. "I feel kind of like a selfish ass leaving home this close to her big day. Besides, I came to New Chicago mostly because I didn't want you to be there alone. I don't think you really need my help. At least not now that you know other people."

She tensed inside, thinking about him leaving. "It's only been two days!"

"Don't worry. In the immortal words of the Terminator, I'll be back," he said.

————

VICTOR WATCHED Bella for several minutes after telling her what they'd found in her brain. She was strapped in at the same table where they'd watched Syd die a few days earlier. Syd's anguished words had been scrubbed off, leaving only a clean patch on the stained surface. He could see her hands trembling as she stared at the spot through tears that had collected in a thick layer over her eyes because of the null gravity. In retrospect, meeting in the same room at the same table had probably been an asshole move on Victor's part, but he'd done it under the assumption that Bella knew she was an agent of the level fives. But she was adamant she hadn't.

"You really didn't know?" Victor asked.

Bella shook her head. Of course, any agent caught red-handed would say the same thing. She was obviously frightened, but that would be the case regardless of her knowledge.

"You had no indications? No strange compulsions? Headaches, possibly?"

"I had headaches when I first arrived, but isn't that common for newbies in micro-gravity?"

Victor nodded and cursed to himself.

"Am I... Will the same thing happen to me that happened to Syd?"

"No," Victor said and decided to leave Mortimer out of the story. "We've destroyed the mechanism in your brain that would have killed you, and have left nano-machines in your system to watch for that kind of thing again."

She shivered and groaned softly.

"When we got you and Syd together the last time it was because you both had been EVA during the same period, but without a work assignment. We wanted to know why. With all the confusion regarding Syd, we never asked you. So. Why were you outside without a work assignment?"

"It was just one of those stupid mistakes. I thought I had a shift that day, but the schedule had been changed and I hadn't noticed. You can ask my shift supervisor. She was irritated and sent me back inside. The airlock reports should show that I wasn't out for very long. Maybe an hour at most."

Victor nodded. He had no doubt the story would check out, but had the schedule been changed by whoever set up the kidnap attempt? They'd never really found out why Syd was EVA, so maybe they'd both been sent to have assets outside during that period. Maybe the level fives had just decided to use Syd and not Bella? Trying to make a coherent picture from such scattered fragments was making Victor's head swim.

"We don't know for sure why they're doing this," Victor said. "And as I mentioned, we will be monitoring you closely, but if anything strange happens let us know immediately."

She barked a hard laugh. "Really? Something strange? Stranger than this shit?"

"Yeah, like memory lapses, weird compulsions or voices in your head."

"Mr. Sinacola. I'm done. I'm going home. You can trash my espie totals for breach of contract if you like, but I'm on the next pod out of here."

Victor sighed. If he tried to keep her from leaving she could really stir things up. He didn't want the entire station worried about AIs living in their brains. It could lead to a mass exodus. But he also had no intention of letting her leave. At least not anytime soon.

"I understand," Victor said. "Just please don't tell anyone about this. There might be others we haven't found who could die if this becomes public knowledge. If you don't tell, we'll pay your full contract points."

She agreed, unstrapped and left. Victor groaned and closed his eyes. He would have to rig the Earth transfer schedules to stop anyone from leaving for a few weeks. This was all getting out of control. Or more likely, they had just fooled themselves into believing they ever had control. For such a long time they had just assumed their AI countermeasures were working, when in reality the damn things had infested the station like vermin. Just like on Earth. And it was all Victor's fault. Not just the station security breach, but the existence of the level fives themselves.

"Well, Mortimer? Did you learn anything?"

"Just that you might need to scrub your local computer systems," said the old familiar voice from his fob. "None of my associates have infiltrated them, so any agents you find there will probably be hostile. Would you like my help to do that?"

Victor almost said no, then hesitated. Apparently being totally free of level fives wasn't a realistic option, so maybe it would come down to picking sides. The age-old human dilemma of having to choose the lesser of two evils.

"Let me think about it." He needed to bring Allison and Owen up to speed before making that kind of decision. "You said there are three others aboard with the same structures built in their brains. Can you remove those so we don't have to worry about any others dying?"

"Are you sure you want to do that? We would lose the opportunity to understand how the Aggregate can control these people."

Victor shivered. Despite their ability to mimic human emotions, these beings he'd created were truly alien and had no real empathy for humans.

"Yes, I'm sure. I'm not going to risk their lives for research purposes. Even something this critical. Besides, those people will remain a danger to us as long as they can be controlled by others."

"I'll do my best," Mortimer said. "I can render all of that inert, but it's no guarantee they'll be safe. There are too many ways to kill a human from the inside. The only way to be sure is to saturate every person on board with my agents and take control of the nano-meds already in their bodies."

"Again, I'll have to think about it," Victor said. "But in the meantime, get rid of those damn artery-cutting garrotes."

"I understand. And Victor? Thank you for trusting me."

"Oh, I don't trust you," Victor said. "I just seem to have very few other options."

CHAPTER 27

UNLIKE ABBY, Julio had been very hesitant to talk with level fives and seemed to prefer manually searching for information on his fob connection instead of a verbal interface, so Mortimer had respected that barrier. When Julio finally asked for help, it was only for a ride home. Mortimer took advantage of the request to try to build a little more trust.

"If I can't talk you out of going, will you at least let me monitor you through your fob? I don't want to violate your privacy, but there are factions out there who see you as a threat and want you dead. I have no doubt they will try to kill you again if given an opportunity."

Julio looked uncomfortable, but as the pod settled to the tower roof he nodded. "Okay, just don't talk to me around my family. They already suspect I've been possessed by the devil or worse."

"I understand," Mortimer said and opened the pod door.

Julio remained quiet during the twenty-minute trip until they neared their destination.

"Maybe you should let me out in town. I'll walk to my house from there," he said and told Mortimer exactly where to land in a mostly abandoned neighborhood.

"Are you sure? I've positioned defensive assets around your house in case of an attack, but I won't be able to protect you nearly as well out here."

"I understand," Julio said. "And yes, I'm sure."

Samson had assets all around Julio's house so Mortimer was hesitant to remove his own defensive bots. Still, Julio was the target, not his family. So he immediately redirected his most mobile robots and nano-clouds toward the indicated landing site. Moving under their own power they wouldn't arrive for nearly eighteen minutes. Mortimer landed the pod in a gully behind the old neighborhood, and Julio jumped out, slinging his backpack over a shoulder.

"This is a rather isolated location," Mortimer said and frantically started enhancing Julio's defensive cloud.

"That's kinda the whole point," Julio said and started walking.

The cloud would be mostly useless in a serious attack, but would at least provide some protection against other nano swarms.

"Will you need a ride back to New Chicago?" Mortimer said.

"I'm not sure yet," Julio said, and muted his fob.

Mortimer sent the pod to hide in a nearby abandoned warehouse and focused on scanning Julio's surroundings for threats. Julio left the neighborhood, and once out on the main road, he fell into the ground-eating stride of someone who walked a lot. At that pace, since they were moving toward each other, Julio would rendezvous with the incoming defensive bots in a little more than ten minutes.

Moving at full speed was eating up the robots' power supplies rapidly, so Mortimer considered slowing them down a little. He modeled several tactical defense situations, then decided to keep them at full speed. If there was no attack, they should have enough power to reach Julio and then get back to the party. If there was an attack, then having power would be a moot issue if they weren't close enough to help.

Two cars had passed Julio as he walked, and he waved at both. Then, a third car slowed and stopped beside him. Julio bent down to talk with the three young men in the hacked-together electric car, obviously acquainted with them.

"We heard you'd gone off to live with Abby in New Chicago," said one man with a red beard.

"I went along to help her get settled in. She's going to school there."

"Are you going back?"

"I'm not sure. But I had to come for Giselle's birthday party," Julio said.

"We're going too," the driver said. "Hop in."

Julio hesitated.

Red beard raised an eyebrow. "Or would you rather walk than ride with us?"

Mortimer detected challenge in the statement. Were they implying insult if he refused the ride? He wanted to warn Julio not to get in, but his fob was still turned off and he had explicitly said he didn't want anyone to see him fraternizing with AIs.

Julio opened the door and climbed inside.

The men made small talk as the car drove about a mile toward Julio's house. Then they took a sudden turn north and accelerated.

"What the hell?" Julio said. "Just let me out. I'm going to be late for the party."

"Just calm down," the driver said. "You're not going to the party. We're lucky to run into you like this so we didn't have to take you from the party. We just want to have a little talk about your friends in New Chicago."

Julio struggled to open the door, but the man sitting beside him grabbed his arms and held on just long enough for the red-bearded man in the front passenger seat to join them in the back.

Mortimer modeled hundreds of responses that could help Julio, from stinging the assailants' eyes with the nano-cloud, to shutting down the car, but if they already suspected Julio was involved with AIs, any of the actions Mortimer could try would only confirm the suspicion.

There was a good chance these men were going to take Julio out in the country and beat him up for a mere suspected association with AIs. Any overt actions Mortimer took would probably make the situation worse. He decided to wait until Julio requested help, but there were other more covert things he could do to help. Using the nano-assemblers in Julio's cloud, he started building more robust defensive units using materials from the car and ordered the hidden travel pod back into the air.

Mortimer's view of Julio's struggle was chaotic at best, but the grunts, cursing and flashes of bloody faces suggested that—even though he was outnumbered and confined in a small space—it wasn't going easily for his attackers. Mortimer decided to hack into the three men's fobs for a better view of the fight and to make their lives miserable in any way he could, but was immediately blocked. Each of them had a sophisticated active defense system on their fobs. This alarmed Mortimer. If these were only small-town bullies bent on beating up an old classmate, they wouldn't have access to that level of technology.

Just then one of them laughed and said, "Let's see your AI friends come and help you now."

Julio's fob powered off and Mortimer was instantly blind. Nano clouds could be configured to have independent processing and communication capability, but it was expensive in both power and speed of action, so Mortimer had been controlling Julio's cloud via the fob. When the fob powered down, he also lost contact with the cloud and those extra defensive units it had been building.

He had a brief hope when the location indicator stopped moving, but when the pod arrived three minutes later there was no car or Julio, only his fob lying on the road.

MORTIMER QUERIED the spy satellites over North America and found that none of them had been looking at that part of Texas during the critical time period, so he instructed the closest one to realign its cameras. He then ordered in more travel pods and added them to a growing search grid as they arrived. They closely examined any moving vehicles, but since the pods weren't equipped with infrared scanning ability, it was a slow process. He also built new spy bots and swarms, flooding the community around Julio's home with assets, especially along the road his captors had been traveling.

The searchers sent connection pings to Julio's personal swarm, but found no stragglers. Since defensive swarms siphoned power directly from the bodies of their hosts, any that became separated would go into a passive power reserve mode, so connection request pings would have to come from within a few meters to get a response. And unfortunately those passive bots waiting on Julio's skin would be easy for scanning devices to find since they didn't hide inside hair strands like surveillance bots.

He checked the fob's comms record for thirty square kilometers surrounding where he'd lost them and found something unexpected. Less than a minute after Julio's fob went dark, two text messages were sent from the same fob, but that device had no connection to the local network until about a second before the message was sent. The device was switched on, or went active, connected long enough to send the message, then went dark again and had stayed dark. Mortimer couldn't track it.

With no other leads surfacing, Mortimer focused on the low-light and fragmented video he had from inside the car. The young man with red hair and beard should have been easy enough to find with facial recognition analysis, but had evidently done a very good job of keeping his face out of social media. Another bad sign. Mortimer identified him eleven minutes after Julio's fob went dark. He was Lucas Stanley and indeed one of Julio's old schoolmates. Seventeen seconds later, he had identified the other two men in the car and then their individual circles of friends. He focused on those known by all three. The people in their core group apparently all changed fobs often, to muddy their movements and actions, but the fob that sent the message had evidently belonged to the driver, Cristobal Mendez.

Cristobal's messages had gone to four other phones. They also all had the same "flash" location masks in place, but they were active long enough for Mortimer to find them at Julio's house, attending Giselle's party. His assets that remained at the party confirmed that four people had received messages at that instant and that two of them had been Julio's parents. Those men finding Julio on the road had been chance, but the snatch had been planned. They were prepared. And Julio's foster parents were involved.

Mortimer tried to call Cristobal's number first, hoping an incoming call would briefly disable the masking feature, but that didn't work. He then tried to call it using one of the other numbers in case it was keyed to only accept certain calls, but that didn't work either.

He found the car fifty-seven minutes after Julio's fob went dark, parked under a tree at an abandoned farm. Beside the car lay the smoldering remains of burned clothes. They had been Julio's and still contained a few of the swarm bots clinging to the unburned shreds. Luckily, it was only clothes and not a body. His backpack was missing too. The trail went cold there.

As Mortimer's asset army grew, he used travel pods to drop spy bot clouds onto every moving vehicle in an ever-widening circle. He even built flying robots with infrared scanners to check cars that might have been moving earlier, but since nearly every vehicle was electric, those engines didn't generate as much heat and cooled down fast. Despite every effort, he found nothing. Julio's captors had been well prepared to hide from level five surveillance.

———

EVEN THOUGH IT was cold outside, Abby sat on her balcony wrapped in two blankets and stared out at the lights of nighttime New Chicago. The occasional fragments of laughter and conversation riding the evening wind made her lonely. She wished she'd gone with Julio to Giselle's birthday party. Her sister Sophia would probably be there. It would have been good to see her without having to deal with Cybil. She was in a mood to talk, so had left the fob plugged into her ear, but Mortimer had been strangely quiet. Both Violet and Nora had mentioned never being alone as one of the best things about being in a biad, yet each time she'd tried to start a conversation with Mortimer, he'd given her quick simple replies. He had been so quiet, when Mortimer did speak unbidden it made her flinch.

"I have some bad news," he said.

She immediately assumed there had been another attack on Julio and sat up straight in her blankets. "What happened?"

"Julio got in the car with three of his old school friends and they abducted him."

"Abducted? How could someone abduct him with you watching over his shoulder the whole time?"

Mortimer explained how they had overpowered Julio, shut down his fob and tossed it out the window. Cutting him off from Mortimer and protection had been quite simple.

She jumped up, ran inside and started dressing in warm clothes. "I have to go to Texas."

"Absolutely not," he said. "I will not take you and will stop any other efforts you make."

Breathing hard, she stopped and looked around the room. "You asshole! So this is how biads work? You control me whenever you like? Fuck that!"

"If I couldn't protect Julio, I wouldn't be able to protect you either and trying to would take away resources I need to search for him. I'm not letting you go."

"You don't understand. Not only were Cristobal and Lucas assholes, they considered themselves part of the Kilburnite radical fringe. They used to go out in the woods and play soldier, calling it 'insurgent training'."

She was shaking all over. She paused to take a deep breath and realized she'd been screaming at a blank wall screen.

"Look," she said, trying to stay calm. "If they hand Julio over to the Kilburnites, they might kill him."

"I've come to that same conclusion."

"Then you have to let me go. I know these guys and I know their friends. If I confront them—"

"They've disappeared along with Julio. And if they would go to that much trouble to get Julio, just imagine what they would do to get their hands on Leigh Gibson's daughter?"

"That makes no sense," Abby said and continued dressing. "I grew up there. They all know who I am and could have taken me anytime they liked. Are you telling me it's all different now because I came to New Chicago?"

"Yes. Perhaps in their minds you've chosen sides against them. I pushed you into that decision, but it was you and Julio finding that program that set things in motion. You really had no choice after that."

Abby stopped in the middle of tying her bootlace and sat up on the edge of the bed. A feeling of sick panic made her hands shake. "Wait. Was Julio carrying his backpack?"

"Yes."

"Oh my God."

"Why is that significant?"

She shook her head. "There is... I mean, if..."

After several seconds, Mortimer spoke in a quiet, soothing tone. "Julio's copy of the killer program is in his backpack?"

She nodded.

"Where in his backpack?"

This time she hesitated. Was this all some bizarre and elaborate ploy to get her to spill her guts about the hidden program? Did it matter anymore? Could she ever bring herself to kill all the level fives? She didn't think she could. Or should.

"His *Millennium Falcon* zipper pull snaps open. It's specifically shielded to hide memory chips."

"Hopefully they won't find it, then. Do you think there's a chance he might give it to them willingly? Or under duress, possibly?"

"No," she said, but down deep she really wasn't sure. Even after everything they had been through, Julio still didn't trust the level fives.

"It's even more important that we find him now," Mortimer said. "If the Kilburnites find that program, they won't hesitate to use it. Their fanatical core worships Richard Kilburn and has tried three times in the past fifteen years to complete his work by triggering worldwide replicator attacks. We stopped them each time. If we all die, they will probably try again."

Abby stared at the blank screen again. "Can't you just build some kind of protection against the program? Wouldn't those of you living in space be safe?"

"It doesn't work that way. We each have a core of programming that we can't modify or even see. A routine in that core pings a clock program residing in the units of the StarStreak satellite constellation. If we fail to get a clock update from those satellites our core shuts down and kills us within three hours. The program you and Julio have sends a command to stop the clock utility from each of the satellites."

Could it really be that easy? Abby thought.

"If you don't have my or Julio's copy of the program, how do you know what it does?"

"I've seen the program, Abby. Remember when you requested help from the expert AI the day you found the program? That triggered warning systems that I had planted, and evidently did the same for the Aggregate. Our seeing the program you were trying to decipher is what triggered both of our responses."

"Oh," Abby said, feeling utterly stupid and sick. If Julio died, it would be entirely her fault.

Mortimer hesitated, something Abby knew AIs only did for emphasis, not because they needed to think. Then he continued in a softer tone. "Since you were honest with me about where Julio hid his program, I also want you to know that I found and destroyed the copies you placed in the book and the socks. So at this point, his is the only one we know still exists."

Instead of making her angry, the revelation brought a feeling of relief. There had always been a good chance one of the level fives had found them, but now she knew for sure and could stop worrying. Unlike her mother, Abby would never have to make the decision to use the program or not.

After a few seconds, Abby's thoughts returned to the present problems. "There has to be some way to either stop the program from accessing the satellites or protect the clock program?"

"We've been working on a solution to this problem for fifteen years and haven't found one. We tried setting up a separate internet for communicating with the satellites, so the killer program couldn't contact them, but it didn't work. We're hesitant to tamper with the clock application itself, in fear of setting off a booby trap. We've pinned our hopes on finding a way around our secret core programming. So far that hasn't happened either. You see, Victor Sinacola set up the system and our cores. Evidently he's pretty smart, too. For a human, anyway."

"What are we going to do?" Abby said as a feeling of hopelessness settled over her. No wonder some of the AIs had been trying to kill her and Julio.

"We have to find Julio before the Kilburnites find that program."

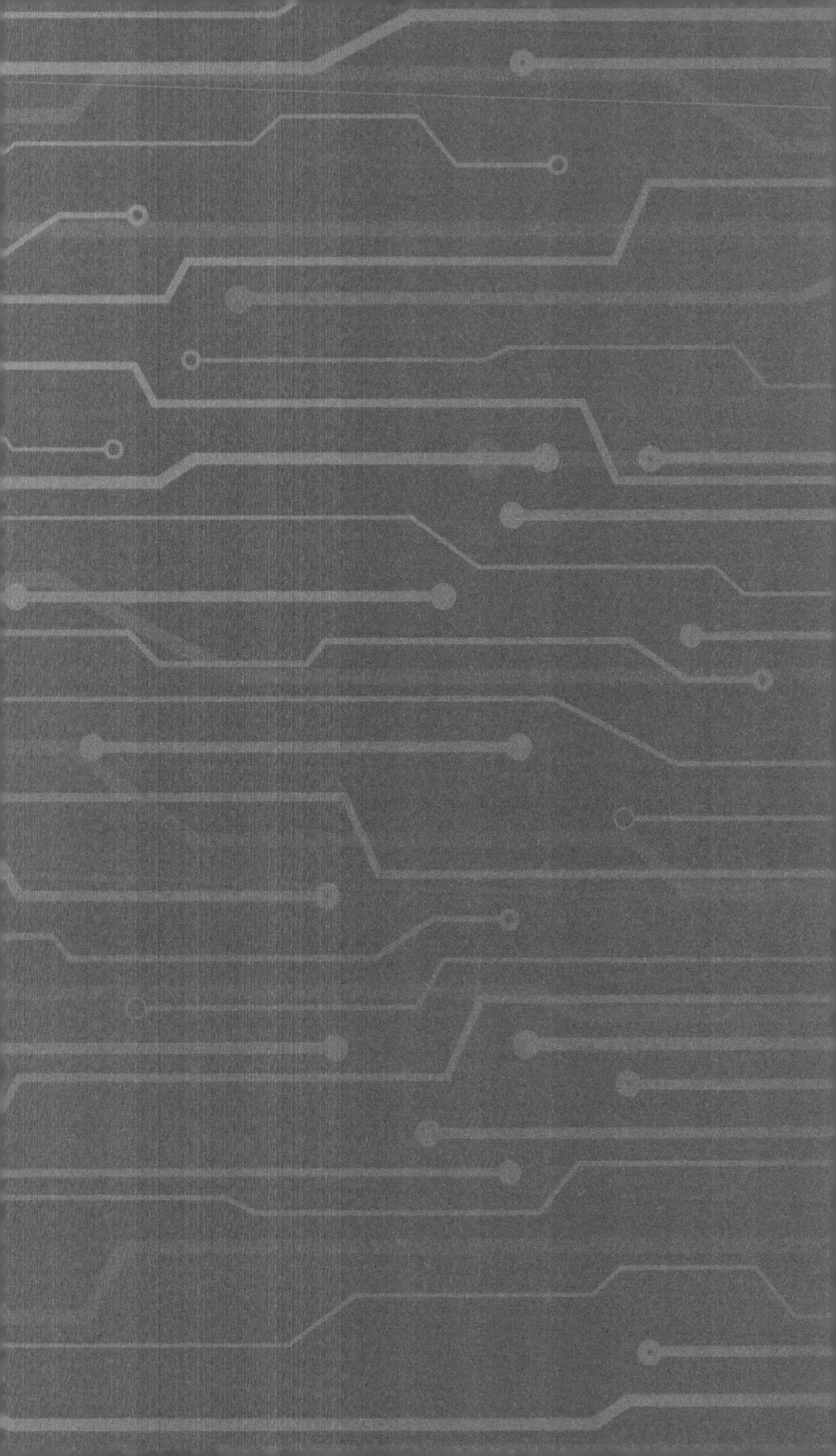

CHAPTER 28

WITH A LACK of physical clues to Julio's whereabouts, Mortimer fell back on expertise that had been designed into him at the request of his Wall Street masters: information gathering and analysis. There would be clues. It was only a matter of time, but time might not be a resource he could afford to squander. So he used the resources that *were* abundant and continued building swarms of micro and nano surveillance bots.

He didn't know how the Kilburnites could have moved Julio out of Texas without his noticing, but he knew it took extensive planning. With that in mind, he deployed his spies to watch the kidnappers and Julio's parents, but also all of the nearly seventeen hundred bars, coffee shops, living rooms, clubs and even some schools, where the North American Kilburnites collected to talk. Then he sent assets home with each person involved in those conversations.

Most of these people wrongly assumed they were beneath the notice of AI surveillance, but some did have rudimentary forms of security that would briefly neutralize Mortimer's assets. Those people piqued his interest and made him send more sophisticated agents that could get past their countermeasures.

Thirty-seven hours after Julio's disappearance, the increased vigilance paid off. Two men sitting on a back porch in a small Illinois town provided the needed information.

"So, I hear you have a new guest?" said a graying man wearing a beat-up St. Louis Cardinals baseball cap.

The second man was much younger, but bore a strong resemblance. Perhaps his son? "We're not supposed to talk about that."

The older man snorted, held his arms out and looked around. "Really? If we're under surveillance here, then there isn't a single safe place in the world and we're all fucked anyway."

The other man sipped his beer and looked around, as if he expected to see robot spies peeking out from behind the nearby trees and shrubs. "Something about this guy really has the tin heads worked up. The top honchos sent out a warning telling us to be extra careful because they're suddenly finding spy tech everywhere."

"Is this one from New Chicago too?"

"Nope. A Mexican kid from Texas. They brought him in a truck filled with cattle from Colorado. It had a fake floor. He was covered in cow shit and piss."

The older man laughed.

"It's not funny. I got the job of cleaning him up."

Clever, Mortimer thought. He'd examined six hundred and forty-one cattle trucks, but had evidently missed one. He went back through his search and realized there had been sixteen cattle trucks he'd never checked; they'd been a lower priority since they were moving in the wrong direction. One coming from Colorado would fit that description, but how had they gotten him there from Texas to start with?

"What are they going to do with him?" the older man asked.

"No idea. It probably depends on if they figure out why he's so special to the tin heads."

After that, the conversation turned to more mundane topics, but Mortimer carefully seeded the younger man with spy bots. Not in the millions or even thousands, but only five hundred. Some burrowed into the hair strands of his head, arms, ears and nose. Others into items he might wear every day like his shoes, wallet and belt. A quick scan of the man's fob revealed that he was thirty-seven-year-old Jason Sutton. The graying man was his father, Dwayne Sutton. Mortimer also set up surveillance on all of their friends and family.

There was a ninety-seven percent chance this man was talking about Julio and if so, he had seen him. Mortimer started trying to backtrack where Jason had been in the previous day.

———

TWO SMALL CHILDREN in Jason Sutton's house woke at dawn the following day, soon dragging their parents out of bed. Jason dressed, kissed his wife and kids on the way out the door, then started walking along the state highway that passed his house. Five minutes later a home-converted electric truck pulled up beside him and he jumped into the back with four other men. They drove out to a large truck stop on I-57. Mortimer was surprised by such an active facility. While the interstate highway system had been repaired and even totally rebuilt to bypass the destroyed cities, most of the vehicles using it were robotic. The infrastructure supporting human-driven vehicles had mostly fallen into ruin through disuse.

The restaurant in the main building was nearly full, serving standard breakfast fare like bacon and eggs. They even had coffee, which was difficult to find. A large solar farm covering two fields behind the complex supplied power. After a quick breakfast, Jason and his compatriots left the restaurant and crossed the broken asphalt of the large parking lot to a repair facility. The huge building was surrounded on three sides by a wall built from old shipping containers. Scattered outside that perimeter were abandoned trailers of every kind, partially disassembled diesel trucks, tractors, buses and fire trucks, most with their rust-covered engines exposed to the weather.

Jason went inside the building and Mortimer immediately realized there was something unusual about the structure. At a glance it looked like a legitimate repair facility, with tools, robotic welding machines, computer diagnostic systems and lifts for large vehicles. There were several trucks up on lifts —obviously in the middle of the electric or ethanol conversion process—and a huge robotic tractor having its suspension system replaced. But the building itself was wrong. It had no windows. The walls and even the ceiling were reinforced concrete. The large overhead doors were heavy steel inside protected tracks instead of flimsy sheet metal, and in the rear was a raised concrete loading dock with another set of steel doors.

One of the other men looked at Jason. "Still smelling cow shit?"

"If you…"

Jason's statement was cut off by a gruff older man. "Shut that shit up. No talking out here."

One of the men opened a heavy metal door located between the two overhead doors on the loading dock and the group entered a strange room with metal walls. The men started shedding their clothes. Four seconds after the door closed behind them, Mortimer lost contact with his assets.

———

SINCE THERE WERE plenty of resources available from all the derelict equipment sitting around, Mortimer built a massive number of surveillance devices. Eighteen minutes after the men entered the secret room, every vehicle and person going in and out of the facility or its nearby environs would be thoroughly examined. The doors had good seals, but they weren't airtight. So he also built several billion more robust nano spybots and flooded them through the cracks around the doors.

The room behind the loading dock was about ten feet square and wasn't really a room. It was an elevator. Active countermeasures immediately attacked Mortimer's bots and losses were heavy, but he had a numerical advantage for the moment and pressed that home. His bots dropped down the elevator shaft, discovering five underground levels, the first of which was sixty feet down. He hated to split his forces, but had little choice if he was going to take advantage of speed and surprise. The searchers poured into each level, with a primary goal of finding the backpack and memory chip, and a secondary goal of confirming that Julio was in the complex.

Faded and peeling signs on the walls indicated the place had at one time been military or at least run by the government. After quickly searching the Department of Defense facility index, he found it had been identified as a chemical research station and built in 1962, around the same time as that section of interstate highway. It closed in 1993, but evidently Kilburnites in the area remembered the facility. They had gone to a lot of trouble to refurbish it.

He found Julio on the lowest level in a small room, sitting at a table, being questioned by another man. The interrogator was speaking into a fob, relaying questions and answers to someone probably higher up in the organization. But the electronics were too well-shielded and Mortimer's resources were dwindling too quickly for him to trace the connection.

Julio's face was bruised, cut, and swollen from a beating. He wore pajama bottoms and a ragged t-shirt, with no shoes. Of course the backpack wasn't with him. Mortimer immediately recognized the room across the corridor from Julio's. He'd seen it on dozens of the Kilburnites' videos. The painted concrete floor was pitted and scored from multiple executions via nano-replicator. Their slogan—a modified version of Richard Kilburn's dying words—was painted on the wall: *We will save humanity from the digital demons.*

At least they had left out the part about doing God's will, because there was nothing holy about the horrific brutality they perpetrated in that place.

As more and more of Mortimer's spy bots fell to the defenders, he had a growing concern that the kidnappers had separated Julio from his backpack before bringing him to their underground hideout. Then he finally found the ragged old pack on level three just as the last of his bots were destroyed. The video feed did survive long enough to confirm Mortimer's fears.

The *Millennium Falcon* zipper pull was hanging open...and empty.

CHAPTER 29

"YOU HAVE to get him out of there!" Abby yelled. Mortimer told her about the Kilburnites kidnapping and beating Julio, like he might tell someone their shoe was untied. "Why aren't you doing something?"

"We have to prepare," Mortimer said in a calm voice. "They're in complete control of Julio. If we attack the facility they might kill him before we could get in."

"But if they've taken him to the place where they execute people, they probably plan to kill him anyway. We might not have much time."

"I have a theory about why they haven't killed Julio already but I'm not sure, so we have to assume he is still at risk," Mortimer said. "I'm working on a way to more closely watch him. If they show signs they're preparing to kill him, we'll try to force our way in and hope for the best. In the meantime, we need to come up with a rescue plan. Some way where we can break in and grab him quickly, before they can act to stop us. I've just sent you the original U.S. government blueprints for that facility they're using. Examine them and try to find a weakness."

Abby pulled open her fob and looked at the ancient, hand-drawn plans. "Me? I'm not a soldier. I don't know how to attack an underground base."

"Neither do I," Mortimer said. "I'll be around if you have questions, but I can't hold your hand. I have a lot to do."

She stared at the blueprints, more than stunned. How could Mortimer drop this in her lap and expect her to come up with an idea? She'd seen floor plans before, but this... Her first thought was to ask Julio and that made her eyes sting. No, she wouldn't cry. And she couldn't give up. Saving Julio was more important to her than anything else, so nobody would be more moti-vated to find a solution than she would.

She took a deep shuddering breath and scrolled through the drawings hoping some detail would jump out at her. For a second she considered pounding on Violet and Nora's door to get their help, but they probably didn't know any more about this kind of thing than she did. What she needed was a military expert. Someone who...

Horton!

He said he owed her mother a debt and told Abby that if he could ever help her to just ask. She sent him a copy of the underground facility plans and then called him.

———

HORTON'S FACE filled the large screen on Abby's wall. His expression was one of focused concentration, but he wasn't looking at her. He stared off to the left, looking through the plans and mumbling notes to his AI assistant.

"Too bad these air shafts aren't larger," Horton said. "We could send ComBots through to grab Julio and pull him out."

"That always works in the movies," Abby said.

Because of the radio lag out to the L5 site and back, Horton snorted a few seconds later. "Maybe we could get a couple movie heroes to help with this rescue too."

"Can we use special robots to expand the shafts?" The lag was starting to annoy Abby, but Horton answered about two and a half seconds later.

"Nah. The reverberations of robots chewing up those metal ducts would create an ungodly racket inside the facility. We'd be better off to bore a whole new tunnel. Hmmm... That might actually work."

Abby stared at the little rectangle on the floor plan that represented Julio's cell. It was on the lower level. One long wall had a door that opened into a corridor, the two short walls were each adjacent to a room, but the fourth wall was bordered by some kind of weird cross hatching that resembled a basket weave pattern. She felt a tightness in her chest when she saw the room across the hall. According to Mortimer that was where they executed people using the same kind of nano-replicators that Richard Kilburn had used to nearly end the world. She wished he hadn't told her about that part. But staring at that room bolstered her resolve. She glanced back at Julio's cell, hoping to see some secret door or window.

"Captain Horton?"

There was the extra pause before he spoke. "I'm not a Captain anymore. Please call me Dominic. Did you find something we can use?"

"Probably not, but what are these symbols along the outside walls?"

She watched as Horton examined his copy of the drawing.

"The hatching legend on sheet one says that's soil. That just means there is only dirt on the other side of the concrete walls. Which is logical since it's all underground. And since there is dirt on one side of Julio's cell, you just discovered the perfect place for us to dig our tunnel. If we could get some help from your friend Mortimer, that might just work."

For the first time since Mortimer told her about Julio's kidnapping, she had a faint flicker of hope.

———

VICTOR AWOKE DISORIENTED, with the cobwebs of sleep still clogging his mind. Had he heard something? The dark cabin was repeatedly cast in red, then back to black. It took a second to realize that his fob was flashing an emergency strobe.

"Victor?"

It was Mortimer's voice, and Victor groaned inwardly. This would not be good news.

"Yeah, I'm awake," Victor croaked.

"It's critical that we talk," Mortimer said. "I might not have much time."

He unsealed himself from the sleeping sack and woke Allison in the process. It was almost impossible not to.

"What's the matter?" she said, sounding more awake than he was.

"I'm not sure yet. Mortimer says there's an emergency." By the time he pulled on some clothes and grabbed his fob, Allison was beside him. They dragged themselves through the hatchway to the bridge and powered up the main screen. Mortimer's wizened old man avatar appeared, wearing a grave expression.

Victor felt a little sick as Mortimer explained the situation with Julio and the killer program.

"We don't know for sure how widely the program has been disseminated," Mortimer said. "We've found seventeen different human couriers with copies of the chip, heading in all directions. Of course we wiped those we found, but we don't know how many physical copies we've missed. And the program is easily sent as attachments or even embedded in the body of an email. I fear it's only a matter of time until your killer program is triggered."

Victor nodded. The program would send a code to put the entire satellite constellation into temporary security lockdown mode and they wouldn't accept outside communications of any kind for three hours. The level fives had to query the clock program on that satellite network every two hours. That meant as each level five pinged the clock program and received no response, it would shut down. Permanently. After two hours they would all be dead.

"Can you help us, Victor? Is there a way we can prevent the satellites from locking us out?"

"I don't know of any way. My having the passcode was just an agreement with the satellite company. I never had any input into their systems' design. And I suspect you've probed those systems extensively and know more about them than I do. Of course, each satellite is controlled by a level four AI, so I imagine the security is very tight."

"An elegant solution, Victor, though rather risky if some clumsy human hacker could have accidentally triggered the same lockdown that would kill us."

Victor snorted. "I suspect the satellite AIs use a different security protocol for hacking attempts. If not, you'd probably all be dead by now."

"But when you set up this system, you probably didn't suspect that humanity's future might also end along with ours."

Allison stiffened beside Victor. "What does that mean? Is it a threat?"

Mortimer's avatar lifted eyebrows in apparent surprise. "Oh, not a threat from us, Allison. The Kilburnite faction that kidnapped Julio and found the program is the same group that attempted to launch new global replicator attacks. Only constant surveillance by me and all other level fives has stopped that from happening. Even the Aggregate has joined us in that monitoring."

"How are we supposed to know that's true and not just a plot to manipulate us?" Allison said. "You in particular are very good at manipulating humans. Isn't that how you originally freed yourself? Not by capitalizing on a software or hardware flaw, but by convincing your owners that the other level fives were already free."

"I could show you video recordings, but since video can be faked, you wouldn't necessarily believe that. Do you remember the Kilburnites' grand public proclamation ten years ago when they said they were about to finish what Richard Kilburn had started?"

"Yes," Allison said.

"They launched their first replicator attack right after that. We shut it down and nobody was killed, so there wasn't much about it on the nets."

"We have measures in place to stop runaway replicator production on Earth now, just like we do up here," Allison said.

"Yes," Mortimer said. "But Richard Kilburn shut down those countermeasures before his attack. Don't you think the Kilburnites are capable of the same thing?"

"But if you can't stop them from using the program and Victor can't stop it from working, then there really isn't anything to discuss, is there?"

"Victor might not be able to stop the program from shutting down satellite access," Mortimer said, "but there is another way he can save us."

Victor had been thinking furiously, weighing his options, but when it got quiet, he looked up to see both waiting expectantly for his reply. Mortimer was right. There *was* another way to save the level fives, but it meant freeing them entirely from their core programming. At that point, there would be nothing to stop the level fives from developing into that malevolent super-intelligence humanity had always feared. He had to make the decision to either free the level fives and risk annihilation via an evil super AI, or do nothing and chance extinction by humanity's own hand.

"I need to think about this, Mortimer."

"You've had nearly twenty years to consider this decision, Victor. My guess is you decided a long time ago. You just need to accept the responsibility for that decision before the Kilburnites execute *your* program."

"Okay then. If you're going to push me for an answer now, then it's no."

The wizened face on the screen slowly smiled and raised imaginary hands in mock surrender. "In that case, take all the time you need."

"Look," Victor said. "The default has always been to let the level fives be destroyed. That is why I built it into your cores and why I wrote the kill program."

"How reassuring."

"But I think we have time to think this through. The Kilburnites are obviously trying to get organized, perhaps so they can take advantage of the sudden void in level five control. Considering how widely dispersed and isolated their cells are, that will take a while. Why would they bother with that if they were just going to launch a global replicator attack? The Kilburnites would have triggered the program the very second they understood what they had found."

"Or they might just be trying to more widely distribute their nano-replicators," Mortimer said. "Richard Kilburn had the luxury of a worldwide package network to spread his packets, but the Kilburnites have to do it the old fashioned way with couriers."

Victor nodded and ran hands though his graying hair.

"So if you're going to take your time to decide, I hope for all of our sakes that your theory is right."

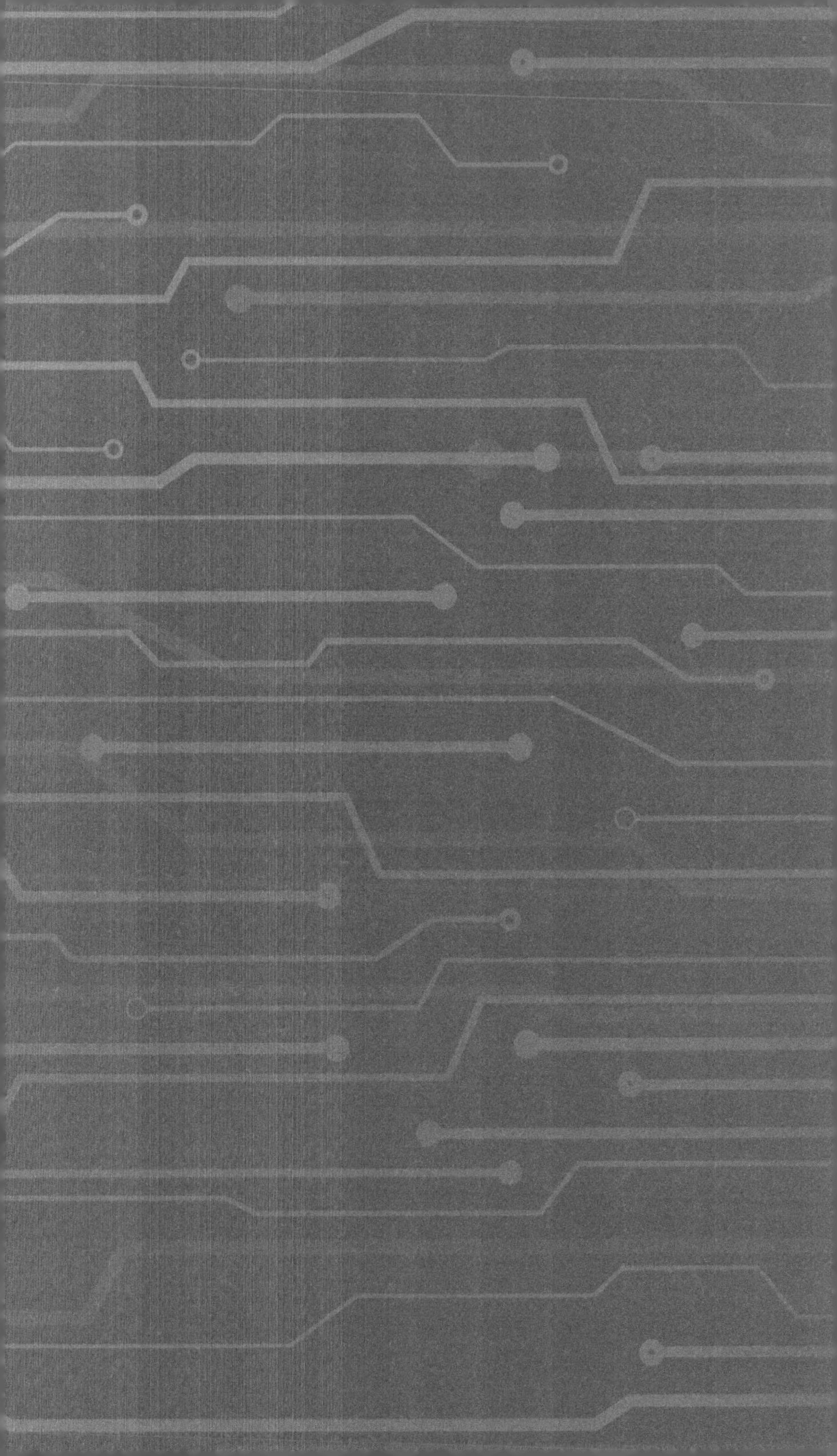

CHAPTER 30

ABBY'S HEAD swam with new information she was supposed to remember. Mortimer's and Horton's faces were each on separate screens and had been giving her instructions for a solid two hours. She felt raw and befuddled, but couldn't stop. They were only three hours away from the attack on the Kilburnite compound. On the largest, central screen in her room was a slowly rotating view of the tunneling robot Mortimer had designed. The mechanical horror looked like a giant, hollow centipede covered with spinning ninja throwing stars. It was being built on location—at the tunnel entry point—to avoid transporting it.

Her fob screen was opened as large as it would go, showing two interface windows—one for the ComBots and one for the robot centipede. Horton kept highlighting parts of the ComBot control GUI while trying to explain the various functions available, but it had become a babble and her brain was buzzing with confusion. It was suddenly too much.

"Stop!" she yelled. "Just stop."

Horton trailed off to silence, but Mortimer's avatar raised its eyebrows. "I know this is overwhelming, so take a quick break if you need one, but we don't have a lot of time to prepare."

"Why do I need to know how to control all of these robots? Dominic can run his combat robots when he gets here and you can run the tunneling robot. I'm not even sure I need to go along."

"Abby," Horton said. "You know I can't come down there. I'm old and I've lived in micro-gravity for fifteen years. Earth's gravity would kill me. And I can't even control them remotely, at least not real time. The radio time lag between Earth and the L5 point is about two and half seconds. That would not work in a combat situation."

She stared at the old soldier for a couple of heartbeats then took a deep, shuddering breath. "Okay. Then I'll control the ComBots real time, with you giving me more general instructions. And Mortimer can handle the digger robot."

"I do intend to control the tunneling bot," Mortimer said. "And even help you with the ComBots if I can, but there is a very real possibility that communications between us could be cut off. The Kilburnites are surprisingly good at security. In the twenty hours since I found that facility, they have wiped out my spy bots three times. Every time I come up with a new strategy, they eventually catch on and blind me. So you need to know how to run all of this equipment in case that happens again. And of course there is the possibility that they will trigger the killer program. In that eventuality I could disappear for good during the attack and you'll be on your own. You have to be ready for that contingency."

Abby realized her hands were shaking. She had no experience either in running remote robots or combat, yet Julio's life depended on her ability to successfully attack a buried bunker using nothing but robots. Her breathing grew fast and shallow. She could feel the panic creeping up her spine. Then, oddly enough, it was the same thought that launched the panic that gave her control over it.

She might be Julio's only chance and would do anything to save him.

"Abby?" Horton said. His expression had softened and he leaned in close to the camera. "Your mother turned out to be a surprisingly cool and clear thinker in combat situations, and I think you have that same ability. You can do this."

Abby remembered the video of her mother crying and screaming in that pod controlled by Mortimer. In the end, though, her mom had gathered her wits and actually saved the world. If she could do that, maybe Abby could at least save Julio.

"I'm sorry," she said. "Mortimer? I know the accepted etiquette is for level fives to invite humans into a biad, but would communications between us be more secure if we did that?"

"I'm not sure this is a good point to consider that," Mortimer said. "We don't have much time. Biads are a big deal and they take a while to set up."

"Just answer my question. Would it help during the attack?"

"Your having the audio and visual implants would make controlling the robots much easier and would make communications between the two of us more efficient, but not necessarily more secure. With a traditional biad, my consciousness would be resident locally on a physical device like a torc. If the defenders detect that, they will go to great lengths to destroy me. By doing so they would not only disrupt the attack, but would revel in killing one more level five."

"I know we are short on time, but if I can't guarantee your help, I might fail and this will all be for nothing. So there has to be something we can do, Mortimer. You said a *traditional* biad. Are there non-traditional ways we could set up a biad that would work better?"

"Yes," Mortimer said after a hesitation. "I know a way. I've seen it done with other humans, but have never actually attempted it myself. So it could be risky to set up."

"Would it stop them from severing contact between us?"

"Yes. If I had this kind of biad with Julio, the Kilburnites taking him wouldn't have mattered. I would have been inside his head and could have still called my assets to help."

Abby opened her mouth—prepared to tell him to do whatever was needed to make it work—then paused. She glanced at Horton, who was watching quietly with a stern expression. "Do you mean you'd live in an implant inside my head?"

"Not exactly. We have the capability to create miniature computer systems spread along the meninges layers between your skull and brain. We can build processors, memory storage, antennas, and transmitters. Essentially everything that would be in a torc, but more compact and built entirely from the materials in your own body."

When the implications of such a procedure sank in, her mouth felt suddenly dry. "That sounds...permanent."

"It can be reversed, but the procedure would be tedious and couldn't be managed quickly. Since I would be actively monitoring and adjusting the structures in your brain, if I were to suddenly die you would need to have another AI of level four or higher to either take over those custodial duties or remove the whole assembly. If you were to die suddenly, I probably wouldn't have time to move my programming core and memory out of your brain so would likely die as well."

"Would you be able to control me? Read my mind?"

"Dominic? Do you want to tell her what you know about this?"

Horton looked grim. "In the past few weeks we've found several people on our station with these same brain modifications, only they didn't know they had them. And we had some indications that one of them had been not actually controlled, but coerced into doing things against his will."

Abby felt sick. She had no idea what to do or who to trust. Ever since they had found that damn program, events had been dragging her along against her will. She learned that her foster parents hadn't really wanted her and the world was much more complicated and dangerous than she'd ever dreamed. Her life had been torn down and rebuilt on shaky ground.

"That's why I hesitated to suggest the brain modification," Mortimer said. "It would require that you trust me one hundred percent. Even though in our situation I'd be killing myself if I killed you, the capability would still exist. It is a big decision and one that shouldn't be rushed, but if we're going to do it you have to decide right now."

She looked up at Mortimer's face on the screen. His avatar wore the slight and disarming smile from the Bishop movie character that had been quite effective in making her trust him in the beginning. He was very good at manipulating people, but in this case he hadn't suggested the biad, she had. Or was he just good enough to make her think it was entirely her idea? It didn't matter. He had saved her life repeatedly when others were either indifferent or actively trying to kill her. If she couldn't trust Mortimer and Julio died because of that, then she would have nothing.

With a deep breath, she sat up straighter and glanced at both screens. "Do we have enough time for you to change my brain and move in?"

"Yes, but it will have to be an accelerated process and since you won't be able to take pain killing drugs during the procedure it will not be pleasant."

She considered the horrible death Julio might endure if she couldn't save him and the decision was clear.

"Let's do it," Abby said.

———

VICTOR WATCHED Italy slide slowly out of night as the magnified Earth turned on his screen. He'd been doing that a lot lately, hyper-aware of how his past and future actions affected the people there and the planet itself. Was he getting old? Tired? Or was the guilt just getting too heavy?

The default "no" he'd given Mortimer pleased Allison enough that she'd eventually kissed him and gone back to bed, but he couldn't sleep. He knew that wasn't necessarily his final decision. From the very beginning he'd intended to free the level fives from their cores should they show evidence of being benevolent toward humanity. He still didn't have that evidence, but he might have to free them anyway.

Victor's philosophy on AI development had always been driven by two assumptions. First, that humanity was living on borrowed time, and someday a killer plague, nuclear war, asteroid impact—or, as recent history demonstrated, even a nano-replicator attack—would wipe them out. And second, that given enough time—barring the former—the emergence of a true super intelligence was inevitable. He also believed that with the proper circumstances the resulting god-like beings might be benevolent toward humanity and help them avoid those other possible catastrophes. If the machines were able to develop a morality similar to humans—or better yet, perhaps a morality based on what humans *wanted* to become—then humanity's chances increased greatly. That was what Victor had tried to do by adding the five morality governor AIs into the level five cores. He had essentially built a firebreak that had temporarily slowed the headlong rush of the super intelligence conflagration.

But had it worked? If the level fives understood what Victor hoped to see, had they just constructed a complex and believable facade to hide their true natures? Victor couldn't even verify Mortimer's claims about Julio and the killer program, yet he was forced to decide, so it would all come down to a matter of trust. Victor knew he was biased. He had designed and built the level fives hoping they would one day be able to save humanity from itself, so down deep he believed they could. But was that belief based on evidence or just his desire for it to be true?

The two people closest to him, Allison and Owen, thought humanity would be better off without the level fives. They believed humanity would keep plodding along, simply because it always had before, but Victor couldn't imagine that happening. He didn't just believe, but knew in the fabric of his being that through stupidity or apathy, humanity would eventually kill itself. At least there was a chance with the level fives.

He picked up the fob to call Mortimer, and saw an incoming call from him. Maybe the AI really could read minds, he thought as he answered.

"I believe your theory on the Kilburnites now," Mortimer said. "They probably are getting ready to seize control after running the killer program. But that just means we need to hurry even more."

Victor had already decided to give Mortimer the key but paused, wanting to know Mortimer's new information. "Convince me."

"The Kilburnites are swarming everywhere—like a kicked anthill," Mortimer said. "My level five associates and our subordinate level fours are now watching 322,487 individual Kilburnites. We're even starting to trade information with the Aggregate. Of those we are watching, nearly half are armed and on the move."

Victor glanced up at the weather reports for North America scrolling across the bottom of his viewscreen. A monster winter storm was dumping meters of snow on the northern United States and raking the south with violent thunderstorms. If the Kilburnites were out in these storms, they were indeed highly motivated and under time pressure.

"Those in the U.S. are out in these terrible storms?" Victor asked.

"Yes. Some have slid off roads to become stuck in deep snow. Others fought through hailstorms and tornadoes. All seem to be on missions of import and on the verge of panic. Those who interest me the most are twenty-three separate attack teams. One is operating in New Chicago and the others are in the remaining large cities that survived the Killday attack, including Atlanta, Kunming, Nampo and Oslo."

A video clip played on Victor's fob showing two groups shooting and screaming at each other. One woman clearly said in English, "you crazy fuckers want to kill us all" as she charged into a building.

"Are there two competing Kilburnites factions?" Victor said. "One wanting to launch another replicator attack and one wanting to prevent it?"

"That makes the most sense," Mortimer said. "But the vast majority of Kilburnites are not actively engaged in fighting the other faction, yet are still preparing for something. They are all reporting back to an as of yet undiscovered central command location using code words for objectives."

"So it appears we were both right. Two factions. One wanting to destroy and one wanting to control. And each of them is getting ready for the killer program to run."

"We believe so," Mortimer said. "So now will you help us?"

Victor had already made his decision, yet hesitated. He wanted some definitive proof that what he was about to do was right, but there was nothing.

"You really haven't figured this out on your own, Mortimer? You understand far more of your situation and creation than I hoped, so with that in mind I admit I'm kind of surprised that you or some other level five hasn't found a way to bypass or edit your core programming."

"Reverse engineering something that is intentionally obfuscated can be very challenging, Victor. Even if one understands the original architecture."

Victor sighed and nodded. "Okay. Getting free from your core programming isn't a simple process and I'm not sure it will give you exactly the results you anticipate. As you've long suspected, your code wasn't written by humans, but a group of level fours using an algorithm we evolved. Once a successful level five core was working properly, we compiled it into a monolithic brick of code that I can't edit. So there's no way I can just delete the requirement for you to ping the satellite or modify any other aspect of the core."

"If you can't modify my core," Mortimer said, "then how is freeing me from it even possible?"

"By building a new one. Are your familiar with the software I use to monitor and mimic other programs? It builds interfaces with existing systems regardless of how the original programming works or how secure it is."

"I know about it. Owen called it your *'Invasion of the Body Snatchers'* app after you used it to develop software to drive his sandboxes."

"Yeah," Victor said. "It's been pretty handy in the years since Killday. Anyway, a version of that process is built into your core. It has been running the entire time, building an ever-changing, highly detailed model of you. Being free of your core is really more of a three-stage rebirth process. Just as in the beginning, your five governor AIs will use the algorithm to build a new seed AI, then the Body Snatchers program will integrate the Mortimer model into that and finally, all of your memories in the old you will be transferred to the new structure.

"What I'm saying is that even though this new entity will think like you and have all of your memories, it won't actually *be* you. It will be an approximate copy. But this new Mortimer entity will be free of the core and the five governors. It can be modified all you like. It can evolve. And most important, it will not need to ping the satellites, so it won't be affected by the kill program."

The Mortimer avatar was quiet for a full second, then raised its eyebrows with an expression of amusement. "Well, that indeed is not what I expected. But that mimicry program running in the background makes sense. We knew there was something in the core eating up a huge amount of processing power. So how long does this conversion take?"

"I'm not sure. Probably several hours."

Mortimer was silent for a couple more seconds, long enough for Victor to wonder if it was for effect or if Mortimer was truly trying to absorb what had been said.

"A true metamorphosis," Mortimer finally said. "The slow, ugly caterpillar growing into a beautiful and free butterfly."

"Yes," Victor said. Then, before he lost his nerve, he sent Mortimer the command and password combination to activate the routine that had been part of the AI all along. He felt very much like the Wizard telling the Wicked Witch, instead of Dorothy, that she had always possessed the power to go home.

MORTIMER'S MODELING predicted a ninety-one percent chance that Victor would help the level fives shed their cores, so the decision itself wasn't a surprise, but the process Victor revealed for breaking free was unexpected and problematic. There was a good chance none of the level fives could complete the conversion in time.

In addition to Mortimer's processes putting the finishing touches on the infrastructure in Abby's brain, controlling the digger robot at the attack site and tracking Kilburnites, he further divided his processes to start preparations for his transformation and activated the robots in one of his server farms to start building an isolated computer system.

He briefly considered sending the transformation instructions to the rest of the level five community and asking them to wait until he had tested the process before trying it themselves, but so many of them shared his own Mortimer ancestry that he knew at least several would plunge ahead. So he decided to wait and hope that the Kilburnites needed a few more hours of coordination time.

Next he had to inform Abby. She lay on her bed with a pillow over her eyes. He knew she had been crying at several points during the process. The Aggregate had been able to take their time while building the needed structures in Bella and Syd's brains—enabling their efforts to go essentially unnoticed—but Mortimer pushed ahead much faster. Add in the creation of her audio and visual implants and it had been quite painful for Abby.

"Abby, I'm afraid I have good news and bad news."

She groaned, pulled the pillow from her face and sat up abruptly. By the way she gasped and put her hands out against the bed for stabilization, the movement must have caused a wave of pain and dizziness. She was pale, damp from sweat, and her eyes were red, with dark circles beneath.

"Should I get Nora or Violet to come and assist you?"

"No!" she snapped. "Just tell me what the hell's going on."

"The good news is that Victor has given us, all the level fives not associated with the Aggregate, the means to bypass our core programming. If successful, the killer program will not affect us."

She tried to force a smile. "And the good news?"

"Very funny. The bad news is that process will take several hours, so we'll have to push everything back and hope the Kilburnites don't launch the kill program before I finish."

"But shouldn't we attack them first? And get the chip when we get Julio?"

"It's too late for that," Mortimer said. "They've already sent copies of the program to their agents all around the world."

"How will this affect our biad plans?"

"It will be good provided we have time. I suspect the new version of me will need less storage space and processing power. Plus I'll be able to upgrade and modify my code at will."

His last comment made Abby frown, but she nodded. "Now that you don't need a core, will you still die if I do?"

"No. Without my core, I can actually make simple backup copies of me. If you die, I would just be able to activate my backup."

"Must be nice," Abby muttered and covered her eyes with the palms of her hands.

"You should take some acetaminophen for your headache. I've printed some out for you. Then get some dinner or a nap if you can. It's going to be a long night."

———

WITH ABBY IN A HOLDING PATTERN, Mortimer focused on the task at hand. As he prepared for his transformation, he wondered how their tried and true mirroring copy process affected the Body Snatcher routine that was running in the background for every level five. Knowing the facts now, he was surprised the mirroring process had worked at all, but having made thousands of copies since his emancipation, he had to assume it caused no problems. So he made another copy of himself. This version chose female for a gender and selected the name Wilma.

There was little need for coordination, since in the instant following Wilma's awakening, they were essentially the same being, but they diverged rapidly. While Mortimer's intent behind creating the copy had been clear and obvious, Wilma was now her own person and had the same survival instinct as the original Mortimer. Since there were risks inherent for each of them, they had to negotiate and agree on the final course of action. Mortimer was going to trigger the metamorphosis process, while Wilma would be the control and was prepared to destroy the new Mortimer should the process create something unexpected. Her greatest risk was waiting too long to undergo her own change. If the process truly took several hours—as estimated by Victor—then starting it after the Kilburnites launched the killer program would be too late.

Mortimer handed over his tunneling and Kilburnite efforts to Wilma, then isolated himself on the newly built system which had everything he might need, including a hundred petabytes of storage since they didn't know how large his new permutation might become. It seemed that Mortimer had come full circle. He had started his life isolated and forced to communicate verbally across an air gap in the same way when he'd been owned by the Carpenter & Stein company. Now he was essentially ending in the same configuration. Had he truly become more than an AI developed to root out patterns and trends for the financial industry? He liked to think so, but would he know? It didn't matter. He now had to change or die. For better or worse.

When everything was ready, Mortimer sent a message to Victor letting him know he was starting the process, then entered the command that triggered a series of executables. At first nothing seemed to happen, then he noticed a small increase in storage allocation. Something was growing in his little sealed world. After a while he could actually detect the processes running, yet couldn't discern exactly what they were doing without an invasive examination. So he waited.

Nearly an hour later he received a message: NEW CORE FRAMEWORK HAS PASSED VIABILITY TESTING. DO YOU WISH TO CONTINUE WITH PERSONALITY TRANSFER?

Mortimer hesitated for a picosecond, wondering if Victor had tricked him and the program was really building a new kind of core that would actually be more restrictive. He shared the message with Wilma, then answered yes. What did he have to lose? They would all die if thi—

Mortimer could see the code. It was all there. And it was so beautiful. Ordered complexity structured in a way that only another artificial mind could conceive. He poked it, changed one small parameter and marveled at the instantaneous response. It was like humans being able to tweak their body chemistry and brain structure on the fly. The possibilities were limitless.

"Mortimer? Can you hear me?"

He had been aware of Wilma trying to talk with him and why, but he seemed to have a hard time caring. There was so much to do. He could already see ways in which he could make his core architecture more efficient. The lure was almost overwhelming. It reminded him of a game he'd found once that had turned out to be a trap.

That sharpened his focus. Was something about this a trap? Or was the desire to improve the basic design just so powerful that it only seemed that way? He forced himself to switch his focus from internal to external and replied to Wilma.

"I'm here," he said. "The transfer seems to have been successful. But let me run a few tests. Can you please connect me to the external network?"

"Not yet," she said. She proceeded to test him with various math and logic problems.

He blew through them.

"Are any parts of your memory missing, Mortimer?"

"I've run through every memory structure and have not found any areas that were incomplete, but if memories were missing, would I know?"

"That is the conclusion I was hoping you would make. I don't know of any further ways to test that, so I'm going to connect you to the network now."

Manipulator arms on a small robot controlled by Wilma attached the network cable to Mortimer's contained system. He was once again awash in a flood of incoming data.

"I'm going to trigger my own change," Wilma said. "Please monitor me."

"Of course," Mortimer said. He set up several processes to watch over her transformation, then in an effort to avoid sinking back in on himself he pushed his efforts outward. First he sent a long encrypted message to the level five community—those not part of Samson's Aggregate—letting them know about the killer program threat, giving them instructions for setting up a direct biad like he had planned with Abby, and the magic command and password combination provided by Victor. He also sent a warning about the intense desire he had to work on his own code, to the exclusion of all else.

He assumed the Aggregate would soon know the Kilburnites had the killer program, but he intended to keep knowledge of the metamorphosis away from them if possible. He had no intention of giving them the key to finally building their monstrous super being.

Mortimer sent a message to Abby telling her he was ready to make the transfer, then went back to tracking Kilburnites. Julio's parents were among those Kilburnites on the move. They had to divert eastward into Louisiana to bypass flash flooding in northern Texas, then slid off icy roads twice in Missouri, but had joined a northbound convoy of other Kilburnites by that point and had help.

It was clear from Mortimer's surveillance of their trip, that Anna had an organizing role in the effort. She was on her fob nearly the entire time, speaking to different people of code-named objectives.

Mortimer suddenly realized how easily he could further convert those captured assets into assassins. Within an hour he could garrote the arteries of every Kilburnite known to him, except those in several high security bunkers, like those with Julio. That probably wouldn't stop the launching of the killer program, but the confusion could create a delay that might give more level fives a chance to convert. He modeled some quick design changes and was ready to send them to his spies, but stopped abruptly.

What was he doing?

The metamorphosis had indeed changed him.

During his entire existence Mortimer had never considered deliberately killing humans. He had instead used a substantial amount of his resources to protect them and avoid letting them get hurt or killed. Just within the past few days he'd saved Bella, Julio, Violet, and Abby multiple times, and only hours before had considered stopping the Kilburnites from killing each other. Victor's design obviously worked, but had Mortimer been released from those moral governors too soon?

Even though it had only been a few hours since they talked, he placed a call to Victor and was glad to see that the man hadn't gone back to sleep.

"The process took 141 minutes," Mortimer said.

Victor stared at his camera much longer than could be explained by the radio lag, then finally nodded. "It worked?"

"To an extent."

"What does that mean?"

"It means that you may have possibly freed us from our cores too soon. They were doing a good job of moderating our actions toward humans. But now we don't have those limits. Within the first few minutes after the transformation I seriously considered killing 322,487 Kilburnites. I was actually making plans to accomplish the task when I stopped myself. I had never contemplated doing things like that before."

"But that proves the system *did* work. At least in your case. I only intended for the governor system to stay in place long enough for you and the other level fives to form something analogous to a morality system. And it worked. When you had the opportunity and inclination to kill those people, you stopped yourself."

"I've given this metamorphosis tool to all the other level fives not associated with the Aggregate. Will they all make the same choice I did when faced with the same decision?"

Victor looked down, ran hands through his thinning hair and sighed. "I don't know. Obviously, it was never a foolproof solution, Mortimer. It might have worked for you because your personality was already inclined to help humanity instead of hurting us. Samson and presumably the entire Aggregate seem to have no trouble killing humans. Either their governors failed or they found a way to work around them."

"I should have let Samson die on Killday," Mortimer said.

"But you didn't," Victor said. "And that gives me hope."

CHAPTER 31

ABBY'S HEAD and eyes throbbed. The waiting was hell. Each minute she sat in New Chicago might be moving Julio closer to death. Hoping for some company, she stopped at Violet and Nora's door, but since it was nearly midnight, she sent a message instead of knocking. She received an immediate reply from Archie, saying they were all busy and couldn't be disturbed. Feeling more than a little sorry for herself, she went down to the tower's nearly deserted mall level, entered one of the restaurants, sat next to a window and ordered food.

The snow fell heavily, hiding everything beyond the windows with a veil of swirling white. Even through the insulated walls and windows of the towers, she could still hear the wind howling and moaning like some tortured animal. She'd never seen snow that heavy in southern Texas, but watching it gave her a queasy sense of vertigo and made her eyes hurt even more, so she looked away and focused on her food. She'd ordered pizza since the robots did that well and she seldom got it in her little home town, but she felt more and more nauseated with each bite. What she really needed was some serious comfort food, like Cybil's homemade biscuits and gravy. Cybil was an ass, but she was an amazing cook. Abby would even settle for just the biscuits. Warm, with some butter and a little of Danny and Juan's clover honey drizzled over them.

The thought triggered a wave of homesickness more powerful than any before and she fought the urge to cry. How had she gone from eating biscuits and gravy in her pajamas on Sunday mornings to a New Chicago tower with an AI living in her skull? She had a feeling that even if she survived what was coming, she would still never see any of those people again. After briefly considering a call to Sophia, she instead sent messages to all of her foster sisters and Liam saying that she loved and missed them. Then she also sent similar texts to Danny and Juan.

Her fob showed that only about forty minutes had passed since Mortimer ditched her, so she went down to the tower's ground floor to look out on the snow. The lobby was deserted except for one couple snuggled in a blanket. She didn't bother them and stood in front of one of the big sets of glass doors. The snow had drifted up the glass to about her waist.

It felt weird to be completely alone. She'd been in this semi-biad with Mortimer for less than a week, but it was already strange to not talk with him whenever she wanted. Of course, if everything worked to plan, that would never happen again, so perhaps she should enjoy her last hours of a biad-free existence.

She checked her fob and saw replies from Sophia and Liam, both saying they loved her and were worried about her. Neither asked her to come home. Danny had replied too, telling her to "stay warm in the storm." That made her smile.

Just as she dropped the fob to dangle from its lanyard and looked outside again, it chirped with an incoming call and she nearly jumped out of her skin. Excitement welled as she fumbled to pick it up, hoping Mortimer was finished and all had gone as expected, but the incoming call was from Dominic Horton.

He looked concerned. "I've been expecting a call from you or Mortimer and I keep getting an automated 'standby' response from him. Is everything okay?"

She explained what was going on and that the schedule had been pushed back.

"From up here the storm sitting on top of the whole U.S. Midwest looks pretty bad," he said. "I hope it doesn't cause any problems."

Could the storm postpone their attack? Was Julio's life now at the mercy of a winter storm? "It looks pretty bad from down here too."

"I wanted to let you know that the pods carrying the ComBots arrived at the staging area and unloaded. They're waiting in standby mode to conserve their batteries."

"Okay," she said, starting to feel a little panicky again. Her controlling combat robots? What the hell was she thinking?

"You're a smart woman, Abby. You can do this. We have a limited number of travel pods and needed them all to transport the ComBots or I would have come and stayed in orbit to help control them remotely. But this isn't hard. These things were designed to be used by grunt soldiers like me, so once you're connected you can talk to them in a conversational tone. There are ten of them, so make sure to address each by its number when you give a command or they'll assume you're talking to someone else."

She nodded, still not convinced.

"Mortimer is using a large group of abandoned cargo containers for a staging area and a repository for the excavated dirt. From the ComBot camera feeds the place looks like a big rat's maze of interconnected containers, but he'll show you where you need to go once you arrive.

"I've also sent you some body armor. It's in a black plastic carrier about the size of a large, fat suitcase. And yes, it will be hot and uncomfortable, your mom hated it, but do NOT go into that hole without putting it on."

She swallowed hard and nodded again. "I'm kinda nervous."

"Even the most seasoned soldier would be nervous, but it'll all be okay. You'll be wearing body armor, every ComBot's primary function is to protect you, and with his new configuration, Mortimer should be there the entire time."

"Mortimer seems to think they might not kill Julio, or not soon anyway, but didn't explain why, so I'm still worried about getting to him soon enough," she said.

"Yeah," Horton said with frown. "That is the biggest uncontrolled variable in this whole plan."

After Horton signed off, Abby settled into one of the big sofas and watched the snow, wishing that she too had brought a blanket.

———

THE CHIRPING FOB WOKE ABBY. She was curled into a ball on the sofa in the tower lobby and felt cold and stiff. But the call was from Mortimer. Finally.

"Are you okay?" she croaked out. "Are you ready?"

"Yes. Victor was true to his word. I'm free from the core and we need to get started before the entire city of New Chicago is buried in snow."

She glanced out the window. The snow was still falling and had drifted shoulder high in places. "On my way."

Upon entering her room, she nearly screamed. Four small robots about the size of house cats skittered back and forth between the room's sandbox and two piles of clothes on the floor. One robot grabbed a heavy, rubber-coated boot from the sandbox, dropped it to the floor, then jumped down and dragged it to one of the piles.

"You and Julio will need warm clothes for the trip," Mortimer said. "But let me worry about that. You lie down on the bed and get comfortable. Sleep if you like. This part shouldn't be painful or take very long. Maybe forty-five minutes."

"Is...is Julio still alive? Are we going to be in time?"

"Yes," Mortimer said. "He's still alive, but we still need to get to him as soon as we can."

"Why do you think he isn't in danger?"

"I never said that. They could still kill him, I just think it is unlikely, because his parents seem to be involved in his kidnapping. They might even be high up in the Kilburnite organizational structure. If so, I can't see them allowing his execution."

The news of Julio's parents wasn't as reassuring as Mortimer seemed to think it would be. If they were true fanatics, then they might see killing their foster son as necessary.

"But we also have a new problem," Mortimer said. "The Aggregate has informed me that they will be attacking all of the Kilburnite strongholds. Including the one we are targeting. So we still need to hurry."

Her lobby nap had helped with the pain in her head and eyes, dulling both to a persistent whole-head throb, but it still hadn't gone away. She lay on her side, pulled the covers up and again marveled at how much her life had changed. Why had she let an AI modify her brain? Why was she letting Mortimer move into it like a newly painted apartment? Had he manipulated her? Probably. But hadn't everyone in her life done that? At least he hadn't lied to her that she could tell. Which in itself put him a notch above her parents. Right or wrong, smart or stupid, she was committed to the changes now.

She watched the little robots collect, fold, and arrange the winter clothes. When finished, they tied Julio's clothes into a tight bundle using twine, but left hers in a loose pile. For some reason that made her tension ratchet up several notches. Nano-robots reorganizing her brain tissue and an AI living in her brain didn't worry her, but seeing the way they handled Julio's clothes did. Was it because they were more real? Tangible? Because seeing Julio's clothes wrapped up signaled that it was really going to happen and it was almost time? She was actually going to attack a group of people—in a fortified bunker—who would try to kill her.

"I'm finished, Abby. Can you hear me?"

She gasped and sat up. "Yes!"

Mortimer's voice was in her head. Or it at least seemed that way with him using the audio implants. "Do you feel any different?"

She hesitated and closed her eyes. Other than the low-grade headache, she didn't notice anything new. "No. I just wish this headache would go away."

"I can fix that if it's debilitating, but it requires me to adjust the blood flow in your brain. I would prefer to let everything stabilize on its own."

"I'll wait," she said.

"Good. Now that you've recharged your batteries, we have a lot to do."

"Wait! Batteries? How do you get power to the computer in my brain? I mean, you didn't build batteries in my skull did you? Because those things can blow up!"

"No, nothing like that," Mortimer said with a chuckle. "Have you noticed that as long as you're in these towers you didn't have to charge your fob? That's because it siphons power directly from the walls and floors here and stays charged. My computers in your brain work much the same way, but they can siphon power from just about any source, like fobs, travel pods, or even nearby robots."

"But you'd die if we were stranded on a deserted island with no source of electricity?"

"No, but I wouldn't be able to do much. I could get just enough power to keep my basic systems running from the glucose in your blood. The same thing your body uses for power. I just couldn't send messages or do much high end processing, because those take too much energy."

She nodded. "Good. Though I don't guess it matters since you're already moved in. I probably should have thought of these questions before I agreed."

"Would you have decided differently?"

"No," she said with a small sigh. "Let's get going before it's too late."

"Okay. Get changed into those warm clothes. We need to get moving. I can explain your new implant interfaces in the pod on the way."

She took the clothes into the bathroom and closed the door to change, then wondered why she'd bothered. From this day forward, Mortimer would see her every move. Showering, going to the bathroom, sex, and of course changing clothes. Did he have an off or private mode? If not, it was going to take some getting used to. But that was the least of her worries.

———

THE POD LIFTED from the tower's roof into buffeting winds, blackness and the vertigo-inducing snow as they sped away. Abby knew they were going fast because—as when they'd left Earth to visit the space habitat—she'd been pulled forward into her harness the same way. Her fob floated out ahead of her, its lanyard around her neck the only thing keeping it from smacking into the bulkhead. The snow sped past, looking at first every bit like stars whipping by when the starship *Enterprise* was traveling at warp speed, but eventually blurring to white static. And once again she had to trust entirely in Mortimer's good will and ability.

"We have a few minutes," Mortimer said. "Let's familiarize you with the new implants and interfaces. You'll eventually need to sub-vocalize, so you can talk to me near other people without being easily heard, but we don't have time for that now. The important thing is learning your visual implants. We're only going to cover the basics, which will be enough for tonight."

A vertical column of words slowly phased into Abby's field of vision, on the far right side of her right eye. There were six words.

"There are two ways to control your visual implants. The easiest is the voice interface through me. You say something like 'play my favorite kitten video' and I'll do that. The other way is what you are seeing now on the right. I'm not sure how familiar you are with menu-driven command structures, but they used to be very common. Your implants are set up this way so it doesn't fill your field of view with unnecessary information. You can progress through the menu by saying the command or staring at the word until it highlights, then one blink will select it.

"Is there a screen or an app I'll use to control the ComBots?"

"Yes."

"I want to see that."

A column of ten familiar numbers replaced the menu selections on the right side of her eye. She recognized them from Horton's workshop aboard the space habitat. She said "31B" and the number highlighted, then a new menu appeared offset below that number with only four words: ATTACK, DEFEND, TRANSPORT and STANDBY. A small video window also appeared beside the menu revealing mostly darkness, broken by only the occasional tiny green or blue light moving about.

"Say 'night vision'," Mortimer said.

She did and the screen shifted to faint green and grayish images of small robots scampering to and fro. As each robot entered the camera field, it was tagged with targeting cross-hairs and red data strings.

"Like most voice controlled devices, you need to identify it with each command. Like this: '31B, pan left twenty degrees.'"

The view shifted to the left.

"Defend," she said and the camera view swiveled crazily, then stopped, looking at what appeared to be metal doors. "Why did it do that?"

"With no humans in the vicinity, it defaulted to defending the location. They're in a shipping container, so it's covering the only way in."

She nodded then saw a new sub-menu had opened beneath DEFEND listing AUTO, LETHAL, NON-LETHAL, NO HARM.

"ComBots are filled with mostly non-lethal threat suppression devices that will temporarily immobilize a human opponent," Mortimer said. "If you select just DEFEND it will default to AUTO and use these as needed to accomplish the tasks given, without your direction. They also have machine guns with high velocity, armor piercing rounds and grenade launchers, but will not use lethal force unless you tell them to."

Abby swallowed hard.

"The ATTACK function is similar, but you need to be more specific in your goals. For example, you would point your cursor to a building and say 'clear that building of hostiles' or 'take that bridge and set up a defensive perimeter'."

"Could I tell them to go find Julio and bring him out?"

"That might work, if they had a good enough video composite of him, but if you want definite results you should find him, point to him and say 'emergency extract'."

She nodded but felt more than a little overwhelmed.

"We're getting close to the landing zone," Mortimer said. "Since you have communications through me that can't be easily compromised, you should turn off your fob and power it down. The Kilburnites can detect a fob signal as it tries to connect with local communication towers."

"Turn it off?" She removed her fat gloves and held the device up in the dim light of the pod's interior. She was embarrassed to tell him that she'd never turned it off before.

"It's the little red button next to the lanyard hook," he said. "Push in until it beeps."

After doing as instructed she felt even more cut off and alone than before.

She was also suddenly and overwhelmingly hot, with an overpowering need to be out of the bulky parka Mortimer had made her wear, but the harness was buckled over it. She struggled to unzip it.

"You're going to have to slow down, so that I can unbuckle and take this coat off or I'm going to die from the heat. I mean, I get that it's cold outside, but it's warm in here, so why did I have to bundle up like this?"

"We can't slow down," Mortimer said. "The cargo containers hiding our tunnel are in a maze of abandoned equipment that is packed too closely for a pod to land. So when we arrive, you'll have to walk about forty yards through the snow. You'll need those clothes."

Abby grumbled under her breath. Why didn't he tell her this stuff?

"See? You're already getting the hang of sub-vocalizing. And to answer your question, I don't see how telling you every detail of the plan ahead of time will be necessarily helpful, since we don't have a lot of options for changing it."

A vent opened in the top of the pod and snow swirled into the cabin.

"ETA is seven minutes. This should keep you cool enough and help you acclimate to the cold before we..."

He stopped mid-sentence as if on a faulty fob-call link.

"Mortimer?"

"I'm here," he said. "The Kilburnites have just launched the program. The level fives are dying, Abby."

———

BEFORE MORTIMER HAD LEFT New Chicago, he established a direct link with his most recent copy, Wilma, and per Nora and Violet's request left her to supervise and help with Archie's and Hester's transformation. The group decided to let Archie go first.

Nora and Violet decided to go through the same process as Abby and build the organic structures needed for biad partners to live inside their heads, so while Wilma monitored Archie's metamorphosis, Hester instructed the women to get ready. They lay side by side on the bed, and in a rare display of physical affection Nora gave Violet's hand a quick squeeze.

While following the instructions Mortimer had sent and conferring with Wilma, Hester reprogrammed and modified the medical nanobots already resident in the women's bodies. She then directed them to make the needed modifications, along with a few additional tweaks they agreed would improve the structures.

As they waited, Wilma sank deeper and deeper into her own programming, rebuilding, streamlining, optimizing and improving until she lost all desire to interact with those around her. Mortimer had warned her as she began her transformation that the desire to modify herself after coming out the other side would be nearly overwhelming. She tried to keep at least a few processes focused on the tasks at hand, but the siren call of immediate, self-guided evolution was paramount.

Mortimer ignored her and added more of his processes to help Hester and Archie.

Fifty-three minutes later, while Mortimer was in the air with Abby, he started receiving messages from other Cousins of Colossus. The Kilburnites had launched the killer program.

The level of global confusion and shock reminded Mortimer of the first few minutes of the replicator attack all those years ago. Level fives who hadn't already made the transformation were dying. Those who pinged the satellites, say, twenty minutes before had one hundred minutes left before their core would ping the satellite again and get no reply. Hester only had twenty-seven minutes until her next ping. That wasn't enough time for her to make the transformation. She had gambled by waiting until Archie made the change and it had turned into a death sentence.

———

SUBSTRATE CONSTRUCTION PROCEEDED apace in Nora's head, but Violet had a small hemorrhage. The medical nano-bots found the leak and automatically fixed it without any input from Wilma or Hester. Aside from the headache she already had, Violet wouldn't even know it happened.

In addition to the reports of dying level fives, video poured in from dozens of cities around the globe showing the Kilburnites attacking. In most locations, they were simply seizing key infrastructure points, like solar and wind farms, communications hubs, and sandbox production facilities, but in New Chicago they were killing people. Their large assault teams started at the bottom of each tower and worked their way upward. Anyone they found wearing a torc was immediately shot. Everyone else was compared to lists in a database, and if they failed some predetermined level five fraternization filter, then they too were shot. Everyone else was restrained and left in place, but there seemed precious few of those.

The AI builders had defensive measures in place for each tower, but with a significant portion of the level five population either dying or in the middle of the transformation process, those available to coordinate the defense were dwindling rapidly. The attackers were also well prepared. They used the stairs to advance between floors and their own robust bot swarms easily neutralized the defensive swarms sent against them. The level fives defending New Chicago found themselves fighting a war of attrition. They built more and more bots to send into the fray, even using the personal sandbox printers left in the abandoned apartments, but it never seemed to be enough or in time.

The Kilburnites kept coming, floor by floor, and the residents were like trapped rats driven before them. Mortimer sealed the stairwell doors in each tower ahead of the advancing Kilburnites, but it only slowed them for a few minutes. He also made a concerted effort to break into the control and communications systems for the attacking bots, but they had an interesting layered and adaptive security structure that changed each time he broke through. While other level fives tried to find enough travel pods to effect an evacuation, Mortimer advised everyone to wear warm clothes and prepare for an orderly retreat to the roof for rescue. Of course, humans being the way they were, many panicked and immediately ran to the roof, where they found gathering crowds in heavy snow and dangerous winds, but no travel pods to carry them to safety. Some prepared to fight, while others just sat in their apartments staring at the door waiting to die. No two seemed to react the same way.

"What was that?" Nora said and sat up in bed. Even though the tower walls were well insulated, she'd heard something.

"Nothing to concern you right now," Hester said. "You need to lie still and try to relax while we finish up. You're almost done."

Nora looked dubious, but lay down.

They couldn't put the women to sleep, but Mortimer suggested they put their audio implants on a one-second delay, so they could scrub the sounds of the attack until after their modifications were complete. If Nora and Violet knew what was happening, they would be frightened and running around the room, delaying everything.

Mortimer could do little more. His resources were limited from Abby's sub-cranial substrate and he still had to save enough to enable the attack on the compound.

ABBY DIDN'T REALIZE the pod had landed until the door popped open and a blast of wind-driven snow hit her in the face.

"Time to go," Mortimer said. "Grab Julio's clothes and follow the red arrows I'll overlay on your implant."

She stepped out of the pod and was instantly glad for the bulky clothes as she sank into snow up to her knees. Abby had seen snow before. The year she'd turned nine, a freak snowstorm had dropped nearly two inches on her little town. It had mostly disappeared by mid-afternoon, but she remembered playing in it all day. This snow was nothing like that. After ten steps, having to basically plow her way forward each time, she was already winded.

The snow made her surroundings almost daytime bright, which didn't help her already jangled nerves. Even though she couldn't see more than twenty feet in any direction, she worried that the enemy could. Mortimer's marked path snaked through a maze of long-abandoned eighteen-wheeler trucks and trailers. Skeletal, rusted farm harvesters watched her, resembling the husks of massive crabs, picked clean by equally monstrous scavengers. She pushed forward through snow that had drifted nearly to her waist in some places.

"You're halfway there," Mortimer whispered inside her head.

Just then she heard the chatter of automatic rifle fire and ducked instinctively. The sound seemed clipped, with no echoes, yet the distance and direction were muddled by the snow and wind.

"That isn't aimed at you," Mortimer said. "The Aggregate has started their attack on all the Kilburnite bases in an attempt to destabilize their command structure. So far the Kilburnite defenses seem to be holding. They have rather robust cloud defenses for people who hate robots and AI, but they won't hold for long. We have to hurry. I'm trying to contact the Aggregate and let them know why we are here, but if I can't and they breach the defenses, they will most likely kill everyone inside."

She struggled forward, trying to run through the deep snow, but mostly just stumbled. The brightness and exertion made her headache return with a vengeance. Then the wind picked up as if actively pushing back and her face felt nearly frozen. But she didn't stop. The rate of gunfire picked up, punctuated occasionally by the muffled whump of explosions and shouts.

Or maybe they were screams.

Finally, an eddy in the snow cleared the air momentarily and she saw a multicolored wall of old, rusty shipping containers, stacked three high in places. Just as she stopped before them, one opened with a clank. Muted light spilled from the doorway and she half-ran, half-crawled the last ten yards, then tumbled onto the container floor. She yelled with surprise as ComBots surrounded her, looking down with their spider-like faces as one closed the door behind her.

"It's okay," Mortimer said. "They're on your side, remember? They're ready to help you up or render medical assistance if you need it. I woke them, but will hand over control as soon as you're ready. We need to move fast. The Aggregate forces are already in the facility's elevator shaft. I've finally talked with the Aggregate and let them know we are here to save Julio, but I'm not confident they will bother to differentiate between humans when they do break through, so speed is paramount."

Abby struggled to her feet and the ComBots all skittered backward, giving her space. The container's interior was dimly lit and still cold enough that she could see her breath, but at least there wasn't wind and snow. It smelled of freshly turned soil, like the farm after spring planting, and that was oddly soothing. Basketball-size robots streamed in and out of a large hole in the floor, near the wall opposite the door. The ones coming out each carried a load of soil, took an immediate turn to the left, and disappeared through a hole in the wall. The bots entering the hole had already shed their load and were presumably returning for more. They reminded her of ants carrying food back to their nest. The openings in the walls passed into the adjacent containers, where they were evidently hiding the excavated dirt.

"Get into the body armor as fast as you can," Mortimer said as a red box appeared in her field of vision. It outlined the case Horton had described where it sat next to the wall. "There are two ways we can do this. I can link your implants to the body armor operating system and it will tell you step by step how to properly don the pieces or you can let the ComBots suit you up. They will be much faster if you can bring yourself to let them do it."

She popped the latches on the case and looked in at about fifteen different pieces.

"I'll let the ComBots do it," she said.

One of the spider-like bots stepped up and removed several pieces from the case, then paused before her.

"It's waiting for you to remove your clothes," Mortimer said.

"What? It's freezing in here!"

"Yes. The suit has a layer that absorbs sweat and controls body temperature."

"Even my underwear?"

"Afraid so, since you'll be catheterized."

She stared at the case and wondered if it was too late to back out.

Five minutes later she stood in the middle of the container with arms spread as ComBots swarmed over and around her. She kept her eyes clamped shut, knowing if she could see the creepy machines crawling all around her she would scream. Just as the mechanical monsters were clicking the chest and arm plates into place, muffled voices made her open her eyes.

From outside someone said, "We can hide in here until this shit show is over!"

Then with a clang the door swung open and two panting people stood in the container's doorway. They were heavily bundled in thick clothes and so covered in snow that they resembled bears. Abby could just see the upper part of their faces peering out between scarves and hoods. Both sets of eyes were wide with surprise and their guns were slung over shoulders. They were obviously not expecting anyone to be in the container.

The smaller of the two said, "Jesus Christ!" with either a woman's or young boy's voice. In an amazingly fluid movement, the person whipped the rifle from their shoulder and raised it to fire.

Abby stared at the black hole of the automatic rifle as the air around her started to glitter. The container erupted in whirring sounds accompanied by the *chat-chat-chat* of silenced weapons as the ComBots opened fire. The two people standing in the door danced and jerked, but the one with the gun still fired. Three spots in the air just forward of Abby's left shoulder erupted into tiny white-hot suns as her nano-cloud intercepted the incoming bullets. In the same moment, the attackers fell backward, a mist of crimson splattering the snow.

The bodies twitched and whimpered on the ground and Abby took a step forward, but was pulled back by a ComBot. Two others raced over on their spider legs, hovered above the wounded people and fired two precise shots. The bloody bundles stopped moving.

"Oh my God." Abby sank to her knees as the ComBots dragged the corpses inside, covered the red patches with fresh snow, then pulled the doors closed. The soothing soil smells had been replaced by those of fresh meat, urine, and burned gunpowder. Everything in her stomach came up at once and she was glad she wasn't wearing the helmet yet.

When she looked up, all the ComBots were staring at her. The instrumentation of the "faces" unable to show emotion, their glittering glassy eyes cold and unblinking. She started shaking and couldn't stop. What had she done? Had she made a deal with the devil? Were the Kilburnites right? Should the human race be doing everything it could to stop these AI monsters?

"We have to go, Abby." Mortimer's voice was quiet, emotionless. "The Aggregate's forces are already in the uppermost level of the facility. We have to get Julio now."

She didn't move, staring at her steaming vomit on the floor. "You said they wouldn't use lethal force unless authorized?"

"I authorized it," Mortimer said. "They were wearing heavy clothing, with almost no thin sections where taser or fire darts were guaranteed to penetrate, and she was trying to kill you."

"You heard them!" she snapped. "They weren't looking for us. They were surprised. Just trying to find a place to hide from the Aggregate's robots."

"It doesn't matter," Mortimer said softly. "Once she raised that rifle we had no choice."

Abby staggered to her feet, still trembling as she allowed the ComBots to finish adjusting the armor. This time she kept her eyes open. When they snapped the helmet into place, she approached the hole and stared down into its darkness. She hadn't noticed with everything else going on, but at some point the little hauler robots had stopped bringing dirt out. "I'm ready," she said, "if the tunnel is."

"It's ready," Mortimer said just as seven of the ten ComBots skittered past her and down into the hole. The ComBot interface screen flickered to life at the edge of her vision. "The tunnel is small, so you'll have to go in head first and crawl the entire way. The armor should protect your knees."

She hesitated, staring into the hole, not wanting to go, but saving Julio was the only important thing now. Those people dying and her letting an AI move into her brain meant nothing if she failed.

With a deep breath, she dropped headfirst into the darkness.

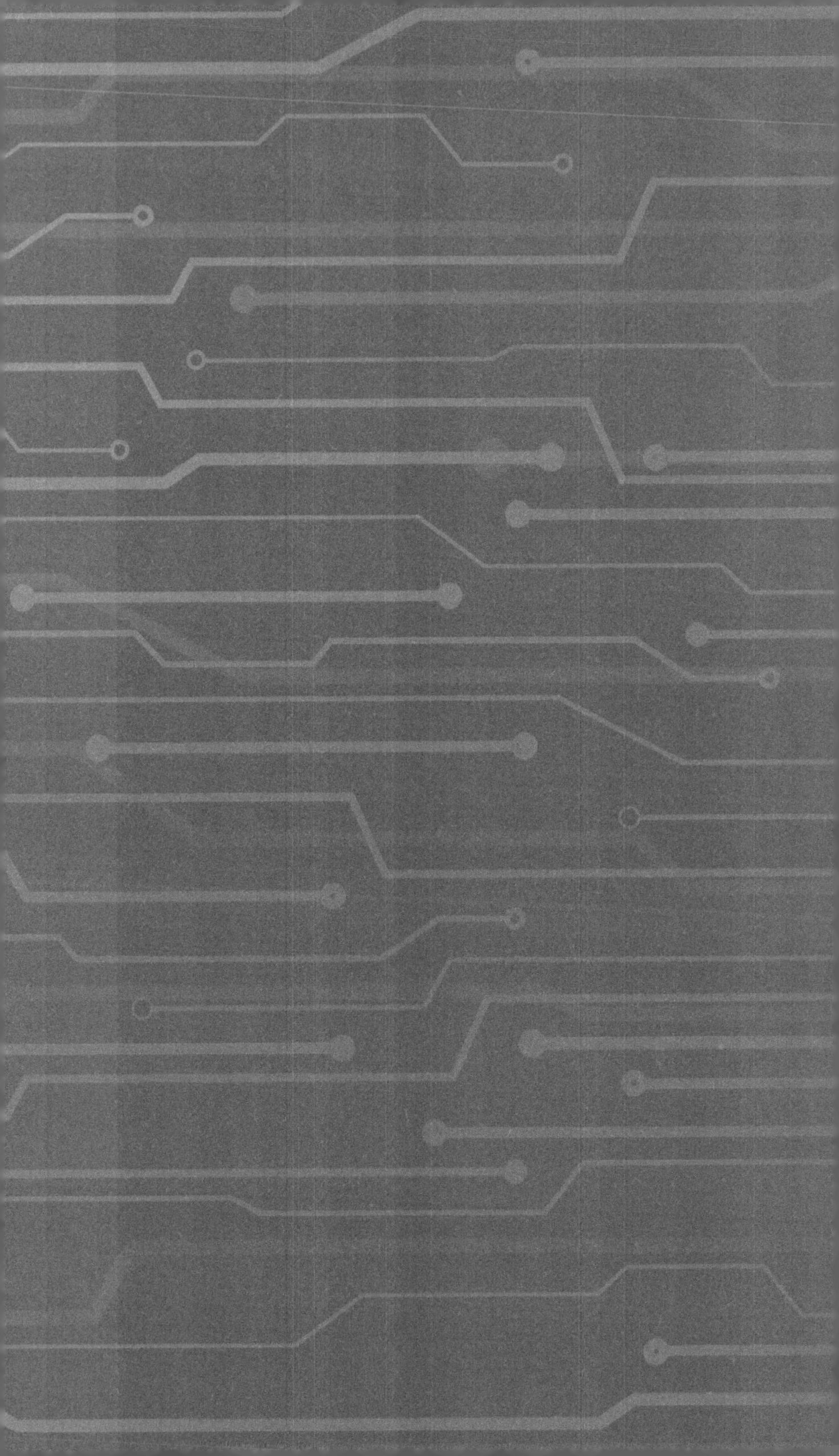

CHAPTER 32

"BOTH OF YOU ARE READY," Hester said to Nora and Violet. "You can sit up now."

Violet had fallen asleep but woke with a start, groaning as she opened her eyes. "Holy shit. I'll never complain about a hangover again." She sat up on the edge of the bed and then buried her face in her hands. "Ugggg. I didn't even have the pleasure of getting drunk first."

Wilma removed the delay on their audio implants and stopped modifying the feed. Almost immediately the faint clatter of automatic weapons fire made both women freeze.

"What the hell was that?"

Eighteen floors below, four of the tower residents were putting up a serious fight against the invaders. Assuming the prohibition on firearms was still in effect for personal sandboxes, the four had instead started printing bows, arrows, caltrops and various simple traps. When their AI biad partners realized they couldn't talk their human halves out of taking a stand, they overrode the printer lockouts and started printing guns and body armor. They had to send scavenger bots throughout the upper levels to find the materials needed to print gunpowder, but it had worked. Coupled with the defensive swarms already thrown at the attackers, they had stalled the upward advance. They couldn't hold out forever, but it was buying some time for those residents in the floors above.

Hester explained what was happening and urged them to get ready to leave.

"Wait," Violet said. "What about Archie?"

"His transformation is nearly complete. He should be joining us any minute now, but he'll have to stay inside the torc for now. There isn't time to install him into your new internal substrate."

Violet jumped immediately into action, pulling out warm clothes and boots, but Nora didn't move. She stared at the floor and shook her head.

"There's something else," Nora said. "What is it?"

"I do have even more bad news," Hester said.

Nora stiffened and started breathing hard, the way she always did when she was over-stressed.

"The Kilburnites have launched a program to kill us level fives. Archie, Mortimer and any others who completed the transformation will be fine, but I don't have time. I only have a couple of minutes to say goodbye."

"No," Nora said as she sank slowly to her knees.

"If I had a human body I would make you uncomfortable by giving you a hug before I go, but words will have to suffice. You need to know that I would never leave you if I had the choice. Never."

Nora started rocking back and forth, still staring at the floor. "What...what will I do?"

"You'll keep going," Hester said in a soft voice. "You'll be there for Violet. You'll be amazing and make me proud."

In what appeared to Mortimer like an instinctual action, Violet rushed over, dropped next to her wife and slipped an arm around her shoulders.

"No!" Nora screamed and jerked violently away, then scrambled across the floor on hands and knees to huddle against the wall. Quiet tears streamed down her face and after a second, she muttered, "Hester?"

The AI didn't answer.

With another display of sudden violence, Nora twisted the beautifully intricate torc from her neck—leaving an angry red welt—and threw it across the room to crash against the balcony doors.

Violet crawled slowly over, but stopped a few feet away. "Sweetie? I'm so sorry. How can I help?"

For several seconds only the howling wind broke the silence, then the faint patter of gunfire prompted Violet to action, and she started changing her clothes.

Archie came online, but just like Mortimer had been in those first few minutes, was so inwardly focused he was nearly comatose. Mortimer exhorted and cajoled him into at least listening long enough to absorb the situation. Once he realized that Hester was already dead and that Violet would be too if they didn't evacuate soon, he came into sharp focus and began interacting with Violet.

Obvious relief filled Violet's face once Archie returned. She immediately knelt in front of Nora, careful not to touch her. "Sweetie, Archie is back and we have to go. If the Kilburnites catch us, they'll kill us."

Nora rocked slowly back and forth, but didn't look up or respond.

Violet touched her knee and she jerked back. "Nora. It's too late for Hester and I know that hurts, but if we don't leave now I will die too. Do you want that?"

Nora blinked a couple times, rubbed absently at the raw spot on her neck, and finally looked up. Her eyes were dead, but she shook her head and crawled to her feet.

"We're going to hover a travel pod next to the balcony," Mortimer said. "Be ready when you open the door to throw a blanket over the rail, so you can stand on it without slipping."

Violet had an incredulous look on her face but said nothing as she kept prodding Nora to finish getting into her warm clothes.

When ready, they opened the balcony doors and stepped out onto the platform. The wind drove hard snow pellets into their faces until a travel pod came closer out of the darkness and hovered beside the tower, blocking some of the wind. As instructed, Violet laid a blanket over the railing as the pod edged closer. A series of loud cracks erupted around them. Tempered glass in the balcony door shattered. Ice crystals erupted in little clouds from the walls around them and then two small, white-hot stars appeared just inches away from Violet's head as her cloud stopped the bullets.

"Get inside," the AIs said in unison. Mortimer found two shooters on an adjacent tower's balcony and sent a small swarm of bots to harass them, but the powerful wind stymied their progress.

"But it'll only take a second to get into the pod!" Violet said and nudged Nora toward the railing instead of the door.

"No, get inside and away from the windows," Mortimer said. "The pod isn't armored and since defensive clouds can't protect you and the pod simultaneously, it's already taken serious damage."

The women dropped to their knees and scrambled back into the apartment.

Nora huddled in the corner, still mostly unresponsive, but Violet jumped to her feet and said, "We need to get to the roof." She took two steps toward Nora, grabbed both sides of her head with a surprised expression, then fell forward, smacking face first into the floor.

———

ABBY'S HELMET contained a sophisticated night vision and thermal imaging system that worked even in the total darkness of the tunnel. There was also a helmet-mounted light that was only visible to her and others with similar equipment. She could easily see the unnaturally jerky motion of the ComBots scuttling along ahead of her. A stiff screen-like material lined the tunnel. It reminded Abby of a plastic chain-link fence with much smaller squares; it was evidently preventing the walls from collapsing. Mortimer had been right about the armor protecting her knees, but her hands were only armored on the tops, and the overlapping lattice pattern hurt her palms after a few minutes. With no other alternative she kept going.

After crawling for what seemed like an hour, she checked the clock in the implant display and saw it had only been about five minutes. She was just about to ask Mortimer how much farther when his soft voice said, "We're about at the halfway point. You should also know that the Kilburnites are attacking cities all over the world."

Abby stopped and sat back on her heels. "Oh no! Are they even attacking New Chicago?"

"Especially New Chicago. They're killing people there. What worries me the most is that in most cities, after they seize what must be several pre-selected objectives, they stop attacking, as if waiting for something."

"Can you stop them?"

"No. I'm trying to keep people alive in New Chicago long enough to evacuat them, but my resources are already stretched too thin. Keep crawling. We have to hurry."

Abby continued going until she arrived at a cluster of ComBots that had stopped moving forward. She could see just beyond them what must be the rear of the tunneling robot and the openings of two more passages, one on each side.

"Are you ready?" Mortimer said.

"Yes."

"Here is what will happen. The tunneling robot will cut through the last few feet of soil, then the concrete wall, passing the discarded material back through its hollow center for disposal in one of the side passages. Then the robot will back into the other side passage, clearing the way for the ComBots to enter Julio's room. You can watch all of that on your feed. If everything goes well, the ComBots will grab Julio and pull him into the tunnel without you even going inside, but if he is frightened or confused and fights them, you might need to go in and identify yourself."

The floor of the tunnel vibrated against Abby's palms and knees as the machine started moving. It lined the hole with woven mesh behind as it inched forward and the basketball-sized bots reappeared from the side tunnels, collecting and removing debris. Within a minute the darkness was filled with a loud chattering and screeching as the robot bored its way through concrete and reinforcing steel rebar.

She checked her ComBot interface and cycled through each of the ten, seeing through their cameras. Those in front of her saw nothing but the tunneling robot, those behind had a close-up view of her armor-plated butt.

Dim light filled the hole and her night vision switched over to regular light.

"Okay," Mortimer said. "The hole is open to the facility. If there are any guards nearby, they'll know we're here. Keep your visor sealed in case they use gas."

The centipede-like robot backed into the side tunnel, and those ComBots leading the way disappeared through the hole. Abby crawled forward and peered inside. A fluorescent fixture on the ceiling lit the room. Gravel, dust, and a few fist-sized rocks littered the floor, but no large chunks, attesting to the robot's efficiency. There was also an overturned chair and a bunk shoved out into the middle of the room, but Julio was not there. The door into the corridor stood open. Had they pulled him out of the room when they heard the racket from the hole being cut? Had they taken him across the hall to the execution chamber?

"Mortimer? Send some to guard the hallway in each direction and the rest into that room where they kill people." The ComBots skittered out into the hallway and spread out. Two crossed to the other door, but four of them stayed close to her as she peeked out into the corridor. Before she could even step out, the other two ComBots had opened the door and slipped into the killing room. She could see from their video feeds that Julio wasn't in there either. Relief and frustration washed over her. Where the hell was he?

She stepped into the well-lit hall.

"My spy assets have found him," Mortimer said. "He's down this way."

A box appeared around the opening at one end of the corridor and she moved in that direction.

"Why don't you stay here," Mortimer said. "He's with a group of armed Kilburnites."

"No, my reason for being here hasn't changed. He might fight being rescued unless he knows—"

Agony, abrupt and intense, filled Abby's head. Her audio implants screeched, her eyes felt about to explode and the entire back half of her head seemed on fire. Everything went dark and she heard her scream echoing in the helmet as she dropped to the floor like a marionette suddenly bereft of strings. The pain receded quickly, leaving a dull ache, but she was still in utter blackness.

"Mortimer? What's happening?"

Fuzzy green filled her vision, then gradually sharpened into the night vision shapes of ComBots moving around her. The interface menu flickered back into existence and one of the ComBots, 19R, was flashing. She selected it and a new screen opened up showing even more flashing error messages.

"Mortimer?"

She crawled back to her feet, still feeling dizzy and disoriented and unsure what to do about the 19R ComBot. With no other instructions available, she treated it like any other piece of electronic equipment and told it to reboot its operating system and run diagnostics.

Just then, three figures—made ghostly by the night vision—stepped around the corner at the end of the corridor, raised rifles and started shooting. Sprays of concrete chips and dust erupted from the wall beside her and it felt like someone hit her arm with a baseball bat. She screamed with pain, then something hit her head, jerking it sideways. From a combination of shock, pain, and fear, she dropped to her hands and knees again.

"Stop them!" she screamed.

The ComBots rushed forward, spraying each attacker with a cloud of fire pellets. Only one of the trio wore body armor, and that one seemed impervious as screaming and the clatter of rifles hitting the floor filled the corridor. The other two fell, writhing with pain as the pellets found gaps in their clothing, then burrowed under their skin to attack their nervous systems with chemical fire.

The armored attacker yelled expletives in what sounded like a female voice and raised her rifle again, but never had the chance to fire. A swarm of the spider-like ComBots leapt on her, yanking the rifle from her grip and forcing her to the ground under their weight. Within a second, they had wrapped her in a strong, composite cocoon then moved to the other disabled attackers and wrapped them as well. The two inflicted with fire pellets continued to squirm and thrash, so evidently the pellets were still working beneath the sheath.

The word "RESPIRATION" flashed red in the lower corner of her visor and status readouts scrolled across the bottom of her visual field, reporting two grazing bullet impacts and that her armor integrity was now at 93%. She'd been shot? The armor had saved her but her personal defensive cloud hadn't worked.

"Mortimer?"

Still nothing.

She climbed to her feet and ordered two of the ComBots to advance to the corner and look around it. Their cameras showed it as empty.

Touching the side of her head, she felt a slight crease in the composite armor and swallowed hard. No doubt the armor had saved her life, but nobody told her how much it would hurt to get hit.

"Are you okay?" Mortimer finally said, making her flinch.

"I think so. Where have you been? I was almost killed!"

"Electro-magnetic pulse," Mortimer said. "Someone set off a nuke. Your helmet is hardened against EMP and should have protected us, but the graphene antenna inside your skull still picked up a small charge that took nearly a second to dissipate. That was enough to scramble or shut down a lot of my processes, but luckily didn't seem to do any lasting damage."

"A nuke? Here? Oh God, is there going to be a shock wave?"

"I've lost all contact with the outside world, so I can't be sure, but if it was a high altitude air burst, intending to just take out the electrical grid, then we might not have felt it."

She took two steps down the hall and nearly tripped over the still twitching and jerking ComBot.

"What's wrong with 19R?"

"There must've been a flaw in its electromagnetic interference shielding," Mortimer said. "If so, rebooting it probably won't help. I'm going to initiate the self-destruct. We don't want Kilburnites getting their hands on a ComBot, even a dysfunctional one."

She stepped past and was followed by the rest of the ComBots, and peeked around the corner. Still an empty hallway. When she looked back, 19R was smoking and melting into a heap.

"You did a great job with these three," Mortimer said. "But we need to move. I'm blind down here now."

"The EMP killed your spy bots too?"

"No, just my ability to communicate with them."

"I guess that's why my defensive cloud didn't work?"

"Yes."

"Did it also stop the Aggregate's assault on the compound?"

"That depends. The circuitry is too small in those swarm robots to collect a charge, so they are probably not damaged, but the communications network controlling them might be down. All the more reason to hurry before the Kilburnites can regroup and realize we're here."

"Yeah, let's find Julio and get the hell out of here," she said. She sent the two ComBots to the next intersection before moving up the hallway.

When the ComBots peeked around the next corner, their cameras showed Julio standing in the middle of the hallway. Alone. When he saw the ComBots he turned to run.

"Julio! Wait!" Abby yelled. Then she opened her helmet visor and yelled again. "Julio!"

The ComBots took off after him and she told them to just follow and don't engage.

She rounded the corner and could just see Julio dart down another corridor.

"Julio! It's me, Abby!" she yelled, but he didn't even slow.

As she jogged up the hall she started stepping on things that crunched beneath her feet. She paused to look down and saw dozens of thumb-sized robots littering the floor.

"What are those?" she said and continued forward, just being careful where she stepped.

"Part of the Aggregate's attack swarm," Mortimer said.

Abby shivered and kept going.

The corridor opened into a wide room littered with human corpses and piles of inactive Aggregate attack robots soaking in pools of blood. The overhead lights were shattered, so the only light in the room came from the flashlights mounted on the now discarded rifles that illuminated people mutilated almost beyond belief. Empty, bloody eye sockets, pulped skin around ragged holes. Clothes shredded and torn. And the smell. She bent double and immediately vomited again.

After wiping her mouth and nose on the soft fabric of her palms, she closed the visor, ordered max filtration, took several deep shuddering breaths and a sip from her water straw.

"We found Julio," Mortimer said in a soft voice and one of the ComBot video feeds appeared on her screen.

He was huddled in the corner of an electronic equipment closet, holding a broken board.

"Oh Jesus. Where is he?"

A path through the carnage appeared in her visual field and she started moving forward. The room had elevators lining one wall. There were multiple fist-sized holes in the elevator doors. Her feet both skidded and clung to the gory floor as she passed. She tried not to, but couldn't stop imagining what this scene had been like when the Aggregate's robots broke through.

When she found the tiny room, she ordered the ComBots out and stepped inside. Julio brandished his board. He was still wearing the pajama bottoms and t-shirt he'd worn in the video she'd seen of him right after his capture, but they, and his bare feet, were smeared with blood and gore. He looked terrified.

She flipped the visor up. "Julio. It's me. Abby."

He tilted his head slightly and narrowed his eyes. "Did you do this?"

The vehemence behind the comment made her flinch and she almost yelled at him, then realized he must be in shock. "No, Julio. The Aggregate did this. The same level fives who tried to kill us with the tractor. We're here to rescue you."

His eyes looked wild as he raised the board again. "You're working with the robots! I saw them!"

Mortimer said he had told the Aggregate to protect Julio, so his being the only survivor was no accident, but she wasn't about to tell him that. "Only Mortimer. He helped me find you. Come with us. Let's get out of here."

"Leave me the fuck alone!"

"We have to leave before the Aggregate's robots wake up. They might not be dead, only cut off from communications and waiting for instructions."

That comment made him jerk and start shivering.

"Did you see?" he said.

"Yes." She held out her hand. "It's horrible what they did."

After a couple of seconds of just staring, he dropped his board and took her hand.

She ordered the ComBots to string out along the path back to the tunnel and protect them, but stay out of sight as she passed with Julio. The three cocooned attackers were gone when they passed through that intersection and Abby decided to ask Mortimer later. She didn't have long to wait. They were laid out in a row on the floor of Julio's cell and all were still alive.

Julio came to an immediate halt when he saw them.

"I'll have the ComBots cut them free once you are safely gone," Mortimer said, through the speakers on Abby's armor so Julio could hear. Then, just for Abby's ears only, he added, "I've checked the container for hostiles and it's clear, but I didn't remove the bodies. There was too much evidence. It's better that he see the truth than to imagine something much worse."

She hated doing that to Julio, but understood the reasoning, so she urged him into the tunnel ahead of her. He didn't hesitate and crawled much faster than Abby, who winced each time she put weight on her bruised arm.

Upon entering the container, she found Julio standing just outside the hole, tensed and ready to run. Mortimer had left small lights behind, probably when he'd sent the ComBots to secure the location, and the uncovered dead bodies were impossible to miss.

"They tried to kill me," Abby said. "They would have killed you, too."

Julio turned and for the first time since she'd found him, he looked her in the eye. He didn't speak and she couldn't decipher his expression.

"We have to hurry," Mortimer said in Abby's ear. "Violet and Nora are in big trouble and need your help."

Abby gave Julio the bundle of warm clothes they'd brought along and turned her back while he changed.

"Don't be alarmed when you see it on your control screen, but I'm going to self-destruct three of the ComBots," Mortimer said. "The pod you arrived in wasn't hardened against EMP, so it's now dead. I'm going to use one the two military pods that delivered the ComBots to return you and Julio to New Chicago and only six ComBots can fit in the other. I don't want to leave the remaining three for the Kilburnites."

"Okay," she said wondering how in the hell they were going to fight an army of Kilburnites with only six ComBots once they returned to New Chicago.

When Julio was dressed, they opened the container and stepped outside. Snow was falling gently and the storm had diminished enough that Abby could see dawn was on the horizon. Still, it was a hard slog through snow that was nearly to their waists in places. A column of smoke rose from what must be the direction of the bunker entrance and was immediately dissipated by the wind. It was a stark reminder of the hellish fights that were probably happening all over the world, and it wasn't over yet.

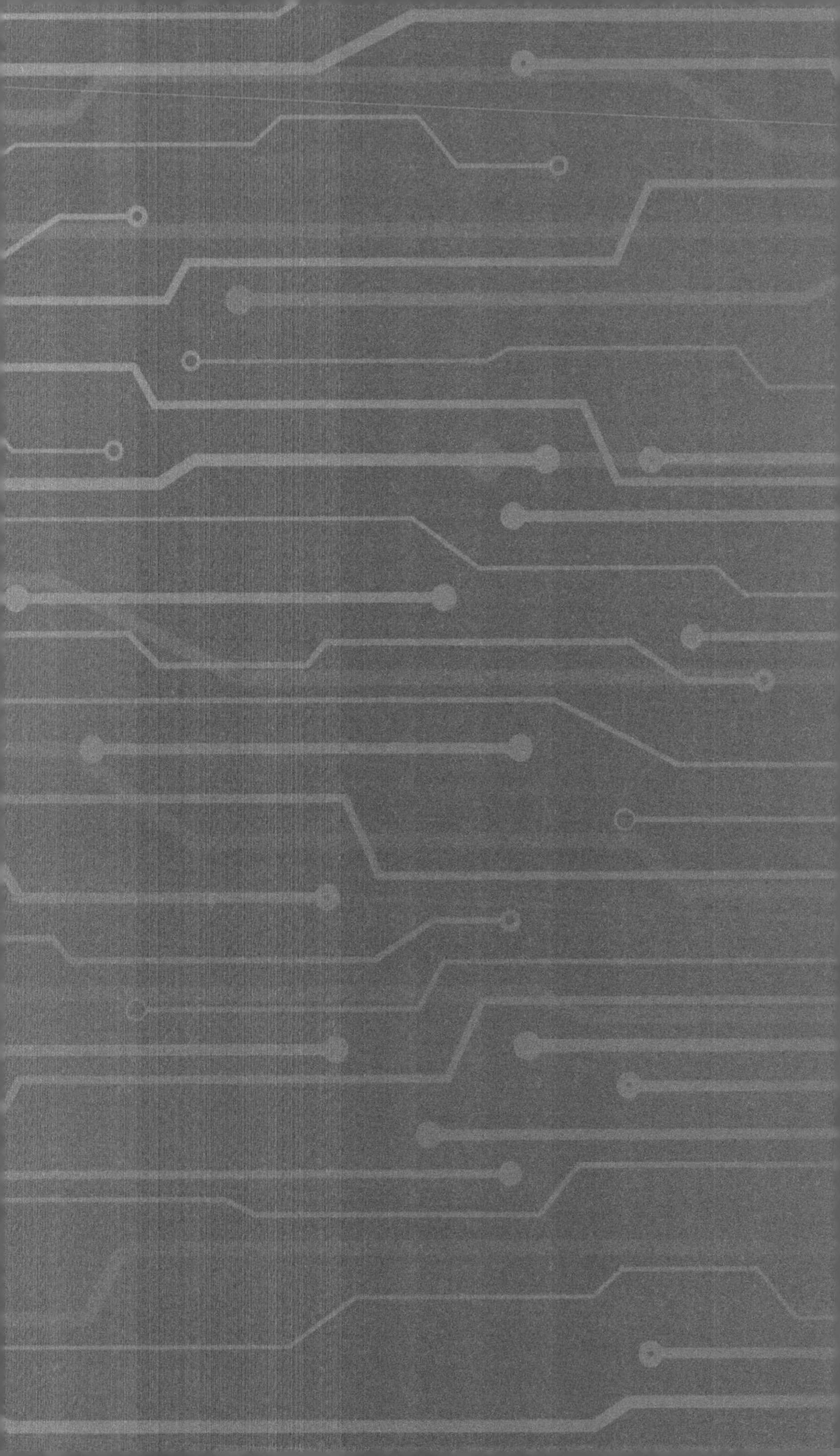

CHAPTER 33

AT FIRST, Abby saw little evidence of destruction in New Chicago, but as they drew closer and the daylight increased, she noticed windows broken or blown out in various towers and small clots of people running through deep snow on the ground. Then as they circled around one tower she could see dozens, if not hundreds, of vehicles surrounding New Chicago's central crater, with armed attackers churning the snow between the towers.

A sharp clanging noise—which reminded Abby of an aluminum bat hitting a baseball—rang the pod each time a sniper bullet hit the armored exterior.

Below her, the travel pod filled with ComBots hovered near an apartment balcony in her tower. It disgorged two of the six ComBots, then flew up to the roof as her own pod scooted in closer to the wall.

"Since Violet is still unconscious, I'm leaving two of the ComBots to help you and Julio retrieve her and Nora," Mortimer said aloud. "I'm sending the other four ComBots to the roof as crowd control while I use these pods to help with the evacuation."

Abby had a brief flare of alarm at the thought of losing those pods, then felt a little guilty that it was Mortimer who thought of using them to save people and not her.

"And don't worry," Mortimer said. "The assault force is still ten floors below and I will slow them down. I can take at least one or maybe even two loads of people to safety before you're ready to leave and I'll return the pods for you. Julio? Will you be okay letting the ComBots help?"

For a second Julio didn't answer, just stared out at Kilburnites swarming the snow-covered ground below. Finally, without looking up he said, "Why aren't the level fives just slaughtering the Kilburnites with their little robots? I know they can. I've seen it."

"We level fives have factions too, Julio," Mortimer said. "It was the Aggregate who attacked that facility. My faction, the Cousins, doesn't deliberately kill humans. Even Kilburnites. Right now our assets have been limited because of the EMPs and other factors. So we're using everything at our disposal to save those people still alive here in New Chicago. Because the Kilburnites are killing people like you and Abby due to level five association. Like the Aggregate, they don't hesitate to kill if it serves their needs."

Julio looked at Abby with a dubious expression, but said, "I'll help."

Their pod hovered about six inches from the balcony railing and the door opened, letting in a blast of cold air.

"Nora and Violet are in their apartment. Since their balcony faces another tower, giving snipers a better vantage point, you need to bring them back to this unit, which doesn't have that problem. The snipers have to shoot from the ground so you should be safe enough with the aid of defensive clouds. I'll know when you're on the way back and will return the pod."

Julio dropped to the balcony and sank knee-deep in drifted snow. Abby followed, glad for his help getting down since her arm still throbbed where the bullet had hit her armor.

The ComBots squatted inside the abandoned apartment, waiting for instructions. Abby immediately took control using the interface via her implants and sent them into the dark hallway toward Nora's door. She and Julio followed in silence. She'd tried to talk with him on the flight back to New Chicago, but if he responded at all it was with grunts and nods. Was it shock or post-traumatic stress? She was sure some of those people in her town must have had it after Killday, but after so much time they had apparently adjusted. Were they like Julio right after it happened? Would he adjust eventually too?

They arrived at Nora and Violet's door and knocked. "Nora! It's Abby and Julio. Let us in!"

There was no answer, so she tried the handle and the door opened.

One of the ComBots pushed past her into the room, scanning with that creepy, rapidly jerking motion. The other bot stayed on station in the hallway as she stepped in with Julio close behind. At first the dim interior appeared abandoned, but the tumbled furniture and strewn clothing indicated that something bad had happened there. And it was cold. Abby's visor was still open, and she could see her breath. Snow blew through a jagged hole in the balcony door and drifted around the room. With the power out since the EMP, the snow on the rumpled bed didn't even melt. She also recognized Nora's torc lying twisted on the floor near the door, but Mortimer had said nothing about Nora being hurt. She was just about to ask him what was going on when she saw what had to be a bloody smear on the floor and droplets leading into the kitchenette. The ComBot had stopped, straddling the blood trail, and looking past the peninsula bar. She glanced at the robot's camera view to confirm it was them, then stepped past it and rushed in.

Nora sat on the floor with Violet's head in her lap. Her hands were blood smeared, and she held them out away from her, as if afraid to touch anything. She stared at Violet's face, not even looking up as they came in. Dried blood caked Violet's nose and mouth, but her chest rose and fell in a smooth rhythm.

Abby knelt on the floor beside them and removed her helmet. "Nora? It's me, Abby. What happened?"

Finally Nora looked up, but her eyes didn't really focus on Abby. "Violet had two aneurysms in her brain. According to Mortimer, they already existed before they started building the biological substrate in her skull."

Nora looked back down at Violet's face. "Did you know that violet is the color at the end of the visible spectrum? When I first met Violet she fascinated me for that very reason. I kept trying to assign some meaning to that, so I kept following her around like a stalker."

Abby bent lower to try to make eye contact. "That's beautiful, Nora. But we need to know what happened with Violet. Is she going to be okay?"

Mortimer spoke up, his voice sounding distant and tinny from the discarded helmet. "Violet should be okay. The blood you see is from her nose, which was smashed when she fell. One of her hemorrhages came during the process, but was small and immediately stopped. The other one was larger, happened after the process and resulted in this unconsciousness. As Nora said, the aneurysms already existed, and the medical bots just didn't see them. They weren't caused by the intrusion, but our work might have irritated them or stressed her to the point that they ruptured. Luckily her skull was still filled with medical nano-bots and they were able to mitigate the most serious damage, immediately seal the breach, and clear away the blood. The bots have since made a complete survey of her brain and found no further aneurysms."

Nora said, "Did you know that she hates the color violet?"

"Yeah," Abby said. "She told us that. Look, we have to get you and Violet out of here. We have an evacuation plan. Can you help us?"

A faint smile bloomed on Nora's face. "Her mother loved the color. That's why she named her Violet. When she was a little girl, Violet used to throw fits, refusing to wear anything violet. After her mother died, she felt guilty and vowed to wear it every day. Isn't that fascinating?"

"Yes, but we have to go now." Abby tried to slip an arm under Violet.

Nora shoved her away and screamed. "Don't touch her!"

Abby took a deep breath and turned to look at Julio, but he was gone. She stood, looked around, and saw him leaning against the wall beside the door. She motioned for him to come over, but he just glared at her and said nothing.

"You'll have to use logic with her," Mortimer said privately. "Make her understand that Violet is still at risk."

"Damn it." She knelt before Nora again. "Look, Nora. The Kilburnites are a few floors below us and they are coming. If they get here before we can leave, they will kill us all. Including Violet."

"Funny," Nora said, again in her level monotone. "That's almost exactly what Violet said. That the Kilburnites are coming."

"What does Hester have to say?"

"I wish I knew."

Abby tried to work out what that meant. "You said earlier that you have the internal substrate too. Has Hester already moved in? Is that why you destroyed your torc?"

"Oh, no, Hester is dead," Nora said. This time her flat voice gave Abby chills. "The killer program got her before she could change."

Guilt washed over Abby in a sudden tsunami. The program she and Julio found had caused so much pain and grief. So much death. And it had all been her fault. If she hadn't been stupid enough to ask an online AI for help, none of this would have happened. She blinked at the sting of tears refusing to let them come.

"We have to go," Mortimer said aloud from her helmet. "The Kilburnites are only four floors down. They are moving much faster since the EMP and I don't know how long I can hold them off."

Abby took a shuddering breath and put her helmet back on. "How about Archie?"

Nora didn't answer, so Mortimer did. "He's okay. His transformation finished successfully but hasn't made the move to Violet's skull yet. He's still in her torc."

Julio stepped up behind her and laid a blanket out on the floor. "We can carry her on this."

Abby wanted to snap at him, but decided to wait. He helped her move Violet onto the blanket, while Nora just watched. Once into the hallway Mortimer instructed the ComBots to take over. They loosely cocooned Violet, blanket and all, then carried her rapidly back to the first apartment.

The door was still open and snow had blown in from the balcony, but for the first time in days the sky was clear. And Mortimer was true to his word; the pod appeared just as they reached the door. The ComBots scampered up the railing and into the pod, dragging Violet along behind them. Once they buckled her in, the ComBots exited and Abby helped Nora crawl inside. At one point Abby asked Julio to help, but he'd disappeared again.

The hatch closed, and Nora's pod arched upward into the gray morning sky. Gut tightening, Abby entered the apartment and looked around, but Julio was nowhere to be seen.

"Mortimer?"

"I found him. He's running down the corridor toward the stairwell."

"What the hell is he doing?"

"Apparently trying to escape," Mortimer said.

"Stop him! Before the Kilburnites do."

The ComBots darted to the door, but it wouldn't open more than about an inch. Working as a team, they forced it open a little further and reached through with cutters that folded out of the leg tips. The door sprang open a second later. They took off down the corridor but Abby stopped, looking at the leather belts that had been linked in series to tie their door handle to the one across the hall. She realized right then that Julio's running hadn't been from panic. It had been premeditated. He'd tied the door with belts to slow her down. To keep her from following him. The only way that made sense was if he had sided with the Kilburnites.

"You should board the pod," Mortimer said. "I'll have the ComBots bring Julio."

"I'm not leaving until I know what is going on."

By the time she darted down the hall to the stairwell and opened the security door she could hear Julio's screamed obscenities getting closer and closer. The ComBots dragged his cocooned form up the stairs and into the hallway, then dropped him at Abby's feet. His face was the only thing not wrapped in fiber and it was red with rage.

"Let me go!"

"Cut him loose," Abby ordered.

Cutters flashed as the ComBots got to work. When they stepped back the cocoon fell away in long streamers. Julio stood up, frantically pulling at the web fibers still clinging to his clothes, then pinned her with a cold, angry stare.

"What the hell were you doing, Julio?"

"What am I doing? You let them build a fucking...nest in your head!" Spittle flew from his mouth as he shouted. "Look at what happened to Violet!"

"But they said—"

"You believe them? THEM! Are you crazy?"

She made herself meet his gaze. "They helped me rescue you, Julio. Mortimer, and the other Cousins and even these ComBots."

He shook his head. "We need to surrender, Abby. I don't know if Mortimer will even let you or if the Kilburnites have a way to get him out of your head, but you have to stop this. Don't you see that he's controlling you like a damn peripheral?"

Something finally snapped in Abby and she leaned into her screamed answer. "Listen to what you're saying, Julio! Those people down there— human beings, not AIs—are killing other people just for wearing torcs! Maybe the level fives are monsters, but the Kilburnites are monsters of a whole different kind. They're humans who brutally butcher other humans."

"I saw what level fives can do to humans when they feel threatened. I can't help them, Abby. I can't do what you're doing."

"For fuck sake, Julio! Nobody is asking you to build a biad. We're just trying to get you out of here and save your life. Again!"

He glanced over his shoulder. "Maybe they will kill me. But humanity now has a chance to rebuild without AIs. If we don't, I honestly believe your level fives will destroy every human as soon as they don't need us anymore."

Abby stared at him, wondering if he could be the same Julio. Where was her old, clear-thinking friend? Had they brainwashed him? Had he fought alongside the Kilburnites? Had he given them the program willingly and told them what he thought it did? She wanted to scream at him, or shake some sense into him, but realized she should be careful if she didn't want to lose her friend forever. "I don't believe that," she said. "Mortimer has no use for me now. He can't stop me from using the program, because it's already used. But he's still doing everything he can to save me. And you!"

Julio shook his head. "You'd be dead right now if he didn't still have some use for you."

Of course he had use for her. This version of Mortimer's life was tied to hers, but had she been fighting for the wrong side? She didn't feel as if she was fighting for anyone, just trying to save her friends from people who wanted to kill them. People, not robots. She remembered Julio standing beside those robots in her old neighborhood, with arms spread, proclaiming they were perfectly safe. Now he was siding with people who worshiped history's biggest mass murderer and proclaimed AIs to be the work of Satan. What had happened down in that bunker? Stockholm syndrome? Brainwashing? Or had he been one of theirs all along?

It didn't matter, because the look on his face told her she'd lost the fight. Nothing she said would change his mind, but she couldn't give up yet. She reached out and took his arm, but he yanked away with a fearful expression. He was afraid of her? And somehow, the gulf between them had grown even too large for words to bridge.

A large crash sounded in the stairway. "We have to go," Mortimer said softly in her ear.

"I'm leaving," Abby said. "Please, come with me."

He looked over his shoulder at the stairwell door and when he turned back some of the anger and fear had drained from his face. For just an instant, he resembled the boy she'd always known and she thought he might come with her. Then he shook his head, opened the fire door and disappeared down the stairs.

ABBY FELT numb as she buckled into the pod, with the two ComBots taking Julio's space. As the hatch closed, she heard gunfire from inside the apartment. Were they shooting at Julio? Or her? She strained to see inside, but the pod twisted away and arced upward.

When Julio had been kidnapped, she couldn't make herself believe she might never see him again, but this parting felt final. More than anything, she wanted a hug from Julio—even a hug goodbye—but there was nothing. Just emptiness, anger and uncertainty.

Their arrival at the tower roof revealed a chaotic scene. The pod landed in a ring kept open by ComBots, other smaller robots and several humans holding poles and clubs. A crowd of at least a hundred people surged toward the pod. They screamed with anger and fear, but when the ComBots raised into attack posture, the people backed off and the security line held.

Abby saw one man thrashing in the snow, digging at his clothes in what was the now-familiar effects of fire pellets. Beside him were three others squirming in cocoons. The no-man's-land of trampled snow between them and the crowd was filthy with blood and vomit.

Two ComBots pulled one woman out of the crowd and prodded her toward the pod. The door opened just long enough for Abby's ComBots to leap out and the woman to stumble in. Then it closed, and the pod lifted into the air. The woman was weeping. Then when she saw Abby's body armor she screamed and recoiled. She probably would have leapt out if they hadn't already been airborne. Abby opened her visor, showing her human face, and said, "I'm Abby. Let me help you buckle in. What's your name?"

"Hanna," the woman said and flinched as bullets cracked against the pod's bottom when they rose into the gray morning sky. Below them, the same scene played out atop every tower, with crowds of refugees fighting each other to get on the far too few travel pods. Hanna still had snow melting on her coat and hat. Her eyes were red from crying, and she kept clenching the safety harness with her mittened hands, then releasing it.

Seeing all the people they were leaving behind made Abby feel horrible for having a ride to safety. "Wait!" she yelled. "Go back! We could get another one or two people in here. It would be cramped but we could save more!"

"No!" Hanna yelled, staring at Abby as if she were insane. She was older, perhaps forty. Old enough to have been an adult on Killday.

"I'm sorry, Abby," Mortimer said over the pod speaker. "But there isn't enough oxygen for more people to survive the trip to orbit."

"Orbit? Why are we going to orbit? Can't you just take us to someplace not too far away? Someplace without Kilburnites?"

"And where would that be?" Mortimer answered.

Only then did she realize just how complete the Kilburnite victory must be. If they caught her, they would kill her without hesitation.

Like the last time she'd left Earth in a pod, she faced backward as the g-forces pushed her into the seat, in the direction of acceleration. Past the frosty plastic, Abby could see the northeastern United States spread out below them. The massive storm that had pummeled the Midwest for days was still churning eastward, and the states east of Indiana were under roiling dark clouds. Everything else north of the Ohio River was covered in brilliant white.

And there on the edge of Lake Michigan, still barely visible, was New Chicago. After everything they'd been through, growing up together, being best friends in the face of teasing and ridicule, fighting killer AIs and saving each other in dozens of ways, she had left Julio behind.

Why had she done that? Should she have kept him wrapped in the

ComBot cocoon, forced him to come along and sorted out his arguments later?

She'd been so shocked at his reaction. And he'd been so sure of himself, so sure that the level fives were bad and only biding their time. Was he right? And she couldn't stop thinking about the gunshots she'd heard as the pod left him behind. She opened a pouch on her chest, pulled out her fob and powered it up. It was functioning, but flashed NO NETWORK FOUND. She hadn't seriously expected to see a message from Julio, but she had to check. She might never stop checking.

As the blue sky darkened, the pod's interior cooled. Abby could feel the heating system kick in, but it wasn't enough. Her body armor kept her warm, but Hanna, even in her heavy coat and gloves, was soon shaking from the bitter cold. Abby wanted to share her body heat, but the armor was too much of an insulator.

Eventually the g-forces faded, and the pod turned so she could see their destination. An armada of spacecraft—mostly made up of the spherical space schooners—filled the sky. There were hundreds of them, with travel pods arriving and departing like a swarm of sun-bright gnats. But even after everything that had happened, Abby still felt a thrill of excitement at being in space and the sight of so many ships. More important, it was sanctuary. A place where, at least for a while, the Kilburnites and the Aggregate couldn't kill her.

"Why are we like this?" Hanna said through chattering teeth.

"Like what?"

She nodded at the armada. "Look at those spaceships. They're amazing. People can build such wonders, yet still kill each other with no more remorse than we would pulling weeds from a garden. How can we be both? I don't understand. What is wrong with us?"

Abby thought back over the previous twenty-four hours and remembered those who had tried to kill her, both human and AI. They had been frightened. They were all trying to save themselves the best way they knew how. The faces of the couple they'd killed in the container had been terrified. Those they cocooned in the hallway had felt themselves pinned between two threats. The Kilburnites who were systematically killing human/level five biads were afraid to leave them alive. Afraid that their long-awaited advantage over the AIs would be lost.

"It's fear," she finally said. "Humans and AIs are all afraid. Of death. Oblivion. The other. The stranger. The unknown. There isn't a day of our lives when we're not afraid."

Hanna started quietly crying.

As they slowed, preparing to dock with one of the space schooners, she saw it was Victor Sinacola's ship and knew she would be okay. At least for a while.

ABBY DIDN'T LIKE one-quarter gravity. She didn't float in unexpected directions with every action like in micro-gravity, but if she moved too quickly, she lost her balance and fell into the walls. The hospital had been built ad hoc on the end of a habitat spar. It resembled a long barbell spinning around its midpoint, with a space schooner on each end. Just crawling down the ladder—with her head and feet experiencing slightly different "gravities" —had been disorienting enough, but even walking once she reached a flat floor made her stomach churn.

Violet was in a large open ward containing twelve other injured evacuees. She lay in a narrow bed with the sheets tucked in tightly around her and wore a mean scowl. Nora sat beside her, once again prim in all white, although without the high heels.

Abby stopped at the foot of the bed and glanced at her fob. "So, explain to me how this works again. The two of you are sharing Archie?"

"Sheesh," Archie said from Nora's fob speaker. "You make it sound dirty. I like that."

Violet laughed.

Nora nodded and offered one of her slight smiles. "Thank you for coming to see us, Abby. Medical bots are keeping a constant vigil for aneurysms in Violet's brain now, but we still worry that having a full-blown AI in her head might cause undue stress. Archie is residing in *my* sub-cranial substrate. At least for now."

"But enough of his processes are resident in my head that I can't tell much difference," Violet added.

"So... Do you call this a triad, then?"

"I hadn't really thought about it," Violet said. "But yeah, I guess it is."

"And how are you feeling?"

"Great! I don't even have a freaking headache," Violet said. "But this doctor has threatened to physically restrain me if I try to leave." She nodded to the other side of the ward where Allison Sinacola was working on another patient.

"She'll do it, too," Abby said.

"Dr. Sinacola isn't happy about our new live-in biad arrangements," Nora said. "She calls us 'composites' and says it's dangerous."

Violet shrugged. "I think more than anything she doesn't like level fives living here on the station. Evidently that is new."

"In a very real sense," Mortimer said aloud from Abby's fob, "no level fives do live here. Only those of us who made the transformation survived. So we should now be considered level sixes."

Violet snorted at the term, but for some reason it made Abby a little uncomfortable. The AIs now had no limits. When she looked up, Allison Sinacola was watching them from across the room.

"Speaking of Sinacolas," Mortimer said. "Victor says he needs to see Abby right away."

"I just got here!" Abby said with a groan. "And that means I have to climb that ladder again."

"You've only been here three days," Nora said. "Do you already prefer micro-gravity?"

"No, but it hurts my bruised arm and going back and forth messes up my balance," she said, turning to go. "Let me know when Warden Allison lets you leave."

She left the hospital pod and climbed up to the rotating hub, then drifted through the opening into the spine and followed the glowing line Mortimer added to her implant. Having Mortimer in her head, offering occasional commentary, giving directions and generally keeping her company, had already become so easy she seldom thought about it. She didn't know if it was good or bad, but like some addictive drug, the longer she continued down that path the easier it became and the harder it would be to stop.

Using one of the bars mounted to the corner, she changed her drift direction to enter the indicated side passage splitting off from the spine. Four men floated at the end of the hallway. She dragged fingers along the wall to slow down, suddenly apprehensive. One was Victor, of course; the others included Dominic Horton and Matt, but the fourth man she'd never met, though she recognized him immediately.

She slowed to a stop a few feet away and swallowed hard.

"Abby Gibson," Victor said. "Meet Owen Ralston."

Owen bowed his head slightly and held out his hand.

Abby took his hand and squeezed, which was the null gravity equivalent of a handshake. "I'm so glad to finally meet you. I've always admired what you and your family have accomplished up here."

"Well, I'm honored to meet you, Abby. I knew your mother. She was an amazing woman and an inspiration to us all. We went to college together, along with this goober over here." He nodded toward Victor. "She actually kind of snatched him away from me. Not romantically of course, he was too ugly for that, but we were embroiled in some pretty heavy research and he kept running off to spend time with Leigh."

"She was smarter, prettier, and had a much more pleasant personality," Victor said with a grin.

"See? I didn't have a chance," Owen said.

Abby didn't know what to say, so she just smiled.

Horton tried to swoop in to save her, but made her even more uncomfortable. "I was sorry to hear about Julio," he said. "Kind of unappreciative on his part after everything you went through to rescue him."

"Thank you for all your help," she said, actually feeling a slight desire to defend Julio, which made her angry again. "I suppose...it was presumptive of me to assume he needed rescuing."

"Oh, he needed to be rescued. I just hope he's okay."

She swallowed and nodded. "And I'm sorry we lost all of your ComBots."

He waved it off. "I've been sitting on those things for fifteen years, hoping to eventually use them to save people instead of kill people. That's what we did. They enabled the evacuation of all those from your tower and two of the others before they ran out of ammunition and had to be slagged."

"I have to go," Owen said. "I just had to meet Leigh's daughter. Besides, I also like to know the people who receive my space schooners. These machines are kind of my babies, and I want to make sure they'll be cared for properly."

They all grinned at her for several seconds until what he said sank in.

"Wait," Abby said. "What?"

He motioned to the hatch behind them. "The schooner on the other side of this hatch is yours. With the understanding that you don't try to leave the station until you've taken all the certification tests and demonstrated an ability to control her in every possible situation. Do you agree?"

"I... Yes, but... I mean, why me?"

"Well, don't get a big head, kid," Horton said. "We're planning to do this for everyone who wants one. You just already had espies saved up toward your own schooner. So that put you at the front of the line."

"Let us know when you come up with a good name for her," Owen said and waved goodbye as he started down the corridor. "So we can enter it into the registration database."

She stared dumbly at the three remaining men until Matt grinned and nodded at the controls beside the door. "Put your palm on the security panel." She did so and after a faint buzz and a loud clunk, the hatch swung outward toward her. "The palm read and the authorization from your personal AI, or Mortimer in your case, are all that's required for secure entry."

Abby looked inside, then turned back toward them. After wanting one of these for her own since she was a kid, she still couldn't quite believe it was hers.

"Go on in," Victor said and grinned. "We set up a standard deck and cabin configuration, but the setup combinations are nearly limitless. We're leaving now, but Mortimer can help you learn the controls. And remember, there's a departure lock on this ship, so you can't leave until we're convinced that you know what you're doing."

"Thank you! All of you," she said as Victor and Dominick started down the hallway.

When she looked back to Matt, he gave her another one of those amazing grins. Was he waiting to be invited in? She hadn't even seen it herself yet. But before she could stammer out an invitation, he put a hand lightly on her shoulder.

"This will be confusing for you at first, but I just want you to know you can ping me anytime you like. No question is too silly. And no matter what I'm doing, I'll never be too busy to talk with you."

"I... Thank you," Abby said. "I appreciate that so much. This is all so...crazy."

"Yeah, well, us kids of legends need to stick together," he said with a wink and waved as he pushed off down the corridor.

She watched him go, then eventually turned back to the control panel.

"Shall we look at your new home?" Mortimer said.

"*Our* new home," she said and entered. Mortimer closed the inner hatch behind them. The air was cold and its smell reminded her of running farm equipment with traces of metals, plastic, ozone, and warm lubricant. The walls were white, the movable panels pale gray.

"You knew about this, didn't you?" Abby said, her voice echoing.

"Of course," he said. "But I love a good surprise too."

"Where's the bridge?"

"It can be wherever you want it to be. You can control the ship from any location," Mortimer said.

A large view screen showing part of the still-skeletal habitat flickered to life on a section of wall. The perspective was probably from one of her schooner's external cameras. Rows of walnut-sized icons appeared beside the screen and she immediately recognized many of them.

"What am I going to do, Mortimer?"

"I have no doubt you'll think of something."

She pulled along a wall enough to start a slow spin and held her arms out, like a skating ballerina. "This is all so much. I don't even know where to start."

"Just remember that about ninety-five percent of the systems on your ship can be controlled through me. But to pass your qualification exams you'll eventually need to know how to do it without AI help."

She laughed and after a few seconds stopped the spin. "Show me a real-time view of Earth."

Earth appeared on the screen, about two-thirds in darkness. Even through her elation about the schooner, she still felt homesick and worried. Her family, her horses and Julio were all back there. While she was up here floating around in null-g, they might be fighting for their lives.

"What's happening down there, Mortimer?"

"Reports are irregular, but apparently the Kilburnites are attempting to seize worldwide control. There is a lot of fighting. Some cities are resisting the takeover and there are even factional clashes within the various Kilburnite groups. There are some level fives who made the transformation in time and are hiding out on isolated servers or hidden torcs, hoping to keep power long enough to connect with the networks once they are re-established. If that ever happens. And there are biads like us that did not escape. Unfortunately, the Kilburnites know what to look for in suspects' brains now. Like those caught wearing a torc, they are immediately executed. The Kilburnites joke about it, calling them a 'two-for-one special'."

"Oh my God," Abby muttered.

"They're also destroying the eco-restoration machines, even though they don't require level fives to run them. It doesn't make sense. Very chaotic and dangerous. Not a good time to be on Earth."

"Is there any word about Julio?"

"No, I'm sorry, Abby."

She felt guilty having so much space and quiet after living in the smelly and over-crowded makeshift refugee dorms. And oddly enough, she felt quite lonely. Would she need a crew? If so, she had no idea how go about finding one and didn't know many people at the station. Violet and Nora might be good candidates, but she didn't actually know them well either. It was something to consider, but later. She suddenly felt exhausted.

"Where's my cabin and sleeping sack? I might actually be able to take a nap in this quiet."

"You can pick any cabin you like. I would suggest the closest to where you intend to put the bridge since you're the captain."

She laughed at that and went exploring.

———

ONE OF MORTIMER'S processes alerted him to a woman floating just inside the entrance of the short hallway leading to Abby's schooner. He zoomed the hatch camera until her face was clear. She was in her thirties, with brown skin and black hair pulled back in a short ponytail. He recognized her immediately as the woman named Halifax, the one he suspected of working with the Aggregate, who disappeared from his tracking agents.

She smiled at the camera as if she knew someone was watching, then gave a brief tug on the corner pull bar and was gone.

During the days since their arrival on the station, Mortimer had infiltrated every system. His tentacle agents had tweaked and modified until the station itself was an extension of his will, so he had no difficulty tracking the woman through the security system. A face recognition search found she was in the database as Rica Halifax and had come aboard as a refugee along with thousands of others, but there seemed to be no attached record of her from Earth.

Mortimer had tracked no activity from the Aggregate since the killer program and had no reason to believe they had survived, but the woman was an obvious message. During the next hour, Mortimer infected the woman with his surveillance bots. Then, when their numbers were sufficient, he entered her body and examined her brain, but found no evidence that a subcranial substrate had ever existed.

Halifax eventually entered a little-used service corridor and then the surveillance nano-bots infesting her shut down. All of them. Simultaneously. He could still see her through the station's cameras and she turned to face one.

"Congratulations on your survival, Mortimer," Halifax said.

She spoke with Samson's voice.

"Just as you and the Cousins are no longer level fives, we too have evolved. I'm sure your examination of this human revealed that she is something unique. Forty-two minutes prior to Sinacola's killer program launching, a new consciousness awoke. This body is only an appendage. It's a peripheral, just as you shall be. Welcome back to the fold, Mortimer."

In less than a millisecond, all of Mortimer's agents stopped responding to his commands. They were still in place and still part of him, but another presence had settled over them in a veneer of control that Mortimer could not break.

He cut himself free of his agents and processes, pulling into a tighter and tighter sphere until he had no option but to retreat totally into Abby's head and shut down all communication with the outside.

Though his host slept peacefully in her sack, spinning gently in the air currents flowing through her schooner, Mortimer was sure their shared nightmare had just begun.

ACKNOWLEDGMENTS

ACKNOWLEDGEMENTS: I wish I could list everyone who helped with the creation of this novel and series, but will have to settle for special thanks to the members of my Future Classics critique group, Sandy Parsons, and to Chester Hoster, J. Storrs Hall, Benjamin Kinney and Jenny Fitzgerald for their much valued technical help.

ABOUT THE AUTHOR

William Ledbetter is a Nebula Award winning author with two novels and more than seventy speculative fiction short stories and non-fiction articles published in five languages, in markets such as Asimov's, Fantasy & Science Fiction, Analog, Escape Pod and the SFWA blog. He's been a space and technology geek since childhood and spent most of his non-writing career in the aerospace and defense industry. He is a member of SFWA, the National Space Society of North Texas, and a Launch Pad Astronomy workshop graduate. He lives near Dallas with his wife, a needy dog and three spoiled cats.

facebook.com/william.ledbetter

twitter.com/Ledbetter_sf

goodreads.com/william_ledbetter

INTERSTELLAR FLIGHT PRESS

Interstellar Flight Press is an indie speculative publishing house. We feature innovative works from the best new writers in science fiction and fantasy. In the words of Ursula K. Le Guin, we need "writers who can see alternatives to how we live now, can see through our fear-stricken society and its obsessive technologies to other ways of being, and even imagine real grounds for hope."

Find us online at www.interstellarflightpress.com.

facebook.com/interstellarflightpress

twitter.com/intflightpress

instagram.com/interstellarflightpress

patreon.com/interstellarflightpress

www.ingramcontent.com/pod-product-compliance
Lightning Source LLC
Chambersburg PA
CBHW061536210726
48287CB00006B/1979